No Screams In Silence

To Kelly,
Hope you Enjoy!

Scott P. Bzdak

Printed in the United States of America

First printing, 2014

ISBN-13: 9780692028322 (Scott Bzdak)

ISBN-10: 0692028323

Cover Art by Tim Bzdak

All inquiries can be made to the author:
sbzdak@yahoo.com

DISCLAIMER:
This novel is a work of fiction. Names, characters, businesses, places, events and incidents are either the products of the author's imagination or used in a fictitious manner. Any resemblance to actual persons, living or dead, or actual events is purely coincidental.

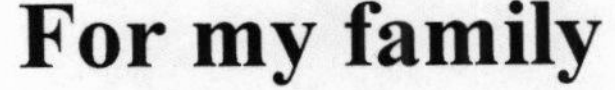

For my family

Chapter 1

Engine One screamed down Spurlock Creek Road into the heart of Stillwell County, with Tanker One tucked in close on its six. The red and white strobe lights on the fire trucks bounced off the darkened trees that lined the narrow unmarked two-lane road. There was no room for error.

"Engine One to Stillwell dispatch."

"Go ahead with your traffic, Engine One."

"Do we have anything further on this call we're headed to?"

"No, Sir. The only thing I was able to hear before the caller disconnected was that there was heavy smoke showing from a residence just past the Baptist church on the right-hand side of the roadway. I tried calling the number back but it goes straight to voicemail."

"Engine One direct. We're only a few minutes out."

The full moon that hung low overhead cast enough light for the officer on the engine to see a faint glow coming from one of the houses as they drove down the narrow winding road into the valley.

"Engine One to Stillwell dispatch."

"Go ahead, Engine One."

"Hold myself and Tanker One on the scene of a two-story farmhouse with smoke and flames showing on side bravo. Tone out for a second alarm and have Tanker Two expedite. We have zero hydrants out here and we're gonna need some serious water."

"Stillwell is direct on your traffic. Chief One is direct and also en route at 22:31 hours."

The fire fight lasted for the better part of an hour before the flames were brought under control. After Chief One was given the "all clear" from his guys, he donned his turn-out coat and leather helmet to start his investigation. It was now his job to determine the cause and origin of the blaze. With his fully charged pumpkin light in hand, he entered the house and cautiously made his way toward where he thought the fire had begun. Paying more attention to the floor than his surroundings, Chief One entered the front room of the main floor of the house. When he felt he was in a safe position, he glanced up to take a careful look at the room in its entirety.

"You've got to be fucking kidding me," Chief One muttered under his breath.

His heart rate immediately shot up and his breathing became shallow as he quickly realized he was somewhere he didn't want to be. He froze in his tracks. Water from the hour-long firefight was seeping from the ceiling and down the walls all around him. He could feel the steady drip of soiled water falling from the holes in the drywall above him onto his leather fire helmet and protective gear as he stood motionless. His breath condensed upward over his gray handlebar moustache every time he exhaled and, in reverse, the pungent smell of burnt wood and plastic that hung in the air hit his nose when he inhaled.

Light from the halogen lamps on the fire trucks in the driveway sparsely lit the room through the broken-out windows. His eyes had trouble focusing at first, due to the red and white strobe lights from the emergency vehicles reflecting off the residual smoke in the air and shattered glass strewn all over the floor. The floor bowing under his feet gave him the uneasy feeling that he was in danger of taking an express trip to the basement, but that was the least of his worries. Using his pumpkin light, he carefully aimed the beam toward the unlit corner of the room and confirmed his worst fear as he took an inventory of the danger.

Directly in front of him, on an old wooden desk, were all of the components of a working meth lab. Empty bottles of diethyl ether, iodine crystals, red phosphorus, and other chemicals were either on the desk top or scattered on the ground next to it. A plugged-in hot plate with two burners and one triple neck flask sat in the middle of the desk. Chief One had never had to deal with meth labs back in Chicago, but ever since he had begun to serve as Fire Chief for Stillwell County, Kentucky, he had come across half a dozen or so. He knew that red phosphorous, when left on the heat source for too long, converts to white phosphorus and is ten times more likely to explode, igniting every other toxic fume and vapor in the room. Even if cooked properly, a meth lab can leave behind a host of toxic byproducts, including phosphine and iodine gases, which are all fatal when inhaled. Depending on the concentration left suspended in the air, death could be mercifully instantaneous, or take it's time like cancer. He had to get the hell out of there. Now!

He spun on the balls of his feet toward the door to make a hasty exit. Half way through his turn, Chief One stopped abruptly. He glanced into an open closet and saw a pair of eyes staring blankly back at him. He walked gingerly over to the closet entrance, shining his light on the face of a badly burned female who was sitting on top of a pile of smoldering clothing. Steam rolled off her lifeless body as its intense heat met the cold December air. Her mouth was wide open, exposing her dried pink tongue and white teeth. Her pupils were completely dilated, with no trace of the iris or any color beyond black. He had seen enough. She was obviously dead. This was now a crime scene, and the problem of the Stillwell County Sheriff's Office. He keyed up the mic on his portable radio and made an announcement to the fire ground and the dispatcher as he carefully walked back outside.

"Chief One to Stillwell."

"Go ahead, Chief One," the dispatcher responded.

"Have everyone evacuate the residence immediately. There's what appears to be a working meth lab in the front bedroom and a dead body in the closet. I need someone from the sheriff's office to meet me in front of Engine One, pronto."

"I'm direct on your traffic, Chief One."

He followed the same treacherous path out of the house that he'd used coming in, and eventually, found his way to the front of the engine to wait for the deputy.

The lone dispatcher switched from the fire department frequency to the sheriff's office frequency and made an attempt to contact the midnight supervisor, "Stillwell to Unit 35."

Several seconds went by in silence, so she tried again, "Stillwell to Unit 35."

"Unit 108 to Stillwell, is there something I can help you with?" Deputy Bobby Smith inquired.

"Are you aware of the structure fire on Spurlock Creek Road?"

"Yes, ma'am. I arrived on scene a few minutes ago and am at the end of the driveway trying to keep the neighbors off the fire grounds. What do you need?"

"Chief One is advising they have a possible meth lab and a dead body inside the residence. He's requesting someone from the sheriff's office meet with him in front of Engine One."

A rush of excitement went through Bobby's body as his adrenaline caused his hands to start shaking. Only seven months prior, he had been standing tall in his uniform, accepting his diploma from the Police Academy. This would be the first major crime scene he had been on since graduation.

"Keep trying to raise Unit 35 on the radio, and I'll go talk to Chief One."

Bobby walked back to his cruiser and made sure his doors were locked before he jogged up the driveway to the front of the engine.

"What's up, Chief?" Bobby asked, out of breath.

"You've got a mess on your hands, son. There's a dead female in the front room and a meth lab right next to her."

"Holy shit! Are you serious?"

"As a heart attack. You guys have your work cut out for you."

Bobby didn't know what to do next. All his training went out the window as he stood there, desperately trying to recall what he learned in his one-hour course on homicide investigation at the academy, but his mind was a total blank.

Chief One calmly put his hand on Bobby's shoulder and suggested, "Try to get a hold of your supervisor, son. He's going to want to be here for this."

"Yes, Sir. I'll let my supervisor know immediately."

Bobby frantically ran back down the driveway to his cruiser to get his cell phone that was charging in the center console. He had to wake up his supervisor, Corporal David Gibbons, who was probably sleeping the shift away over at Jenny C. Wiley State Park, on the other side of the county. The phone rang, but went to voice mail on the second ring. Bobby tried again with the same result. He was about to try a third time when he heard Corporal Gibbons chime in over the radio.

"Unit 35 to Stillwell?"

"Unit 35, I need you to head to Spurlock Creek Road for a structure fire. Chief One is on scene and is advising there is a possible meth lab inside, along with a deceased female."

"Unit 35, I'm direct and en route. Do you have an address?"

"I don't have an exact address at this time, but the original caller stated it's just down past Stillwell Baptist Church on the right."

"I'm direct."

Bobby closed his eyes and took a deep breath. After pulling himself together, he remembered that he needed to rope off the scene with yellow tape and start the crime scene log. He pulled out the fresh roll of yellow *Sheriff's Office Do Not Cross* tape from his trunk and carefully tied one end to the mailbox. He stretched the roll over to a small sapling on the other side of the driveway and tied a tight knot half way up the trunk. Satisfied with his work, Bobby retrieved a pre-printed *Crime Scene Log* from the file folder he kept in his seat organizer and walked around the grounds, documenting all the names of the fire personnel who were on scene. He was more than half-way through recording their names when he heard a familiar voice from over his shoulder.

"Bobby, where's Chief One?" Corporal Gibbons asked.

"He is over there, Sir." Bobby stated, pointing up the driveway toward the garage.

Gibbons abruptly turned from Bobby and walked toward Chief One, leaving him to finish his task. Bobby stopped to watch the interaction between Corporal Gibbons and the chief from where he was standing. Although he couldn't hear what was being said, he could see Gibbons become more animated as the conversation progressed. Bobby could tell he was getting flustered. When the conversation was over, Gibbons walked back to Bobby.

"Okay, Bobby. You already have the driveway blocked and the crime scene log started, so go ahead and post-up by the mailbox. You can get the remaining names of all the firefighters who were here later. For right now I need you to stay as far away from the house as possible, I don't want you inhaling any chemicals. Make damn sure you keep everyone out of here. You got that?"

Bobby stood silently with his mouth agape, nodding his head.

"I'm going to get Sergeant Bishop from CIB and the narcotics task force guys started, okay?"

"Yes, Sir," Bobby responded.

Gibbons pulled his cell phone out of his shirt pocket and walked over to his cruiser. After he slammed the door behind him, he scrolled through his contact list and hit *send* when "CIB Sergeant" was illuminated.

On the third ring, Gibbons was greeted with a groggy voice, "This is Bishop."

Sergeant Gerard Bishop, a twelve-year veteran of the sheriff's office, had done his time in the trenches to earn his promotion to the head of the Criminal Investigation Bureau. Prior to becoming a sheriff's deputy, he was honorably discharged from the Marine Corps after serving three years as an MP at Camp Lejeune, North Carolina. He quickly realized when he was halfway through boot camp that he wanted to give orders and not take them. Fortunately he had a C.O. who didn't do things by the books or Bishop would have spent all three of his years in the brig. He didn't re-enlist, for obvious reasons.

"Hey, Sarge. I'm sorry to bother you this late, but we have a problem at a residence down here on Spurlock Creek Road."

"Where?"

"On Spurlock Creek Road. We're just down past the Baptist Church on the right."

"Yeah, what the hell's the problem?"

"We were called to assist the fire department with a structure fire. After the fire was out, Chief One was doing his investigation and found a dead female along with a possible meth lab inside the residence. We already have the area cordoned off and the crime scene log started. Is there anything else we can do before you get here?"

"No, just hold what you've got and I'll be there shortly."

"Will do, Sarge."

For the next fifteen minutes, Bobby waited next to the trunk of his cruiser at the end of the driveway, with the crime scene log under his crossed arms. As he stood there shivering, he stared up at the house wondering who the victim was and how she had met her untimely demise. He had never seen a burned body before and he desperately wanted to go inside to have a look. Maybe the homicide detective would let him have a peek before they sent it off to the medical examiners for the autopsy. He would just have to wait and see.

While Bobby froze in the cold December air, Gibbons sat comfortably in his cruiser with the heat going full blast. He was satisfied he had done everything he was supposed to do, but decided he had best check on Bobby to see if he was filling out the paperwork correctly. Reluctantly, he emerged from his warm cruiser and walked over to the end of the driveway.

"Hey, Bobby. You understand what it is you're supposed to be doing?" Gibbons asked.

"Yes, Sir. I've got it under control." After a minute or so he continued the conversation, "The last couple of days have been crazy, huh? I just finished putting the final touches on that fatal car accident report from last night, and now this."

Gibbons didn't respond. He obviously wasn't in the mood for small talk and luckily he was saved by the arrival of Sergeant Bishop. Gibbons turned away from Bobby and walked over to Bishop's driver's side door just as he was getting out.

"Do we know anything about the deceased female yet?" Bishop inquired.

"No, Sir. We don't. The meth lab has kept us out of the house. Is Steckler on his way down here?"

Bishop looked over toward all of the flashing red lights in the driveway and then over at the partially burned house.

"Yeah, Steckler's on his way. I called him five minutes before I got here," Bishop said as he pulled a small laminated schedule out of his wallet to see which CIB Detective was on call. When he realized who it was he muttered, "Damn it!"

"What is it, Sarge?"

"I just remembered that Adam is on call this week. I'm still trying to recover from the last major case he worked," Bishop sneered.

Bishop looked down at his cell phone and scrolled through his contact list until he got to Adam's number, which he had saved under the name "Detective Smart Ass."

Adam Alexander was a transplant from Detroit, Michigan, where he had attended the University of Detroit Mercy on a full track and field scholarship. He had the street smarts of a career criminal and the mouth of a sailor. He got his start in law enforcement directly out of college as a probation officer working for the city of Detroit, monitoring high-risk repeat offenders. All his coworkers were shocked he wasn't killed in the first week because of the way he talked to his parolees. He made no attempt to play nice with anyone. He did things his way.

Adam picked up the phone on the third ring, "If you're calling to check on your wife and my kids, you've got the wrong number, Gerard."

"Adam, shut your damn mouth! We have a crispy critter and a meth lab down here that need your attention."

"Where are you guys?"

"Half way down Spurlock Creek Road. You can't miss us."

"I'm on my way, Sarge."

Bishop hung up the phone and walked past Bobby up the driveway. He stopped at the rear bumper of Chief One's chase vehicle to get a better look at the scene. The engine had all four of its exterior light poles fully extended, casting an almost blinding light onto the house and front yard. He pulled out a new pack of smokes from his pocket and pulled the brown tab to take the cellophane off the top. He flipped back the top to the hard box, pulled out a cigarette, and gently tapped the filter on the pack before placing it in his mouth.

Just as he was lighting up he saw Chief One come into view with his hand extended, "Mitch Allen, Fire Chief."

Bishop put his lighter in his pocket and met the outstretched hand with a firm hand shake, "Gerard Bishop, with the Sheriff's Office. Good to meet you, Mitch."

"Is there anything we can do for you guys right now?"

"No, Sir. Just getting a look at the house and trying to figure out what to do next. My lead detective is on his way and should be here any time. He only lives a few miles up the road. I'll make sure he meets with you as soon as he gets here. And, let me apologize now for his behavior."

Chief One turned away without saying another word and walked back up to the front bumper of the engine while Bishop finished his smoke. Just before the red glow reached the filter, he mashed the cherry in the gravel, making sure to put the crushed butt in his pocket, and walked back down the driveway to contact the rest of the supervisory staff. As he passed under the crime scene tape, he saw a guy in a bright red long-sleeve shirt walking toward him.

"What the hell, Adam? Jeans and a Red Wings jersey!" Bishop yelled.

"Yeah, my wife just got it for me. Do you like it?"

"You get back to your car and take that fucking jersey…"

"Settle down, Gerard. I'm here to investigate a dead chick, not get bitched at for my wardrobe. What do we know so far?"

Bishop wanted to read Adam the riot act, but knew this wasn't the time or the place. Civilians from a handful of houses had already started to gather in their driveways and along the narrow tree-lined road to see what the commotion was. Word had traveled fast, and more people were arriving by the minute.

"Go over to Chief One and get the low down from him. I don't even want to look at you right now," Bishop scorned.

Adam turned away from Bishop, unscathed by his gruff words, and ducked under the crime scene tape. As much as he wanted to hang around and push Bishop's buttons a little more, he decided against it. Adam knew Bishop was pissed off and could sense that another disciplinary write-up would be in his personnel file before the night was over.

He slowly walked up a small incline and stopped briefly where the gravel driveway leveled off to look at the mess he had just inherited.

"Damn fire department. I can already tell this is going to be a disaster."

In the distance he saw numerous firefighters in full turn-out gear scurrying around the property. To him, they looked like little wind-up toys, darting from the front of the fire engine, only to return to be wound up again. Adam didn't care too much for firemen. He thought they were glorified janitors who did nothing but cook, clean, and sleep all day. According to him, any woman could do their job.

His eyes scanned the front yard and all he could see were two fully charged hoses leaking water at the couplings, creating several mud pits, empty air bottles, pike poles, and other assorted fire department equipment scattered on the grass. They had better hope that this was just a meth explosion, or there would be hell to pay.

"Fucking evidence destruction team, I swear."

He had to regain his composure before going any further, or the exchange between him and Chief One wouldn't be very pleasant. After a brief pause, Adam continued up the driveway toward the front of Engine One and located an older man barking out orders to each of the firefighters.

"Are you Chief One?" Adam asked.

"Yes, and you are?"

Adam extended his hand, "I'm Detective Adam Alexander from the sheriff's office. I was told by Sergeant Bishop to come and talk to you about what's going on."

Chief One looked Adam up and down before shaking his hand.

"We were called to a structure fire at about 10:20 tonight. When we got here the fire was just starting to get going, so we dropped our lines and hit it hard from inside. After we got the fire extinguished, I started my investigation to determine the cause and origin. I made my way through the middle floor and up to this front room right here," Chief One turned around and pointed to the front left window on the main floor of the house before turning back around. "I was paying closer attention to the condition of the floor than my surroundings as I walked into the room. That turned out to be a BIG mistake."

"Why was that?"

"Because when I looked up I was standing in the middle of a meth lab. There was a glass tube with three necks sitting on top of a hot plate and a lot of chemical bottles nearby. I turned around to leave and that's when I saw a pair of eyes staring at me from inside the closet. I made sure she was dead and I got the hell out of there."

"She? How do you know it's a she?"

"Her clothes were burned off her body, exposing her breasts. I'm pretty sure it's a female in there."

"In your opinion, does this look like a cook gone bad?"

"Yeah, it looks like she was cooking when something went wrong. She may have tried to take refuge inside the closet and got trapped by the flames."

"Anyone else inside the house other than the dead chick?"

"One of my guys went upstairs to search all the rooms when we first got here, and another one went down to the basement. We're confident that she's the only one inside."

"And they missed the dead girl in the front room. Sounds to me like they did a bang-up job during their search."

"Excuse me, Detective."

"Don't worry, Chief. We'll pick up your slack on this one. I'll get back to you if I have any other questions."

Adam didn't give the chief a chance to respond before he pulled his portable radio from his belt and made contact with Bishop on the talk-around channel, "Bishop, you copy on ops?"

"Go ahead, Adam."

"Do you have Detective Steckler en route to this thing? I could use his help taking care of this meth lab."

"Yeah, I called him out. He should be here any minute with the narcotics task force."

Adam turned away from the Chief and walked over to an older model Toyota Corolla parked in front of the attached two-car garage. As he circled around it, he noticed that the Toyota had passed its prime a long time ago. Several rust spots had started to form along the rear quarter panels and the driver's side door. The rear passenger door had a huge dent in it, as did both front quarter panels, and a *My Kid is an Honors Student at Stillwell Elementary School* sticker was prominently displayed to the right of the license plate on the bumper.

Adam keyed up his radio to contact dispatch, "Unit 77 to Stillwell."

"Go ahead, Unit 77."

"Yes, ma'am. Can you run Kentucky K1G-98L for me, please?"

After a short pause the dispatcher responded, "That returns to a 1998 Toyota four-door to Melissa Anne Dwyer of Stillwell. There are no warrants on file for the registered owner and the vehicle returns clear."

"I'm direct on your traffic. Can you print out that information and I'll pick it up from you later?"

"10-4, Unit 77."

Adam clipped his radio back on his belt and pulled out the mini-flashlight he always kept in his pocket to look inside the car. It was spotless. Trying to decide what he could do next, he looked down at his watch and saw it was just before midnight. He knew he had a few more minutes to kill before Bernie's arrival, so he decided to make a quick lap around the house. He walked past the garage and into the back yard. Without the lighting from Engine One, Adam wasn't able to see anything beyond the trees. He would have to wait until morning to get a better look. He did notice the door to the basement was open, so he poked his head inside. An inch of water covered the bare cement floor, and more dripped from the ceiling. Cardboard boxes were stacked from floor to ceiling, obstructing Adam's view of the full basement. It resembled the basement of a hoarder. He hoped the rest of the house wasn't as cluttered, or this investigation would turn from a disaster to a nightmare.

"You should really have an SCBA on if you're going to be this close to the house," Chief One cautioned.

"I'll be fine. You go do… whatever it is you do."

Chief One shook his head in disgust and walked back around the garage. Adam pulled his head out of the basement door and continued on his way around the rest of the house. The remainder of the yard didn't raise any suspicions, so he walked back down to the end of the driveway to wait for Bernie to arrive. He ducked his head back under the crime scene tape just in time to see Captain Cubbage pull up with the sheriff's office command bus.

"Ah yes, the disgrace of the sheriff's office fleet," Adam chaffed.

The 1980 E-One ambulance with a Stillwell County Sheriff's Office star plastered on the side came to a halt behind Bobby's cruiser. It had all the necessary tools and lighting that Adam was going to need inside the house, but it was still an ambulance. As soon as the bus was idling in park, Bishop leaned against the hood to warm himself on the engine compartment. He pulled another cigarette from his front pocket and lit it, never taking his eyes off of Adam.

"Could you wear that shit to work in Detroit?"

"I worked in probation and parole. They didn't care what we wore as long as we showed up once in a while. What the hell is your problem anyways? Didn't your wife give you any this week?"

"Why can't you just go with the damn flow, Adam? You always have to go against the grain?"

Bishop took a long drag off his cigarette and blew the smoke up into the air. The two stood silently glaring at one another, expecting the other to break the silence, but no one did. Adam was a damn good detective in Bishop's eyes, but the way he did things made Bishop angry. At least once a week, he was handling a complaint from an irate citizen about the way Adam had treated them. Just once, he wished Adam would play by the rules and not constantly bend them. Bishop finished his cigarette, and was about to light up another one, when he and Adam were illuminated by a pair of headlights coming toward them.

"Good, Bernie is here. Now we can get this investigation started. And this isn't over, Adam, you can bet your ass on that."

Adam let his words roll right off his back as he walked up the street to meet Bernie.

"What's up, Adam?"

"There's a dead chick in a closet and a meth lab on a desk in the front bedroom. Chief One thinks she was cooking and the lab caught fire. She got trapped by the flames and headed into the closet. Burned to a crisp, like my wife's cooking."

"Did he give you any indication about what kind of lab it is?"

"All he said was that he saw a glass bottle with three necks on top of it, sitting on a hot plate with chemical bottles nearby."

"Okay, my guys from the task force are on their way, along with the DEA clean up crew. They should be here in an hour or so. You get the search warrant yet?"

"No, I just got here half an hour ago. After we meet with Bishop and Cubbage, I'll head to the office and type one up."

"Did Bishop yell at you for wearing your jersey?"

"Yep."

The two detectives had a good laugh as they continued to walk over to Bishop and Cubbage, who were standing in front of the command bus.

"Out of shirts, Detective Alexander?" Captain Cubbage asked.

"Nope, I was half asleep when I put this on. Can we please focus on the case, gentlemen?"

Adam looked over at Bishop and Cubbage and saw they both had a look of disgust on their faces. That write-up was imminent now. Trying to change the subject from his inappropriate attire to the investigation, he pulled out the small notebook from his back pocket and flipped to a blank page.

"The way I see it, we're going to need a search warrant for the house,"
Adam suggested.

Cubbage immediately protested, "No need for that. Just get in there. If you run into something that looks suspicious, then get the warrant. We're losing valuable time here."

Bernie had kept quiet up to this point but felt he had to interject, "With all due respect, Captain, Adam is right. We already know there's a meth lab inside the house, which means she was probably distributing. If we go in now, without a search warrant, we run the risk of any potential narcotics cases being tossed out due to a bad search. Let's slow down and do this right."

Cubbage threw his head back in disgust and disappeared into the confines of the command bus. It had been at least fifteen years since he had worked the streets, and it was apparent that pushing paper from behind a desk had taken its toll on Cubbage's knowledge of the legal system.

Bernie looked over at Adam and then back at Bishop, "Did I say something wrong here?"

"No, you're right, Steckler. Don't worry about him. You guys figure things out, and I'll talk to Cubbage. Adam, you go and get that search warrant ASAP. You hear me?"

"You got it, boss," he replied.

Chapter 2

Bishop disappeared into the command bus, leaving Adam and Bernie to talk over their game plan. As he opened the door to the rear cab of the one-time ambulance, a warm blast of air hit him in the face, along with the aroma of freshly brewed coffee. He immediately craved a cup. Climbing in, he took a seat on the bench that ran along the wall just inside the door and inspected his surroundings. The first thing his eyes gravitated toward was the coffee pot that was mounted securely to the shortened counter and a small microwave directly above it. The walls were lightly stained from years of hard use and the linoleum flooring was in desperate need of replacing. This was the first time he had been inside the command bus since it was purchased at an auction a few months back. Although it was a little run down, Bishop thought it would serve their purposes just fine.

"Coffee, Bishop?"

"Sure."

Captain Cubbage poured the coffee and set it on the small table that separated them. Bishop quickly picked up the piping hot cup of black coffee and gingerly took a sip. He could feel it warm his insides as it traveled down his chest, and eventually settling in his stomach.

"This is the first time I've been in here, Cap," Bishop said.

"Yeah, I had to fight for the coffee pot and the microwave, but I think the sheriff will be happy he gave in to my requests when he gets here."

"The sheriff's on his way down here?"

"Yeah, he is. I told him he didn't need to, but he insisted on it. He said it would look good if he made an appearance, because of the upcoming election later this year."

"That must be stressful, having to worry…"

"Cut the bullshit, Bishop. You and I both know your job is on the line here. All because of your nasty attitude and your inability to keep your troops in line."

"My troops listen to me just fine."

"Oh, do they? Alexander looks real fucking pretty in that bright red shirt out there. You need to show the sheriff that you can get the job done and do it without being a pain in his ass."

"My wing has a 78% case resolution rating. Higher than when you ran the unit, Eddie…"

"That's what I'm talking about, Bishop. It isn't about the numbers. It's how you play the game. And right now, you aren't a team player. I'm tired of sticking my neck out for you all the time. Play nice or get demoted. It's that simple. Oh, and by the way—I had an 80% case resolution rating. Make sure you close the door on your way out, Bishop."

Bishop picked up his Styrofoam cup and stepped out of the bus without saying another word. He walked past Adam and Bernie, who were still talking about the case, and returned to his spot against the warm engine compartment. After placing his cup on the hood, Bishop pulled out a cigarette and lit it. He took long drags, like any chain smoker would, as he stared into the dark distance. He was so angry at this point, that his hands were shaking and the cold air stung his red hot face.

"Problem, Sarge?" Bernie asked.

"No, just get going, you two."

Adam turned his back on Bishop, pulled out his notebook, and wrote *1894* on a blank page—the house number he had gotten from the mailbox. He would need the exact address for the search warrant.

"Okay, Bernie, I'm headed to the office to fill out the search warrant. After it's typed up, I'll swing by Judge Watson's house to get it signed, which should put me back here in a little over an hour. When the rest of the task force guys get here, tell them to suit up and do a cursory search of the house, to make sure there are no more hidden secrets or dead bodies inside, and then get out. Tell them not to open any drawers or cabinets that a body can't fit in."

"You got it. I'll go talk to Chief One and see what I can figure out."

Adam closed his notebook and took one last look at the house up on the knoll before getting into his car. Thankfully, the engine was still somewhat warm from when he first arrived so it didn't take long for the heat to warm up and thaw him out. As he drove up the winding road out of the valley, he contemplated calling the judge, but decided to wait until he was almost to the office. There was no need to wake him up any earlier than he needed to.

Bernie walked over to Bobby and checked in before ducking under the crime scene tape. He pulled out his flash light and aimed the beam at the wooded area that lined the right side of the driveway. While he was walking up to meet Chief One, he searched the ground for empty bottles, plastic containers, used coffee filters, or matchbook striker plates. But it was clean. Not even an empty soda can or candy bar wrapper.

"Can I help you?" Chief One called out from near the rear bumper of Engine One.

"Yes, Sir. I understand you were the one who found the meth lab and the dead lady in the front room."

"That all depends on who you are."

Bernie turned off his flash light and walked over to the chief with his hand extended, "I'm Detective Bernie Steckler from the sheriff's office. I'm also the narcotics guy from the Appalachian Mountain Narcotics Task Force." (AMNTF)

"Don't any of you guys wear a uniform, or at least some form of identification any more?"

Bernie laughed before answering, "Well, Adam marches to his own drummer and I'm sure you noticed that he can be kind of a prick."

"Yeah, I picked up on that. What would you like to know, Detective?"

Bernie and the chief went over his exact movements through the first floor and everything he had seen in the front room. He also questioned him extensively on the chemicals on the floor, the type of cooking implements, and the heat source that was used for the cook. Bernie was now confident this was a red phosphorous lab that he would be dealing with. Luckily for him this one had already exploded, so his only real worry would be the deadly gasses that were left behind.

Ten minutes later, Adam turned right off of Spurlock Creek road onto Route 114. As he crossed over the bridge into the town of Stillwell he pulled out his cell phone and dialed Judge Watson's home number to alert him that he would be stopping by shortly. It took two tries, but he was finally able to get the Judge to answer.

"Hello, Your Honor. This is Detective Adam Alexander."

"Good Lord man, do you know what time it is?"

"Yes, Sir. I'm aware of the time. The reason I'm calling this late is because we have a deceased female inside of a residence on Spurlock Creek Road, and I'm going to be on your doorstep in the next forty five minutes to get a search warrant signed."

"Sorry to hear that. Do you know how she died?"

"It appears it was a meth lab explosion. The house went up in flames pretty quick, and she got trapped in the closet. Chief One said she's burned pretty bad."

"You know where I live, detective. Try not to take too long, please."

"I won't, Sir. Be there shortly."

Adam hung up the phone and made the right off of Route 114 onto Main Street. All five of the traffic signals were now on flashing yellow, making the short trip to Court Street even shorter. He considered getting a cup of coffee, but the only business that was open this late on a Sunday was the *Grub-N-Gas* on the other side of town. Nine times out of ten the local drunks hung around the front of the convenience store begging for spare change, or getting drunk behind the building. Normally, it didn't bother him, but tonight he didn't feel like dealing with career alcoholics, so he went directly to the sheriff's office. Roughly a mile down the road, Adam made the left onto Court Street and an immediate right into the sheriff's office parking lot. He pulled up to his assigned spot in the rear of the building and wasted little time getting inside the modest three-story brick structure to his office on the second floor. Adam had written so many affidavits for a search warrant that it only took him about 20 minutes to get this one typed up and ready for Judge Watson to sign.

With the finished affidavit in hand, Adam made the 15 minute drive north to Hagerhill, just outside the small town of Paintsville. As he drove in silence, he remembered being dragged down to Paintsville by his parents to visit relatives for just about every holiday when he was a kid. He dreaded the seven-hour car ride from Detroit, but loved being able to run around town without having to worry about a drive-by shooting every minute. That's what drew him to the area after he was laid off.

Adam pulled into Judge Watson's driveway and parked right behind his black Lincoln Town Car. As he walked up the steps to the front porch, he could see the outline of a man slumped over in a recliner through the living room window. The only light on inside the room came from a flat-screen television that hung on the wall over the fireplace. Adam hated to wake him, but he had no choice. Carefully, he opened the storm door and knocked on the heavy wood door. It took a few minutes, but eventually the Judge opened the door.

"Good morning, Your Honor. Thanks for doing this so late. I certainly do appreciate it."

"Come on in, Detective. My wife made us some coffee in the kitchen, if you'd like a cup."

"You have no idea how good that sounds, Sir."

Adam followed the judge into the kitchen, took a seat at the table, and graciously accepted the cup of coffee that was offered to him.

"Now, let's get down to business, shall we?" The Judge stated as he took the affidavit from Adam, walked into the living room, and sat down behind his desk.

Adam took a few sips before noticing the cup he was drinking from cheerfully declared: "Global Warming, The Homeless Give It Two Thumbs Up!" Adam started to chuckle as he turned the mug to see a homeless cartoon character staring back at him with two thumbs held high in the air.

"You like that, huh? My wife's brother picked that up for me somewhere. It might be a little politically incorrect, but I find it humorous."

Judge Watson took a few minutes to read over Adam's affidavit before raising his right hand and asking, "Is all of the information contained within, true and accurate to the best of your knowledge?"

Adam raised his right hand and responded, "Yes, Sir."

"Well, everything seems to be in order here. How many copies of the search warrant would you like, Detective?"

"Three, please. One has to be left at the residence, one for me, and the original that needs to be certified with the Circuit Court when we're finished."

"You got it."

Judge Watson filled in the blanks on the search warrant with all of the information Adam provided in the affidavit and hit the *print* button. Within five minutes Adam had his search warrant and was driving like a man possessed to get back to the fire grounds. Precious time was being wasted. But nothing could prepare him for what waited for him when he got back.

"What in the HELL is going on here?" he yelled.

The road was completely blocked, forcing Adam to double back and park in the Baptist church parking lot. He angrily grabbed the search warrant, shoved it in his leather notebook, and walked the quarter mile to the command bus. The entire area was lit up like a Friday night football game.

As he got closer, he could see Sheriff Joseph Lawson pacing back and forth at the end of the driveway. It was official—Adam was walking into a giant cluster fuck.

"What's going on here, Bishop? Who are all these damn people?"

"Calm down, Adam. It could be a lot worse, trust me. The fire department has to decontaminate everyone who was inside the house and they wanted to do it in the driveway. But I convinced them to do it out here on the road. The three white box trucks are from the DEA cleanup crew. The seven cars in front of the command bus are all Bernie's guys. Those three cars over there are more volunteer firefighters who came late to rubber neck, and …"

Adam put his hand up to silence Bishop and walked up the driveway to find Bernie. He found him huddled up with his crew in front of the stairs leading to the covered porch. "Hey, Bernie! Gather your crew and come on over here, please."

Bernie and the rest of the AMNTF had just finished gearing up in their hazmat suits and full SCBA, so they did as they were instructed and gathered in front of Adam to get their assignment.

"I have the search warrant signed by the judge, so don't worry about opening something that you shouldn't. If you guys see anything that will help us in the investigation, tell Bernie, and he'll let me know. I appreciate all your help."

Bernie led the team of four up the stairs and into the living room. He gave instructions for two guys to head upstairs, two to go into the basement, and he would take the middle floor with the gas meter. Before heading off, everyone was advised that once they had completed their sweep, they were to meet on the front porch to debrief.

"Remember to open any windows that haven't already been broken by the fire department. We need to vent this place as much as possible. Any questions?" Bernie asked.

No one had any, so they all moved off to search their assigned portion of the house. Bernie hit the power button on his portable gas meter, expecting to find some level of dangerous gasses in the air, but the backlit needle didn't budge. He pulled the device toward his ear to make sure it was cycling air through the particle filter. Once he was satisfied it was functioning properly, he slowly ambled through the first floor, moving counterclockwise. He stopped in each room, making sure he took adequate air samples from each of the four corners and the middle. Shockingly, there were no toxic levels in the kitchen, family room, or the dining room. Bernie continued slowly down the small hallway that passed the half bathroom, and on to the front bedroom. He had encountered more than a dozen meth labs since joining the task force, but this was the first one that had a body associated with it.

He hesitated at the door and looked down at his gas meter to see how high the levels were, but it still read zero. He looked into the corner to see the meth lab sitting on the table, so he knew he was in the right room.

"Is this damn thing even working?" he thought to himself, as he hit the side of the black box.

Enough procrastination, it was time for him to go in. Reluctantly, he took a deep breath and slowly walked into the room. He had seen many dead bodies throughout his career, but it never got any easier. This was one of the reasons he had left general investigations and moved over to the narcotics position. Dead bodies always forced him to face his own mortality, keeping him up at night. After much deliberation, he had come to the conclusion that he wasn't scared of dying, but he was terrified of being dead.

Bernie had to snap himself out of his trance to get his tasks completed. He eased himself further into the center of the room and took a mental inventory of what was in front of him. Out of the corner of his eye, Bernie saw the badly burned female sitting upright in the closet. Quickly, he again turned his attention back to the gas meter in his hand and the meth lab.

"What the fuck?" Bernie muttered to himself.

He hit the side of it again in an attempt to make it magically start working, but no matter what he did, or how hard he hit it, the needle still hovered over the zero. After a few minutes of fumbling with the meter, he put it down to start looking at the lab set-up. The first thing he noticed was that there was no ventilation device to pull the toxic fumes away from the hot plate as it cooked. He looked down at the hot plate itself and made sure it was turned off before looking inside the triple-neck flask to see if any sludge had settled in the bottom. The flask itself was charred black with soot from the fire, but there didn't appear to be any residue left inside. This was strange to him, but maybe one of the bottles of ether had caught fire before she could start the cook. Or maybe while she was separating the red phosphorous from the match books, one had accidentally ignited. That little flame could have set off some residual gas that hung in the air. Anything was possible.

Bernie picked up his portable gas meter, turned, and walked out of the bedroom to rendezvous with the rest of the AMNTF, who were already on the front porch.

"You guys find any other bodies?" Bernie asked.

No one else in the crew had seen anything out of the ordinary, but they were highly interested in what Bernie had seen. He described the scene to them, in all its gory detail, as they walked back toward Adam.

"Are we all good?" Adam asked.

"As good as we can be with a dead chick and a meth lab, I suppose," Bernie laughed.

Adam and Bernie retreated back to the command bus while the rest of the task force assisted the DEA in setting up their gear. Everything that came out of the house had to be placed on large plastic tarps and separated into chemical classifications. After the evidence was separated, samples had to be taken out of each container and sent off to the lab to be analyzed. During a trial, it's easier to make your case with samples from each stage of the process, so the defendants can't say they were simply mixing chemicals trying to come up with a new laundry detergent. After all the samples were gathered and labeled, what was left of the items was placed in plastic fifty-five gallon drums to be destroyed at a special DEA facility in Louisville.

Bernie opened up one of the side compartments on the bus and retrieved the digital video recorder and a fresh tape, while Adam put on a TYVEC suit.

"Do we need full SCBA on this one, or will a respirator mask do?" Adam asked.

"You know, I'm going to downgrade to level C and just use a mask. I think that all the residual gas is long gone from inside."

Adam pulled the respirator over his face and waited for Bernie to get the video recorder ready. Bernie hit the *record* button and trained the camera lens on Adam.

"It is now 01:11 hours, on Monday, December 19th. It is approximately thirty-one degrees out this morning, and the moon is almost full, hanging midway in the sky. The light being cast by the moon is excellent, and visibility without an alternate light source is roughly one hundred feet. The house is a two-story farmhouse with deep red wood siding and a covered front porch. There are four windows across the front of the bottom floor and there are five windows across the top floor. The tin roof appears to be a light green color. All of the windows are broken. There is obvious charring around the roofline and around each of the windows. First impression of the exterior of the residence is that it appears to have held up well considering what it just went through. There's an attached two-car garage which appears to have been added after the construction of the house, and the two garage doors are closed and in the locked position. Located in the driveway there's an older model Toyota Corolla bearing Kentucky registration K1G-98L. The car appears to be dark grey in color. Beyond the house, to the right, there's a barn-style utility shed with open doors."

Adam continued to narrate as he walked around the perimeter of the house a second time, looking for anything out of the ordinary. But nothing revealed itself to him. After completing the full lap around the house, he walked up the wooden steps that led to the font door. Using his flashlight, he was able to see what was in front of him, and more importantly, what he was stepping on.

"I am entering the residence at exactly 01:14 hours through an open front door. Looking at the door-frame, it appears that forced entry was made into the residence. Company One was first on scene and attacked the fire from the front, so I will check with their personnel to see if any of them kicked the front door in. I am now in the living room of the house, just inside the front door. The house has a normal flow, and you can move through each room freely. Every room appears to have two entrances, so I will be moving through the first floor counterclockwise until I return to my point of entry. To my right is a fake Christmas tree that is unlit, but still plugged in. The ornaments have all melted onto the hardwood floor from the heat of the fire. To my left is a coat closet and the stairs leading to the upper level. In front of me are the couch, love seat, and coffee table, which are all burned. Looking at the walls, the charring appears to be normal from floor to ceiling."

As he walked into the next room, Adam noticed there weren't any family pictures on the walls, and there was a lack of furniture, like the occupants had just moved in. He was thankful that his suspicions about this being a hoarder's residence weren't proving to be true.

"I'm now moving into the kitchen, directly behind the living room. There is charring along the walls in this room, as well. The sliding glass door is in the closed position and is locked."

He unlocked the heavy glass door and moved outside to take a better look at the deck and the back side of the house.

"The deck off the kitchen doesn't appear to have been damaged. There aren't any char marks on the wood. On the railing next to the door is an ashtray that's not been emptied in a while, and there's water in the base. The siding on the back of the house is intact. I see nothing out of the ordinary on the deck, so I'll be moving back into the kitchen. There is a hallway to my left that has two doors. The door on the right is a pantry, and the door on the left is the door to the basement."

He knew he was getting close to the origin of the fire because the charring on the walls and ceiling were getting darker, but he wasn't there yet.

"Further down the hallway is another room. As I stand in the doorway, there's a large hutch to my immediate right. There aren't any plates or glasses displayed in the hutch. Along the back wall is a window that was broken out—during the fire, I'm assuming. Directly in front of me is the dining room table, with exactly six chairs around the table and two additional chairs in the back corners of the room. All of the furniture has sustained significant fire damage. So far, this is the only room I have been into that has carpeting, and all of the fibers have been melted. There's no other furniture in this room, and it looks like there may have been a picture hanging on the wall, but it is now missing. Moving to my left, there's another hallway."

Walking down the hallway, Adam was able to see the char marks on the wall were dark black from the intense heat and flames. He was almost at the origin.

"I'm walking down the hallway, and I see there's a door on my right that leads to a half bathroom. A quick look into this room reveals that the left wall is burned through in two places, and in daylight conditions I would be able to see into the front room. The fire appears to have been the most intense in that front right room."

Adam stopped and looked over his shoulder to make sure Bernie was still directly behind him and filming.

"You ready, Bernie?" Adam asked.

"As ready as I'll ever be."

Chapter 3

Bernie took a deep breath at the door, not wanting to go back inside, but he persevered and pushed past his anxiety, making his way in.

"As I enter the room I notice that the walls and ceiling are badly damaged by the fire," Adam narrated.

Bernie stopped in the center of the room and slowly spun clockwise, recording everything Adam was talking about.

"The wall to my immediate left has the remnants of a dresser and a television. The television is melted and not plugged in. Along the far wall, which is the front of the house, the window has been blasted inward, from what I am assuming is the pressure coming from the fire department's hoses. To the left of that window is a small wooden desk that contains the possible meth lab that Detective Bernie Steckler will be dismantling and sending off for chemical analysis. Along the wall to my right there's a box spring and a mattress being supported by a metal bed frame. The mattress is badly burned, exposing the metal infrastructure."

Adam continued to turn to his right and looked into the closet.

"As I turn to my right, I'm looking into a closet with double sliding doors. Inside the closet on top of a pile of burnt clothing is a deceased female in the typical boxer's position. She's thin and partially clothed. Her height is estimated at five feet, three inches tall, and her approximate weight is 115 pounds. No hair color or eye color can be discerned at this time. She's wearing jeans that have melted partially into her skin and a black sweater that has also melted into her skin. Due to her exposed genitals, it doesn't appear that the female was wearing a bra or panties at the time of death." Adam looked back toward Bernie, "You can stop the video, Bernie."

Bernie hit *stop* on the recorder and placed it on the floor next to the doorway. Although he had already seen the lab setup, he took a more detailed look around the room to make sure he hadn't missed anything.

"I need to photograph everything before we start moving stuff around. You got the camera, Adam?"

"It's in the evidence kit on the front porch. I'll get it."

Adam walked out the door, returning a few minutes later with the evidence kit. He placed the hard plastic pelican case on the floor and opened the cover to find the camera mixed in with all the other paraphernalia. He reached in and picked up the camera to inspect it for damage. After blowing the dust off the LCD monitor, he opened the battery compartment to see the memory card slot was empty. He hoped there was an extra one in all that mess, because if there wasn't, he would have to drive all the way back to the station to get another one. It took a minute, but luckily Adam was able to pull out a new memory card that was buried in the bottom of the kit.

"Here you go, Bernie."

"Damn, and I thought I was unorganized."

"You can go get your evidence kit if mine isn't good enough for you."

"Don't get your panties in a wad, Detective Sensitive."

Bernie quickly began snapping pictures of the room, giving most of his attention to the meth lab. After he finished, he turned and handed the camera back to Adam.

"I'm going to take my samples from the stuff off the dresser and get all this shit outside for the DEA guys to dispose of."

"Dispose of? Don't you need any of that for court?"

"Nope, all I need are the photographs and the chemical analysis from the DEA chemists. In a minute, I'm going to put in a new tape and set up the video recorder to record my every move as I take all my samples. When I'm done I'll take everything out into the front yard and put it on that big blue tarp. The DEA clean-up crew will take it, package it up in those blue fifty five gallon plastic barrels, and destroy it for us at their facility. What I'm going to keep is good enough—besides, judges tend to get a little pissed off when you bring toxic chemicals into their court room."

"I never thought about it like that. As soon as I finish here, do you mind giving me a hand getting the body outside?"

"Yeah, sure." he said hesitantly.

Adam turned away from Bernie and started to photograph the closet and the dead woman inside. He took multiple pictures from every angle to make sure he accurately recorded the scene in each picture. The body was in terrible shape and the smell was almost unbearable. Adam began to gag as he thoroughly looked over the body. He didn't see any gaping wounds or any unidentifiable holes, just burnt flesh. Adam placed his hand under her chin and lifted up her head, exposing the only unscathed patch of white skin on her otherwise blackened body. Her eyebrows and eyelashes were completely singed off. Her hair was almost completely gone, except for one small patch in the back that appeared to be blonde with dark-colored roots. Adam shined his flashlight into her gaping mouth and saw the light reflect off of the four fillings that were in her molars.

"Looks like the medical examiner is going to have to positively identify her through her dental records, since we won't be able to do that here," Adam stated.

Adam gently put her head back in its original position and retrieved two medium-sized paper bags from his collection kit. He turned back around, placed the bags on the ground next to her thigh, and picked up one of her hands to look under her fingernails.

"Doesn't look like there's any skin under the nails, and the prints are all but burned off. I sure hope we find a driver's license or social security card for this lady, or it's going to set us back a few days. Identification through dental records takes a while."

Adam placed her left hand inside the brown paper bag and sealed it tightly with evidence tape to preserve any debris, skin cells or foreign contaminants that may have survived the fire under her fingernails. He did the same with the other hand, just as cautiously. It was time to get the body out of the closet, so he gently pulled her forward, exposing her back with one hand and photographing with the other. Her sweater was relatively intact and hung on to her body by the fibers that had fused into her skin. Adam had never investigated a burning death before, and was intrigued by the way her body had reacted to the intense heat. He could feel her waxy skin, which was still warm, through his latex gloves as he grabbed her around her shoulders.

"I can't even tell if this lady had any tattoos, she's so burnt. Bernie, can you give me a hand getting her out of the closet and into the body bag?"

"Sure thing. Hey, why did you call it a boxer's position earlier?" he asked, as he walked over toward the closet.

"You see how her body is right now? Her arms are flexed at the elbow and her wrists are held out in front of her body. Just like a heavyweight boxer. When a body is exposed to heat for too long, the water evaporates from the muscle and the proteins coagulate, causing it to contract into this position. Unfortunately, the body reacts to heat like this no matter if they die before or during the fire, so the true test will be if there's smoke in her lungs."

Adam put one hand under her armpit and the other under her thigh while Bernie did the same on the opposite side. They lifted the stiff body and brought it into the center of the room.

"It's just like my wife's overcooked thanksgiving turkey, and smells just as bad," Adam noted casually.

"Man, that's gross. Why do you have to say shit like that?"

Adam started to laugh as he took the body bag out of its plastic housing and placed the two toe tags that were inside on the pelican case. He unfolded the heavy nylon bag and placed it flat, next to the body.

"Good luck getting this thing zipped up. She's stiff as a board," Bernie added as they positioned the body in the middle of the bag

"Yeah, and I don't have a lot of information to put on the toe tag, either. She's gonna have to be "Jane Doe" for now, because even if we do find her driver's license I won't be able to positively identify her."

Adam placed one of the tags on the victim's left toe and zipped the bag up tight. It looked like they had placed a large cube in a bag that was designed for the body to lie flat. He placed the second tag on the two zippers, along with a biohazard sticker on the outside of the bag, because of the possible contamination from the meth lab. With Bernie's help, he carried the body to the front porch for the funeral home to transport to the coroner's office in Lexington.

"It looks like it's up to the medical examiner to figure out who she is and how she died," Adam said.

Bernie called out to Sergeant Bishop, "Hey, Sarge, she's all ready to go to the medical examiner's office in Lexington. Can you call the funeral home and get someone to take her down there?"

"Dr. Edwards specializes in burn victims, and I think he would be better suited for this investigation. See if he can do the cutting on this one," Adam added.

Sergeant Bishop gave Bernie and Adam the thumbs-up, and called for Deputy Smith to leave his post at the end of the driveway to stand near the body, in order to maintain a proper chain of custody.

"You ready to head back in, Bernie? We've got a long night ahead of us."

"Yes we do."

The two detectives walked back inside the house to continue their investigation. Adam returned directly to the front room to start the more thorough search of the closet while Bernie finished packaging up the lab and bringing it out piece by piece to the front yard. Adam stood inside the walk-in closet where the body had been to give Bernie more space to work. He sifted through each piece of burned clothing, making sure there were no secrets contained within. Toward the bottom of the pile, he made a discovery.

"Get a load of this, Bernie."

Adam pulled out a melted red plastic gas can and held it up for Bernie to see.

"What could this be used for?" Adam asked.

"It's used as an HCL generator."

"What in the hell is an HCL generator?"

"At the end of the cooking process, the meth is suspended in a liquid and needs to be turned back into a solid. These guys take muriatic acid and mix it with rock salt inside the gas can, creating a reaction that yields hydrochloric gas. When you run that gas through your liquid with the suspended meth in it, it binds with the meth, making it a solid again. All you have to do then is run the liquid through a coffee filter. The solid that's left behind in the filter is pure methamphetamine hydrochloride."

"People actually put this shit in their bodies?"

"Yeah, and what's worse is the fact that a lot of these first-time cooks screw up so badly, that their initial batch kills people."

"I guess this belongs to you, then."

Adam handed the melted can over to Bernie to add to his collection of evidence and returned to the closet. Finding nothing of any particular use to him, Adam decided it was time to go and look through the rest of the house.

"Let me know when you're finished here, Bernie. I'm going to go upstairs and have a look."

"You got it."

Bernie turned back around and continued to focus on his task, while Adam grabbed his camera and digital recorder. He walked out of the room and turned to his right, leading him down the dark, narrow hallway toward the living room. When he got to the front door, he turned right again, and stood in front of the old staircase leading upstairs. After a quick visual inspection for any charring, he gently put the ball of his foot on the first step. Satisfied it was going to hold his weight, he raised his second foot onto the step and stood motionless for a few seconds. When he didn't hear any unsettling noises coming from underfoot, he moved on to the second step. He repeated this tedious process for what seemed like an eternity until he successfully reached the top. Once successfully on the second floor, he paused and took a deep breath. He looked back at the stairs he had just climbed before turning his full attention to what was in front of him. Using his flashlight, he was able to see that he was standing at the beginning of a long, wide hallway with four doors on either side. He was pleasantly surprised that the fire had not destroyed anything he could see, but had only left a heavy odor of smoke.

With his digital recorder still turned on, Adam began to describe everything he was seeing as he walked down to the first door. It was a frustratingly slow process because every time he snapped a picture, his vision was impaired by the flash, and it took his pupils a few seconds to readjust to the inadequate lighting. It took a few minutes, but he finally arrived at the first door to his left, which was a full bathroom.

"The upstairs bathroom is clear of any evidence. There is no blood in the sink, and there are two toothbrushes in a clear glass cup next to the faucet. As I pull back the shower curtain, I can see that the tub is clean and free of any blood or bodily fluids."

He walked out of the bathroom and across the hall to the next door. He opened the door and walked in.

"This room is pink with a lot of posters of boy bands and porcelain dolls throughout. The bed is made and the room itself is neat and orderly. Clothes are folded and placed neatly on the chair that is next to the dresser. There is a middle school yearbook on the shelf above the dresser."

Adam pulled the yearbook from the shelf and opened the front cover. As he read the well wishes from a few of the students, he noticed they were all addressed to a girl named "Addison". But as he flipped through the 7th

grade class, he counted 3 Addison's within the first 5 pages. He gently put the yearbook back on the shelf and directed his attention to the medium-sized oak jewelry box that sat on top of the dresser. After opening the lid, he saw several expensive-looking gold and silver chains, along with ten silver rings, lovingly housed in the green velvet-lined box. He gently closed the lid and pulled open both of the small drawers, exposing several pictures of an adolescent girl, standing next to a mid-twenties looking man at Disneyland. They both looked so happy in the pictures. Adam could see her holding his hand tight, and smiling like she didn't have a worry in the world.

He carefully placed the pictures back where he found them, and restored the box to its original condition before saying out loud, "There is no blood or anything out of the ordinary in this room."

After exiting that room he walked a little farther down the hall to the second door on the left which was another child's room.

"This room is painted blue and is in the same orderly condition as the other. Clothing is neatly folded and on the chair next to the dresser. There are race car posters hanging on the wall, and there's a baseball mitt on the bed."

He walked over to the closet and opened it to see a pint-sized three-piece suit hanging neatly in front of him. On the floor were several plastic boxes full of building blocks, Matchbox cars, and green army men. Nothing was out of place.

"Again, there isn't any blood or anything out of the ordinary."

Adam's next thought was about the safety of the children. He needed to quickly identify these two and make sure they weren't kidnapped. He went to retrieve his portable radio from his belt to contact Bishop, but was quickly reminded he didn't have it, when he reached down and grabbed at nothing. He would have to go outside. Adam went down the stairs, not paying as much attention to their weakened state as he previously did, and out the front door.

"Hey, Bishop!"

"Yeah, Adam. What's up?"

"It appears that two kids live in this house. See if you can get a hold of our school resource deputy and ask if he can do a search of the students by address. If not, the last name on that tag in the driveway returns to a Dwyer. See if that turns up anything. If we can't find them soon we may need to issue an amber alert."

"I'll call the school resource deputy for the elementary and middle schools now. You said the last name was Dwyer?"

"Yeah, and let me know what you find out."

Adam turned around and went back to the second floor to finish his search. He bypassed the little boy's room and continued down the hall to the next room on the right. Slowly he opened the door, expecting to see heavy damage, since this was the room directly above where the fire had started, but was amazed to see the bedroom wasn't in terribly bad shape. Aside from the stench of smoke and a little water damage, everything was in good condition.

"This looks like the master bedroom. The door to this room is located in the middle of the wall, leaving equal distance on either side of me as I enter. To my left is a book-shelf, and to my right is a small table with a television on it. The wall that is back and to my left is the front of the house. The two windows are not intact, and again I'm assuming they were taken out by fire personnel. The glass is shattered inwards and is on the hard-wood floors, along with a small amount of water. On the back wall there is a bed with two small tables on either side. On the wall to my right are two doors. One leads to a closet and the other leads to the master bathroom."

Adam photographed the room before beginning a more thorough search. The first items of interest were all in plain view. He focused on the bookshelf and the items that rested on each shelf. There were three small pictures and one large one of a slim white female and two small children. Adam picked up the large picture and stared at it for a minute. He recognized the train in the background as the steam engine that ran around the Dollywood theme park in Tennessee. He had been there several times when he was younger. He put the picture down and went on to the next shelf. Small pieces of jewelry adorned each shelf along with little trinkets that appeared to have been made by a child during arts and crafts time at school. Although the items didn't have any real monetary value, it was obvious the owner cherished them enough to display them.

Not finding anything that was helpful to the investigation on the bookshelf, Adam turned around and looked at the back wall. On the first of the two bedside tables were an old wind-up alarm clock, an antique glass lamp, and two school pictures—one of a boy and one of a girl. The only drawer contained a small pocket-sized bible, a deck of playing cards, some aspirin, and a bottle of Percocet. Adam pulled out the medicine bottle and found the name Melissa Dwyer printed on the label. Next he looked for the fill date. It was filled 03/04/08 at the local pharmacy and was prescribed by *Physician, Dr. Jarvis Watkins*. The label indicated that the prescription was for thirty pills, and after opening the bottle, Adam counted out twenty nine.

"If she was a junkie, these pills would be long gone. Something is not right here," he thought.

After jotting down all the necessary information from the pill bottle, Adam closed the drawer and moved over to the neatly made queen-sized bed. There were three pillows, all tucked under the comforter at the head, where they should have been. Adam began to dissect the bed one layer at a time, meticulously scouring the linens for any clues that might emerge. When he was satisfied that the comforter had nothing to offer, he peeled off the top sheet, and then the fitted sheet, exposing a dark brown stain that was about a foot in diameter, in the exact middle of the mattress.

"BERNIE! Get up here with the collection kit."

It took a few minutes, but eventually Bernie arrived with the kit and a portable battery-powered light source.

"What did you find?"

"This stain, here on the mattress. It looks like it may have been here for a while, but then again, the heat from the fire may have dried it faster. Either way it's getting sent to the lab."

Adam pulled out a cotton swab on an elongated wooden stick from a sterile package and dipped the cotton tip into a bottle of saline solution. Carefully, he dabbed the wet cotton on the mattress until the tip was the same color as the stain. He placed the sample in a biohazard container and placed the tube in the top drawer of his kit.

"Help me flip this mattress, Bernie."

Bernie walked to the opposite side of the bed and grabbed hold of the mattress. With one steady pull, the mattress was off the box spring and leaned up against the front wall.

"What in the world are those?" Adam asked.

"Looks like four envelopes to me."

Adam picked up the camera and photographed the four business-sized envelopes that were concealed under the mattress.

"This envelope is dated yesterday, this one ten days from now, this one for next month, and the last one is dated for February," Adam said.

He reached down and ripped opened the envelope that was dated 12-18-08 to find a stack of twenty dollar bills, totaling $140. One by one, he opened the remaining envelopes and placed the contents on the box spring.

"All the envelopes have money in them. Two have $140, and the other two have $300 in them. That's what, $880? Bernie, what is meth going for these days?"

"Depends on the grade, and if it's crystal. Typically it goes for around $100 per gram. Crystal is the purest form of meth, but we rarely see that stuff around here. That goes for around $150 to $200 per gram."

"Why is crystal more expensive?"

"Normally, meth has a pink tinge to it because they don't get all of the red gel coating off the Sudafed pills. With crystal, they clean out all the red junk and other impurities, leaving behind almost one hundred percent pure meth. But that cash couldn't be proceeds from drug sales; it isn't enough. One cook should yield a lot more than $880 worth of dope, right?"

"That all depends. Maybe this was all that's left after she paid someone to deal it for her."

Adam put each of the individual envelopes in evidence bags and placed them near his collection kit. He did the same for each of the bed linens, because of the stain he had found on the mattress.

"Can you start taking this stuff down to the van while I finish up in here, Bernie?"

"Yeah, I can do that."

Bernie picked up the packaged items from the room and stacked them by the front door, just outside the house, while Adam snapped a few pictures of the remaining bedside table. Since there was nothing on top of it, he had little faith that there would be anything inside its tiny drawer. To his surprise there was a small book with a blank brown leather cover. After photographing it in its original position, he picked up the book and opened the cover. Three social security cards and an old Radford University student identification card, that had been nestled in between the front cover and the first page, fell to the floor. Adam quickly picked them up to keep them from getting damaged from the residual water on the floor and read the three names that were printed on the cards, Melissa Anne Dwyer, Addison Michelle Dwyer, and Aiden Christopher Dwyer. The name on the *Radford University Express* card was Melissa Anne Herzog and had a picture of a younger version of the female Adam had seen in other pictures in the room. This had to be their victim. Adam walked over to the broken-out window and stuck his head out to get Bishop's attention.

"Hey, Bishop! I've got three names and three social security numbers for you when you're ready. It appears that the last name I gave you earlier might be the right one, and I think we can safely assume our victim is going to be Melissa Anne Dwyer."

"Yeah, we know. But thanks for screaming that information to the neighborhood."

"No problem!"

Adam pulled his head back inside the window and directed his attention back to the book. He started to read the first page and discovered it was a complete chronology of Melissa's life. Adam finished reading the first few paragraphs before quickly thumbing through the remaining pages.

"Holy smokes, there has to be at least fifty or sixty hand-written pages here," he thought.

He placed the book in an evidence bag along with the social security cards and retrained his attention back to the open drawer. There were a few scrap pieces of paper and receipts for oil changes and groceries. Adam heard Bernie come back upstairs and walk down the hallway toward the master bedroom.

"Is there anything else you need?" Bernie asked.

"Check this out, Bernie. There are three separate receipts for pregnancy tests in this drawer. All of them dated within the last four months. This just keeps getting more and more interesting."

Adam continued to look through the drawer and found three passports as well as two more prescriptions for Percocet that were never filled. Everything was packaged up as evidence.

"I just have the closet and the bathroom to go through and the upstairs is finished," Adam said.

"Take your time. Oh, by the way, Bishop asked me to tell you to refrain from yelling information about the case out the window."

"Screw that guy. He's just being a dick."

Adam walked over to the first door on the right wall, which opened to the walk-in closet. The shelves were lined with shoe boxes and other collectables, but once again there was nothing out of the ordinary. A small four-drawer dresser was stashed in the back corner, but it only had clothing inside of it. After the search of the closet was finished, Adam moved over to the other door, which opened to the master bathroom. A search of every available space failed to turn up any more clues.

"Did you make it into the basement, Bernie?"

"Yeah, there's a ton of boxes down there. I looked in a few, but they all had junk in them. I think they were in the process of moving in, but never finished. I'll go down there and finish looking with my crew while you go to the station and fill out all the lab request forms. Leave the search warrant on the table at the front door, and I'll complete the evidence inventory on the second page."

"Thanks, Bernie. See you back at the station."

Chapter 4

Adam was lost in his thoughts about the case as he ambled toward his cruiser. The investigation was already off to a slow start because of the meth lab, and ideally he would have been out of the house hours ago. Adam rarely second guessed himself, but tonight, for some reason, he was doubting himself—"have I forgotten anything? Or did I move too quickly and overlook something obvious?" There were too many variables that just weren't adding up.

He was in mid-thought when his concentration was broken by Bishop yelling his name.

"What?" Adam yelled back.

"Are you deaf? I called your name three times. Come over here and brief the captain and sheriff on what you know so far."

Adam walked over to the back of the command bus with the full box of evidence in his hands. Adam could tell that Bishop wanted him to hop in the back compartment for an in depth briefing, but he didn't want to. Instead he leaned his head inside the rear double doors.

"Good morning, Sheriff Lawson, Captain Cubbage. Do you two need anything from me?" Adam asked.

Sheriff Lawson was sitting in the captain's chair towards the front. His head was down and he was picking at his lower lip. Adam could tell he was deep in thought, but with Sheriff Lawson, you could never tell what was going on inside his thick skull, because he only spoke on rare occasions.

"What's that? Um… No, I don't need anything from you right now." The sheriff stammered.

"What about you, Captain?"

"Nothing comes to mind right now, Detective. Let us know if you need anything."

"Sure thing, Cap."

Adam turned back to Bishop and stared blankly at him for a few seconds before walking away. Bishop closed the double doors to the command bus and caught up with Adam as he was walking back to his car.

"I was able to track down some info on Ms. Dwyer and the kids. Fortunately, the kids are safe, with their aunt and uncle in Buffalo for the first week of Christmas vacation. According to the school resource deputy, the principal of Stillwell Elementary confirmed that Jeff and Kim Norris picked the kids up from school and drove to the airport in Louisville. They're supposed to get back sometime this week. I have yet to get in touch with them, but we do have their contact information. Also, I had them pull the contact information forms that are on file at the school. Ms. Dwyer is a manager at the BMB Textile Mill outside of town and had another address listed inside Stillwell town limits. We think she failed to update the forms at the beginning of the year. So far that's all I have been able to come up with."

"Well, that would explain all the unpacked boxes in the basement. Okay, I'm headed to the station to get going on the lab request forms to get this stuff analyzed. When did the funeral home come and get the body?"

"They came about an hour ago. I had Deputy Spencer follow them."

"Good, I'll call the medical examiner's office in a few hours and see if they can move our girl to the front of the line. See you back at the station, Bishop."

Adam placed the box of evidence down at his feet and was in the process of taking off his TYVEC suit when chief one came running over toward him.

"You need to be decontaminated, Detective. You were just exposed to toxic chemicals."

Adam quickly peeled off the entire suit and dropped it on the ground at chief one's feet. "No thanks, I'll be fine," he said as he turned around, picked up his box of evidence, and made the long walk back to his car in the church parking lot.

"You're a real prick, Detective. You know that?" Chief One yelled.

Adam didn't even break stride when he responded, "I've been called way worse, by way better than you, Chief."

On the drive to the sheriff's office, Adam was trying to think of possible scenarios as to what went wrong at Ms. Dwyer's house. The first theory that immediately popped into his head was the meth lab put off too much toxic gas, caught fire, and smothered the victim who had sought refuge in the closet. That, coupled with the money that had been found under her mattress, meant the victim was possibly involved in some illegal activities. The second theory that came to mind was this was possibly a homicide. Ms. Dwyer could have been murdered in a drug deal gone bad, placed in the closet, and the house set on fire to cover it up. Fortunately, he didn't have any evidence to support the second theory. It was almost Christmas, and a homicide investigation was not what he wanted to close out his holiday season.

As much as Adam hoped it was a bad cook, he still had a ton of unanswered questions. Like, why didn't she just run out the door when the fire started? The lab was positioned near the front wall of the room. Any fire over there wouldn't have prohibited her from running out the door. Maybe the toxic chemicals clouded her judgment and she thought she was running out the door, but instead she ran into the closet. And if she were murdered, why wasn't there any evidence on her body that suggested foul play, like a gaping wound of some sort. He would just have to wait for the medical examiner's report to get those answers.

Adam turned onto Court Street and parked in his assigned space in the sheriff's office parking lot. He walked around to the trunk of his car, and was in the process of taking out the box of evidence when he noticed a news truck pull up to the front of the office. The crew quickly emerged from the white van, and hurried down the street towards him, with the camera rolling.

A slender and attractive young woman, with a *News Channel 15* microphone spoke excitedly about the incident to the camera before turning to Adam and asking, "Are the items in your hands evidence from the suspicious death on Spurlock Creek Road? Was it in fact a meth lab explosion that killed the person?"

Adam gave the reporter a puzzled look before responding, "The remains of a female were found inside a partially burned residence last night, and we're working feverishly to get a positive identification on her. The cause of the fire is still under investigation by the fire marshal and we'll know more shortly. Thank you."

Adam turned around and walked into the rear door of the sheriff's office making sure to let it slam behind him.

"How in the world did they get this information so quickly? It must be a slow news day if they're all the way out in the country doing a story on this," he thought to himself.

Meanwhile, back at the crime scene, Bernie and his crew spent the remainder of the morning looking through all of the boxes in the basement, but were unable to find anything of importance to the investigation. Satisfied they had looked everywhere, Bernie picked up the original copy of the search warrant, filled in the remaining blanks, and drove it to the clerk of the circuit court to have it certified. Just before he walked into the courthouse, Bernie called Adam to make sure he didn't forget anything.

"Hey, Bernie. What's up?"

"Just making sure you listed everything you took from the house on the back of the search warrant before I go in and get it certified. The clerk's office opens up here in a few minutes."

"Yeah, I wrote everything down that I took before I left. It should be ready to file."

"Sounds good."

Bernie ended the call and walked into the lobby of the courthouse, bypassing the deputies at the metal detectors with a flash of his badge. He continued past first floor courtrooms and took the elevator up to the third floor. At exactly nine o'clock he opened the heavy glass door to the clerk's office and walked up to the counter, where he was greeted by the receptionist.

"Can I help you?"

"Yes, ma'am. I need to get this search warrant certified."

"Hold on one second and I'll get the clerk for you."

Bernie watched as the receptionist disappeared into the maze of filing cabinets toward the back of the office. Once she was completely out of sight, he walked over to the floor to ceiling window in the waiting room and looked down on Court Street. He let out a laugh when he saw the line of pissed off citizens, each with his or her bright yellow piece of paper in hand, waiting to get inside the warm courthouse. He was just about to look for familiar faces in the line when he hard someone behind him trying to get his attention.

"Can I help you, Sir?" the Clerk asked.

"Yes, ma'am. I need to get this search warrant certified."

"Please, raise your right hand."

Bernie raised his right hand and swore that the information was true and correct before putting his signature on the bottom, and handing the warrant over to the clerk for her to do the same. With that very important task completed, he walked back across the street to the sheriff's office to check in on Adam and his progress.

"How goes it, Adam?"

"Good. Just getting all my ducks in a row here. Did you get the search warrant over to the clerk's office?"

"Sure did. Do you need any help with anything?"

Before Adam could answer Bernie's cell phone rang.

"Detective Steckler."

Adam didn't know who was on the other end of the line, but he could tell by Bernie's angered tone that it wasn't a conversation he wanted to be having.

"Are you serious? Again? Okay, keep his dumb ass there. I'm on my way."

Bernie hung up the phone and looked over at Adam, "Sorry, Bro. One of my informants just got stopped by Deputy Harris, for going 100 miles per hour. That idiot doesn't even have a driver's license and I need him on the street. I'll be back in a little bit."

"Anyone that I know?"

"Yeah. It's JT again."

Bernie rushed to his car and headed out of town on Route 80. It didn't take long before he came across a sheriff's cruiser with flashing blue lights sitting behind a red Ford Mustang. Bernie stepped out of his car and walked up to Deputy Harris who was sitting on the hood of his car watching JT's every move.

"Sorry to bother you, Detective Steckler, but this guy says he knows you."

"Yeah, he's one of my informants. What happened?"

"Well, I was headed down to see my girlfriend in Martin when my radar starts screaming at me on this straight stretch of road. I looked over at the receiver and saw that the target vehicle speed was already at 75 and climbing fast. I pulled over to the side of the road and switched from moving radar to stationary mode and clocked him at 105 in a 45 mile per hour zone. It took me a bit to catch up to him at that speed, but when I got up to him he pulled right over."

"Was he an asshole when you pulled him over?"

"No, sir. But he's been really fidgety this whole time and that's why I'm out here watching him. I figured I might have to shoot him if he keeps it up."

Bernie walked past Harris and up to JT's driver's side window.

"What the fuck is your problem, JT?"

"Sir, I was being chased, Sir. This dude was chasing me, Sir, and I was just trying to get away. He said he was going to kill me."

"You were up at Bubba's trying to score again, weren't you?"

"No, Sir. Not to score. But I was there for a little while just hanging out. I was trying to get some information for you, Sir."

Bernie turned back to Harris and asked, "You mind if we move off the road. I don't want to be seen talking to him out here."

"Not at all. There's an abandoned body shop up the road a ways, off of Porter Lane. We can head there if you want."

Bernie, Harris, and JT all drove to the body shop and pulled around back into a gravel and mud parking lot. The dilapidated brick building was long enough to shield them from any unwanted onlookers. Bernie got out of his car and slammed the door behind him. JT was already out of his car and slowly walking towards Bernie with his hands in the air.

"What the fuck were you doing at Bubba's, JT? And don't you dare lie to me," Bernie asked.

"I went up there to hang out like I always do. Every Monday afternoon I'm up there. I can't start doing crazy stuff now or he'll think I'm a rat."

"Put your hands down, you look like an idiot. What happened that you had to be going 100 miles per hour, and you better not owe him money for dope?"

JT stood silent for a minute. He took a step backwards and crossed his arms while thinking of what to say.

"Detective Steckler, you've always been good to me so I ain't gonna lie. I was up there to score some dope. But when I got there Bubba and C.W. chased me off. C.W. pointed a gun in my face and told me he was gonna kill me, so I got the fuck out of there."

"Why would they want to kill you? How much money do you owe them?"

"About a grand. I was supposed to sell some dope for him to work off the debt but they told me my services were no longer needed and that I needed to come up with the scratch or I was a goner. I need your help, detective. I'm scared."

"Go home and lock your doors, JT. And don't even think about leaving until I give you a call. If you want my help then we are going to do things my way. Oh, and you are gonna set up another three deals to work off the driving on suspended and reckless driving charge you almost got yourself tonight."

JT walked back to his car with his head hung low. Bernie and Harris watched as his beat-up Ford Mustang pulled out of the parking lot and headed toward the highway.

"So is he good for three more deals, Detective?"

"Yeah, JT used to have a good job, but got hooked on meth. He has his nose in the drug trade and knows some pretty high up dealers. I just hope he didn't burn any bridges with Bubba and C.W. tonight."

Harris had aspirations of one day following in Bernie's footsteps, so he took every opportunity to learn all he could, about the local thugs and how they pushed their poison in Stillwell.

"How many buys do you need before you can get the search warrant for Bubba's place?"

"I've got two already, but I want to gather as much intelligence on his place as I can. So I'm going to send JT in a few more times before I get the warrant. The more buys I can make, the more nails I can put in his coffin in court."

"Won't Bubba know it was JT that ratted him out?"

"There's no way in hell. From the time of the next buy I have 72 hours to get a search warrant and 14 days to execute it. That gives me 17 days total to hit the house taking as much heat off our informant as possible. Bubba deals with a lot of people in 17 days. He can point his finger all he wants, but the truth is he'll have no clue who did him wrong," Bernie explained.

"So how bad is the meth problem here in the county? I grew up just outside of Louisville and crack was the drug of choice up there."

"Let me put it to you this way, Harris. Do you remember that old trailer that blew up in Lackey?"

"No, sir. Bobby and I got out of the academy a few months ago. I think that happened just before we got hired."

"Well that was one of Bubba's meth labs. His cook got too high on his own stuff and let the red phosphorus boil too long. The red-p turned into white phosphorus and exploded. Bubba has several trailers around the county and has a stronghold on the meth trade here. We estimate that he has around five labs in the county with 10 or so people working for him. That's not including all of the other little mom and pop cooks that are popping up all around us. Right now there are roughly 10 to 15 working meth labs here in Stillwell. I have my work cut out for me, that's for sure."

"Who is Bubba exactly?" Harris asked.

"Bubba's real name is Derwin Bolden. He is a transplant from Boone County, West Virginia, and arrived here about five years ago. I ran his criminal history once and the damn printer ran out of paper. All his years behind bars gave him a lot of time to think about how he got caught and how to better hone his trade. After he got released from prison the last time he moved here and brought all of his bad habits with him. His right hand man is Eddie "C.W." Rogers. C.W. fancies himself a real bad ass and he is the enforcer of the operation. It's been rumored that he's killed dozens of folks he thought were informants. As much as I would like to say that he's all bark and no bite, I can't. There are way too many missing persons reports in Stillwell and the surrounding areas to be coincidental. Unlike Bubba, C.W. has never been in trouble for anything, not even a speeding ticket."

They talked for a little while longer about narcotics before going their separate ways. Bernie drove back to the station to make good on his promise to help Adam with cataloging all of the items removed from the house. But when he entered the criminal investigations wing of the sheriff's office, he noticed that there was no one around.

"Adam, you here?" he yelled.

"Get in here and shut the door. You aren't going to believe this shit," he heard Adam yell from down the darkened hallway.

Bernie walked into Adam's office, turned on the lights, and took a seat across from Adam's desk.

"What shit am I not going to believe?" Bernie wanted to know.

"I just got off the phone with Dr. Edwards. He did a full body x-ray of our victim and guess what? There is a medium caliber bullet hole in her chest. The fire cauterized the hole so we didn't see the entrance wound. It entered just below the sternum and lodged itself in the spinal cord. That's why there wasn't an exit wound. He moved our victim to the head of the line because this is a homicide and he's performing the autopsy now. He also called in for her dental records and is hopeful that he can make the positive identification by the end of the day."

"Did you tell Bishop and Sheriff Lawson yet?"

"Yeah, they're both on their way down here now. What the hell is going on here, Bernie?"

"I have no idea. But it looks like someone may have been pissed off that she was selling on their turf."

"You think that Bubba and his crew might be behind this?"

"I wouldn't put it past them. I'll keep my ears open on the streets."

Adam and Bernie were in the process of coming up with a new game plan when Adam's office door flew open. Sheriff Lawson and Sergeant Bishop walked in and wanted to know everything that was going on.

"Sarge, we need to go back to the house. Now that we know she was shot, we need to find that spent casing. This is going to be extremely labor intensive and we need some help. Possibly from the State Police."

Adam looked over at Sheriff Lawson and saw his face crumple up in disgust. Sheriff Lawson wasn't keen on asking any outside agency for help, especially the State

Police. In his eleven years as sheriff he'd had many disagreements with the State Police over procedural and administrative matters. Not one of which was ever resolved pleasantly.

"The reason I ask, Sheriff, is because we still need to canvass that entire 10 mile road and knock on all the doors. There are several fields that are in walking distance to the house, not to mention all the trails through the woods. They also have access to all the cool gadgets and luminal that we're going to need to go over that house with a fine-tooth comb. And to be honest with you, we don't have the manpower."

Sheriff Lawson didn't say anything as he stood up and walked out of Adam's office, closing the door behind him. Adam was used to his reclusive behavior so he kept talking.

"I need to get a timeline started of Ms. Dwyer's last few days here on earth and subpoena all her phone records. We also need to go to BMB Textiles to see if they will let us look in her office, Bernie."

Adam jotted down his to-do list and arranged the assignments in order of immediate importance. After a short discussion, they all agreed that Adam and Bernie would both stay at the station and get all the forensic analysis request forms filled out and ready to ship to the lab first thing the next morning. Once that was completed, Adam would look into the victim's cell and home phone numbers because subpoenas would be needed to obtain that information. While they were busy doing that, Bishop would be returning to the house with two other detectives and a patrol deputy to look for the spent casing.

"When you're finished searching the house Bishop, get Chief Allen back in there to determine if the meth lab was the real cause and origin of the fire or if it was put there to throw us off. Also someone needs to get in touch with Mr. Norris to see when he's coming back with the kids. Bernie and I have more than enough here to keep us busy until the end of the day, so let's meet up tomorrow morning."

Bishop made his usual hasty retreat to his office to type up the new search warrant to get to the judge for his signature before 4:30. Bernie continued to plug away at all the lab request forms while Adam did a name search in the National Crime Information Center Database (NCIC) for any records of Melissa Anne Dwyer. The only arrest on file was for an underage possession of alcohol from Radford back in 2000.

"Hey, Bernie. This chick has no priors for any narcotics violations anywhere. Not here and nothing nationally. Let's get all your samples packaged and sent off first. Lord knows we don't want any toxic evidence in here."

Bernie held up three completed forms for Adam to see, "Already done. The DEA guys took it with them when they left this morning."

"Really? That was fast. Well, I guess we had better get started on my stuff. We're going to be here for a while."

The two detectives worked throughout the night getting all of the paperwork and subpoena's prepared for submittal to the state lab, the cell phone company, the local phone company and the courts. In between forms, Adam looked over at the clock with his burning eyes and saw it was already three in the morning. They had been going non stop for the last twenty eight hours sustaining themselves only on coffee and cold pizza. With the last forensic analysis form finished, Adam started on the time line of everything that they knew so far while Bernie put his feet up on the desk and closed his eyes.

"If you close your eyes, Bernie, it's all over."

"Nah, I'm good. I won't fall asleep."

Within a minute of his eyelids closing, Adam could hear faint snores coming from the corner where Bernie sat. As much as he wanted to close his eyes, there was still too much that needed to get done. Instead, he poured himself another cup of coffee and kept on typing.

As the sun started to rise on day two of the investigation Adam rudely kicked Bernie's feet off the desk to wake him up.

"Rise and shine, cupcake."

"How long was I out?"

"Long enough. Let's go to Monica's and get a bite to eat. I'm starving."

Adam turned off his office light, locked the door, and followed Bernie down the hall toward the front of the sheriff's office. As they rounded the corner to the lobby they saw the sheriff and some guy in a suit, whom they had never seen before, walking toward them.

"Adam and Bernie, do you two have a few minutes to fill First Sergeant Parr from the state police in on what we know so far?"

Both Adam and Bernie looked at each other with a puzzled gaze. Neither of them had expected the sheriff to ask for help from the state, but they welcomed it. As it was, Adam and Bernie were already doing the work of four detectives and any more delays would set them back even further. They followed the sheriff and the first sergeant into the conference room and sat down at the large oval table in the center of the room.

The meeting lasted for a little over three hours. They discussed numerous strategies as to how to proceed with the investigation and what roles each agency was expected to play. In the end, it was agreed that the sheriff's office would maintain the lead and the state police would intervene only when asked. First Sergeant Parr had no problem loaning one of his investigators to Adam and Bernie to help with anything they needed. He also said the state police would take over the canvassing of Spurlock Creek Road and its surrounding area, which was a huge burden lifted off their shoulders. Just as they were about to conclude the meeting, the sheriff's secretary poked her head into the conference room with a message for Adam.

"Detective Alexander, you have an urgent phone call parked on line 114."

Adam reached over to the phone in the center of the table and picked up the receiver.

"Hello, this is Detective Alexander."

Dr. Edwards was on the other end anxiously waiting to give Adam the autopsy report.

"Can you hold on a second, Dr. Edwards? I'm going to put you on speaker phone for the sheriff and first sergeant to hear."

Adam pressed the speaker button and put the phone back on the base, "Can you hear us Dr. Edwards?"

The voice on the other end came through loud and clear.

"Hello, gentlemen. This is what I've found out. Of course the hard copy of my official report won't be finished for a few days, but this is what it is going to say. The victim was positively identified through her dental records as Melissa Anne Dwyer. I already told Detective Alexander that an intact bullet was lodged in her spinal column. I removed the lead and found it was a 9 mm. It has already been sent upstairs to the lab for analysis. I photographed every step as I removed the bullet and those pictures will be sent to you along with the copy of my report. Also, Ms. Dwyer had no petechiae in the eyes or mouth and there wasn't any smoke in her lungs. The cause of death was the bullet piercing the ascending aorta resulting in massive internal bleeding, not smoke inhalation. She was dead before the fire started. The cause of death will be ruled a homicide in my report."

"Thank you for the phone call, Dr. Edwards. I'll be waiting for your report."

"No problem at all, Detective. I'll get it out to you as soon as I can."

Now that the case was officially labeled a murder, Adam and Bernie needed to get going on the tasks they had set forth for the day, but first they needed to get something to eat.

"Hey Sheriff, we're going out to for a bite to eat before we get back in the game. Is there anything else that needs our immediate attention?" Adam asked.

The sheriff shook his head, and with that the two detectives were out the door and on their way to Monica's Restaurant. The food had not been on the table for any more than three minutes before it was devoured and Adam was asking for the check.

"Have you called your wife in the last two days?" Bernie asked.

"Shit, I knew I was forgetting something."

Adam excused himself from the table and walked out to the street corner to make the call. Bernie watched as he walked out the door and put the phone to his ear. The next thing he saw was Adam staring at the phone, before putting it back in his pocket and walking back toward the table.

"She hung up on you didn't she?"

"Yep."

Adam picked up the tab and in no time they were back at the office tying up all the loose ends on the lab requests so the property room deputy could take the evidence to the state lab for testing. Once that tedious task was completed, Adam spent the remainder of the morning and most of the afternoon typing up and faxing the subpoenas for Ms. Dwyer's phone and financial records. After every subpoena had been faxed, Adam called the investigations division for each company and expressed how important it was to get the information as soon as possible. He had just hung up the phone with the last company on his to do list when Bernie walked into his office.

"Are you ready head down to BMB Textiles, Adam?"

"Yeah, we can do that."

On the ride down, they discussed how they were going to handle the investigation at the textile plant. Adam had been there a couple times before investigating check frauds and an occasional assault that took place on the production floor. There were some pretty shady characters who worked there.

"Hey, Bernie. Let's not mention the presence of anything in the house. Just let them talk and see if they know anything and maybe we can get in her office to have a quick look. If they tell us we need a search warrant then you can hold the scene while I go and get one,"

"That sounds good to me, but we better hurry. It's almost quitting time."

BMB Textiles sat just east of the town limits off Gibson Drive. Adam parked in a space reserved for visitors and both detectives got out of the car. A steady stream of employees moved toward their cars in the parking lot as Adam and Bernie approached the double glass doors.

After the last group of slow moving office workers ambled through the doors, the two detectives walked into the large lobby and were greeted by the receptionist, "What can I do for you two gentlemen?"

She stared cheerfully up at Adam and Bernie with her hands resting on top of the desk, waiting for a response.

"Yes ma'am. I'm Detective Alexander and this is Detective Steckler from the sheriff's office. We'd like to speak with Melissa Dwyer's boss. Is he or she available?"

"That would be the plant manager, Byron Glanham, but he's not available. Is there something I can help you with?"

Bernie and Adam looked at each other and asked the receptionist if there was someplace they could go that was a little more private.

"Certainly, detectives. The conference room is just over here."

They followed her across the lobby to the conference room. After she turned on the overhead florescent lights, they walked into a large, bright room with three glass walls that looked back into the lobby. Adam closed the door behind them and motioned for her to take a seat at the large oak table. She hesitantly sat down in the chair closest to the door while Adam and Bernie walked around the table and sat with their backs to the wall.

"I'm sorry, but we didn't get your name," Adam stated.

"My name is Lisa Butler, and I'm the head receptionist for the plant. I'm also Ms. Dwyer's assistant. What's this all about?"

"We want to ask you a few questions about Ms. Dwyer if that's all right with you?"

Before he could begin, Lisa nervously asked, "Is she okay? She's my best friend in this world. Please tell me she's okay? I tried calling her several times today and she didn't answer. I knew I should've called you guys, I just knew it."

Tears started to roll down Lisa's cheek as she anxiously looked over at Adam.

"Why should you have called the police, Ms. Butler?"

"While I was talking to her Sunday night at about ten, she said there was someone at her door and that she was going to have to call me back. Just before she hung up the phone I remember hearing a man's voice asking who owns the cows down the road because they had gotten out."

Adam looked over at Bernie and half-grinned. Both he and Bernie had been almost trampled by an 800 pound dairy cow when they had worked the street. Unfortunately, loose-cattle calls were an almost daily occurrence in the sheriff's office.

"Did you try to call her back at all?"

"I tried to call her back at around 10:30, but there was no answer. I kind of thought I should go over to her house, but then I thought I was being irrational so I let it go. She was supposed to go to Frankfort yesterday morning so I figured I wouldn't hear from her for a few days. I was going to try calling her again tonight to check on her."

There was a long silence and Ms. Butler was looking at both detectives with such despair that they had to let her know. Adam reached across the table and placed Lisa's hand in his.

"She's gone, Ms. Butler. Melissa Dwyer was murdered Sunday night."

"MURDERED?"

Lisa let out a loud scream, put her head down on the table, and started to cry hysterically. Bernie looked around the room for a box of tissues, but unfortunately, he couldn't find any. All they could do was watch and wait as she sobbed into the sleeve of her sweater. After a few minutes, she gradually regained her composure and Adam was able to continue with his questions.

"Did you recognize the voice in the background by any chance?" Adam asked.

"No sir, I didn't. The funny thing is that I can't imagine what he was talking about. There isn't a single cattle farm on that road, at least not that I know of."

"What were you two talking about that night?"

"You know, the usual things girls talk about."

"I'm sorry, but I have no idea what girls talk about. Can you elaborate on that a little bit?"

"We were just talking about our lives and our children. You know, every day stuff."

"Did she ever tell you anything about her financial situation?"

"She let me in on a few things here and there, but for the most part she was doing okay. She got $1,000 a month, to help with the kids and bills, from an aunt and uncle who live outside of Buffalo."

"Was she into anything illegal that you know of?"

"Oh, good lord no! Mel is… I mean was, a law abiding citizen who has never gotten into any trouble. Why on earth would you ask that question?"

"No reason, Ms. Butler. We just need to be thorough if we're going to solve this case. Is there anything else you can think of that might help us out here?"

"No, nothing stands out in my mind."

"Bernie, do you have any questions?"

Adam looked over at Bernie who was shaking his head and then back at Ms. Butler, "If you can think of anything else, anything at all, will you please let us know?"

"Absolutely, Detective."

"Oh, one last thing. Would you mind if we looked in her office for a minute or two?"

Ms. Butler stood up from the conference table and led the detectives to a small office just behind her desk.

"I'll be here until 6:30 or so. I'll also call Mr. Glanham to let him know what is going on."

"One more question Ms. Butler. This happened on Sunday night and it's now Tuesday. Everyone in town has heard about the murder, how come you haven't?"

"I live in West Virginia and I had to take yesterday and today off because my kids are sick. The only reason I'm here tonight is because I had to come in and get the payroll done. Mel is the only person I talk to from here. And now I don't even have her anymore," Lisa said as she dabbed her eyes with the cuff of her sweater.

"Thanks, Ms. Butler. We'll make sure we talk to you again before we leave."

The two detectives started to look around the eight by eight office space. It was difficult for both of them to move around without bumping into one another so Bernie moved back and stood in the doorway. Adam looked down at the desk and saw there was a docking station for a laptop computer instead of a CPU.

"Did you see a laptop back at the house or inside the car, Bernie?"

"No, I sure didn't."

Adam pulled the brown leather chair out from under the desk and took a seat. One by one he opened the three drawers on the left side of the desk, but all he found were office related papers, a few personnel files and some office supplies. He tried to open the center drawer but it was locked.

Adam looked past Bernie into the hallway to make sure nobody was looking before he asked, "Can you pick this lock, Bernie?"

Bernie pulled out his pocket knife and took Adams place in the leather chair. It took him a minute, but he was able to jimmy the lock open. In the drawer were several pieces of folded paper with Melissa's name printed on the outside.

"This is interesting," Bernie said. "There are several notes from a guy named Al in here. They all say the same thing, that he misses her and is thinking about her. I wonder who that is."

Bernie closed the drawer, but didn't take the time to lock it back up. Satisfied they had seen everything, Adam and Bernie walked out of Ms. Dwyer's office and into the lobby.

Adam walked around to the front of Lisa's desk and saw that she was on the phone. He waited patiently for her to finish her conversation, but when it became apparent that she wasn't going to hang-up anytime soon he held his hand up and interrupted her with one final question, "Do you know who Al is? We found several notes in Ms. Dwyer's top drawer with his name on them. Does he work here?"

Lisa's cheeks became flushed and she looked down at her desk as she muttered,

"No, Sir. I've never heard that name before."

"Okay, well, I appreciate all of your help today. We'll be in touch," Adam said as he placed his business card down on the corner of her desk.

While walking back to the car, all Adam could do was shake his head, "She knows something, Bernie. Did you see her get all red and flustered when I asked her who Al was?"

"Yeah, that was pretty strange."

"She's lying about not knowing who Al is. But why?"

"I guess we'll have to find out on our own."

"Yes, we will."

Chapter 5

The short drive back to the office was a quiet one. It was just after six and the sky was already completely dark. Bernie stared blankly out the window at all the Christmas decorations in the store windows on Main Street and thought about which informants he had that are close to Bubba and his crew. Unfortunately, only JT came to mind. Adam drove past the station lot on Court Street and dropped Bernie off near his car.

"Thanks for all your help, Bernie. See you tomorrow."

Bernie closed the car door behind him and walked up the street to his undercover car. He seldom parked in the station lot because he didn't like the bad guys knowing what kind of car he drove. The longer he kept it a secret, the better chance he had of blending in.

Adam drove around the block and parked in the station lot. He wanted to check his e-mail and phone for messages before going home for the night. He hit the power button on his CPU and looked down at his phone to see there were no messages waiting for him. Just as he was about to log onto his computer, Sheriff Lawson walked into his office and slammed the door behind him. Adam could tell he was angry, but he had no idea why.

"Just what in the hell is your problem boy?"

Adam opened his mouth to answer, but Sheriff Lawson didn't give him a chance.

"It isn't your responsibility to talk to the fucking media. It's mine! From now on, if I hear you breathe one word of this case to anyone, or if I see your ugly mug in front of another camera, it's gonna be your ass! You understand me?"

Adam nodded in agreement and apologized.

"You may be able to get away with all the shit you pull with Bishop, but let me tell you something Yankee, you're on thin ice with me. If you show up for work wearing anything other than what's listed as appropriate attire in the general orders, I will fire your ass."

Sheriff Lawson turned, opened Adam's office door and slammed it behind him after he walked out. Adam, completely bewildered, sat in silence for a few moments trying to process what had just happened. Sure, he was used to getting yelled at by Bishop all the time, but the sheriff brought it to a whole new level. Then suddenly, it dawned on him. Adam remembered the impromptu news conference he gave wearing his Red Wings jersey and it all made sense. He contemplated turning out the lights and calling it a night, but decided to gut it out another few more hours before going home. He looked across his desk at the brown leather diary that he had found in the bedside table. It was time to get to know his victim, Melissa Anne Dwyer.

Adam propped his feet up on the only available uncluttered square inch of his desk, and opened up to the diary to the first page.

04/01/94: Well, my mother thought it would be a great idea for me to start keeping a journal. Now that I'm headed off to college and starting a new chapter of my life, I do think that it will be neat to read this ten or fifteen years from now and remember how my life used to be. I was accepted to Radford University and I will be going there in the fall to study business administration. I know that the university is only fifteen minutes from my house, but it will still be fun to live on campus. I hope the party scene is as crazy as everyone says it is.

8/1/94: I'm so excited I can hardly stand it. I'm all packed up and ready to move into my dorm on Saturday. I called my roommate for the first time today and talked to her for an hour or so. She's from northern Virginia and she seems really nice. We laughed that they stuck us in Pocahontas Hall, which is the all female, all freshman dorm, for our first year. I wonder how strict they'll be about letting guys in after hours. I guess I'll find out soon enough. This is going to be the best time of my life and I intend to live each moment like it's my last.

Adam rolled his eyes and thought to himself that if the rest of this diary was like this then it was going to be an extremely long night. He dreaded the thought of having to read through the drama filled life of a college girl.

2/10/95: I just met the most interesting and handsome boy. His name is William Dwyer and he is a sophomore from Buffalo, New York. He lives in the next dorm over from me and is also a business admin student. He is in Alpha Sigma Phi fraternity and invited me to a party this weekend at the Palace. I just might go. I hope he doesn't turn out to be a big jerk like the rest of those frat guys.

2/15/95: Just got back from the party with Billy and I must say I had the best time. He took me to The Palace on Grove Street and one thing is for certain, if you're with a brother you don't have to wait in line for the bathroom or a beer. I just might get used to this. Billy was a perfect gentleman and we talked the entire time. He made me feel like I was the only girl in the room all night long. He even walked me back to my dorm. He wasn't even going to ask for a kiss, so I just kissed him. He's really a nice guy and I hope this works out.

Adam sat back in his chair and rubbed his burning eyes. He wanted to keep reading, but decided he had better take a few minutes to call his wife and tell her goodnight.

"Hey honey…"

"Don't 'hey honey' me, Adam. You've been gone for two days and this is only the second time you've called to check on me."

"I know, but we hit the ground running with this case. I just have one more thing to do here and I'll be home tonight. I promise."

"I'll believe it when I see you. Goodnight."

Rennae hung up the phone before Adam could tell her goodnight. He looked down at the receiver in his hand and wondered how many more people he could piss off before the day was over. After hanging up the phone, he skimmed over the rest of Melissa's college days and found himself immersed in her post-graduate life.

05/06/99: Well, I finally did it. Today is graduation day and I couldn't be happier. Bill came back to see me walk across the stage and take me away with him to Jacksonville, Florida. He said that we can get an apartment on the beach. I can't wait to start the next chapter of my life with him.

05/07/99: I can't believe it!!!! Bill just proposed to me in front of The Palace. It might not seem that romantic to some, but it's where we had our first date and it was perfect. Of course I said YES!!!!!

07/12/99: Bill and I are getting settled in our new apartment and as he promised, it's three blocks from Jacksonville Beach. I've started looking for work, but the pickings are slim in this area. Luckily for us, Billy has a great job as a project manager in the aerospace field, and the money is fantastic. A girl could get used to all this pampering.

11/15/99: I just called home and talked to my mom. She told me that there's almost a foot of snow on the ground. I think I'll put on my bikini and go catch a few rays. I made sure to rub that in before I hung up the phone. Yeah, this is the life for me.

05/10/00: Bill came home today and said he's tired of waiting. He wants to get married by the end of this month. I'm so excited I could scream! I have so much to do and so little time to do it in.

06/01/00: This is my first Official entry as Mrs. Melissa Anne Dwyer. We got married yesterday on the Beach in front of our closest family and friends. It was better than I ever could have imagined. I can't wait to start our family together. My life is almost complete.

As he read through the years of entries, Adam was struck by how perfect their marriage was and took notice of how different it had been from his. Bill had been rewarded for all his hard work with two promotions and made amazing money. They had traveled the globe for the first year they were married, but eventually decided it was time to settle down and expand their family. Within three years, the happy couple had had two children and had moved to a larger home on the south side of Jacksonville. It had every luxury anyone could ever want, including five bedrooms and a view of the golf course. But something wasn't making any sense. How did she go from a five bedroom palace to a three bedroom farm house in the middle of nowhere? As he continued to read, everything became clear.

02/21/05: We laid Bill to rest today. I still don't know how I'm going to make it through this without the help of my best friend. It's been almost a week now since the car accident and I haven't stopped crying. How am I going to live? Billy didn't have any life insurance and the bills are starting to pile up. I don't have a job and I can't afford this house. I just don't know what I'm going to do.

As Adam read the next five pages, he was able to see his victim slip further and further into depression. It was obvious that Bill meant the world to her, and that she depended on him for more than just financial security. On the first few pages after his death she wrote about the fond memories they shared together on their travels around the globe, and how happy they were after the birth of their second child. But then her writings took a dark turn. She found herself turning to alcohol and contemplating suicide to end her grief. But the one thing that kept her going, and eventually made her put down the bottle, was the thought of her children living as orphans.

01/04/06: Well, I've drank away the better part of a year and it's time to stop feeling sorry for myself and clean up my act. My kids are scared that I'm going to go away like daddy, and I just can't bear to see them like this. Today is the day that I make a change in my life for my children's sake.

03/12/06: I just accepted a contract on the house and am going to move back to Radford with my mom. I sure hope I don't have to stay there long.

03/21/06: Thank God for Bill's Uncle Jeff and Aunt Kim. They've picked up the tab for all of my moving expenses and have even offered to help pay for child care. It seems that there is an Angel in Heaven looking out for me. Thanks, Bill. I love and miss you.

2/15/07: It would appear that my luck might be turning around. I just got word that I'll be the new plant manager for BMB Textiles in Stillwell, Kentucky. I'll have to stay in a motel until I can get a place for the kids and me, but I'm really excited. The starting pay isn't the greatest but it's a step in the right direction. Now I can start to regain my independence. It will be nice to be able to have enough money to take the kids out to eat every once in a while.

2/24/07: Work is going great. I really like my new job and the people here are really hard workers. I have already increased production by a narrow margin and the boss has taken notice of my hard work. My secretary, Lisa, is a great person and is recently divorced with kids. Although we've just met, I've found that we have so much in common and I feel like I can tell her anything.

4/15/07: I went out with Lisa and a few people from work last night to the local watering hole. Everyone there had a great time even though the house band was horrible. How can you screw up "Free Bird"? There was one guy in particular who was extremely funny and not too bad looking either. The only problem is that he's married. We talked until the bar closed down and they kicked us out. I needed an evening like that. It was nice to get out and meet new people.

4/21/07: We all went out again last night and Lisa was in rare form. She got so drunk that I had to literally pick her up off the floor a few times. In between babysitting her and trying to keep myself under wraps I was able to talk to the same guy that I met last time a little more. His name is Allen Livingston and he is a very interesting guy. People around here call him Rocky and he owns Rocky Top Landscaping here in town. He drives a beautiful 1969 Pontiac GTO that he has fully restored. He and the guys who work for him fix up old cars and they even have a race car that they run on the weekends at the local dirt track. He invited the kids and me to come out to one of his races. I just might take him up on that offer.

Adam's jaw hit the floor as soon as he realized that Rocky was "Al" in all the love notes in Melissa's desk drawer. He grabbed the phone and called Bernie.

"Bernie, you're never going to guess what I just found out."

Before Bernie could answer Adam blurted out, "I just found out that Al in the love notes is Rocky from Rocky Top Landscaping."

"You're kidding. He's married to a hot piece of ass if I'm not mistaken. Ouch!"

Adam started to laugh because he knew Bernie's wife had just slapped him on the back of his head.

"Yeah, he's married and when this gets out the shit is going to hit the fan. Oh, I also read that Lisa and Melissa went out a few times after work and Lisa was there when Melissa met Rocky. I knew she wasn't telling us the truth."

"There was no doubt in my mind that she knew more, but why would she hold that back from us?"

"I don't know, Bernie."

"I'm thinking we need to go back tomorrow and question her a little more. If she still wants to play games then we'll bring her back to the station to talk. And if she still jerks us around we charge her with obstruction."

"Sounds good to me. See you in the morning."

Adam hung up the phone and continued reading the diary with a new-found interest.

5/7/07: I took the kids to Al's garage today to see his race car. He offered to take me to dinner sometime at one of his favorite restaurants just outside of Cincinnati. He wants to drive me there one afternoon in his Corvette and have dinner. I know that he is married and that I shouldn't be doing this, but it sounds like too much fun to turn down. Looks like it's time to find a sitter for the kids.

5/15/07: Dinner was fantastic. The drive took a little under three hours and the food was exquisite. Al was a perfect gentleman and he explained that he and his wife are not doing very well. He also said that he's a few months away from leaving her for good, but her illness guilt's him into staying. Apparently she has some disease that is attacking her nervous system and he doesn't want to be known as the jerk that left his sick wife. I can appreciate where he is coming from. Why does he have to be married?

5/28/07: Well, I guess I really messed up this time. Al came over to the house tonight to return my sunglasses that I left in his car the last time we went driving. Thank goodness the kids were having a sleepover at the neighbors because our clothes hit the floor as soon as he walked through the door. We made love for hours. I have not felt this way in quite some time. The sex was absolutely incredible. We are going to see each other again really soon I hope.

7/12/07: I have officially been swept off my feet. Al has been there for me in ways that I never knew possible. I sure do hate all the secrecy about our relationship, but I'm just going to enjoy his company and see where this takes us. I told Lisa about our torrid love affair yesterday. It was like I was in high school again, confiding in my best friend that I have a crush on the captain of the football team. I have a really good feeling about this one.

09/13/07: My boss, Mr. Glanham just informed me that he's giving me a raise. It seems that the plant, under my expert eye, has increased its productivity and is actually turning a significant profit. He says if I keep it up, I'll have his job when he retires. It's time to celebrate.

12/14/07: Al is taking me out to dinner tonight. He hasn't been able to see me lately because his crazy wife is claiming she's sick all the time. This is starting to make me a little bit angry and also a little bit suspicious that maybe he doesn't have any intention of leaving her. If he cancels dinner tonight then we're going to have to have a serious talk about what's going on. I realize that I have no control over his relationship with his wife, but I also deserve to be treated better than this.

Well, Al called tonight and canceled our dinner. UGH!!!!!!!!

2/11/08: Things between Al and me have gotten a little better. He's actually kept our last three dates and is coming over tonight to hang out for a little while. The last time he came over was a week ago and it was wonderful. We made love three times and each time was better than the last. I just wish he wouldn't leave right after. It makes me feel more like a hooker than a girlfriend.

4/18/08: I HAVE HAD IT! I can't believe this is happening to me. He actually had the nerve to tell me that he and his wife had talked about their lack of sex and what it was doing to their relationship. Apparently they now have this understanding that he can sleep with whomever he wants just as long as she doesn't find out about it. Now he has no intentions of leaving her and asked if we could keep our relationship physical. Oh yeah, he still wants to keep it a secret too. This is such bullshit!!! Maybe it's time I let him know who is really in charge here.

04/21/08: Al stopped by my place tonight and wanted to come in. I just shut the door in his face and turned off all the lights. Maybe he'll take the hint.

04/27/08: Al has been so sweet. He's left flowers on my doorstep every day this week and has even called to apologize a few times. Maybe it's time I back off a little. I think that I made my point.

5/12/08: It's the middle of racing season and Al is in first place. The kids really enjoy spending time at the race track and being able to go into the pits before each race. It's amazing how he's able to drive around that dirt track. I never really considered myself a redneck until now. I haven't missed a single local race but I have missed a few that are too far away for the kids and me to go to. Even Lisa has come to a few races with us. It's all so exciting!

6/21/08: It was raining all day today so Al and his crew stopped by the house to hang out while the kids were at the neighbor's house playing. We all hung out in my newly built garage and talked the afternoon away. It was weird but while they were here some strange people kept pulling into my driveway. Al would motion for them to leave and they did. I asked him what they wanted and he said that they were just friends of his that were stopping by to say hello. I told him that I didn't mind if they came in and joined us but he insisted they stay away.

7/18/08: It's Friday night and it's almost time to go to Thunder Ridge Raceway for some dirt track action. Al is so far ahead in points that the championship is in the bag for him and his crew. The kids and I are headed out there in a few hours to cheer him on. All he has to do is finish the race tonight he will get invited to race at Charlotte Motor Speedway for the Dirt Track Finals in the late model stock class. Keep your fingers crossed. We just might be headed to Charlotte, North Carolina.

8/4/08: If it were not for the incredible sex, I would have ended things a long time ago. I think he's starting to lose interest in me though. The last time I took the kids to the garage to see him, he was very distant. He took the kids for a short drive and afterwards asked if he could have some time to be with his friends. He said he would call me later, but I won't hold my breath on that one. I also noticed that there are a few strange people that like to hang out at the garage from time to time. I asked him what they were doing the other day and he told me to mind my own business.

10/10/08: He still ignores me every time I come to the garage and he makes me feel like I'm invisible. Why am I doing this to myself? Maybe I should just call it quits and leave him. I'm a smart and successful woman. I can definitely do better than him. I just don't understand why he doesn't like me anymore. I'm starting to wonder if he and his wife actually have an agreement like he said they do. That might be something I need to look into.

Adam turned to the last page of the diary and saw that the last entry was dated the same day as the homicide. The hairs on the back of his neck stood up as he read the words on the page.

12/18/08: Well, Al says he's going to come over tonight and I bet he's going to want to have sex as usual. But I have a HUGE surprise for him. I'm going to tell him that he either leaves his wife for me or I'm driving right over to his house tonight to confirm that there is an "agreement" between them. I've had enough of this bullshit. Thank goodness the kids are with their aunt and uncle in Buffalo for the week because this is going to get ugly.

Rocky went from person of interest to prime suspect in a matter of seconds. Adam looked over at the clock and saw it was already three in the morning. He had been awake now for nearly forty eight hours and coffee wasn't helping anymore. It was time to head home and recharge his batteries.

He closed the diary and placed it on the corner of his desk before turning off the lights and walking out to his car. On the ride home he thought about what he was going to say to Rennae when he walked through the door to smooth things over. Luckily for him, he didn't have to say anything because all the lights were off in the house. After parking his car, he quietly went upstairs to their bedroom, and climbed into bed next to his sleeping wife. Maybe she would be in a better mood in the morning.

Chapter 6

It seemed as though Adam had just closed his eyes when his alarm screeched in his ear. He looked over at the culprit and slammed his hand down on the snooze bar giving himself a ten minute reprieve from reality. On the second set of annoying buzzes, Adam reluctantly gave in to the demand and got out of bed to start his day. Within fifteen minutes he was showered, dressed appropriately, and back on the road to start day three.

Now that he had a few hours of sleep under his belt he was energized and excited to share his new-found information with Bishop and Sheriff Lawson. He walked into the station, retrieved the diary from his desk, and headed toward the kitchen to get a cup of coffee before the meeting. With coffee in hand, he walked down to the conference room and waited for everyone to arrive. At eight o'clock sharp, the sheriff and the first sergeant walked into the room and closed the door.

The sheriff sat back in his chair and gave Adam the nod to start the meeting. Just as Adam was about to drop his bomb shell the door to the conference room opened and in walked Sergeant Bishop, Bernie, and someone he had never seen before. Adam looked at the new guy's hip and saw he had a State Police badge clipped to his belt right next to his duty weapon.

"I found these two wing nuts out in the lobby and figured they needed a job," Bishop joked.

"This isn't a time for your wise-ass remarks, Sergeant. Now can we get going here please, I have another meeting in an hour," Sheriff Lawson barked.

Adam looked back at the sheriff and was once again given the nod to start the meeting. Adam waited for everyone to get settled before he started to speak.

"I spent most of last night reading Ms. Dwyer's diary which we found in her bedside table. To make a long story short, she was seeing, actually sleeping with, someone in town whom we all know—Alan "Rocky" Livingston, the owner of the Rocky Top Landscaping."

Adam looked around the room and saw the look of shock on everyone's face, so he picked up right where he had left off, "Ms. Dwyer kept a thorough journal about her life from college right up to the day she died. In it she mentions that she told Lisa Butler about her relationship with Rocky, which means she lied to Bernie and me. The most interesting entry, by far, was the one she made on the morning of the day she was murdered. She said she was going to tell Rocky that he needed to leave his wife or she was going to tell her about their relationship."

Adam waited for a few seconds to let everyone digest what he had just said. Alan Livingston was one of the more revered citizens of Stillwell County. He always donated to the Shop with a Cop program which gives Christmas presents to needy children and their families, and he organized several motorcycle Poker Runs throughout the year to raise money for leukemia research since he had lost his middle child to the disease a few years back. Exposing Rocky as an adulterer and possible drug dealer to the entire town would be catastrophic to his reputation. They needed to tread lightly.

Sergeant Bishop broke the silence, "We can handle this discretely to a certain point, but eventually we are going to have to go after the guy if we find out he did it. What do you think, First Sergeant?"

"Well, this is ultimately your investigation, Detective Alexander, but I think you should talk to Lisa first and ask her why she lied. While you guys talk to her, another group should head to the garage and talk to Mr. Livingston. See if we can't get him back to the station to answer a few questions."

"What about the canvass of Ms. Dwyer's street? Who is going to handle that task?" Adam asked.

"I already have four of my guys out there going door to door on Spurlock Creek Road asking the neighbors if they saw anything out of the ordinary on the day of the murder. They'll keep us posted if they find out anything. In the meantime, this gentleman to my right, who was late this morning, is Investigator Eric Jenkins from our criminal investigations bureau. He's here to help you out, Detective Alexander, should you need any assistance."

Investigator Jenkins stood up and shook hands with Adam and Sheriff Lawson before sitting back down.

"Do you have anything you would like to add, Jenkins?" Bishop asked.

"I agree with First Sergeant Parr. It's obvious we need to talk to this Mr. Livingston, but it's also obvious we need to talk to Lisa again. I say we hit them both at the same time. That way they don't have the opportunity to compare notes, if they haven't already. Since you guys made contact with Lisa yesterday, and you can prove she lied, why don't you take a second crack at her? First Sergeant Parr and I will go and talk to Mr. Livingston and see if we can't take him back to our station for a chat. Is this good with everyone?"

Bernie raised his hand to interject, "I have something to add if you guys don't mind?"

"What do you have, Bernie?" Bishop asked.

"After Adam called me last night, I got to thinking about Rocky and who he's got working for him. One of his crew used to be an informant of mine, but it's been a while since I've talked to him."

"Who is he, and do you think he'd still talk to us?" First Sergeant Parr asked.

"His name is Stuart Winston and he got popped a few years ago for marijuana possession and driving suspended. He used to be a good kid before he started hanging out with the wrong crowd. I drove past Rocky's garage on South Railroad Street this morning to see if he was there."

"Was he?" Adam asked.

"Yeah, he was there with four other Woodchucks in the parking lot. I recognized all but one of them from prior narcotics arrests."

"What in the hell is a Woodchuck?" First Sergeant Parr asked.

"It's what we call the guys that work in the landscaping business. They trim trees and shit, kind of like a woodchuck. I ran their criminal histories and DMV transcripts for you guys to look at. Well, everyone but the fifth guy. I'll try to find out who he is later on today."

Sergeant Bishop leaned forward to look at all the paperwork Bernie had gathered on Rocky's employees while Bernie picked up his notebook and continued to talk.

"We have Stuart Winston, whom I already mentioned. This second guy is Richard Easton. He's just your run-of-the-mill local thug. His license is revoked for habitual DUI charges along with one assault and a domestic violence charge on his old lady. Next we have Charles Lipscomb. Ol' Charlie just got out of prison six months ago for burglary and possession of a firearm by a convicted felon. He also has a possession with intent to distribute schedule one and schedule two drugs. I busted him for manufacturing meth a few years ago and he was out on bond when he committed that last burglary. Guess he's out again. And last but not least, we have Stephen Barton. Stephen has two DUI charges and a malicious wounding to his credit. I also found out he was charged with brandishing a firearm but he was never convicted. It says that the disposition was never received on his criminal history. Nice group, huh?"

"So we have a deceased female who was shot, a married business owner who was allegedly sleeping with the deceased, a meth lab in the front room of her home, and a bunch of shady characters all with criminal histories to contend with," First Sergeant Parr summarized.

Bernie flipped to the last page of his notes, "Not everyone, Sir. Rocky is as clean as a whistle. Not even a speeding ticket on his record."

First Sergeant Parr's cell phone started to ring just as they were getting ready to conclude their meeting, so he excused himself, only to return a few seconds later.

"What color are Rocky's landscaping trucks?"

"They're dark green with bright yellow block style lettering on the sides and rear window. His enclosed trailers are the same," Bernie answered.

"Okay, because my guys out doing the canvass said that they've talked to several people along Spurlock Creek Road who all saw that same truck in the driveway on Sunday morning and again Sunday afternoon. They also said that people saw that truck regularly parked in her driveway. It looks like this case is coming together."

Adam looked over his shoulder at the clock to see that it was already 9 o'clock. The town and county of Stillwell were open for business and it was time to get a move on. They ended the meeting with the understanding that everyone would reconvene in a few hours to discuss how their interviews had gone.

Adam drove with Bernie out to the textile plant and although neither of them had much to say, they were both curious as to how Lisa would receive them the second time around. Adam rounded the corner into the parking lot and was headed toward the visitor parking spaces when Bernie looked over his shoulder and saw Lisa's car in the back row.

"I think that's Lisa car parked over there, Adam."

"Is she in it?"

"I couldn't tell. But there's exhaust coming from the tailpipe. Let's go check it out."

Adam made an abrupt turn and drove across the lot, not paying any attention to the markings on the pavement, and pulled into a parking space a few down from her car.

"She's in there," Adam advised.

Both detectives approached with caution, but as they got closer it was obvious that Lisa was distraught and crying hysterically. Adam knocked on her driver side window to get her attention but she just sat there sobbing into her hands. Adam knocked again, this time a little bit harder but got the same result. Bernie looked down and noticed the passenger side door was unlocked so he lifted the handle and opened it.

"What's going on, Lisa?" Bernie asked.

"I just want to die! I feel responsible for Melissa's death. I lied to you guys. I should have called. I just want to die."

Lisa put her hands back over her face and began to cry again.

"You did lie to us yesterday and that's why we're here. Can we go down the road a little ways and talk about this? I don't want everyone here to see us talking."

"Yes, Sir. We can go to the elementary school parking lot down the street. The kids are still on break so there won't be anyone there."

Adam and Bernie followed Lisa down the road to Stillwell Elementary School to have a more thorough and private conversation. Both cars traveled around the building to the school loading dock where they would be totally concealed by the building and surrounding landscape. Bernie stepped out of the car and held the passenger door for Lisa to sit up front with Adam. After he closed the door behind her, he climbed into the back seat, behind Lisa, and prepared to take notes on the interview.

"Now Lisa, I need you to calm down and start from the beginning. Tell me everything you know and don't leave anything out this time," Adam explained.

"Everything I told you guys about Sunday night was the truth. There was a knock on Melissa's door and there was someone asking about the cows down the road. I didn't recognize the voice but I do know it was a man's voice. That's when the phone hung up and I never heard from my best friend again."

Adam gave Lisa a stern look before continuing, "What about Melissa and Rocky? What do you know about their relationship?"

Lisa looked back at Adam and nodded her head while she wiped away her tears with her jacket sleeve.

"They met one night when we were out having a few drinks. They had a great time together but had to keep their relationship a secret, for obvious reasons. This is a small town, and when word gets out you're doing something wrong, well, let's just say people like to judge. They hung out quite regularly. Mel would even bring the kids out to the garage to see the racecar and take a drive from time to time. The kids really liked Rocky. From what Mel told me, their relationship was really nice right up until they started having sex. After that, Rocky started to change. She also said something about Rocky and his wife having an agreement that he could sleep with whoever he wants because she can no longer have sex. She just didn't want to know about it."

"That's an odd arrangement," Bernie added.

"Tell me about it. My feeling is, if you give a man that kind of leeway, then you better expect him to use it. But to be honest with you, I think that Rocky is just a lying asshole, and he said all of that just to get in her pants."

"Earlier you said that Rocky changed. Exactly how did he change?"

"Mel said it started out just like most relationships do. They were always on the phone with each other, constant text messages back and forth, and he would leave little notes on her car. Then, after they started sleeping together that all stopped. It was almost impossible to get in contact with him, he hardly ever returned any of her phone calls, and the only time he showed up on her door step was when he wanted sex. Every time she would bring her kids to the garage, he would talk to them but ignore her. He also wouldn't talk to her when his friends were around. It was like he was ashamed of her being there. Mel told me that one night when he was over at her house, she questioned him about their relationship and where it was headed. Rocky got very upset that she would even bring that up and yelled at her. Mel said it was like she was looking at someone she had never met before. It scared her. She thought he was actually going to hit her."

Adam glanced over his shoulder at Bernie before turning his attention back to Lisa.

"Do you know who his employees are at the garage and what they might be into?"

"I know who they are from the racetrack. We've all hung out a few times down at the Old Still House Saloon, but other than that I only know their first names. I've had my suspicions about what they might be into, but I don't have any hard proof of anything. They have this pickin' party every Friday night down at Rocky's garage and they are the only ones that are allowed to attend."

"I'm sorry. Did you say pickin' party?" Adam asked.

"Yeah, it's kind of like a little fraternity, and a good way for Rocky to get out the house every Friday night. They all get together and play bluegrass for a few hours at the garage. Afterwards, they all head to one of the local watering holes for a few drinks to unwind. As a matter of fact, Mel met Rocky on a Friday night after one of their pickin' parties. They hit it off immediately. Rocky is quite the charmer."

"Does anything else go on at this pickin' party or is it legitimate?"

"From what I can tell it's legitimate. They're there for about two hours or so and sometimes they invite other racecar drivers to attend. Mel made the mistake of going down there one Friday night to check up on Al. She had her doubts about what was really going on. When she got there the front gate was closed, and she couldn't get in. I guess Al was late to the meeting and drove up behind her. He was so pissed that he told her if she ever came back without his permission she would regret it. The next day he gave her a dozen roses and apologized for his behavior, so she forgave him. He said what she did reminded him of how his wife acts from time to time and he just snapped. He also reassured her that they were there for a pickin' party and that was all."

As Bernie listened to everything Lisa was saying, a red flag went up in his mind. With the hooligans that Rocky employed, and their ability to move about the state from racetrack to racetrack, that would be a perfect cover for moving narcotics. Not to mention different drivers from other parts of the state coming to Stillwell during the off season just to hang out. All of it was making perfect sense to him and now he had to figure out how deeply they were involved in the drug trade.

Adam continued asking Lisa questions, "Who are the guys that he hangs out with?"

"There are five of them including Rocky. They are Richard, Stuart, Charlie, and Stephen. Like I said earlier, I only know their first names. The other drivers that show up—I don't have any idea who they are."

"I saw a fifth guy out there this morning with them. Is there anyone else that comes around regularly?" Bernie asked.

"Not that I'm aware of. But I started having doubts about what they're up to as soon as I heard Mel say that Rocky almost got violent with her. You have to understand, that's why I lied to you about knowing who he is. I'm scared for my life. Who knows what this guy is capable of doing."

"Don't worry, Ms. Butler. We'll get to the bottom of this and believe me when I tell you, Rocky will never know that you talked to us. Bernie, do you have any questions?"

Bernie looked down at his notes for a brief moment before asking, "What doubts were you having about the guys in the garage?"

"Come on Detective. These are hard times and I know that all of those guys can't be doing as well as they say they are by mowing grass and chopping firewood. I mean, they are always hanging out at the garage. I never see them working. Mel made the comment to me a few times in the past about how she rarely sees the guys working. This area has a bad drug problem, as you already know, and those guys are at that garage an awful lot. And if they aren't there, then they are on the road going form track to track every Saturday night and some Sundays."

"Did Ms. Dwyer go on any of these weekend trips with them?"

"She told me she wanted to go with them, but every time she brought it up Rocky would tell her there wasn't enough room in the truck for her. She told him she would drive separately but he didn't want her to have to do that, so no, she never went on any of the trips. Mel and Rocky did take weekday trips to various locations, but those were only for the day and they never stayed overnight anywhere that I know of."

Bernie looked over at Adam and said, "That's all I have, unless you have anything else to add."

Adam looked back at Lisa and handed her a business card, "Thanks for all your help. I know this wasn't easy for you to do, but we really appreciate everything you've told us. If you remember anything else you feel might be important, please give me a call. Do you have any questions for us?"

"Yes, as a matter of fact I do. I remember you asking if Mel was into anything illegal. I knew her pretty well and there is no way she was involved in anything illegal. If she was killed because of anything, it's because of what she knew and not what she did. Do you guys think Rocky may have done this to her?"

"Ms. Butler, we still have a long ways to go in this investigation and thanks to you we have a lot more leads to follow up on. As soon as we know anything, you'll be the first to know," Bernie answered.

With that final assurance, Ms. Butler got out of the car, returned to hers and drove back toward BMB Textiles. Adam and Bernie headed back into town to the sheriff's office and found the first sergeant and Investigator Jenkins waiting in the back lot by the door. With near zero temperatures, everyone shuffled inside to the warmth of the conference room to collaborate on their interviews.

"Well, how did it go with Rocky?" Adam asked.

Jenkins laughed out loud before he answered, "We weren't in there for more than two minutes before he told us to get out. He also told us that any further questions we had needed to be addressed to his lawyer."

"Did he say anything at all before he showed you to the door?" Adam asked.

"Nope, he pretty much lawyered up immediately and told us to get the hell out."

Adam was about to tell them how his interview with Lisa had gone when Jenkins continued, "However, the trip wasn't a total waste of time. Just before we left, his office manager, Sheila Potts, asked to see us outside. She asked us why we were nosing around the shop. We told her we were investigating the homicide of Melissa Ann Dwyer and that Rocky and Ms. Dwyer knew each other intimately. Ms. Potts went off. And when I say she went off, I thought we were going to have to go in there and save Rocky's ass. She ran back inside that garage and started yelling at him, calling him a cheating bastard. She called him a few other choice words too before she walked back outside toward us. I asked her if she knew where Rocky was Sunday night and she told me to fuck off."

Bernie and Adam both started laughing.

"Looks like Melissa Dwyer wasn't the only lady Rocky was sleeping with," Adam commented.

"How did you guys do?" First Sergeant Parr asked.

"Our interview wasn't as funny as yours, but we got what we needed."

Adam told them everything that Lisa had said, as well as her concerns about the possible illicit activities of Rocky and his employees. Everyone knew that it was time to turn the heat up on everyone in Rocky's inner circle.

"It looks like we just identified our suspect gentlemen. Let's get a list together of all our objectives, as well as a list of all the equipment you guys are going to need to accomplish them. I'll tell you now that a majority of our surveillance equipment is in Frankfort so it will take me a day or two to get it here," First Sergeant Parr remarked.

Adam, Bernie, and Jenkins brainstormed for the better part of an hour putting together a wish list of all the gadgets they wanted to use. They all agreed that the most important device they were going to utilize was the wireless GPS unit called a Birddog. Since multiple vehicles would need to be tracked throughout the county, a Birddog is the best way of tracking all of them without having to actually tail the suspect. The state did have more modern GPS units that could transmit a live feed to a laptop computer but they ran through their batteries every week. The Birddog could run off a single battery for over a month because it's only activated when the vehicle is in motion. First Sergeant Parr took the list and left for the State Police Headquarters to put in the request for the equipment while Adam and the guys came up with their new assignments.

"I'll take care of the subpoenas for cell phone records for Rocky and his Woodchucks. Bernie, you're going to have to press all of your informants for information and see if you can get back in Stuart Winston's good graces. Jenkins, you have the hardest part of all. Since Bernie and I don't have any experience with the Birddogs, I'm going to need you to get them installed on all the bad guys' vehicles when they arrive and monitor all of them for us. Is that okay?"

"Not a problem at all. I've been permanently assigned to you guys as of this morning."

"Excellent. Let's get started."

Chapter 7

They were already halfway through the third day of the investigation and Adam felt they were headed in the right direction. Every lead they had received so far pointed to Rocky and his woodchucks, but he knew they needed a little more to tie them to the crime. Adam had excellent circumstantial evidence but he wanted the smoking gun, that one piece of evidence that would make a jury of Rocky's peers hand down the death sentence for capital murder. He quickly finished with the subpoenas for everyone's cell phone records and walked next door to the courthouse the get them signed by the judge. With signature on paper, he faxed them to the phone providers' investigations division and waited patiently by his fax machine for a return.

Adam sat back in his chair for a brief minute, put his hands behind his head and looked out his window at the hillside. The leaves had all fallen from their branches leaving behind a brown lifeless landscape. The creek that wound around the base of the hill was almost completely covered with dead leaves and had been reduced to a trickle. He thought about how horrible it must have been for Melissa Dwyer to be murdered the way that she was. What did she think about before she died? How much pain did she feel when the bullet entered her chest? For the first time since the investigation started, he put an actual person with the crime. How in the world could someone be so cruel as to take another person's life like that? He wanted the answers that only Rocky could give and he was going to get them… now.

Grabbing his jacket, he walked out of the sheriff's office and got into his car. He pulled out of the office lot and turned west on route 114 getting angrier and angrier as he drove. His mind raced as he thought about how to approach Rocky and what he was going to say. Before he had had time to really think about what he was doing and how it could negatively impact his investigation he was pulling onto South Railroad Street. As he approached the garage he saw one of Rocky's green trucks pull out of the parking lot and head toward him. He slowed down enough to see Rocky behind the wheel, shaking his head in disgust as they passed one another.

Adam thought that if he continued down the street to the garage then Rocky would turn around and follow him to kick him off the property. But he didn't, he just kept driving in the opposite direction. Once in front of the garage, Adam parked on the street and looked over in the lot to see a car that he had never seen before.

He keyed up his radio and ran the license plate on the car, "Investigator 16 to Stillwell, tag check please."

"Go ahead with your tag, Investigator 16," The dispatcher answered.

"Kentucky registration 1FL-673Z"

Adam sat silently for a few seconds for the dispatcher to return, "That tag returns to a Sheila Potts from Cliff, Kentucky. Her license status is valid and there are no outstanding warrants for her arrest."

"I'm direct on your traffic, thank you."

Adam thought for a minute and decided he had nothing to lose by going in and talking to Ms. Potts. Maybe she had calmed down enough or better yet, she was still pissed and wanted to tell Adam everything. He walked into the business office and was greeted by a slender red head, wearing a low cut shirt that accentuated her large breasts, sitting behind a cluttered desk. Her pleasant demeanor abruptly turned to hostility once she realized who he was.

"I knew that you'd be coming back here at some point and I ain't got nothing to say to you."

"Why is that, Ms. Potts? You're the one who's been betrayed here. I'm sure Mr. Livingston told you that you were the only one for him and that he was going to someday leave his sick wife for you. It has to hurt knowing that all along he was saying the same shit to another woman."

"You're the one that's full of shit, Detective. He never told that woman any of that. You're a damn liar."

"Can you explain why his trucks were seen at Ms. Dwyer's house on several occasions?"

"Because Rocky and his guys built that garage for her over the summer. I still have the invoice where she owes us a lot of money."

"How much money?"

"$15,000 dollars to be exact."

"That's a lot of money. Has she been paying you on time?"

"She stopped paying about three months ago and I was about to send her to a collection agency but Rocky told me not to. He said he would take care of getting the rest of the money from her."

"And you don't find that odd? How many times has Rocky done that for any of his clients?"

"He's never done that."

"Exactly. Ms. Potts, I have a diary Ms. Dwyer kept that details her affair with Mr. Livingston and let me tell you, it gets pretty steamy. She talked about how good the sex was and how she was deeply in love with Rocky."

"I want you to leave now, Detective."

Adam turned around and walked out of the office. The door had barely closed behind him when he heard Sheila screaming into the phone at Rocky. He stood by the front door and listened to her screaming obscenities until he heard the phone slam down on the receiver. A smug smile came to his face as he turned and walked toward his car. He almost had his key in the door when he heard Sheila yell to him.

"Hey, Detective Alexander. Let's take a ride."

Adam watched as she locked the office door and walked over to his car. He unlocked the passenger door and allowed her to slide gracefully into the seat.

"Where to, Ms. Potts?"

"Anywhere but here. And please call me Sheila."

Adam pulled onto South Railroad Street and back toward the highway. He figured they could chat while he drove around the more remote parts of Stillwell County.

"I'm going to drive out to the state park. Is that okay with you?"

"That's fine by me. Listen, Detective. As pissed off as I am right now and as much as I want to get Rocky in trouble I can't. He was with me on Sunday night. We watched the Redskins game, we had sex and then I went to bed. He left my place around 9:45 or 10:00."

"What time did he get to your place?'

"Around 4:00 I think. Yeah, it was just before four. The game hadn't even started yet."

"Was he acting funny when he got to the house?"

"Nope, he was his usual self. He couldn't keep his hands off of me. I even had to ask him to calm down a little bit because I wasn't feeling well. Plus he needed a shower, he stunk."

"What did he smell like?"

"It was a weird smell, like he was around chemicals all day. All I know is that it was making my headache worse."

Adam continued to drive while Sheila talked about her life and how she ended up in Stillwell working for Rocky. Her mother had been killed in a car accident when she was really young leaving her alcoholic father to raise her and her younger sister. He sexually abused both of them until she ran away at age 15 and never looked back. She moved from town to town for several years until she ended up in Stillwell and met Rocky. He took her in, gave her a job, and helped her get established.

"He isn't a bad guy, Detective. But I also understand you have a job to do. I just don't think he's capable of murder. He has such a kind and giving heart."

"Does he have a substance abuse problem that you know about?"

"After his son died he was never the same. He started to lose weight and he became more and more irritable. I've had my suspicions but he's never done any of that shit in front of me. He knows my father was an alcoholic and that I don't put up with any of that nonsense."

Adam drove Sheila back to Rocky's garage and dropped her off. He thanked her for the information and drove back to the office to type up a supplement detailing his most recent interview. The folder on the case was starting to look more like a novel than a file. He looked over at the clock and saw that it was only two in the afternoon, so he picked up his phone to call Bernie.

Bernie answered on the second ring, "What's up Adam?"

"Hey, Bernie. Can you break free in a little bit to interview Stephen Barton with me?"

"I can't. I'm in the middle of something with my guys. We're about to make another controlled buy from Bubba's place with a new informant."

"Where are you now? Do you need any help?"

"We're down here behind the old body shop getting ready to move out. I think we have enough people on this one, but thanks for offering."

"Okay, I figured it's time to start in with these guys and see if they're willing to talk. Have you gotten hold of Stuart Winston yet?"

"Not yet, I'll try to get in touch with him after I'm finished here."

Adam hung up the phone and thought about going out to Stephen Barton's house by himself until he pulled out his criminal history from the case folder and saw the malicious wounding and the brandishing charge staring back at him. He decided he had better call Jenkins for some help. There was no need to go out there by himself if he didn't have to.

Bernie put his cell phone back in his pocket and got out of his car with a new *Reliable Confidential Informant Agreement* form in hand. His newest informant, Rusty Flynn, had contacted Bernie after JT recommended him as being reliable.

Rusty extended his hand toward Bernie as he walked up to him, "It's nice to meet you, Sir."

"I don't shake hands with anybody. It's nothing personal. Now tell me, why do you want to be an informant, Rusty?" Bernie asked.

"Because I need the money. They gonna turn my power off if I don't pay them on Friday."

Right away Bernie knew Rusty was lying. He was just as hooked on crack as JT because they both had the same mannerisms when they wanted a fix. Rusty's hands were shaking and he wheezed loudly every time he took a breath. On the third wheeze, Rusty would let out a small cough, catch his breath and continue to talk. JT did the exact same thing. Bernie called it the "Crack Cough".

"Okay, Rusty. This is a form that you have to read and sign. It pretty much says that you won't buy dope without us being present and if you get yourself killed it isn't our fault."

While Bernie explained the rest of the form, one of his guys searched Rusty's car to make sure he didn't have drugs with him.

"Why is that guy searching my car?"

"Because in the past I've had informants bring fake dope with them and try to pass it off as the real deal. They'll go up to a house, shoot the bull with the homeowner without buying dope, and come back to me with the fake stuff. Then after I pay them for making the buy, they go buy real dope from someone else."

"Come on man. I ain't got nothing, I swear."

"I don't know you and you don't know me. If you want my help, then you play by my rules. Understood?"

"Yes, sir."

"Good. Now empty your pockets and kick off your shoes for me so we can get this ball rolling."

Rusty turned his pockets inside out and took both of his shoes off for Bernie to see that he wasn't carrying any drugs or paraphernalia. After he finished his search, Bernie pointed back to the *Reliable Confidential Informant Agreement* form on the hood of his car and told Rusty to keep reading and sign it when he finished.

Instead of doing like he was told, Rusty picked up the pen, signed his name at the bottom of the form, and handed it back to Bernie, "I get paid for doing this right?"

"Not this time, but next. I've got to make sure you can do what you say you can and then you start getting paid. You got that?"

"Yeah, I got it."

"Good. This is Frank," Bernie turned and pointed over toward the task force member searching his car. "He's going to stay back here with you while the rest of us go and get set up. You're to stay put until you hear from me. What's your cell phone number so I can call you and tell you when to move in?"

Without hesitation, Rusty rattled off, "It's 606-555-9821."

He entered the cell phone number into his contact list and hit save, "You'll be hearing from me soon."

Bernie and the task force strapped up and drove towards Bubba's house at the end of Beaver Valley Road just outside the town of Martin. Unfortunately, they had to park off of Coal Street and walk about half a mile through dense woods and brush to get set up. As soon as the house was in sight, Bernie knelt down behind the largest oak tree he could find and dialed Rusty's number.

"What the fuck? Why isn't he answering?" Bernie whispered to himself.

He hung up and called Frank's cell to see what was going on.

"Hey Frank. Is Rusty's cell phone ringing? I'm trying to call him."

"It hasn't rung since you guys left and he's been standing next to me the whole time. Hold on a second."

Bernie could hear Frank's muffled voice asking Rusty if his cell phone was turned on, but he couldn't hear Rusty's response.

"You ain't gonna believe this Bernie. Rusty gave you Bubba's cell phone number by mistake. You just called Bubba."

"Are you serious?"

Bernie sat silently for a minute contemplating their next move, but ultimately he knew that they had to cancel the buy. It just wasn't safe to send Rusty in after he had called Bubba.

"We're on our way back now. Keep an eye on that idiot and don't let him leave."

The half-mile walk through the woods gave Bernie the extra time he needed to calm down and remember that he was dealing with a crack addict. Toward the end of the walk Bernie looked over at Jimmy and started to cuss under his breath.

"Still pissed off, Bernie?" Jimmy asked.

"Hell yeah, I'm pissed off. One of the stupidest crack heads in Stillwell County gave out their supplier's personal cell phone number to the police. That dipshit knows Bubba's number better than he does his own. What's that tell you?"

After everyone had walked safely from the woods, they drove back to the body shop where they had left Frank and Rusty. Bernie got out of his car, walked over to Rusty and ripped up the confidential informant agreement form right in his face.

"You and I will never work together, Rusty. Thanks to you, the biggest dealer in Stillwell has my cell phone number. How could you be so stupid?" Bernie asked.

"All I can say is I'm sorry Detective Steckler. I was nervous. I'll do better next time, I promise. I need this money. Please," Rusty pleaded.

"We're through Rusty. Wait here a few minutes after we leave and go home."

Bernie and the task force members got back into their cars, and left Rusty standing in the parking lot. While Bernie drove toward town, he shifted gears and thought about how he could salvage the afternoon. Immediately he thought about a Nip Joint at the end of Main Street that the local ruffians frequented. No matter what time of day, people were always there getting drunk on illegal moonshine or high from whatever they could get their hands on. Bernie picked up his phone and called JT.

"Hey Detective Steckler, how did it go?"

"It didn't go JT, and now you owe me a favor for your friend's screw up."

"What did he do?"

"He can tell you all about it later, but tonight you're gonna go into Darren's house and ask about our dead chick. Be ready to go in fifteen minutes and don't be late."

Bernie hung up the phone before JT had the opportunity to say no and keyed up his in-car radio to let the guys know that they were going to town.

"Okay guys, one more short assignment and then we'll call it a day. JT is gonna go into the Nip Joint for an hour or so and see what he can find out about our homicide victim. Frank, I need you to set up on Second Street and get eyes on the back of the house. Jimmy and Derek, you guys park on Main Street and Zach and Tim, you guys park in the grocery store lot with me and watch the front of the house. Let's get a move on. It's getting late."

They had to get back to town to get set up around Darren's house before too many people started showing up. Bernie drove into the parking lot of the *Buy Fresh* grocery store and parked between two cars facing Main Street and the house. He pulled out his binoculars from the center console and kept watch while the rest of his guys got into place.

Bernie keyed up his radio again, "Everyone ready to go?"

After everyone marked 10-4, Bernie called JT and gave him the instructions.

"JT, you're gonna go into the house and ask around about the dead girl that we found Sunday night on Spurlock Creek Road. Be casual about it though. When the time is right ask them if they heard about the murder and see what they say. Someone in there has to know something."

"I know I can't smoke up, but can I have a few beers or a shot of shine to fit in?"

"You can have two beers JT and that's it. Are we clear?"

JT assured Bernie that he understood what he was supposed to do and that he wouldn't get high.

"How soon can you get here? We're all set up and waiting on you?"

"I can be there in five minutes."

JT lived in an apartment over the Hardware Store so it only took him a few minutes to get to the house. Bernie watched him as he slowly walked up the stairs onto Darren's front porch, and eventually through the front door. They had to pay close attention to the front and the back doors because the last time he was here, JT snuck out the back and got high in the tool shed. For the next twenty minutes Bernie watched just about every local drunk and drug user walk into the house.

"Any sign of JT around back," Bernie asked?

"Nope, just a bunch of the locals drinking on the back patio. I've got good eyes on the back," Frank advised.

Thirty minutes later, JT came stumbling down the front steps, high as a kite and headed toward his apartment.

Bernie, extremely irritated, called JT on his cell phone, "Did you find anything out or did you just get stoned the entire time?"

JT had a slur to his speech, "Well, sir. They was talking about it when I got there. I didn't have to say nothing. They had the newspaper article and was looking at the picture wishing they had known who she was because of how pretty she is. None of them guys knows nothin'."

Bernie was surprised when he heard this. He thought that out of all the dirt bags he had watched go into the house, someone had to know who she was.

"Okay JT. Go home and stay there. I'll be in touch."

"How much you payin' me?"

"I'm not paying you a damn thing. We went over that before you went in."

Bernie hung up the phone before JT had a chance to complain. He was finished listening to that fool for the night.

He reached down for his in-car radio and keyed up the mic, "Hey guys, you all can stand down for the rest of the night and we'll meet up tomorrow sometime. Thanks for the help."

Bernie thought about calling it a night himself, but ultimately he decided there was a lot more he could be doing with his side of the investigation. It was time to call in a few favors that were owed to him from his informants that had screwed up over the years. Every once in a while, Bernie and his guys would look the other way on a driving suspended charge or a bullshit petty larceny, but made it known that they would be calling on them one day for a favor to work off the charge.

"Hey, Slim, it's Bernie. Can you meet me at the usual spot? I need to ask you a few questions and possibly send you into a few places."

"Sure thing, Detective. I'll be there in a few if I can get my knees to cooperate with me. They been acting up here lately."

Eugene "Slim" Davenport was a large man who had an insatiable appetite for crack cocaine. Back in the day he was considered to be the best mechanic in town until he got hooked on prescription pain killers after a nasty shop accident. He was quickly labeled as a pill popper by the medical community and after they stopped prescribing to him he found that self medicating with crack cocaine dulled the pain just as well.

Bernie drove north out of town and turned right on Jane Brown Branch Road next to the junk yard. A few miles back in the hollow, there was a 30 acre piece of property that the county owned. Bernie often used this spot to meet up with his informants because it was secluded. There were mountains on three sides of the property and the nearest house was at least five miles away in any direction. He drove down the long dirt driveway to the center of the property where a dilapidated farmhouse stood. Behind the ruined house was a small two stall barn where the local teenagers sometimes came to drink and carry on. Bernie made a quick lap around the property to make sure no one was lurking in the shadows and waited for Slim to show up. He was a little bit early so he picked up his phone to call Adam.

"What's up Bernie, you got anything interesting?"

"No, JT was a bust so now I've got Slim meeting me down at the county yard to talk. Do you have anything new?"

"No, I still need to talk to Stephen Barton. I'm sitting here in front of his house with Jenkins waiting for him to show up. I wouldn't think that a Woodchuck would have too much to do in the middle of winter."

"Okay, let me know how it goes."

Just as Bernie hung up the phone he saw an older model Pontiac coming up the gravel drive toward him. As he got out of his car, he recognized the passenger as Slim, but had no idea who the female driver was. The Pontiac came to a stop next to Bernie, and Slim slowly got out of the passenger side and shut the door.

"Can we go around the corner, sir? I don't want the misses to hear what we're talking about."

Bernie glared at Slim as they both disappeared behind the farmhouse.

"What in the world are you thinking, Slim? You know that we don't need anyone finding out about this place. If people know we come here then those woods will be crawling with idiots looking at us."

"I know sir, but I didn't have a ride and you know my license is revoked. Plus I needed the money."

For the third time that day Bernie took a deep breath to calm his nerves.

"Okay Slim, first of all, what can you tell me about the dead lady we found on Spurlock Creek Road, Sunday morning?"

Slim took a giant step backwards and by the look on his face was about to have a heart attack.

Bernie quickly addressed his uneasiness, "Calm down Slim. We don't think you had anything to do with it, but we did find a meth lab in one of the rooms."

"Meth lab? You know I don't touch that shit," Slim exclaimed.

"Slim, I know you don't touch the stuff, but you have friends who do. I need to know if Melissa Dwyer was selling or not. Can you do that for me?"

Slim looked away to act like he was disinterested in what Bernie was saying.

"And trust me Slim, if you find this out for me, I'll make it worth your while."

Bernie produced three hundred dollars from his front pocket and showed it to a salivating Slim.

"Give me one day, and I'll find out everything."

Bernie gave Slim twenty five dollars for meeting him on such short notice and sent him on his way. Bernie followed him as he walked back toward the passenger side of his car. He watched as Slim and his girlfriend drove down the driveway and off the property. Once they were out of sight, Bernie flipped open his phone to move on to the next informant to get them working on the case.

The next name he came to was Timmy Jameson. Timmy used to work for Bubba back in the day, but he ended up using more than he sold, so he was lucky he was only fired and not killed.

Timmy was another local who was born and reared in Stillwell County. He was raised by his aunt and uncle because his mother had been in and out of jail for prostitution and his father was serving a twenty year sentence for bootlegging. The Jameson clan was known throughout the county as a fighting and partying bunch. Timmy got into some drug trouble a few years back and worked off his charges with Bernie. They had crossed paths not too long ago and although he claimed to be drug free,

Timmy's emaciated body and open sores on his face told Bernie otherwise.

"Hey, Timmy. It's Detective Steckler. You got a few minutes to talk, or better yet can you meet me at the property?"

"No sir, I can't make it to the property tonight. I got some things going on out here at the farm. Can you just tell me what you're looking for over the phone?"

"Did you hear anything about a house fire on Spurlock Creek road three days ago?"

"I did. And I heard you guys are looking heavy into who the woman was. You got folks talking out here something awful. Even Bubba is trying to figure it out."

"Bubba is looking into this too? I wonder why?"

"I'll tell you why. It's because that dumb ass JT was up at his house poking around yesterday and today. He better watch his ass because they ain't gonna play with him like that no more. They're just gonna kill him and dump his body down a mine shaft. Bubba already thinks he's a snitch."

"So it's safe to say that you have no idea who Melissa Dwyer was?"

There was a few seconds of silence on the other end of the line.

"Well, I can tell you that I don't know who she was. But Bubba is pissed because he thinks this chick was dipping into his customers, so now he wants to see who she was working with, if you know what I mean."

"Thanks for the info, Timmy. I'll give you a few bucks for your time tonight. We can meet in a few days to settle up. Just do me a favor and keep your ears open. Oh, and I'm paying four hundred dollars to whoever can tell me who Melissa Dwyer was selling to."

"I'll ask around."

Bernie hung up the phone and immediately tried calling JT. The phone rang, but no one answered. Bernie jumped in his car and sped off the property toward town. He feverishly kept trying to call JT but all he got was his voicemail. His next call was to Adam who picked up on the first ring, "Yeah Bernie."

"Hey bro, where are you?"

"I'm still sitting outside of Stephen Barton's house. What's going on?"

"JT was asking around about Melissa Dwyer for me and apparently he got Bubba all pissed off. Now I can't get hold of his dumb ass and I'm headed to his place to check on him. Are you close to town because I need some backup?"

"I'll drop Jenkins off at the sheriff's office and meet you in the parking lot of the Dollar Store in five minutes."

Bernie pulled into the dollar store parking lot to find Adam already there. The sun had gone down about an hour earlier so the cover of darkness helped to hide their approach to JT's apartment. The entrance was down an unlit alleyway on the back side of the Hardware Store. Carefully and silently the two detectives bounded down the narrow "fatal funnel". Normally, officers try to bypass any areas that create a choke point, but this time it was unavoidable. The alley was the only way. As they rounded the corner Bernie noticed JT's car half in its parking space with the driver's side door open. Looking just beyond the car, Adam could see the front of the apartment.

"Fuck Bernie, the apartment door is open too. Hold the channel, we gotta go in."

Bernie reached for his portable radio and had the dispatcher clear the frequency so they could make entry into the apartment. With guns drawn the two detectives cautiously walked up the stairs and into the one bedroom apartment announcing their presence the entire way.

"Sheriff's Office! JT, you up there?" Bernie shouted.

At the top of the stairs, Bernie went to the left while Adam went to the right to get out of yet another fatal funnel. It only took a minute to clear the tiny apartment and to realize JT wasn't there. Bernie had the dispatcher clear the channel for routine traffic and reholstered his gun.

"Well, this place is an absolute shithole, that's for sure," Adam sneered. "I wouldn't let my dog stay here."

Adam stood in the center of the apartment and turned clockwise taking in the foul apartment. A rancid stench from overflowing garbage hit his nose and almost took his breath away. Filthy clothing was strewn all over the floor and furniture. Adam walked into the kitchen and saw that the double sink in fact did double duty. The left side housed all of his dirty dishes and the right side with the garbage disposal served as his toilet. Adam could see and smell urine and feces in the bowl.

"Bernie, this is fucking disgusting! How can someone live like this?"

"I don't have a clue, but I need to find this guy. I would hate to think he got killed because of something I asked him to do."

"He knew damn well what he was getting himself into. You don't mess around with dope dealers and not expect to have something happen to you eventually."

Adam stepped carefully on the cockroach laden floor and walked back downstairs to check out JT's car, while Bernie started canvassing the neighbor's to see if anyone had seen or heard anything out of the ordinary. After striking out with the neighbors, Bernie came back down the stairs to see what Adam was up to.

"You see anything Adam?"

Adam took out his flashlight and shone it in the red two-door Mustang and was startled to see blood on the headrest.

"We have a big problem here," Adam stated.

Bernie came around to where Adam was shining his flashlight and looked inside.

"Holy Shit! This isn't good Adam. This isn't good at all."

A pool of blood had collected in the driver's seat of the Mustang leaving Bernie to think the worst had happened. Adam noticed that the plasma had already started to separate from the coagulated blood letting him know that it had been there for more than an hour. Frantically, Bernie called JT's cell phone over and over but got his voicemail each time.

"We can go back to the office and have dispatch try to ping the phone," Adam suggested.

Bernie locked JT's apartment door while Adam locked up the Mustang. If they needed to, they could always call the town police and let them handle the missing person's case. A few minutes later the two detectives were at the sheriff's office and headed to the dispatch center on the second floor.

"Hey there boys, what can I do for you tonight?" Ms. Crags asked.

"We need you to help us ping a cell phone please," Bernie asked.

"Sure thing honey, what's the provider information and the number?"

"It's a prepaid phone from Mountain Wireless and the number is 606-555-4671," Bernie answered.

Ms. Crag's took the information and contacted Mountain Wireless. If the phone JT had in his pocket was equipped with GPS then the cell phone company could send out a signal to his phone. It wouldn't give an exact location, but it would indicate which cell tower the phone was closest to.

"Well, it looks like that phone is somewhere near Cincinnati, Ohio," Ms. Crags stated.

"I guess there is nothing we can investigate down here, Adam. Why don't you head on home and get some rest. I can make a few calls from here and check out the Ohio connection tomorrow," Bernie stated.

Adam didn't need to be told twice, he walked out the door and went home for the night.

Chapter 8

Adam rolled over to look at the alarm clock on the table next to his head. His eyes slammed shut from the bright sun shining through his bedroom window hitting him directly in the face. It took a few blinks, but when his eyes adjusted to the light he was able to see that it was seven fifty in the morning and the annoying buzz was set to go off in ten minutes. He lifted his head off the pillow and looked over toward the opposite side of the bed to see Rennae still asleep next to him. He quietly turned off the alarm clock and slowly sat up putting his feet on the cold hardwood floor. Reluctantly, he prepared himself for another long day.

Satisfied with his appearance, he walked downstairs and directly over to the coffee maker. While he stood in front of the sink, rinsing the glass pot with hot water, he stared blankly out the window and thought about the events of last night. He thought about his flashlight revealing the pool of blood on JT's car seat and the foul smell of his cockroach-infested apartment. Why did people choose to live that way? His trance was broken by the feeling of hot water running over his hand causing him to drop the pot.

"Are you okay?"

Startled, he looked over to see Rennae, still in her nightgown, looking at him.

"I'm fine, just got some hot water on my hands."

Over the years Adam had learned how to read a perp's body language because his mouth had gotten him into more trouble than it gotten him out of. His life depended upon knowing whether someone was going to take a swing or go for their waistband to pull a gun, but Rennae was different. She rarely showed any emotion at all, and the look she had on her face was neutral. Adam had no idea if she was still angry at him for not calling so he figured the best thing to do was give a half-hearted smile and go on making his coffee.

"Are you any closer to solving the murder? I don't like you being away all the time."

"We've got a good suspect developed. During the canvass people remembered seeing a dark green pickup truck in the driveway on Sunday morning and again that night. We found out the truck belongs to Rocky from Rocky Top Landscaping, so now we've got to follow him and his employees around. Don't say anything honey, that's between us."

"I won't say anything. I got some good news yesterday."

"Yeah, what's that?"

"My application has been accepted at Stillwell Elementary for next year. I'm going to be teaching kindergarten."

"That's great. Lord knows we could use the extra money. We should celebrate by going out to dinner tonight."

"I can't wait, Honey."

Adam turned and put the water into the coffee maker while Rennae sat down at the table with the morning paper. As soon as the coffee was ready, he grabbed his travel coffee mug from the cabinet next to the sink and poured himself a cup. He leaned over and kissed Rennae on the cheek and walked out into the cold morning air to his frost-covered car.

"We've gotta move to Florida," Adam thought to himself as he scraped off his windshield. Completely frozen to the core, he got in his car and pulled out of the driveway. He was just starting to warm up when he pulled into the parking lot of the station. The de-icing of his car had made him late so he hastily made his way into the conference room.

"Am I late and everyone left without me?" Adam asked.

First Sergeant Parr laughed, "Your Sheriff is at another meeting this morning, Bishop is running late and Detective Steckler is looking for his lost junkie, so it's just the three of us for the time being. Do you have anything new to report Detective?"

"Well, sir, I interviewed Rocky's office manager, Sheila Potts."

"You got her to talk to you? How in the world did you do that?" First Sergeant Parr asked.

"Hell hath no fury like a woman scorned. I just went in there and told her some of the more intimate details about Rocky and Ms. Dwyer's relationship. I figured he was feeding her the same line of shit that he fed to Melissa and I was right. He's been sleeping with her, too. I do have some bad news though. She gave Rocky a half-assed alibi. She said he arrived at her place just before 4:00 on Sunday afternoon. They watched the Redskins game, had sex and Rocky left around 9:45 or 10:00. The fire was called in at 10:20 so he still had time to kill Ms. Dwyer, but not much. Then she went into her life story and I dropped her off back at the garage. What about you, First Sergeant? Do you have anything new to report?"

"All of the equipment you requested is on its way to us from Louisville. The boys from Frankfort are using all their equipment on a meth lab that they've been working for the last few months. As soon as it gets here, Jenkins will get it installed on the cars. What's the game plan for today?"

Adam looked down at his to do list to see what he had laid out.

"First and foremost, we need to talk to Stephen Barton. I would've taken care of that yesterday, but Bernie can't keep his junkies under control. Then we can work on talking to the rest of the Woodchucks. Since I am down a detective for awhile can you come with me on the interviews, Jenkins?"

"Sure, what time do you want to get started?"

"As soon as we finish here we can get going. I'm figuring that they were out partying all last night and are still home sleeping it off. Let's go and give them an early morning wake up call."

"Sounds good to me. Just let me make a few phone calls and we're out the door."

Adam pulled out the list of Rocky's Woodchucks and their last known addresses from his file while Jenkins made his phone calls. He plotted out which address they would visit first based on its proximity to the Sheriff's Office.

"You ready to go?" Jenkins asked.

"Let's hit it."

Adam pulled out of the station lot and drove north out of town. During the short drive down to Stephen Barton's house the two detectives talked about what it was like working for their respective agencies. They were in the midst of talking about how much money they didn't make when Adam made the left turn onto Allen Avenue and slowly drove down the street.

"This is less than two blocks from Rocky's garage," Jenkins noticed.

"Yeah, Stephen Barton and Richard Easton both live here I think. Which is good for them because neither of them has a driver's license. They're both either suspended or revoked. I pulled the tax records a few days ago and found out that Rocky owns this place."

Adam pulled past the house and parked on the street a few driveways down from their destination. He wanted to have somewhere to retreat to if the interview took a turn for the worse and they had to make a fast break for safety. He put the car in park and both detectives got out, paying close attention to their surroundings. They were in Woodchuck territory, which gave home-field advantage to the bad guys. Within a minute, they were standing in front of a run-down, single-story house with black plastic trash bags piled waist-high in front of the door and in the yard. Every so often Adam got a whiff of the same rancid garbage smell that he had encountered the night before.

"Look at this shithole. Have you ever been in a place like this?" Jenkins asked.

"Yeah, last night. And trust me, this place is nothing compared to JT's apartment. His place almost made me puke."

Adam looked at the garbage strewn all over the front yard wondering if every wild animal in Stillwell County had been there chewing holes in the bags looking for a free meal.

"Well, I guess knocking on the front door is out of the question. Let's head around back." Adam suggested.

They walked up the gravel driveway toward a detached garage that sat roughly 50 feet from the house toward the back of the property. The door to the garage was open, and a light bulb attached to a bright orange extension cord hung from the ceiling casting light on an old muscle car that was up on jack stands. As they rounded the corner of the house, Jenkins noticed a second building just inside the woodline that he never would have seen if the leaves had been on the trees. He tapped Adam on the shoulder and pointed toward the building, making sure that he saw it too.

"Just what the fuck you two think yer doin'?"

Both detectives stopped abruptly in their tracks and turned around. Standing on the back porch was Richard Easton in a pair of coveralls without a T-shirt and a pump-action shotgun in his hands. Adam started to walk toward Mr. Easton but stopped when he racked the forend of the shotgun making that all-too-familiar sound. The hairs on the back of Adams neck stood up on end.

"The way I sees it, you two is trespassin'. You got a warrant to be here, detective?"

"No sir, we're just here to talk to you is all," Adam managed to spit out.

"Well, I ain't in the mood fer no talkin'. So you and yer friend need to get yer sorry asses off my property before we have ourselves a problem."

"Sure thing, Mr. Easton. Is Mr. Barton home?"

"He ain't here."

Mr. Easton lowered the shotgun and went back inside his house, slamming the door behind him. Adam laughed hysterically as they walked back to his car.

"What in the hell's so funny, Adam?"

"I think it's funny that out of all four of those idiots, he's the only one that isn't a convicted felon. If it had been anyone else, we could have arrested them."

"I fail to see how that's funny. I think I shit my pants!"

"Don't be so dramatic. We were safe the entire time. I could see into the chamber of the shotgun as he racked it. There weren't any shells in the tube."

They both got back into Adams car and drove toward Rocky's garage on Railroad Street.

"Did you happen to smell anything funny, like a chemical smell anywhere near the house?" Adam asked.

"No, why?"

"Because when I interviewed Sheila Potts, she said that on Sunday night Rocky smelled like he was covered in chemicals. The smell was so bad she made him take a shower. I was just thinking that maybe they were cooking here, too."

"Well, that's interesting. Maybe Rocky was cooking in Ms. Dwyer's front room when they started to argue about their relationship. Rocky flips out, shoots her and lets the cook explode to cover up what he did. How long would it take for the meth to boil over and cause an explosion?"

"I have no idea. We need to ask Bernie about that when he gets back."

Adam pulled into the empty parking lot of Rocky's garage and parked in front of the office door.

"Stay here. I'll be right back," Adam said.

He got out and walked to the office door to see if anyone was inside. He pulled on the handle to the door but it was locked. Jenkins did as he was told but he kept a close eye on his partner. Adam looked through the glass front door and saw that Sheila's desk was empty. He took three steps back and looked down the long brick building. At one point it had served as an actual automotive garage before Rocky bought the property and turned it into his landscaping business and racing headquarters a few years back. There were three bay doors to the right of the office that opened into one large room and one small room at the end. Adam walked down the front of the building, stopping at each bay door to look through the oval glass windows. The first two bays were filled with lawn mowers, weed eaters and a large Kubota tractor. The last bay door didn't have any glass for him to see through, but the door was open about an inch on the bottom. Adam got down on his hands and knees putting his face as close to the ground as possible. He could clearly see two boots walking around toward the back of the bay. Adam stood up and knocked on the bay door. A few seconds went by with no answer so he knocked again.

"I know someone's in there, I can see your feet. Open up, please."

Adam flinched as the electric motor started to growl on the door opener. He moved back behind the brick pillar that separated bays two and three just in case whoever was inside decided to start shooting. Adam put his hand on his gun as he watched the door slowly open.

"I ain't gonna shoot you detective. If I were, I would have done it when you first pulled up."

Adam looked toward the back of the bay and saw Stephen Barton with his head down in the engine compartment of Rocky's late model stock dirt track car. Just over Barton's shoulder, proudly displayed on the back wall was a shelf full of trophies along with pictures of Rocky standing in different victory lanes within his circuit.

"Nice looking hardware you got there. I heard Rocky won the championship last year," Adam said.

"Did you come here to talk about racin', or did you come here to talk about the killin'?"

"A little of both I guess. Up in Detroit we don't have a lot of exposure to race tracks which is odd considering it's where most of the cars are manufactured."

Adam slowly walked inside the garage and over to where Barton was working. The engine had the air filter removed and the heads taken off.

"What am I looking at, Mr. Barton?"

"An engine."

"What kind of engine?"

"It's an engine that I built from the ground up. She puts out just over 800 horsepower. Now if you don't mind, I got work to do."

"How well did you know Ms. Dwyer?"

"I told you, I got work to do."

"Why are you guys being so elusive, Mr. Barton? If you've got nothing to hide then you shouldn't mind answering my questions."

"First, don't come around here usin' them fancy words like yer better than I am. Second, I ain't killed that lady and I don't know who did. Now I'm telling you to leave!"

Adam turned around and started to walk toward the parking lot when he noticed a dark green Ford F-350 dually pulling into the lot. Rocky sat behind the wheel glaring at Adam as he ambled out of his garage. Adam took his time and even turned around as if he was going to walk back in to talk to Mr. Barton again. Rocky flung open his truck door and sprinted over toward the bay door.

"Get the fuck out of my garage!" he hollered.

Adam smirked at Rocky, turned around, and headed back toward his car. He could feel Rocky's cold eyes watching his every move until he was off the property. It was all a mind game, and Adam was winning.

"I thought he was going to kick your ass, Adam."

"Nah, not in broad daylight. I guess we're headed to Charles Lipscomb's place next."

Adam looked down at his notes and saw the address of 354 Pennington Lane so they drove north on Interstate 460. Since this address was a little further out in the county they had a little more time to talk about their hobbies and personal interests. Adam mentioned that he liked to run and participated in a few marathons every year while Jenkins took full advantage of the vast mountain bike trails that ran all throughout the eastern part of the state. Once on Pennington Lane, Adam pulled up to the address listed but something didn't look right. How in the world could a three-time convicted felon afford such an expensive house?

"Good Lord, that place is three times the size of my house!" Jenkins exclaimed.

"Yeah, that's every bit of 5,000 square feet. I'll have Bishop get the tax records for us."

Adam pulled out his cell phone and called Bishop.

"Hey, Sarge. Can you see if you can get the tax map for 354 Pennington Lane and tell me who the registered owner of the property is, please?"

Adam waited for a response while he sat in his car, astounded by the three story brick colonial perched in the middle of two well manicured acres.

"You there, Adam?"

"Yeah Sarge, go ahead."

"It says here that the property is owned by Charles F. Lipscomb Sr. Is that the same guy?"

"I don't know Sarge, but we're about to find out."

Adam hung up his phone and placed it on the center console. He drove the rest of the way up the driveway and parked in front of the attached two car garage. He and Jenkins both got out of the car and walked up to the garage door to look in. The first stall was empty, but the second had a beautiful older model Porsche 911 turbo parked inside. Dumbfounded, the two detectives turned around and followed the pavement around to the back of the house.

"Holy shit!" Adam yelled.

The asphalt stopped at a detached three car garage with a brick front that resembled the main house.

"Even the garage is bigger than my house," Jenkins exclaimed.

Adam walked up to the first of three garage doors and looked into the window. Sitting in the first bay was a black 1967 Camaro SS with two white racing stripes in mint condition. The second bay housed an old Model T in a state of disrepair but it still appeared to be in running condition. The third was, in Adam's mind, the crown jewel of the collection. In front of him, with the hood up was a polo white, 1953 Chevrolet Corvette with red interior, and the original six cylinder Blue Flame engine. Adam was floored by how someone in today's hard economic times could afford all these luxury items on a landscaper's salary.

"He must have inherited all this," Jenkins said.

Adam turned around and walked to the front door of the house with Jenkins close behind. He rang the doorbell, hoping no one would answer so they could continue to snoop around, but unfortunately someone did.

"Can I help you?"

An older gentleman in his late seventies answered the door wearing a bath robe and slippers. Directly behind him was a woman, about the same age, wearing a red sweat suit and tennis shoes.

"I'm Detective Alexander from the sheriff's office and this is Investigator Jenkins from the state police. Can we have a moment of your time, Sir?"

The frail old man motioned for the two men to come into his home. They followed him, as he walked very slowly to the kitchen where the elderly lady offered to put on a pot of coffee. Adam graciously declined the offer and went right to work trying to figure out who he was talking to.

"What can I help you two with?"

"Yes, sir. What's your name?" Adam asked.

"I'm Charles F. Lipscomb, Sr. and this is my wife, Linda."

"I'm assuming that your son lives here with you?"

"No, he was here for a short while after he got out of jail the last time, but we had to kick him out four months ago. To be perfectly honest with you, we don't even know where he is right now. We got tired of spending our retirement money trying to get him sober. What's he done now?"

"So you're aware of all the trouble he's been in over the years?"

"Aware? Hell, I'm the one that had to pay all his attorney's fees. I still owe one damn lawyer six grand for the last time he was in trouble. Dumb kid had a pistol in his waistband when he robbed our neighbor's house down the street. I can't even drive to town anymore without people yelling at me."

Does he still have any of his personal belongings here, Mr. Lipscomb?"

"It's all here, down in the basement. You two are more than welcome to go down there and see for yourself."

Adam turned his head toward Jenkins, who had a look of uncertainty on his face. Adam thought for a minute about the legal expectation of privacy that Mr. Lipscomb Jr. would have inside his parent's house. Ultimately he concluded that since Mr. Lipscomb Jr. had been asked to leave four months ago and had not returned to pick up his property it could be considered abandoned at this point.

"You only let him stay for a little while, why was that?" Jenkins asked.

"Because I could see he was back to his old tricks. Since he did his time outright he didn't have a probation officer to report to, so when he got out it was right back to getting high and coming home late. After the second month of talking to a brick wall we told him to pack his bags and get out. You still haven't told me why you're here."

"We're investigation a homicide, Mr. Lipscomb and your son's name came up."
Adam looked over toward Linda and saw her eyes tear up.

"Hold on a second, Mrs. Lipscomb. We don't think your son committed the murder, but we do believe he knows who did."

"It's those damn fools he works with isn't it?" Mr. Lipscomb asked.

"It could be. That's why we're here. Do either of you know where he was on Sunday night?"

Both Charles and Linda shook their heads no.

"Like I said before, we haven't seen him in a while."

"Do you mind if we look around in the basement? After that I promise we'll get out of your hair."

Charles pointed over toward a closed door in the hallway and told them that was the basement door. He also told them that neither he nor his wife had been down there since their son left four months ago.

Adam and Jenkins walked over to the stairwell and down into the basement. Adam looked to his right and saw a beautiful oak bar with four Chevrolet bowtie bar stools sitting in front. Just beyond that was a dartboard hanging on a strip of corkboard. To his left was a competition billiards table, a flat screen television, an old jukebox from the fifties, and a leather sectional couch. Adam and Jenkins were in man-cave heaven.

"We shouldn't be down here, Adam."

"Why not, he's been gone for four months and his parents gave us permission to come down here. After a few months all his property becomes abandoned and he has no legal right to call this his residence. We're more than covered for being down here."

Adam left Jenkins standing at the base of the stairs and walked down the hallway that was directly in front of him. The first door he came to on the left was a full bathroom and it was filthy. The sink and tub both had black mold growing around the fixtures and the toilet looked like it hadn't been flushed in years. Adam went through the drawers under the sink but didn't find anything. He backed out of the bathroom and walked across the hall to the basement bedroom. He opened the door and slowly crept inside. For a minute he thought he was back in JT's house because of the foul conditions Junior had chosen to live in. The rancid smell of stale vomit, rotten food and soiled clothing hung heavy in the air causing him to leave quicker than he had wanted to. Adam stood in the hallway trying to catch his breath when he noticed that an uncapped hypodermic needle was sticking out of the sole of his shoe.

"This is ridiculous," he said to himself.

He reached down and carefully pulled the needle out of his shoe being extra careful not to stick himself with it and tossed it back inside the bedroom on the floor. He turned to his left and walked down the remainder of the hallway to the last unopened door. He reached for the knob and found that the door was locked.

"This door doesn't have a keyhole. I wonder what's in here?" Adam thought to himself before turning around and going back to Jenkins at the base of the stairs.

"There's nothing here but a nasty mess. Let's go upstairs and break the bad news to Junior's parents."

Both Detectives walked back into the kitchen and saw Mr. Lipscomb sitting in the exact same place as when they left. He had tears in his eyes as he stared out the sliding glass door toward the hillside.

"Mr. Lipscomb, are you okay?" Adam asked.

"Yes, sir. I'm fine. I hope you never have to go through what we've gone through with our son. Did you know Charlie had a 4.0 grade point average all through high school? He had a scholarship to play basketball at Morehead State but decided to take a year off instead. Although we didn't like it, we supported his decision and even told him that we'd pay for school when he wanted to go back, but he never did."

"When did he start using drugs?"

"I don't even know. One minute the boy was fine and the next he was stealing money out of his mother's purse to buy that garbage. We've sent him to three rehab facilities and each one has kicked him out in under a week. Seems as though he isn't ready to get help yet."

Adam placed his hand on Mr. Lipscomb's shoulder and tried to console him as a single tear rolled down his cheek.

"You're both good parents and you've done everything that you could to get him clean, but like you said, he isn't ready to get help."

"Yeah, well I keep telling myself that but I'm having a hard time believing it."

"Can you tell me what's in that locked room at the end of the hallway downstairs?"

"That's my woodshop. I had to lock the door from the inside to keep Charlie from stealing and pawning my tools. You have to go outside and use the side entrance to get in."

Adam told the Lipscomb's about the mess that they encountered in the basement before putting one of his business cards on the table and walking out the door. On the drive back, Adam asked Jenkins if he was in the mood to grab a bite to eat, but neither of them had an appetite.

Chapter 9

Adam and Jenkins decided to go their separate ways for the remainder of the afternoon. Jenkins had a ton of paperwork to catch up on from his current cases plus the Dwyer murder and Adam was way behind on his reports.

"Meet back here at 6:00? It's Friday, so I'd like to go to Rocky's garage tonight and see who shows up for this pickin' party," Adam said.

"That sounds good to me."

After dropping Jenkins off at the State Police Barracks, Adam drove slowly back toward town. On that particular drive, for some reason he took notice of his surroundings in a way he had never done before. He drove past the Big Sandy Ridge Coal Mine and saw the parking lot was only half as full as it had been in years past. He noticed that one in every eight or nine businesses he passed were closed down. It upset him that the times were so bad and it upset him even more that the people of his county were slowly turning to the elicit drug trade to subsidize their income. Bernie really had his work cut out for him.

Within the next few minutes Adam pulled into the parking lot of the Sheriff's Office and parked in his assigned space. He walked to the rear door and punched in the security code to gain access. As he rounded the corner to the investigations unit he heard a familiar voice from over his shoulder.

"Hey, Adam. How's the case going?"

A sly smile came to his face as he turned around to see the Commonwealth's Attorney, Alexis Leighton, standing in front of him with her arms full of case folders. Adam looked her up and down discretely, admiring the skin tight black pants suit and white button up blouse she was wearing.

"It's going well, Ms. Leighton. We currently have a person of interest and a ton of circumstantial evidence, but I want to make sure this case is air tight for you. I'm hoping to seek the death penalty on this one."

"From what I've read about the crime scene, it meets all the criteria for capital murder. But like you said, it has to be air tight."

Adam enjoyed talking with Ms. Leighton and took every opportunity to do so. She had a contagious smile and flirtatious personality that made their time together pass way too quickly.

"Do you have some time so I can fill you in on the investigation? It'll only take a minute." Adam asked.

Alexis nodded her head slowly and followed Adam down the hall to the conference room.

Alexis Leighton was in her second term as Commonwealth's Attorney for Stillwell County and her third term was all but guaranteed come November. She was born in Frankfort, Kentucky, to Dillon and Linda Leighton and was the only grandchild of James Leighton, proprietor of the multi-million dollar Fox Hunt Bourbon Plantation in Lexington. Her financial backing from her grandfather and his political connections made her a shoe-in for the position; so much so that she had ran unopposed in the last election. She was powerful and extremely beautiful, both qualities that Adam was attracted to.

He waited for Alexis to enter the conference room and closed the door behind them. He inhaled deeply, taking in the delicious aroma that wafted from her body as she passed by. She placed the files on the table and turned around to face him, but she didn't sit down. She stood there with her arms crossed waiting for Adam to say something.

"Sorry to hear about your divorce Ms. Leighton," Adam stated.

"When you work eighty hours a week and your husband wants a family, things deteriorate over time. Plus I wasn't quite ready to trade in my Porsche for a minivan. Not just yet anyways. And how many times am I going to have to ask you to call me Alexis?"

Adam smiled as he looked down at his notebook. He had never heard Alexis tell anyone to call her by her first name in the entire eight years that he had known her.

He quickly changed the subject, “So, Allan “Rocky” Livingston had a physical relationship with the deceased, Melissa Dwyer, and of course he won’t talk to us. We tried talking to his employees and none of them would talk to us either.”

“Are they just afraid of their boss’ retaliation or could they have something to hide, too? Do any of them have criminal histories?”

“Yes, they all do. Ranging from DUI’s all the way down to Brandishing, robbery and manufacturing narcotics.”

“Sounds like a fun group.”

“No kidding. We also found out Rocky was sleeping with his office manager, Sheila Potts, at the same time he was having sex with our victim. She talked to me a little bit and gave Rocky an unverifiable alibi. She said he was with her from 4:00 until 10:00 that night. The house fire was reported at 10:20 by a passing motorist so he’s still my number one suspect.”

“How far does Sheila live from the victim?”

“Only about ten minutes or so. Sheila lives outside town limits and Ms. Dwyer lived a few miles away in the county. The meth lab in the front room may have been the cause of the fire, but obviously we need to know who put the bullet hole in Ms. Dwyer. We’re going to start following Rocky and his guys around and see where that leads us.”

“Does Rocky have any weapons at his disposal?”

“Funny you should ask. I don’t know about Rocky, but I know that his employee, Richard Easton does. He pulled a shotgun on Investigator Jenkins and me earlier this morning. Plus there’s no way to tell if Rocky has any weapons. You don’t have to register them here like you do in Detroit.”

Adam continued to fill Alexis in on the finer details of the investigation in hopes that she would give him an avenue he had not thought of, but no new ideas developed.

"Well, if you need anything Adam, you know how to get a hold of me. My cell phone number hasn't changed."

Alexis stood up and brushed her hand across Adams shoulder as she walked out the door. Adam flashed a huge smile at her as she sashayed past him and out the door. He sat motionless for a brief spell taking in the moment he had just had. A few minutes later, Adam came back to earth and remembered all the work he had come in to do. A mountain of reports waited for him before he went out to the garage with Jenkins. Adam walked into his office and sat down behind his desk. He pulled out his notebook, turned on his computer, and was in the process of typing his reports when he heard a knock at his door.

"Hey, Detective Alexander. How's it going?"

Sheriff Lawson stood in the doorway wearing a black suit which was a far cry from the BDU's and polo style shirt he usually wore.

"It's going fine, Sheriff. We're really trying to get under Rocky's skin, but he and all his buddies are refusing to talk. I'm getting all my reports caught up on so we can go out to his garage tonight to see how legit this pickin' party of theirs is."

The sheriff moved three steps inside Adam's office and stood there motionless for an awkward few seconds.

"You need anything else, Sheriff?" Adam asked.

"No. Oh, here are all the financial and phone records you requested on Monday and Tuesday. I already looked at them and I didn't see anything that looked out of place. All of Melissa Dwyer's phone and credit card activity stopped on the day of her murder," Sheriff Lawson added.

Adam extended his hands to accept the stack of papers from Sheriff Lawson, but before he could say thank you, the sheriff walked out the door and back to his office. He put the file down next to his keyboard and started typing.

The reports on the day's short interviews only took Adam about half an hour to complete. All he could type was *Refused to Talk,* next to each one of their names because each interview yielded zilch. He pulled out the case folder and decided it was time to update it by adding all of the information Sheriff Lawson had just handed to him. Adam looked carefully at all of the cell phone records and noticed that a few of the pages were missing. He looked at the page numbers in the upper right hand corner and saw that it skipped from page two to page five. He stood up and walked back to the sheriff's office to see if Sheriff Lawson had forgotten to give him a few of the pages. But when he got there he saw the sheriff was already gone.

Adam returned to his office with the intention of asking the sheriff about the missing pages first thing Monday morning. Once back at his desk, he looked over what pages he did have. According to the land line phone, Ms. Dwyer didn't make any calls to anyone inside the county except BMB Textiles. The only other number that popped up frequently was Lisa Butler's in West Virginia. Her cell phone information was essentially the same thing, except for a few phone calls that were made to Rocky and her aunt and uncle in Buffalo, New York. If she was into the drug trade then she either hid it extremely well or she had a throw-away phone under another name that she used to conduct her business.

Adam took a break from the case and decided to try to get a hold of Bernie to see what he was up to. He hadn't heard from him in a while and he wanted to see if he had found JT's body floating face down in Dewey Lake.

Bernie's phone went directly to voice mail so Adam left him a message, "Hey, Bernie. It's Adam. Give me a shout when you can. Jenkins and I are headed to stakeout Rocky's garage tonight to see who shows up to this pickin' party. I thought you might want to be in on that."

Adam hung up and went right back to scouring his case file looking for that one piece of evidence that wanted to jump off the page and smack him in the face. He knew that he had to be missing something. He continued to look through the file until he got to the last page, which contained the original outline of the information that he still needed. Looking over the outline, he saw that the only thing that wasn't checked off at this point were the official autopsy report and ballistics information. Adam picked up the phone and called the state lab in Lexington to talk to the ballistics tech working on his case. The phone rang three times before an automated message prompted Adam to press one for English. After mumbling his disdain for having to take this extra step, he was prompted to press zero to talk to an operator.

"Hello, Kentucky State Police Division of Forensic Science Lab, this is Vicky, how can I help you?"

"Hey, Vicky. This is Detective Adam Alexander with the Stillwell County Sheriff's office. I have a bullet that was taken out of a victim and I was wondering if I could get a status update."

Vicky asked Adam to hold while she transferred him back to the ballistics department.

Adam was only on hold for a few minutes when his good friend and leading ballistics expert, Darren Walker, picked up the phone. "What's happening Adam?" Darren asked.

"Hey, Darren. I'm calling to check on the status of my case. Dr. Edwards pulled a bullet from a dead lady on Monday afternoon that should have gotten to you guys by now."

"Yeah, it's here and it has been logged into our system. Hate to be the bearer of bad news but we're on a six to eight month backup on all cases, so before you ask what I know you're going to ask I'm gonna have to say no."

"Come on Darren. This is a big capital murder case we're investigating over here. A dead chick with a meth lab has to take precedence over all the other stuff you've got going on?"

Adam chuckled after his last statement because he knew Darren had at least thirty or so more cases ahead of his, all with circumstances just as horrific.

"You'll be the first to know when I'm finished, Adam. I promise you that."

Adam and Darren talked for a little while longer about each other's families before disconnecting. Adam went right back to work glancing over his file and scratching his head trying to figure out if he had missed anything. He was so ensnared with his file that he failed to notice Sergeant Bishop hovering over him.

"Alexander? Earth to Alexander."

Adam dropped the piece of paper that he had in his hands on the desk and looked up.

"Oh, hey Sarge. What's up?"

"I thought you might want to talk to Jeff Norris. He's in the lobby and is available to talk."

Adam had a puzzled look on his face as he stood up, "Jeff Norris?"

"Melissa Dwyer's uncle from Buffalo."

"Oh, Jeff Norris. I was wondering when he was going to come back. Have you spoken to him at all about the case?"

"No, but I've been in touch with him all along. I told him it would be best if he kept the kids in Buffalo for a few more days while we investigated but he decided it was time to come back and make the arrangements to get her body to Radford, Virginia, for the funeral."

Bishop turned around and walked out the door while Adam grabbed his notebook and followed behind. Adam had a few questions floating around in his head that needed to be answered and he hoped that Mr. Norris would be able to provide them. As the two walked into the conference room, they were met by an extremely well dressed man in his late sixties. Adam wasted no time in getting the interview started.

"Mr. Norris, I'm Investigator Adam Alexander and I've been working on your niece's case. First let me say that I'm truly sorry for your loss. I also want to tell you that we've been working tirelessly and will continue to do so until the very end."

Adam extended his hand toward Mr. Norris and was greeted with a very firm handshake.

"Investigator Alexander, I just want to say thank you from myself, my wife, and our entire family. I know there isn't a lot you can disclose to me at this point, but do you have a suspect?"

Adam looked over at Sergeant Bishop who gave him the go ahead to tell Mr. Norris what they knew so far.

He then transferred his attention back on Mr. Norris, "Yes, Sir. We do. And I promise to answer as many of your questions as possible, but do you mind if I ask you a few questions first?"

Mr. Norris had a tear rolling down his cheek as he told Adam he would help out any way he could.

"Did Melissa have any dependencies on anything like drugs or alcohol that you knew about?"

"For a short time there, she turned to the bottle to help her cope with Bill's death. That's not a secret. But once she got her act together she wouldn't even take aspirin for a headache. She had surgery on her left hand a few months ago and her doctor prescribed Percocet for pain. She called me in pain at least twice that week. She refused to take the pills because of all the horror stories she had heard about people becoming addicted to them."

"So there's no way she could've been involved in anything illegal that you know of?"

"What are you getting at detective?"

"We found a meth lab in the room where her body was found."

Mr. Norris interrupted Adam, "What in the hell are you talking about? Mel was never involved with any drugs or the making of any drugs. There's no way she would bring that around the children."

Adam attempted to calm him down, "Mr. Norris, please listen to me. You asked me to fill you in on everything that we have so far and that's what I'm doing. I can't change the facts of the case, but with your help I can try to explain them. For all I know, the suspect placed these items in the room to throw us off their trail."

Mr. Norris hung his head and spoke softly, "I'm sorry, detective. This has been hard for the kids and our family. We've had to deal with some pretty tremendous losses over the past few years, and as you can imagine, it has taken its toll on all of us all. Please continue with your questions."

"I completely understand that. We found some envelopes with money under her mattress with different denominations in each one. Do you know why she did that?"

"How much money was there exactly?" Mr. Norris asked.

"Almost nine hundred dollars."

"After school care for the kids is roughly $880.00 for three months. I gave Mel the cash to pay for that up through February."

"Did Melissa ever tell you about any of her love interests? Or if she had been dating anyone in the last few months?"

"No, she didn't say anything directly to us. But to be perfectly honest with you, my wife and I wished she would start dating again. We both agreed she had grieved long enough and deserved to be happy. She was a beautiful woman, with a lot to offer." Mr. Norris looked at the floor for a few seconds and then back up at Adam, "So you can't tell me about her boyfriend, Alan Livingston?"

"How do you know about Mr. Livingston?"

"We still have family and friends in the area, so we knew about him a few days after this tragic incident happened. This is a very small town and the people here like to talk. Hell, I was eating a late lunch at Monica's Restaurant before I came here and I heard that Mr. Livingston's wife was moving out of their house as we speak. And she wasn't going quietly, if you know what I mean?"

Adam looked over at Bishop who was standing up and on his way out the door.

"Mr. Norris, I do apologize, but we need to cut this short and get over to Mr. Livingston's house. Here's my card and my personal cell phone number. If you need anything please don't hesitate to call, okay?"

"Okay, Detective."

Adam escorted Mr. Norris out of the secured section of the sheriff's office and into the lobby.

"Once again, I'm sorry for your family's loss Mr. Norris."

"Thank you, Detective. I'll expect to hear from you sometime in the near future with an update."

"Yes, Sir. I'll call you as soon as I know something."

Adam didn't wait for him to leave the building before he ran back to rendezvous with Bishop in the rear parking lot. Both of them got into Adam's car and headed out of the parking lot north toward Rocky's house. As they passed Big Sandy Community College, Bishop looked over at Adam and started to laugh.

"I've got a feeling that this is going to resemble a bad talk show."

Adam started to laugh as well, "Yeah, it would be funny if when we got there all of Rocky's shit was in the front yard. But I do feel bad for his wife. Lisa Butler told us that she has something medically wrong with her. I guess we're about to find that out, huh?"

Adam turned off of Rural Route 3 and onto Rocky Top Lane to find a large yellow moving van in the driveway and a Sheriff's Office cruiser parked behind it. Rocky was busy chasing his wife around the yard waving his hands frantically as she was loading suitcases and other household items into the van. Deputy Aldridge was two steps behind Rocky trying to reason with him and keep him under control.

As soon as Rocky laid eyes on Adam's cruiser, he immediately bolted toward them yelling, "YOU TWO NEED TO GET THE FUCK OFF MY PROPERTY!"

"No, Rocky! They can stay. This is my property too, so you can just shut the hell up. Need I remind you that this is all your fault? If you had just kept your dick in your pants this wouldn't be happening."

That was all the invitation they needed to stay so Adam and Bishop exited the car and walked up to Ms. Livingston.

She extended her hand and introduced herself, "I'm Angela, Rocky's soon to be ex-wife. I just need to get a few more things and then I'll be out of here."

Rocky was now in a fit of rage. What Angela had just said, coupled with Adam's presence threw him over the edge. So much so that he pushed Aldridge to the ground as he ran toward Adam. The deputy quickly scrambled to his feet and gave chase to Rocky, eventually catching him. The fight was on. Aldridge hurled himself through the air, tackling Rocky from behind and taking him to the ground. Adam and Bishop both ran over to assist Aldridge as he attempted to bring Rocky under control. Adam and Bishop did what they could to try to get Rocky's hands behind his back but he was thrashing around so much that they couldn't get him under control. Aldridge took the brunt of the beating because he had Rocky's legs wrapped tight and wouldn't let go. Fist after fist hit him on the top and the back of his head while Angela was screaming in the background for Rocky to stop.

Chapter 10

Rocky was able to break free from Aldridge's grasp and regain his footing. His large frame and immense strength made it difficult for the deputies to get control of any part of his body. Adam and Bishop were both in the process of getting to their feet to re-engage Rocky, when he struck Aldridge so hard in the temple that it knocked him out. Rocky stood upright and started to walk toward his house with a blank stare on his face. Adam and Bishop, now both on their feet, made a mad dash toward Rocky. They both knew there were guns inside the house that he was on his way to get to level the playing field. In one last ditch effort, the two detectives simultaneously dove toward Rocky, taking him to the ground. Rocky took most of the impact as both Adam and Bishop landed on top of him. Adam immediately grasped his handcuffs and got Rocky's wrists secured behind his back before he could regain his wits.

"That was fucking stupid, Rocky!" Adam snapped.

"Fuck you! You two assholes are ruining my life!"

"You were the one having two affairs, Rocky, not me. You ruined your own damn life."

Before they could exchange another round of verbal assaults, Bishop chimed in, "Both of you shut the hell up, you sound like my wife! Rocky, you're in a ton of trouble boy, and you just added two counts of assault on a police officer and a malicious wounding to your tally. Adam, get him to Aldridge's cruiser while I get rescue and another unit here."

Adam helped Rocky up off the ground and led him over to Aldridge's marked sheriff's office cruiser. Rocky took a look at Aldridge who was on the ground and bleeding from the side of his mouth and the back of his head.

"FUCK!" Rocky shouted.

Angela ran toward Rocky screaming at the top of her lungs, "I'm going to take you to the cleaners you cheating asshole. You'll never see your children again. Do you hear me?"

Rocky's demeanor changed from absolute anger to sadness in an instant. His eyes welled up as he looked over at Angela, "You don't have to worry about that, Angie. I've already made the decision to go away. You won't have to worry about me screwing up again."

After Rocky was searched and secured in the rear of the cruiser, Adam came back to Bishop and Aldridge to see if he could help. Bishop was tending to the wounded deputy by making him remain still and on the ground to reduce the risk of any further injury. Over his shoulder, Adam noticed Angela pacing back and forth wildly while talking on her cell phone. Adam walked toward her to make sure she was okay, but before he made it to her, she disappeared inside the house. Adam followed her onto the front porch until he was able to hear her inside, still talking on the phone. From what he could make out she was talking to Rocky's attorney.

Adam stood at the front door and listened as Angela excitedly spoke, "Yes, he's in custody. I don't know, he just went crazy. He punched three cops repeatedly and Lord knows what he would have done to me if they weren't here to take the brunt of his anger."

Adam stood silently on the porch for a few more minutes. He didn't hear Angela say anything he didn't already know, so he decided to walk back to join Bishop and Aldridge.

Off in the distance a pair of sirens could be heard getting closer, until an ambulance and an additional sheriff's cruiser pulled into the driveway. By this time Aldridge was regaining his senses and wanted to get up off the gravel driveway.

"Aldridge, stay put. The medics are here and they're gonna take you to the hospital to get looked at," Bishop told him.

"I'm okay, Sarge. I just need to get up."

"Stay put. You're going to the Emergency Room and that's an order."

Adam reached down and took off Aldridge's badge and gun before the medics knelt down to assess his injuries.

"They'll be waiting for you at the office when you get back to work, Aldridge."

Adam turned and retreated to his car. He sat in the driver's seat, closed the door, and took a deep breath. He held his trembling hands up in front of his face to see that his knuckles were bloody from scraping the gravel driveway during the fight. With the adrenaline rush starting to ware off, he could now feel a sharp pain in his side which, prompted him to take an inventory of his injuries. After a quick assessment, it appeared the only casualties were his hands and a torn pair of pants. Suddenly it occurred to him that he hadn't heard from Bernie in awhile. He pulled out his cell phone and dialed his number.

"Hey, Adam, what's up?"

"You aren't going to believe what just happened to Bishop and me. One minute I'm at the office interviewing Jeff Norris and the next we're in a fight for our lives with Rocky."

There was silence on the other end of the line.

"Are you there, Bernie?"

"Yeah, I'm here. That's just a lot to take in, especially since I'm on my way back from Cincinnati."

"What the hell were you doing up in Cincinnati?"

"JT's mom lives up there. Last night after he left Darren's house he went over to Bubba's to score some dope. Two of Bubba's goons chased him all the way back to his place and roughed him up a bit. After they kicked his ass, he had Rusty drive him up to Cinci so his mommy could nurse his wounds. Now start over, what's going on with Rocky?"

Adam detailed the whole chain of events leading up to Rocky being put into the back of Aldridge's cruiser.

"Holy Shit! Sounds like you've got your hands full."

"You have no idea Bernie. How far out are you?"

"I can be there in about an hour. What do you need?"

"Just meet me back at the office when you get in."

Adam ended the phone call, got out of his car, and walked over to check on Bishop and Aldridge. By the time he got to Bishop, the ambulance was just pulling out of the driveway and headed to the hospital.

"You think he's gonna be okay, Sarge?"

"Yeah, he got his bell rung pretty good, but he should be fine. Can you keep an eye on Rocky while I get Cubbage on the horn and let him know what's going on?"

"Sure thing, Sarge."

Adam walked over to the trunk of Aldridge's car and watched Bishop on the phone explaining the details to Cubbage. All he could do was chuckle while he watched Bishop become more and more animated throughout the conversation. A few minutes later Bishop hung up his cell phone and walked back over toward Adam with a pissed off scowl on his face.

"The Captain wants me to fill out the incident report and the workers comp forms for Aldridge. You know how long it's been since I've filled out a damn report?"

Adam started to laugh but soon stopped when Bishop shot him a nasty glare.

"So Bishop, are you getting the warrants for Rocky or do you want me to do that?"

"No, I'll get them. But I need you to drive Rocky to the jail in Aldridge's cruiser and I'll drive yours. No stops, Adam. Go straight to the jail."

"I think a little country justice is called for in this instance, don't you?"

"No, go straight to jail, Adam."

Rocky didn't say a word on the way to the Adult Detention Center; instead he just stared out the window. Before Adam pulled into the Sally Port, he placed a call to the jail and asked them to send out a few Deputies to assist in escorting Rocky inside. He didn't want a repeat of the fight he had just gone through.

Once Rocky was secured in a holding cell, Adam walked over to the sink behind the booking desk and washed the dried blood off his hands. By the time he finished, Bishop had walked into the jail and did as Captain Cubbage had requested. He booked Rocky in on two felony counts of assault on a police office and one felony count of malicious wounding.

"All you had to do was keep your mouth shut, Rocky. None of this needed to happen," Bishop said as he rolled Rocky's fingerprints on the digital scanner.

"It doesn't matter. My life is over anyway."

Bishop put Rocky back in the holding cell and looked down at his watch to see that it was only 3:00 pm. He could be a jerk and let Rocky sit in jail all weekend, or he could call over to Judge Watson's chambers to see if he was available to set a bond over the video conference system.

"Judge Watson."

"Hey, Judge. This is Sergeant Bishop. Are you available for a bond hearing?"

"Who's the suspect and what are the charges?"

"The suspect is Alan Livingston and the charges are assault on a police officer and malicious wounding. There was an incident at his house today."

"Sure thing. Just let me put on my robe and I'll be ready."

Bishop hung up the phone and wheeled the TV with the video camera over to Rocky's holding cell. He turned on the power to both the camera and TV to see Judge Watson sitting at his desk wearing his black robe and reading glasses resting on the end of his nose.

"Raise your right hand Sergeant Bishop. Do you swear and affirm that all of your testimony will be true and accurate under penalty of perjury?"

"I do, Your Honor."

"Can you tell me what happened, Sergeant?"

As Bishop went over the story, the judge's jaw hit the floor.

"Rocky, I've known you for twenty years. What possessed you to do something like this?"

Rocky just sat in the holding cell looking down at his feet.

"Is there anything you would like to say about the incident before I decide on bond?"

Rocky's eyes left the floor and looked the judge in the eye for a brief second before he said, "No sir. I have nothing to say."

"Okay, Rocky. Based on the Sergeant's testimony, I hereby deem that enough probable cause exists for the issuance of two felony counts of assault on a law enforcement officer and one felony count of malicious wounding. Your bail is set at $8,000 apiece for the two assault charges and $10,000 for the malicious wounding charge. So that's $26,000 total. Do you understand?"

Rocky just nodded his head.

"Thank you, Your Honor," Bishop said before turning off the camera.

He wheeled the television back to the booking desk and exited the jail to find Adam waiting next to Aldridge's cruiser.

Bishop looked over at Adam, "The judge set bond at $26,000. I've never seen a bond that high in my life."

"He was trying to kill us, Sarge. There's no doubt in my mind."

While they walked back to the station they were approached in the street by an arrogant looking gentleman who was extremely well dressed in a pressed black suit.

"Can either of you tell me where they took Mr. Alan Livingston? I'm his attorney, William Mastus."

He extended his hand and presented a business card to Bishop.

"Well Mr. Mastus, he is being held on $26,000 bond at the adult detention center," Bishop answered.

"That's just fine. I've got a bail bondsman on his way down here right now. He'll be out of there in twenty minutes," he said in a condescending manner.

Adam took a step toward Mr. Mastus but Bishop grabbed him by his collar and pulled him back before he had a chance to shoot off his big mouth.

"Is there a problem, Detectives?" Mr. Mastus smirked.

Bishop kept a firm grasp on Adam's collar and directed him away from Mr. Mastus. Once they were safely across the street, Bishop released Adam and continued to walk toward the office.

Adam laughed for a second before looking at Bishop, "Sucks don't it?"

"What sucks?"

"That Rocky will be out of jail before you can even figure out what paperwork you need to fill out."

Bishop didn't find Adam's comment very funny. There was too much truth in it, but he managed to eke out a smile regardless.

Adam walked into the lobby of the Sheriff's Office with Bishop close behind. He was hoping that Bernie was already waiting for him on the CIB wing so he headed in that direction while Bishop went to the dispatch center. Since it was the Friday before Christmas, the halls were abandoned. As Adam rounded the corner toward his office he could see that all of the office doors were shut, except one.

"Bernie, is that you?"

He waited for a minute but received no response. As he called out the second time, a familiar figure walked out of Bernie's office and closed the door behind him.

"Hey, Sheriff. How's it going?"

Sheriff Lawson turned toward Adam with a perplexed look on his face.

"Are you alright, Sheriff?"

"I'm fine detective. Have you seen Detective Steckler? He still owes me some reports from a while back and I need them ASAP."

"He should be here in about ten minutes, you want me to tell him you're looking for him?"

There was no response from the Sheriff. He just turned around and walked away down the dark unlit hallway. Adam stood motionless for a few seconds trying to figure out what had just happened, but he couldn't come up with any reasonable explanation. That was just the sheriff's nature, he left everyone confused about what he was thinking.

"Hey, Adam, you see a ghost or something?"

Adam turned around with the same perplexed look on his face that the Sheriff just gave him.

"That was weird, Bernie. The Sheriff was just in your office looking for you. He said you owed him some old reports."

Bernie pushed past Adam and opened the door to his office. He flipped on his light switch to find scattered papers on his desk and his top file cabinet drawer wide open.

"This is kind of fucked up, Adam. Why the hell was he going through my shit?"

Adam just stood there silently, watching Bernie go through his files to see if anything was missing.

"I can't find anything missing. As a matter of fact, the only file that looks like it was gone through was the Mary Jo Conyer's murder. Why would he be looking through that file?"

Adam thought about what the Sheriff had said to him and asked Bernie, "Do you owe him any reports?"

"No, all my paperwork is up to date. I even put copies of everything on his desk yesterday."

The two detectives just looked at each other. They were both totally bewildered.

"Did he go through your office too?"

Adam turned around and walked out of Bernie's office. As he stood in front of his door, he reached down and felt that the handle was sill locked and there was no light shining from underneath, just like he had left it. He used his key to open his door, turned on the light and sat down behind his desk. Nothing appeared to be out of place but he had a feeling that someone else had been in there. The contents of his desk remained untouched to the best of his recollection so he turned to his file cabinets. He opened each drawer and scanned over his files to see if anything was missing. When he reached his "Unsolved Homicide" drawer he noticed that his Mary Jo Conyer's file had had been rifled through as well.

"Hey Bernie, he went through my file on that murder too. Everything appears to be here, but it's not in the same order I left it."

A few seconds later Bernie's head popped into Adam's office door, "Well this is strange to say the least, but everything's still in my file that I can see."

Adam closed the file and placed it back in the cabinet where it belonged. Bernie walked in and took the seat across from Adam and propped his feet up on his desk.

"Something's up with the Sheriff, Adam. He's acting stranger than usual. I know it's an election year and all, but something's up."

"He's acted like this for as long as I've known him. Hey, I was thinking about tonight and how Rocky and his boys always have that pickin' party every Friday. I still would like to go over there and see what's going on, if you have the time?"

"Isn't Rocky locked up for kicking your asses today?"

Adam shot Bernie the thousand yard stare before answering him, "His dickhead attorney bailed him out just as Bishop and I were leaving the jail. He's probably home and drunk by now."

"What did you have in mind?"

"The way I see it, you and I can head up there and at least see who's coming and going. The entrance to Archway Park is just off of Main Street and the evergreens will give us some cover to sit and watch. I need to get in touch with Jenkins and see if the Birddogs have come in yet because tonight would be the perfect night to get them installed. Grab your binoculars and a notebook and I'll call Jenkins."

Bernie disappeared for a few minutes and returned with what he had been asked to retrieve. Adam was already on the phone discussing the logistics with Jenkins.

"Sounds good to us. We'll be sitting at the entrance to Archway Park. From there, we can see Rocky's garage and his front parking lot. You guys pull further down into the park by the gazebo and we'll call you when everyone is there."

Adam hung up the phone, grabbed his binoculars and the two detectives were off.

On the way to the park, Adam decided to swing by Rocky's house to see if he had bonded out of jail and if any of his cars were in the driveway. It wouldn't make any sense to continue if the main suspect was still incarcerated. As they slowly passed by, Adam noticed that Rocky was sitting on his front porch in the only rocking chair just staring off in the distance. The moving van was gone and Angela's Mercedes wasn't in the driveway. Adam looked over at Bernie who was shaking his head in disbelief.

The silence in the car was broken by the sound of Adam's cell phone going off, "Detective Alexander."

"Hey, this is Jenkins. All my guys are ready to go. Just give me a call before we move in and give us the tag numbers of the vehicles you want these things installed on."

"10-4."

The remainder of the ride to Archway Park was silent. Both Adam and Bernie were physically exhausted from constantly being on the go for five consecutive days with very little sleep. They were both thinking about the possibility that Rocky had nothing to do with Melissa

Dwyer's murder and that maybe one of his employees committed the crime. Adam concealed his car in a clump of evergreen trees just inside the entrance to the park and turned off his headlights. Through his binoculars he could see that Rocky's parking lot was empty with the exception of Sheila Potts' car parked right next to the door. Adam looked down at his watch and noticed that is was only six o'clock.

"We have an hour before people start showing up to this thing, if they show up at all considering today's events. So what really happened with JT the other day?"

Bernie started to laugh as he filled Adam in, "JT's a big idiot and he's lucky to be alive right now. He went over to Bubba's house, like I said earlier, and tried to score some dope. Once they figured out he had no money, they ran him off the property. They also said he was asking too many questions and accused him of being a snitch. Well, Bubba wanted to send JT a message and sent two of his guys after him to ask why he was nosing around about our dead chick. Instead of saying he was just curious, he tried to punch one of the guys in the face. We all know how the rest of the story goes. He got his ass kicked and he went running home to mama."

Adam let out a hysterical laugh as he thought about JT trying to hit someone. He was only five feet three and just over one hundred pounds. A punch from JT would feel about the same as getting hit by a fly.

At 6:45 pm, Sheila closed up the shop and went home for the weekend. Five minutes later two SUV's and two pickup trucks, all nose to tail, were moving toward the parking lot. Adam recognized three of the four as belonging to Rocky, but the fourth was one that he hadn't seen before.

"Bernie, car number three in line, did you happen to get a tag number?"

"No, it was too close to the car in front of it. Just wait till they park and I'll be able to see it through the binoculars."

Adam and Bernie watched as the two SUV's and two pick up trucks pulled onto the property and through a gate that was to the right of the building. Bernie saw Rocky get out, close the gate behind them and quickly disappear around the corner.

"Shit, now what are we supposed to do?" Bernie asked.

"Let's get out and walk to the building. There is a deer trail that runs along the outside of the fence that we can walk to try to get a closer look."

Adam called Jenkins to let them know that all of their target vehicles had arrived and that they were going to scout out the location before sending them in to install the Birddogs. Adam and Bernie cautiously made their way down Main Street toward South Railroad. The closer they got to the garage the louder the sound of music could be heard in the distance.

"Is that bluegrass?" Adam asked.

"What kind of hillbilly shit have you got me into Adam? If we get ass raped I'm gonna be pissed."

"That's really what you're thinking about right now?"

They slowly walked up to the gate and saw that the entire back side of the property was surrounded by a chain link fence.

"Did you know this fence was here, Adam?"

"No. Let's walk around back and see if we can see anything."

They walked around the outside of the fence and saw all of the cars were parked on the back side of the building, near an opening that led to a medium sized room under the garage. Adam knelt down and grabbed his binoculars out of his pocket to get a better look. After he quickly scanned the property, he whispered all the tag numbers of the vehicles for Bernie to jot down.

"You get all those, Bernie?"

"Yeah, I got them all."

"Good, let's keep going."

They continued to make their way around the back of the fence until they were about 30 feet from the back of the building. There were five guys all standing in a semicircle playing instruments around a fire barrel and drinking out of red Solo cups. Adam immediately recognized the fifth guy as Rocky's lawyer, William Mastus.

"Well I'll be damned. These guys actually sound pretty good. I guess the pickin' party is legitimate," Adam said.

"How are the state boys going to get in there to get the Birddogs on the cars? They're practically parked right on top of these guys," Bernie asked.

"Wait here, Bernie. I'm going to see if I can find a way inside the fence."

Adam crawled along the fence line to the far back left-hand corner of the property. There, he noticed a hole in the fence that was large enough for a person to slip through. The only problem was that once you got through the hole there was no way to stay hidden because it was just an empty field. They'd have to follow the fence line to the back side of the building and then over toward the parked cars. And if they got spotted inside, there was no way to easily jump back over the barbed wire at the top of the fence. Adam crawled back to where he left Bernie.

"There's a hole in the fence further down, but it's too risky. There's no way those guys can get through that hole and over to the cars without being seen. Let's go back and I'll call Jenkins to let him know we'll have to try again tomorrow.

The walk back to the car only took a few minutes. Adam and Bernie both opened their car doors when Adam's cell phone rang again.

He answered his phone, "Hey Jenkins, I was just getting ready to call you. Listen, the gate to the fence….." Adam paused in mid sentence before continuing, "Shut the fuck up. There's no way. Okay, we will meet you back in the park."

Adam hung up his phone with a dumbfounded look on his face.

"What's up Adam?"

"Jenkins said they got the Birddogs on all four of the vehicles. Did you see those guys go in there?"

"There's no way. I was looking in that direction the entire time. How the hell did they get in there?"

Confused, the two of them jumped into Adam's car and drove deeper into the park to meet with the guys from the State Police. Adam pulled in behind the gazebo and next to the softball field. He eased up to the rear bumper of one of the blacked out Chevy Suburbans and put his car in park. Adam could see two guys with Jenkins, dressed in all black standing next to one of the SUV's.

"How the hell did you guys get in there?" Adam asked.

"The gate wasn't locked, so Jim went in and installed the devices."

Bernie looked over at Adam and started to laugh, "Way to go detective. You didn't even bother to check the gate. I'm recommending to Sarge on Monday that you be taken off this case and moved back to patrol."

"Shut up, Bernie. You didn't notice the gate was unlocked either."

Jenkins handed Adam four small black boxes that each ran off of a single AA battery.

"Okay, I have each of the receivers labeled with its corresponding license plate number. All you have to do is get within fifty feet of the car you want to download the information from and hit the black button. If you're in range the red LED light will go on letting you know it's downloading the information. Once it's finished the green light will blink and you're done. All you have left to do is use this laptop to download the information. You have to use this laptop because the program is secure and we can't download it on any other computers because of the licensing agreement. This isn't live feed, meaning you can't look on a computer screen and see where they are currently. This only keeps a record of where they've been."

"How long will the batteries last on all this stuff?"

"They'll last about three months before we have to change them out. Just get with me in February sometime and we'll get them changed out for you."

Adam took his new found gadgetry and dropped Bernie off at his car before heading back to the Sheriff's Office.

"Hey Bernie, go ahead and take tomorrow off. I've got a few things I can be working on that won't require two people."

Bernie looked over and gave Adam a salute as he got into his car and left his parking spot squealing his rear tires all the way down Court Street. Adam decided to take this time and get familiar with the program he would be using to track Rocky and his crew. After parking in his spot, Adam entered the five digit code to get into the building and went directly to his office. In the back of his mind, he still couldn't understand why the Sheriff was in his and Bernie's offices earlier in the day. Until he was finished with this investigation, he would just have to dismiss it as the sheriff being his usual elusive self. Adam sat behind his desk and looked over at his phone. He picked up the receiver and called his wife to let her know he was still alive and that he would be home right after he figured out what he was doing with the Birddogs. It only took a few minutes for him to figure out the program so he was home in no time. He was true to his word and took Rennae out to dinner like he had promised in celebration of her new job and was home again before ten.

Adam woke up to start day six of the investigation, much to the dismay of Rennae.

"Come on, Adam. It's Christmas Eve and you promised to help me get things ready for my parents who are coming to town tonight."

Adam had totally forgotten it was Christmas Eve and that he hadn't even been shopping for gifts yet.

"Adam, don't you dare tell me you haven't even done any of your shopping yet."

Adam hung his head for a few seconds before telling Rennae that he hadn't even started. This was the third holiday in a row he was going to ruin because of his job. Easter had been cut short because of a suspicious death that he'd had to investigate and Thanksgiving dinner had never taken place because of a fatal auto accident that had involved three high school football players.

"Rennae, I'm sorry. I've just been so caught up in this investigation that it totally slipped my mind."

"You're telling me that every time you drove down Main Street and saw the Christmas lights you weren't reminded that Sunday is actually CHRISTMAS!"

Adam wanted to yell back, but he knew he had royally screwed up this time.

"Rennae, I promise I'll make it up to you. I just need to look at one thing today and then I'll get my shopping done. Is there anything you need me to get while I'm out?"

"Yeah, a new husband!"

"Rennae, I said I was sorry and I am. I'll do everything that I can to be back at a reasonable hour. What time are your parents supposed to be here?"

Rennae turned around and stormed off toward their bedroom. Adam could hear the all too familiar sound of the door slamming shut a few seconds later.

"DAMN!" was all he could say.

Adam walked out his front door toward his cruiser. As he sat behind the wheel a myriad of emotions went through his mind. He was angry at himself for forgetting about Christmas. He was angry that he hadn't gotten Rennae a present earlier. His wife was pissed off at him and rightfully so for all the holidays he had screwed up because of work. It was at that moment he decided to do the right thing and drive up to Ashland to get Rennae the new carbon fiber bicycle she had been wanting for some time. If Bishop or the Sheriff got pissed at him for taking the next two days off, then so be it.

The round trip to Ashland took just over three hours. When he pulled into his driveway he could see a Chevrolet Malibu with Michigan tags parked in his spot. With no other options, he parked behind Rennae's car and got out. Adam pulled the bike out of the trunk and thought about hiding it in the back shed until tomorrow, but decided he had better give it to her now to smooth things over. Just as he was walking up the driveway the front door opened and Rennae walked out onto the front porch.

"Merry Christmas, baby." he chimed.

"Adam, you didn't have to do this. This is too much!"

"Well, I figured since I haven't been around much I better not skimp on this year's gift. Listen Rennae, I'm really sorry about everything. I've been a royal jerk and I'm sorry. I've been thinking about it and decided that if you want me to go back to general investigations, or even the road, so I can be around more, I will. Maybe even try to have our first kid."

Rennae stood there in amazement.

"Adam, this morning I was being a brat and I apologize. The victim's family needs you, too, and I forgot that. So if you need to go to work, it's okay with me."

"No, not tonight or tomorrow baby. Come hell or high water, I'm staying home with you."

Chapter 11

December twenty sixth came way too fast for Adam. He toyed with the idea of calling out sick, but knew he would catch hell from Bishop if he did. He raised his head off the pillow and looked over at the alarm clock to see how much time he had until he had to get up.

"Damn, 4:55 already?" he grumbled.

Since the alarm was due to go off in five minutes, he gently kissed his wife on her cheek, turned off the alarm, and emerged from underneath the warm covers to start his morning routine. Today was his first day to download the data from each of the Birddogs, so he wanted to give himself plenty of time to find all the trucks before the meeting at eight.

Adam staggered to his car, still half asleep, and headed off into the early morning darkness. He figured the best place to start was Rocky's Garage so he turned off Main Street onto South Railroad and down toward the building. The light over the office door was the only light Adam could see from the road. As he got closer the building, he noticed Rocky's SUV was parked all the way at the end of the parking lot near the gate to the rear of the property. He parked his car on the street, grabbed the remote from his center console, and walked toward the SUV. When he was almost to the property, he noticed that the windshield was all frosted over.

"This thing's been here all night. I wonder where he is?" Adam thought to himself as he hit the button on the remote receiver and waited for the light to turn green before heading off to find the other two pick ups.

Luckily it was still early enough that he was able to find them parked in Richard Easton's driveway. He hit the buttons, collected the data and was off. The last stop on his list was Mr. Mastus's house on Church Street. Adam didn't think that he participated in any extra-curricular activities with Rocky other than the Pickin' Party on Friday Nights, but he wanted to be absolutely certain.

He parked at the intersection of Church and Second Street and saw Mr. Mastus in his front yard walking his wife's Pomeranian. Adam watched him pace back and forth in his front yard for a few minutes, dragging his poor dog on the end of the leash. And every time he would flail his hands the poor dog took flight. Adam wasn't close enough to hear what he was talking about and the sunrise was about to compromise his position. Luckily, Mr. Mastus was only outside for a few more minutes so Adam took his cue and quickly walked up toward the driveway with the receiver in his pocket. He pressed the button, hoping that the receiver was doing its job and walked back to his car. He had everything he needed.

Adam drove to the Sheriff's Office and walked directly toward the investigations wing. He turned on the State Police laptop and transferred all of the data from each of the receivers to the hard drive. With the transfer complete, he printed out all the maps and placed each of them side by side on his desk. Rocky and Mr. Mastus's vehicles remained parked all night, so he moved them to the side and looked at the maps for the two pickup trucks.

"I'll be damned," he said under his breath.

The two pickups left Richard Easton's at exactly 3:14 pm and drove out into the county in two different directions. They wove around the back country roads in random patterns, never once passing each other. At 4:07 pm, the pickups met up at Bubba's house in Martin, stayed for fifteen minutes and drove back out into the county. They navigated around in more random patterns and returned to Richard Easton's at 5:04 pm.

Adam started a new folder for all of the Birddog information and thought it best if he handed it off to Bernie. Now that he knew there was a connection between Rocky's Woodchucks and the largest Meth manufacturer in three counties, he figured Bernie would want to keep an eye on the situation. For the next thirty minutes Adam typed his supplement to the case, checked his e-mail, and his voicemail. After he was finished with his administrative duties, he looked over at the clock on his wall and saw that it was 7:45 am. He gathered up the maps, the receivers and the laptop and walked to the conference room for the meeting. Along the way he ran into Bernie in the hallway.

"How was your Christmas, Bernie?"

"Not too hateful. The wife and I went to her parents house in Ohio for the day. Her mom is one hell of a cook. Other than that I caught up on my sleep."

The two detectives entered the conference room and took their normal seats at the front of the room. Bishop, First Sergeant Parr, Jenkins and Sheriff Lawson were already seated, eager to get started. Adam was about to begin when he looked over at the Sheriff, who was sitting on the edge of his seat and biting his fingernails.

"Everything okay, Sheriff?" Adam asked.

"Yes, fine. Let's get this meeting started shall we."

Adam stood up with the folder of maps that he had started and placed it on the table in front of Bernie.

"With your permission, Sarge, I'd like to hand the Birddog responsibilities over to Bernie. Since these guys might be distributing narcotics in their off time I think that this information will prove to be more useful to him in his part of the investigation."

Bernie shot Adam a nasty look, "Yeah, like I don't have enough to do already, jackass."

Adam opened up the folder marked "Birddog" and pulled out four separate maps. He laid the two pickup trucks maps side by side on the table for everyone in the room to see.

"If you place these maps next to one another you'll see three similarities on Christmas day. First, they leave Richard Easton's at the same time. Second, they both get to Bubba's at the same time, and third, they get back to Richard Easton's at the same time. I'm thinking something illegal is going on in the shed that Mr. Barton didn't want us getting too close to."

Bernie scoured over the three maps in amazement. This was the first time he had heard of Rocky's Woodchucks being tied to Bubba in any way.

"Holy shit!" Bernie exclaimed.

"Yeah, I figured you wouldn't mind after you saw that."

Adam handed over all four of the receivers to Bernie and looked over at First Sergeant Parr who had his notebook out.

"Do you have anything, First Sergeant?"

"I do, Adam. First of all, my guys finished the canvass of Spurlock Creek Road and aside from Rocky's vehicles in the driveway from time to time, they didn't find anything useful. We did a grid search of the fields and walked all the foot paths through the hills. We weren't able to find a thing."

Bernie waited for a lull in the First Sergeants synopsis to ask, "Did any of the neighbors remember seeing a lot of vehicle traffic in and out of there at all hours of the night?"

"My guys did ask that question Detective, and everyone said no. Ms. Dwyer was always quiet and polite to everyone. She hardly ever had any guests over to the house and she was never loud. The principal at her kid's school is my neighbor. She said that Ms. Dwyer attended every school function; she volunteered at most of the events; and she never missed a parent teacher conference. Her kids have straight A's and are model students. This just isn't characteristic of a person using, let alone dealing narcotics."

Sheriff Lawson stood up and started to move toward the door without saying a word. Bishop stood up to walk out with him but was told to sit back down.

"I have a few things to take care of. Ya'll just stay put and continue with the meeting."

The door to the conference room shut behind the sheriff with a loud bang.

"He's a man of very few words," First Sergeant Parr sarcastically said.

Adam stood up and started to pace by the dry-erase board at the front of the room.

"We've tried to talk to Rocky directly and he shot us down. What do we all think about reaching out to his lawyer and try to set up a meeting?"

Adam scanned the room and didn't see or hear any objections from anyone. Bishop produced the business card of William C. Mastus, Attorney at Law, and handed it to Adam who put the phone on speaker and dialed the number. The phone rang and rang but there was no answer. After hanging up, Adam turned the card over to see a cell phone number scribbled in pen so he tried the number.

After three rings someone answered, "Hello, this is William Mastus."

"Hello Mr. Mastus, this is Detective Alexander from the Stillwell County Sheriff's Office. I'd like a minute of your time if you can spare it."

"Why sure detective. It's only 9:00 in the morning the day after Christmas. How can I help you?"

"Well Mr. Mastus, I was wondering if we could schedule a sit down with you and Mr. Livingston to discuss a few things."

"Have you lost your damn mind? You guys are on a fishing expedition right now because you have no case against my client."

"What gives you that impression?"

"If you had anything at all, you'd be calling me to inform me that my client is currently in your custody and he's requested his attorney. You've indicated neither."

"Quite the contrary, Mr. Mastus. Our investigation is moving right along and we have plenty of evidence to support our hypothesis. We were just giving you a courtesy call to see if Mr. Livingston wanted to give us his side of the story."

"On behalf of Mr. Livingston, I'm telling you that he'll never answer any of your questions unless he's on the witness stand. Are we clear on that?"

"Absolutely clear, Mr. Mastus. He'll be in court pretty soon for his three felony assaults, so I guess we'll talk more then."

"Good day detective. Oh, and just one more thing. I represent all of Mr. Livingston's employees as well, so you need to back off of them, too. They don't wish to speak to you, either."

The next sound echoing through the conference room was the familiar click of the phone hanging up.

"I thought that went extremely well." Adam scoffed.

The room fell silent before First Sergeant Parr spoke up, "What do we have at this point, gentlemen. We've got to be overlooking something."

Adam stood up and moved to the dry-erase board. With the red and blue markers in hand, he started a chronology of the events leading up to this moment the day after Christmas.

12/18 – Ms. Dwyer was on the phone with Lisa Butler. She hears an unknown male asking about the ownership of cattle in the area.

12/18 – Structure Fire where Ms. Dwyer was found shot and severely burned in the front room of her home. The remnants of a meth lab were found inside that room.

12/19 – Rocky Livingston is identified as the main person of interest through the diary that was located in the master bedroom.

12/20 – Lisa Butler gives us information that indicated Rocky was abusive toward Ms. Dwyer in their relationship. We know that the relationship was sexual in nature. We also know that Ms. Dwyer was going to give Rocky an ultimatum and threatened to tell his wife.

12/20 – State Police receive information that a dark colored crew cab style pickup with some sort of business lettering in the rear window was seen in the driveway the day of the murder, which is consistent with what we already know about Rocky's vehicle.

12/20 through 12/23 – We attempted to interview Rocky and all his employees and were told to pound sand.

Sheila Potts indicates that Rocky was with her the night of the murder and he came to her house reeking of chemicals. We also learned that Ms. Dwyer was not well known by any of the local drug users or sellers.

Adam stood back and looked at his handy work on the board.

"This looks like shit guys. We've been going essentially non-stop for over a week and this is all we know? First of all, this isn't enough to get a warrant and second, if we did, Rocky's attorney would have a field day making us look like fools. There has to be something we're missing."

Adam was obviously frustrated by the course of the investigation. The lack of any real tangible evidence was leaving them guessing about what happened. Bernie could tell Adam was starting to get angry, so he stood up and walked over to him.

"Adam, there isn't a lot to go on here because the fire really screwed things up. Plus, we're still waiting for a lot of stuff to come back from the lab. Maybe when all of it comes back it will steer us in the right direction."

"I know Bernie. I'm just thinking that if this thing drags on for too long, then it might go unsolved. What the fuck are we missing?"

Adam stood back and just stared at the board while the others sat in silence for a few moments.

Bernie broke the silence by saying, "Adam, let's let these guys go, we all have a lot of work to do today."

The meeting adjourned while Adam stood silently looking at the board with his hand covering his mouth. In his head he was remembering walking through the house on the day of the murder. He recalled traversing each room, walking gingerly on the weakened floor; and when he closed his eyes the odor of Melissa's burnt flesh still lingered in his nose.

"Adam, erase that shit and come on. I've got a search warrant to do later on tonight and you're coming with me. The house we're going to hit is just outside of town and I figured you would want to ask the dopers about Melissa Dwyer while we search. You never know, maybe something will turn up."

Adam turned his head and gave Bernie a slow nod with a blank look on his face. It was painfully obvious to Bernie that a feeling of defeat was starting to seep in.

For the first time in a while, Adam sat quietly in the shotgun position while Bernie drove the half hour to the task force office.

"You're awful quiet. What's up?" Bernie asked.

"Just thinking is all. Not in a talkative mood right now."

The Appalachian Mountain Narcotics Task Force office was centrally located in a little house off of Rock Knob Road, just outside of Staffordsville. Members from the Kentucky State Police, Stillwell County Sheriff's Office, Pike County Sheriff's Office, Martin County Sheriff's Office, Johnson County Sheriff's Office and Knott County Sheriff's Office made up the seven man task force. Each member was dually sworn through their Sheriff's Office and the State Police giving them the ability to work narcotics cases throughout the entire state of Kentucky.

Bernie pulled off the main road onto an unmarked gravel driveway that extended about half a mile into the heavily wooded property. At the end, perched atop a small knoll was a yellow stucco Cape Cod. Bernie followed the driveway around to the back parking lot and parked in his normal spot.

"Is this the first time you've ever been here, Adam?"

"Yeah, this is the first time."

The two detectives made their way through the back door of the house and into the kitchen. Adam was immediately brought back to his college days in Detroit when the heavy odor of stale marijuana hit his nose.

"Damn, I think I just got a contact high."

Bernie started to laugh, "We have a vault in the kitchen pantry that we keep our confiscated weed in. You'll get used to it after a while."

Adam's head was on a swivel trying to take everything in. The house was decorated in a frat house meets *High Times* motif with posters of marijuana leafs, Bob Marley, and magic mushrooms on just about every wall.

"Make yourself at home, bro. I have to finish typing up this affidavit for my search warrant and operations plan before we can brief on the raid."

While Bernie walked down the hallway and disappeared into the living room to his office, Adam poured himself a cup of coffee, and sat down at the kitchen table. It wasn't long before everyone started showing up and crowding the kitchen.

"So what kind of trouble will we be getting ourselves into tonight?" Adam asked.

"No clue. All Bernie told us was that we were hitting a house just outside of town. None of us has been there before. How's your investigation going?" Jimmy asked.

"It's at a stand still right now. Rocky isn't talking and we have absolutely zero physical evidence. Everything is circumstantial. I'm hoping that Bernie can get him on a dope charge and get him to confess his mortal sins."

Adam looked over his shoulder and saw a foosball table begging for some attention.

"Any of you guys up for a game?"

Adam hadn't played foosball since his college days and was easily defeated in less than five minutes. While the rest of the guys continued to play, he walked toward Bernie to see if he needed any help. He rounded the corner into the living room to see Bernie sitting behind his desk putting the finishing touches on the warrant.

"Just a few more minutes, Adam. Go and get the rest of the guys and meet me upstairs in the conference room."

Adam did as he was told and herded the task force guys up the stairs to the conference room. True to his word, Bernie was there in no time ready to brief the team about their objective. He stood in front of the white board and drew the first and second floor layouts so everyone could see.

"This is a one story ranch style house located just outside of town limits on Water Gap Road. It's the second house on the left when you turn onto Water Gap from South Lake Drive. The main door is centrally located in the front of the house with four steps leading up to a small patio. There's a carport on the left hand side of the house with another door that goes directly into the kitchen. On the back side of the residence there's a small deck with a sliding glass door that leads into the family room. There are no other entrances or exits other than those three; unless people want to dive out the windows."

Bernie continued to give the layout of the house as well as team assignments to each of his guys.

"Supposedly there are three pit bulls chained up to a shed in the back yard. This is where they say the dope is stashed. According to my informant, our target has just re-upped and is selling pretty heavy. We're looking at approximately four to five pounds of weed, a kilo of cocaine and some crystal meth. If all goes well, this should be a pretty good score for us. Are there any questions?"

No one raised their hand or expressed any concerns so Bernie drew the meeting to a close, "Okay guys. I've got to go to the court house to get this warrant signed by the judge. We'll meet at the Sheriff's Office at eighteen hundred hours for one final briefing and then we'll go kick this door in. We've only got one uniformed deputy accompanying us tonight, so make sure you shout *Police* before you enter every room. I've also got animal control and the medic crew at station two on standby just in case shit breaks bad on us. I'll see you all tonight."

With Adam in tow, they drove back to the Stillwell County Judicial Center. The two detectives walked into Judge Watson's afternoon session of traffic court, just in time to hear him lecture everyone on the importance of safe driving. After the last case was heard, Bernie walked up to the bench and placed his affidavit for a search warrant on his desk.

"You have another search warrant, Detective Steckler?"

"Yes, Sir."

"You're a busy individual these days. Please raise your right hand. Is everything contained in this affidavit true and accurate to the best of your knowledge?"

"It is."

"Good. Give me a few minutes and I'll be back with your search warrant."

It didn't take long for the judge to type out the search warrant and hand it back to Bernie. After he proofread it for mistakes, he thanked the judge for his time and walked back to the sheriff's office with Adam to wait for everyone else to arrive.

At eighteen hundred hours all the task force members and uniformed deputy were gathered in the back parking lot, ready to hit the road. Bernie loaded everyone up in the Sheriff's Office Work-release van and drove south out of town. Adam could feel the knot in his stomach start to tighten and his adrenalin was kicking in. It had been a long time since he'd felt this way. The van made a right onto Water Gap Road and the ram man opened the rear sliding door just before the mass exodus.

Bernie brought the van to an abrupt halt in front of the house and a rush of Narcotic's Officers, clad in all black, with fully automatic weapons at the ready, swooped out of the van. They traveled in unison up to the front door like a swarm of angry hornets. Bernie was the first on the porch, followed by Derek who had the ram. Jimmy, Frank, and Zach were stacked right behind them. Adam took his post around the rear of the house so he could catch anyone that tried to run out the back while the deputy covered the car port door. There was a split second of silence, and then.

"SHERIFF'S OFFICE, SEARCH WARRANT!"

There was a loud bang as the ram made contact with the front door, splintering the jam into a thousand pieces.

Next, Adam heard what sounded like a stampeded of wild elephants going through the house coupled with a steady stream of obscenities.

"DON'T YOU MOVE, ASSHOLE! KEEP YOUR FUCKING HANDS WHERE I CAN SEE THEM! IF YOU MOVE ONE MORE TIME I'LL BLOW YOUR DAMN HEAD OFF!"

After the shouting stopped and everyone was in custody, Adam heard the all clear from Bernie over the radio. He holstered his weapon and walked around to the front door.

"Did you happen to see any pit bulls in the back yard, bro?" Bernie asked.

"Nope, but I stayed outside the fence line," Adam replied.

Bernie turned to the home owner with a puzzled look on his face and asked, "Where are the dogs?"

"They should be in the back yard. If they ain't there, then I don't know where they are."

Bernie took out a copy of the search warrant and explained it to his suspect while Adam and the guys started to look around the house.

"Why the hell does everyone have to live like a pig?" Adam asked. "Once, just once, I'd like to go into a house that doesn't make me feel like I need a shower and a tetanus shot!"

He walked into the kitchen and was met with the foul stench of garbage. Trash cluttered every square inch of the counters and spilled onto the cockroach-laden floor. Adam turned toward the living area and discovered more of the same. There were used, uncapped needles lying all over the coffee table. Cocaine residue was on just about every bare flat surface and soiled clothing lined the floors. In the dining room Adam found several small cages with dead rodents, birds and a dead boa constrictor. He just wanted to put two rounds in the back of this guy's head and call it a day, but he knew he couldn't.

"I've had enough of this shit, Bernie. I'll be outside."

Adam walked back outside into the fresh winter air and waited for Bernie to finish with his suspect. He didn't have to wait long because a few moments later, Bernie came out of the house with the suspect in cuffs.

"Hey Adam, he's all yours. He's been searched and mirandized. He says he's willing to listen to you."

Adam walked over to the subject and led him over to a waiting marked sheriff's office cruiser. He put the subject in the back seat and shut the door. Adam walked around to the driver's seat of the cruiser and got in closing the door behind him. He got out his notepad and a pen prepared to take notes on their conversation.

"What's your name?"

"Louis Jefferson Wilson," the man replied.

"Mr. Wilson, I'm not going to ask you any questions about what's currently going on inside your residence. I'm here to ask you for some help and if you can help me with some information, then I just might be able to return the favor."

"I ain't a fucking snitch. I got nothing to say to you guys, period. I want my fucking lawyer."

"Mr. Wilson, please calm down and listen to what I have to say? Just listen. And after I finish, if you don't want to help then I'll leave you alone. Deal?"

Mr. Wilson sat back in his seat and turned his head toward Adam, "I'm listening."

"Have you heard about that lady who was murdered on Spurlock Creek Road a little over a week ago?"

Mr. Wilson's eyes got really big as he stammered, "Everyone's trying to figure out who that bitch was. You're the fifth person to ask me that."

"Well, do you know who she was, or what she was up to?"

Mr. Wilson shook his head and shrugged his shoulders, "Man I got no clue who she was or who she be runnin' with. Bubba came round here askin' me that shit."

"So you have no idea who she was? What if I offered to pay you for the information? Would that help you remember anything?"

"I can make up some shit and take your money."

"I appreciate your honesty Mr. Wilson. If you happen to hear anything or remember anything that I might find useful please let me know. I promise to make it worth your while."

Adam closed up his notebook and got out of the driver's seat of the marked cruiser, leaving Mr. Wilson secured in the back.

Adam looked over at the deputy standing at the trunk of the cruiser, "Are you going back to the station any time soon?"

"Yeah, I was told to take this guy to the jail after you finished with him."

"Can you wait a second? I'd like catch a ride back to the station with you."

"Sure thing. I'll be right here."

It took Adam a few minutes, but eventually he was able to find Bernie in the back yard of the house.

"You guys find anything good so far?"

"Hell yeah! We found over five pounds of weed and some crack. Now we just need to find his cash and this will be a good night. What about you? Did our bad guy tell you anything?"

"He didn't tell me anything that I don't already know." Adam looked over his shoulder at the flashing blue lights and then back at Bernie, "Listen, this has been fun and all, but I'm going to catch a ride back to the station with the deputy. That is unless you need me to stick around."

"Go home man, and thanks for your help. Something will turn up sooner or later."

"I hope you're right Bernie. I hope you're right."

Chapter 12

Adam poured himself a bowl of cereal and took a seat at the kitchen table in the early morning hours. The aroma of freshly brewed coffee was starting to permeate the air as he shoveled stale cornflakes into his mouth. He listened intently for the sounds of percolation to stop so he could pour himself a cup and read the local paper that was waiting for him on the edge of the kitchen table. With his nectar in hand, he opened up the paper to see his and Bernie's faces on page one. The caption read, "Cops Bust Local Drug Dealer, But Homicide Still Unsolved." Adam read the article that was filled with inconsistencies and quickly remembered why he never bothered with the local paper. All the reporters cared about was creating a scandal and printing misleading articles that contained half truths at best.

"This is bullshit," Adam mumbled.

"I think I'm starting to get sick, Adam."

Adam turned quickly to see Rennae standing behind him in her bath robe carrying a box of tissues.

"That's not good news. I sure hope I don't come down with it."

"You're not home long enough to catch a damn thing. Let me guess, you're working all day and tonight too?"

"Rennae we've been over this. As soon as I finish this investigation I'll put in for the transfer. I don't need this shit from you right now."

"What did you just say to me?"

"You heard me. The job is the job and I have no control over it. I don't need your shitty attitude right now. I'm doing everything I can."

Tears began to stream down Rennae's face immediately. She stood in the kitchen trembling with anger and hurt, waiting for Adam to apologize, but he didn't. She whipped around and headed back upstairs to their room, slamming the bedroom door behind her. Adam sat motionless, desperately wanting to take back what he had said, but the damage was done.

Adam poured the remainder of his cornflakes into the sink and washed them down the garbage disposal. He grabbed his travel mug from the cabinet and poured the remainder of his coffee into the mug before walking out to his car. He sat behind the steering wheel contemplating whether or not to go back inside and apologize, but decided it was best to let things calm down before he tried to talk to her. He put the car in reverse and pulled out of his driveway. As he drove toward the office with the tranquil sound of Pink Floyd in the background, he hoped that Bernie was already there. He wanted to get a look at the Birddog maps and see what Rocky and his Woodchucks had been up to last night. Adam picked up his cell phone and made the call.

"Hey, Bernie. You got the Birddog info downloaded yet?"

"Sure do, and I'm pulling into the office lot now. I should have them all printed out when you get here. Oh, and I talked to Stuart Winston. He told me that he didn't think Rocky was a killer and never to call him again."

"Yeah, all of our interviews went exactly the same way. It's going to take a miracle for us to get one of them to talk. I'll be at the station in a few minutes, Bernie."

Adam hit the gas and made it to the station a little quicker than normal. He walked directly into Bernie's office and sat down in his usual spot to look at the maps.

"That's strange, Bernie. Rocky's SUV hasn't moved from the garage parking lot for a few days. Let's go down there and see what the deal is."

The two detectives left the office and got into Adam's car for the short drive to South Railroad Street. They rounded the corner to see Rocky's SUV was still parked in the same place Adam had seen it before. He darted into the gravel parking lot and came to a skidding halt next to the front door.

"Was Rocky's SUV parked in that same spot when you were here earlier downloading Birddog info?"

"Yeah, why?"

"Because it's in the exact same place it was when I was here yesterday."

He jumped out of the driver's seat and hastily walked down the building looking into each bay door window.

"FUCK!" Adam yelled.

Bernie watched as Adam picked up the nearest rock and smash out the small oval glass window on the second bay door. He reached his hand inside the jagged hole trying desperately to find the button to open the large white door. He fumbled around for what seemed like an eternity before he finally located and pressed the *open* button. The quick jolt of the opening door shoved a shard of glass into his forearm as he pulled it out of the hole. The slowly opening door was only a quarter of the way open when Adam dropped to his knees and scurried underneath, leaving a trail of his blood on the concrete floor. Bernie, who was already out of the car at this point, ran from the passenger side of the car to the slowly opening bay door and looked in.

He could hear Adam inside yelling, "Get me a knife Bernie! Get me a fucking knife!"

As the door opened, Bernie could see a pair of feet suspended in midair, followed by a torso and eventually Rocky's lifeless face. He ran in as Adam tried to take the pressure off of Rocky's neck by putting his arms around his waist and lifting him up. Bernie saw that Rocky had already evacuated his bowels, which was an indication that all of his vital life functions had ceased. He grabbed Adam by the arm and pulled him away.

"Adam! He's dead. Let him go!"

"He can't be dead, Bernie. He's my only lead in my case! I need answers!"

Bernie took Adam by the shoulders and led him out of the garage to the car. He could tell Adam was upset, and rightfully so. All of his efforts in linking Rocky to Melissa

Dwyer were for naught. They had zero physical evidence to go on and the only suspect they had wasn't ever going to talk again.

Bernie looked Adam directly in his eyes to make sure he had his attention, "Call Bishop and tell him to get his ass down here. I'll go back in and check the building for any other bodies."

Adam stood still for a few minutes before pulling out his cell phone and calling Bishop. He couldn't believe what had just happened.

"Bishop here."

"You need to get down to Rocky's garage now!"

"What the hell did you do now, Adam?"

"Nothing. Rocky hung himself. He's dead Sarge."

"Holy Shit, Adam. I'm on my way."

Adam hung up his phone and stared into the opened garage door as Rocky's dead body gently swayed back and forth. Why would he do this if he were innocent? It didn't make any sense.

Bernie came out of the garage a few minutes later carrying a piece of paper in his hands. He could see that Adam was in no mood for games so he was careful with what he said, "You made quite an impression on Rocky, Adam."

"How's that?"

"I found this on his desk."

Bernie held up a single sheet of paper with the following written in bold black magic marker: "I may be a lot of things but I ain't no killer. FUCK YOU DETECTIVE ALEXANDER. YOU RUINED MY LIFE."

"That's bullshit, Bernie. He ruined his own damn life."

"I also found a glass pipe and a bag of crystal meth on his desk next to the note. I guess his problems went a little deeper than we thought."

Adam looked over Bernie's shoulder to see Sergeant Bishop and Sheriff Lawson driving toward them. They parked on the street next to the gravel entrance and walked over to Adam and Bernie.

"What do we have here boys," Sergeant Bishop light-heartedly asked.

Bernie held up the piece of notebook paper he found inside the garage for everyone to see. Even the Sheriff got a hearty laugh out of the love note.

"Damn son. I guess I'm not the only one that's thought about killing myself after meeting you," Sheriff Lawson joked.

"No, Sir. I guess not."

Adam turned to Sergeant Bishop, "What the hell am I supposed to do with this case now?"

"Well, looks to me like you can close it out due to the death of the offender."

"Sounds like a good idea to me, Bishop. You did a great job on this one, Adam, and I'm proud of you, boy. Only the guilty ones do foolish things like this. Now, let's put this dog to rest and move on," Sheriff Lawson said gleefully.

Adam stood there quietly not knowing what to think.

Bishop looked over at him and saw blood trickling down his arm.

"What the hell happened to your arm, Adam?"

"It's nothing, Sarge. I cut it when I busted out the window to open the door."

Adam pulled up his sleeve pulling off a spot of clotted blood and exposed a large gash on his forearm. Blood started to ooze out of the gaping wound causing everyone around him to wince.

"Damn it, Adam. Now I have more workers' comp paperwork to do. You want me to call you an ambulance?"

"I would rather bleed to death than ride in the back of one of those unsanitary meat wagons, Sarge. I'll drive myself."

"Okay, then get your ass to the hospital and get that sewn up pronto. After that you can head back to the station and close this homicide out. Bernie and I will take care of tagging and bagging Rocky."

"Call Jenkins and tell him he can take the Birddogs off the cars. I guess we won't be needing them anymore," Adam said.

"I'll have Bernie do that now. But in the meantime, you get your happy ass on down the emergency room to get that arm stitched up."

Adam pulled his sleeve back down and drove himself to the hospital. Eleven stitches later, he was back at the station to do what he was instructed to do. He pulled into the parking lot and went directly to his office. After he plopped down in his chair, he stared off into the distance. His mind went blank.

"FUCK IT!" he yelled.

Adam stood up and walked out of his office without closing the case as he had been instructed to do. He was done for the day and he didn't care if he got a write-up for disobeying a direct order. On his way out the door he thought back to what he had said to Rennae before he left the house that morning. If he had any hopes of salvaging his New Year's Eve, he had best go home and apologize to her. He pulled out of the parking lot and drove towards his home, thinking about what he was going to say to smooth things over. But before he could come up with a good apology, he found himself pulling into his driveway and parking in his normal spot. After locking his car, Adam walked through the kitchen door and saw Rennae sitting at the kitchen table drinking a hot cup of tea.

"You look horrible. I take it you're still not feeling well?"

"Nope. I have a fever of 102.4 and it's not going away anytime soon."

"Listen. I'm sorry about earlier. I don't have any excuse for my behavior."

"I understand you're under a tremendous amount of pressure, but don't you ever talk to me like that again, Adam. Do you understand me?"

"It won't happen again. I promise."

Adam stood up and walked through the kitchen and into the living room. He plopped down on the couch and turned on Sports Center to check the college football scores and to see how his beloved Red Wings were doing in their quest for the Stanley Cup. But no matter how hard he tried, Adam just couldn't relax. Every time he closed his eyes he saw Rocky swinging from the rafters in his garage. How could he, in good conscience, close this case without any solid proof that Rocky was the killer. The only good thing that would come from closing the case prematurely would be that he could move back into patrol and get Rennae off his back. But deep down he knew what he had to do—push on, beginning with turning up the heat on the Woodchucks. They might be able to shed a little more light on the situation. In mid-thought, Adam's cell phone rang.

"Hey, Bernie. What's up?"

"I just got a call from Ms. Leighton. She's having a party at her house tonight and she asked me to invite you. You better bring a designated driver, because there's gonna be free booze."

A rush of excitement came over Adam as a sly smile spread across his face.

"What time?"

"She said to be there around eight or so."

"I'll be there."

Adam hung up the phone, and for the first time since December eighteenth he was excited to be doing something outside of the investigation. He got up off the couch and walked into the kitchen to ask Rennae if it was okay for him to go to the party.

"Hey, honey. There's going to be a party tonight at the Commonwealth Attorney's house. If you're feeling up to it, would you like to go?"

"Adam, I'm going to take some NYQUIL and knock myself out for the night. You can go if you want to."

Adam kissed Rennae on the forehead and walked upstairs to their bedroom. He picked out his best slacks, shirt, and tie for the evening and laid them on the bed before hitting the shower. His routine only took twenty minutes to complete before he was dressed and ready to leave. In the time it took him to get ready, Rennae had drugged herself and was out like a light on the couch with the TV on. Adam didn't want to disturb her so he quietly walked past her and out the door.

While on his way to town, Adam looked down at his watch and noticed that it was already 7:30. He pulled his cell phone out of his pocket and gave Bernie a call.

"Hey Bernie, you ready?"

"It's only 7:30, brother. You a little anxious or something?"

Adam started to laugh nervously because he knew Bernie was right.

"No. It's just that this is the first night I've had to myself in a long time and I want to make the best of it."

"Well, I'm going to have to meet you there a little later. I promised the wife I'd take her out to dinner tonight."

"Isn't she coming with you?"

"She's not sure yet. But either way, I'll be there."

"That sounds good to me. I'll see you there."

Adam ended the call and drove aimlessly around town for a little while. He didn't want Alexis to think he was overeager by being the first one there. At 8:30 he decided that he had waited long enough so he started to drive toward the party.

Alexis lived just outside of town in a hilltop mansion that could be seen from town. He drove through the stone arch that marked the driveway and up the winding road to the top of the hill. He parked along the grass on the side of the driveway and walked up to the main house. There were four huge white columns that stretched magnificently from the first to the third story providing a covered front porch which looked like a picture out of a home and garden magazine.

He was about to ring the doorbell when he noticed a note taped to the inside of the storm door that read, "Please come on in, no need to knock."

Adam took a look to his left before walking through the door and saw the town of Stillwell shimmering in the distance. He opened the front door and walked down an elegant hallway toward the noise in the back of the house. The décor reminded him more of a museum than a home the farther he wandered in.

"Adam!" A familiar voice shouted. It was Alexis. Adam smiled as she ran up to him.

"I wasn't sure if you were going to make it tonight."

Adam laughed, because nothing in the world could have kept him away.

"I took the night off just for you, Ms. Leighton."

A smile came to her lips and her eyes narrowed. Adam could smell the alcohol coming from her breath as she lunged forward and gave him a hug.

"Adam, please come on in. I want you to meet my Granddaddy."

She took his hand in a firm grip and led him into the family room. On their way through, Adam saw just about every local attorney along with a few faces he didn't recognize. Adam did, however, recognize the face of an older gentleman who was sitting on a love seat near the television in the sunroom. He was focused on the Fox News channel and paying close attention to the stock ticker that was scrolling across the bottom of the screen.

"Granddaddy, I want you to meet Detective Adam Alexander from the local Sheriff's Office. Adam this is George Leighton."

Adam extended his hand toward Mr. Leighton, "Sir, it's an honor to meet you. I've heard so much about you from your granddaughter, all horrible things of course."

Mr. Leighton let out a healthy laugh, "That doesn't surprise me in the least. She has the spunk of her grandmother and her mother. They both hated me, too."

They all three exchanged pleasantries for a few more minutes before Adam excused himself to find the restroom and a drink.

"Sir, I'm sure we'll see each other later on in the evening, but right now I 'm hoping to enjoy the fruits of your labor."

Adam graciously excused himself from Mr. Leighton and leaned in to quietly ask Alexis, "Can you please point the way to the restroom."

"It's this way."

Alexis walked Adam over to the bathroom and opened the door for him.

"Let me know if you need any help, Detective."

Adam shook his head and smirked at her comment because he knew she was drunk. He walked in the restroom and closed the door behind him. After finishing his business, Adam turned around and looked into the mirror, checking himself over thoroughly. In the recesses of his mind he had a scenario playing over and over involving a long embrace followed by passionate sex, but he knew that it would never happen. With a sigh, he washed his hands and headed back to the party just in time for Bernie's arrival.

"Hey, Adam. Where can a guy get some bourbon in this joint?"

Adam started to laugh as he walked down the hall toward his good friend. He gave Bernie a hearty hand shake as he wished him a happy new year.

"Where's your wife?" Adam asked.

"This isn't her thing. I told her I was only going to stay for an hour or two and then come home to spend the rest of the night with her. We might make it to the fireworks at the high school later on if she's up to it. Where's Rennae?"

"She's sick with the flu so she stayed home. Let's go and find us some alcohol, my friend."

After a few minutes of searching, Adam was able to find the fully stocked bar in the sunroom. Behind the solid oak bar stood a slender gentleman wearing a tuxedo, who would later become Adam's best friend.

"Goodness gracious, that's a ton of booze!" Adam exclaimed.

"Yeah, there might be quite a few people passing out here tonight," Bernie added.

They carefully examined their choices from just about every kind of liquor known to man before making their decisions.

"You want a bourbon and coke, Bernie?"

"Sounds good to me."

Adam looked at the nametag on the left lapel of the bartender and saw that his name was *Lou.*

"Hey, Lou. We'll have two bourbon and Cokes, please," Adam requested.

"We've got several kinds of bourbon. Which would you prefer?" Lou asked.

"The best Fox Hunt you've got back there."

"That would be the *Reserve*. Good choice."

Lou reached underneath the bar for an oddly shaped crystal bottle. He poured a generous amount of the caramel colored liquid into two highball glasses and splashed it with a little bit of Coke.

"Here you are, gentlemen."

Adam grabbed his glass from the bar and took a big swig. The first drink went down smooth and fast. The second one was a little smoother and went down just as fast.

"You'd better pace yourself, or it's going to be an early evening for you, Adam."

"I'll be fine. Let's go and mingle with the rich folks for a while."

The hour passed by quickly and Bernie was true to his word. He said his goodbyes to everyone and headed home to spend the rest of New Year's Eve with his wife. Adam, on the other hand, was starting to feel no pain.

"Hey, Lou. One more of these please, and don't hold back on the bourbon this time."

Lou just chuckled and did as he was told. After he had his new beverage, Adam walked among the ever growing crowd and took the opportunity to meet new people.

"Detective Alexander, may I have a word with you?"

Adam recognized the voice even before he turned around.

"Mr. Mastus, what can I do for you?"

Standing before Adam was a very intoxicated man who was swaying back and forth with a cocktail in his hand.

"I just wanted to talk to you about Mr. Livingston."

"He's dead, does it really matter at this point?"

"It certainly does, to me. Mr. Livingston isn't the cold blooded killer you think he is, Detective. Truth be told, Mr. Livingston was at my home on the afternoon of Ms. Dwyer's murder, chemically sealing my foundation. He was going to finish my basement for me but he needed to fix a few cracks first. And as wrong as it may have been, he was with his secretary until 10:30 that night. So, you see, he couldn't have killed her."

"Why didn't he just tell me that to begin with? It could have saved us all a lot of trouble."

"Why would we make it any easier for you? If he had said one poorly worded sentence, you would have jumped all over him, maybe even based your entire case around it. I find it best to let the evidence speak for itself, and in this instance, you didn't have any."

"Then why did he kill himself if he was innocent?"

"Mr. Livingston was a control freak and always had to be in charge no matter what the situation. Your exposing his adultery threatened his sense of control and put him in a downward spiral. His wife left him, Ms. Potts stopped talking to him, and more than half of his customers called to cancel their contracts. This is a very small community in the Bible Belt of America, Detective. It's hard to make a living in this economy, and it's even harder when your entire community has already labeled you a murderer. All of his control was taken away from him, Detective."

"That was all on him, Mr. Mastus."

"You're correct Detective. That was all on him, and things got even worse when you showed up at his house on the day his wife left him."

"Once again, that was all on him."

"Would you let me finish, please? I agree that he did something he shouldn't have, and when we talked about it in my office after I bailed him out of jail the other day, even he said it was uncalled for. Let me ask you something, when was the last time you've seen Judge Alexander place a bail that high on someone?"

"Never. That was the highest I've ever seen."

"Exactly, he was going to make an example out of Mr. Livingston. We could both see that. I'm good at what I do Detective, but I'm not that good. You had him dead to rights on those felony charges and although I don't think he would have gone to prison, he would have done some time behind bars. And Mr. Livingston couldn't live with that. So I'm assuming he left this world just as he intended to—on his own terms. And a little lesser known fact about Mr. Livingston is that he had a substance abuse problem. I guarantee that when the toxicology report comes back his blood sample will be full of prescription pills and meth."

"So he was dealing drugs with Bubba."

"Hold on a second, Detective, I never said that. Mr. Livingston surrounded himself with people who supplied him with what he needed. And I'm sure you know exactly who those people are. But I digress. I've said way too much already. Have a pleasant evening, Detective."

Adam walked over to the bar to get another drink when he felt a tug on his arm.

"There you are detective."

He turned his head to see Alexis looking wide eyed at him and with a huge smile.

"I was wondering if I could talk to you for a minute? In private?"

Adam nodded his head and followed her down a hallway to a flight of servant's stairs on the back side of the kitchen. She moved down the flight of stairs and into the basement and continued to walk down a long narrow hallway toward the wine cellar. Once they were inside, she walked over to a large shelf filled with wine bottles and pulled on one of the bottles.

"I had this safe room built when I added the wine cellar a few years ago. No one knows that it's here except for me, and now you."

She turned around and pushed on the large shelf which exposed a small door. She ducked her head down and walked in with Adam close behind.

Adam didn't have time to take in his surroundings before Alexis lunged at him and began kissing him passionately. Their lips locked together and their hands began to wander, finding areas of each other's bodies that they both had wanted to become intimately familiar with for some time. Alexis pulled away from Adam and began to undress. Adam took his cue and did the same until they were both standing in front of one another fully exposed.

"Do you like what you see, Detective?"

All Adam could manage to stammer, "Um, yeah."

Alexis grabbed Adam's hand and led him back to a large oversized couch in the corner of the room. She pulled him close as she fell backwards on the soft cushions with Adam landing squarely on top of her. The moment was perfect, better than he could possibly have imagined. Adam could hear Alexis moan with excitement as the two became one and brought each other to climax.

Out of breath and more than a little worried, he climbed off of her, "Please tell me you're on some sort of birth control?"

Alexis laughed as she stood up and turned around, "It's a little late to be asking that question now, don't you think? And yes I am, so no worries."

Adam breathed a sigh of relief while he looked around for something to clean up with.

"I guess we could have planned this better, huh?"

Alexis and Adam both moved into the half bathroom on the other side of the room and began to clean themselves up. Adam kept looking over at Alexis as she tended to herself.

"Listen, I'm glad this happened and all but…."

Alexis walked up to Adam and kissed him gently on his lips to shut him up.

"Adam, I've been divorced from Derrick for ten months now. And in those ten months I've gone through more batteries than humanly possible. I don't want any more than what you can give me, okay? But I will say this. From the day I met you, I knew you were a sure thing." She leaned up and kissed him again on the lips, "And if you can keep this just between the two of us, I see it happening a lot more in our future."

Adam leaned forward and took Alexis in his arms, "It's a deal."

The two quickly got dressed and sauntered back up to the party making sure they staggered their reappearance into the crowd. In their absence, several more guests had arrived and were looking for their hostess. Adam went back over to his old friend Lou and ordered another drink. While he sat at the bar, he wondered if he could continue to see Alexis. Surprisingly, he felt no guilt at the present moment, but he figured he would as soon as he saw Rennae. He guzzled three more drinks before he felt the need to rejoin the party.

It was now 11:30 and the champagne was just starting to flow. Alexis sought out Adam and once again pulled him to the side. This time she dragged him upstairs to the rear balcony. There was an outdoor fire pit with the fire already burning. A bottle of French champagne and two glasses were sitting on a nearby table.

"I got this bottle when I went to Paris right after Derrick left. I always said that I would only share it with someone special. I want to share it with you, Adam."

Alexis tore off the foil top and handed the bottle to Adam to open. He carefully popped the cork and poured two glasses.

"This has been a wonderful evening, Alexis, and I want to thank you."

He leaned over and gave her a kiss on the lips. She just looked back at him and smiled.

Adam stood behind Alexis with his arms wrapped around her, next to the fire pit for warmth. Neither of them said a word as they stared at the tiny lights of the town of Stillwell in the distance. The moment they were sharing was perfect enough without being spoiled by useless words. Adam was about to lean in and give Alexis another kiss when the French doors behind them flew open and the entire party spilled out onto the balcony, ruining their romantic moment. Adam dropped his hands to his side and walked around to the other side of the fire pit, away from Alexis, while everyone continued to file out of the house.

"Five, four, three, two, one….. Happy New Year!" they all shouted.

Like clockwork, when the countdown reached one, the fireworks lit up the midnight sky. Adam desperately wanted to be alone with Alexis during this moment and hoped that she was feeling the same way. Once the fireworks were over, he walked back inside the house and down to the bar for a few more drinks.

For the rest of the party, Alexis and Adam stayed away from one another but kept close enough to give each other a smile from time to time. At two in the morning, Adam decided that the night had run its course and it was time for him to go home.

Adam woke up on his couch in the living room at one in the afternoon fully clothed and with a pounding headache. He vaguely remembered getting into his car and driving through town, but after that, things got little a fuzzy. He raised his head and saw Rennae sitting at the kitchen table eating a small bowl of cereal and some toast.

"It's about time you woke up. And I'm absolutely fucking pissed that you drove home in that condition."

Adam used the rest of his strength to stand up and walk into the kitchen. He grabbed three bottles of water from the fridge, eight hundred milligrams of ibuprofen and a banana.

"Sorry baby, but I didn't feel that bad when I started to drive home. It kinda' snuck up on me. Now if you'll excuse me, my head is pounding and I'm going to go upstairs and have my hangover in peace."

Adam closed the bedroom door behind him and turned on the small box fan. He popped the ibuprofen, chugged the three bottles of water, and ate the banana before closing his eyes. He was asleep for the entire afternoon and a good portion of the evening when Rennae came into their bedroom to wake him up.

"Adam, wake up. Your sergeant is on the phone and wants to talk to you."

Rennae handed him the cordless phone and walked out of the bedroom.

"What's up, Sarge?"

"Get your ass down to the sheriff's office."

He didn't give Adam a chance to answer before he hung up the phone. Adam did as he was told and dragged himself out of bed. He walked into the shower and tried to compose himself as best he could. The cold water on his face felt good as it slowly brought him back to reality.

Dressed in jeans and a sheriff's office polo, Adam walked down the hallway to the kitchen. Rennae had made him a cup of coffee and poured it into a travel mug for him to drink on his way to the office.

"Thanks, baby. I'll call you later and let you know how long I'm going to be."

He leaned over and kissed her on the forehead and walked out the door. On the short drive to the office Adam chugged his coffee and was craving a second cup. He stopped off at the Grub-N-Gas to purchase a second cup along with some breath mints to mask any remaining smell of the alcohol he had had the night before.

The sun was setting on the first day of the New Year as Adam pulled into his parking spot, in the station lot. He immediately noticed that Sheriff Lawson, Captain Cubbage, Sergeant Bishop, and Bernie were already there. He put his car in park and slowly walked into the office. The lights were all on in the CIB wing and Adam could hear voices coming from Bishop's office. The door was open, so Adam walked in to see everyone sitting and staring at the television. Adam grabbed the only remaining chair, turned his attention to the screen, and focused in on a male reporter standing in front of a house that was smoldering. There were fire and police personnel scurrying in the background as the reporter was talking about the fire.

"911 was called at about 3:30 this afternoon for a report of a fire in this brick home behind me. Shortly after the call was made, firefighters arrived on the scene to find the house engulfed in flames. It took them 45 minutes to bring the fire under control. There are no reports of any fatalities at this point. Back to you, Donna."

Bishop turned to Adam, "I was at home enjoying an Adam-free day with my family when my phone rang. It was a buddy of mine who is a homicide detective with the Frankfort PD. He told me it would be in my best interest to turn on the TV and follow the broadcasts closely. Just before he hung up, he told me to ignore the report of no fatalities. As I watched I was able to put two and two together. House on fire with dead people inside, does this sound familiar to any one of you?"

All of the residual inebriation left Adam's body in a split second.

"What do we know so far?" Adam asked.

"Nothing. I know absolutely nothing. But you and Bernie might be taking a trip down there in a little while, depending on whether or not my buddy calls me back. He said that his lieutenant is telling him to keep his mouth shut and that he can't tell us anything."

The room fell silent as everyone's attention was redirected back at the television.

Adam was watching the broadcast intently when Bishop's cell phone rang. The conversation was short with whoever was on the other end of the line, but Bishop was extremely excited.

He hung up and pointed toward Adam, "There was a dark green colored pickup truck with yellow lettering in the rear window seen leaving the scene."

Adam jumped to his feet and clapped his hands together in excitement.

"But, you guys can't go down there just yet. They found a family of four brutally murdered in the basement. He'll let me know when their investigation is far enough along to let us in on what they have."

The mood in the room lightened enough so that everyone had a smile on his face. Even Sheriff Lawson was excited.

"Well, this is a load off my mind. I sure hope they can track down these idiots. The sooner I can hold a press conference telling people to calm down the better."

Having said that, the sheriff stood from his chair and walked out of the room without saying another word.

"It's a good thing he didn't hold the press conference today telling people that Rocky was the killer. He would be looking pretty stupid right now," Bernie stated.

"As soon as Sheila Potts told me that Rocky was at her house late that night, I had a hunch he might not be our guy. But that alibi still doesn't absolve the Woodchucks. I mean, they still have access to those pickup trucks. One, or all of them could have driven down to Frankfort and killed this family. Bernie, did you tell Jenkins to remove the Birddogs yet?"

"Yeah, I did that yesterday right after Bishop told me to."

"And has he taken them off yet?"

"Yep, I helped him take all of them off that afternoon."

"Damn! That could have helped us out."

"Sorry, but I was just following orders."

"Well, I guess we'll have to see where this takes us. I sure hope there was a witness that saw someone leaving that house in Frankfort."

Adam moved over to the sheriff's more comfortable seat and continued to watch the news, while Bernie and Bishop talked about his previous search warrant on Water Gap Road. The bust had yielded quite a bit of dope and Bishop was curious if it was related to Bubba in any way.

As Adam continued listening to the news, he suddenly remembered what he had done the night before. He sat motionless in his chair and smiled as he played the events over in his mind. It had been perfect. He wanted to call Alexis to make sure she was still okay with what had happened, but he figured he would wait to ask her the next time he saw her in passing.

Chapter 13

For six agonizing days, Adam and Bernie did their best to find out where the Woodchucks had been on New Year's Eve, but no one was willing to tell them anything. Even Rocky's pick-up trucks couldn't be located. Bernie had called his entire list of informants and even upped his usual gratuity of $100 to $400, for anyone who could give him credible information, but everyone he talked to told him that they didn't know. On the sixth morning of getting door after door slammed in their faces, Adam's cell phone rang.

"Hey, Bishop. What's up?"

"Come to the station and get the gas card. You two are going to Frankfort to meet with Detective Howell. He's expecting you this afternoon."

Adam turned his car around and made a mad dash for the station. With gas card in hand, they found themselves on their way to Frankfort to meet with Bishop's connection, Detective Richard Howell. Bishop had been in constant contact with Howell over the last few days, but little information had materialized since the only solid lead they had to go on was the dark green pickup with yellow lettering in the windows. And making matters worse, any potential evidence left at the scene was destroyed by the fire.

Adam punched 308 West Second Street into the GPS and arrived at the front door of the Frankfort Police Department two hours and twelve minutes later. After parking their car on the street, the two detectives walked past three news vans with camera crews at the ready, anxiously awaiting any news related to the quadruple homicide on New Year's Day.

"Look at that, Bernie. Six days later and the vultures are still camped out, looking for a story. It pisses me off that they get paid to be assholes."

"You get paid to be an asshole. What's the difference?"

"Hey, Bernie. Fuck off."

Bernie let loose with a hearty laugh as they walked toward the sheriff's office. Once inside the lobby, Adam and Bernie walked up to the receptionist who was sitting in a small room behind a thick sheet of bullet-proof glass. She motioned for Adam to pick up the phone that was hanging on the wall just to the left of where he was standing.

"Can I help you two?"

"Yes, ma'am. We're detectives from the Stillwell County Sheriff's Office here to see Detective Howell."

Adam and Bernie both produced their credentials and held them up so she could see them.

"Just one minute, detectives. I'll get him right out to you."

Two minutes later a door to the right of the receptionist's office opened and out popped a heavy-set gentleman in his mid-fifties. His shirt was half untucked and his hair was a mess. If he had really tried, Adam could have identified exactly what he had had to eat for the last three days, from examining the various stains on his tie.

He walked briskly toward Adam and Bernie, extended his hand, and introduced himself, "Hello, I'm Richard Howell. We seem to have a new development in our case. Please follow me."

Adam looked over at Bernie and then followed Detective Howell back through the same door he had emerged from. They walked down a series of hallways making sure to yield the right-of-way to the numerous detectives darting in and out of the office doors. Howell seemed to walk with a real sense of urgency to the end of the final hallway and turned left. He led them to a conference room where several detectives sat staring at the television with their feet propped up on the large oak table. Adam stood inside the door with his arms folded while Bernie gravitated to the white board, which was next to the flat panel television, with hand written notes all over it. Just as he had started to read the notes, he heard an announcement for breaking news coming from the monitor.

Bernie looked up to see an attractive female with a microphone standing outside the entrance to a run-down duplex. Directly behind her were two police cars, blocking the ingress to the neighborhood, with their blue lights activated. Two police officers stood in the street making sure no one came any closer to the scene.

"We're here, live, at 1121 Lost Circle in Bowling Green. We don't have a lot of details at the moment, but from what we've been told by authorities, there are three deceased people inside unit number two. If we can get a closer shot of the front of the residence, you can see that the police are going in and out, but we've yet to see them bring any bodies out. We'll bring you up-to-the-minute details as soon as we get them."

The cameraman panned closer toward the unit, making sure he got as much police activity in his lens as possible while the reporter did her best to describe what they were looking at.

Adam and Bernie were both startled when one of the officers in the room stood up, pointed at the screen, and shouted, "Look! There's our dark green pickup truck with yellow writing in the rear window in the parking lot!"

Immediately, Adam saw that the lettering on the truck wasn't the same as the lettering on Rocky's trucks.

Adam turned to Bernie and said, "Well, I guess that answers that question."

"Yeah, I guess it does."

Everyone but Bernie, Adam, and Detective Howell stood up and ran out the door.

"See, I told you that we had some new developments."

"Is there anything that Bernie and I can do to help you guys?"

"Not right now. If you just want to follow me around for a little while and pick up on what you can, you're more than welcome to do so. I'm going to call Bowling Green to try to get that pickup truck back here so we can process it for prints. We also need to find out what vehicle our suspect or suspects are in right now. They obviously left the scene somehow and we need to broadcast an APB for that vehicle."

Howell walked out of the conference room, turned left, and proceeded down the hallway until they came to an open door with a "Homicide" plaque hanging overhead. Adam and Bernie followed him through the door and into a large room with five desks scattered around the perimeter. Four of the five desks were occupied by men in shirts and ties, taking notes while talking on the phones.

"They've canceled all our leave and made it mandatory for us to work until we get these guys in custody. I haven't been home for more than a few hours since our murders."

Howell walked over to the only empty desk and sat down with Bernie and Adam following close behind. He picked up the phone and dialed the Bowling Green PD to see if he could get an update on their situation. He had been on the phone for less than a minute when he hung up and ran out of the office. Bernie and Adam just stood there trying to take in everything. On the far wall next to the windows were five cork boards with a series of graphic photographs with hand-written notes on them. Adam walked over to the boards to see if he could see what, if any, similarities there were between these murders and his. He counted four different victims and according to the information on the board they were all members of the *Dutch Family*.

There were several photographs of the outside of a modest ranch style home that was brick on all four sides. The next series of photographs were of the inside of the house—inside the front door, the kitchen area, each of the three bedrooms, the stairs leading to the basement, and eventually the actual crime scene in the basement. The photographer had followed protocol and started taking all of his far away photographs first. The basement was unfinished with a wooden staircase that came down right in the middle of the large room. The walls were exposed cinderblock that had been painted white. Along the wall at the front of the house were three shelves that housed different boxes which were labeled *Christmas Decorations, Easter decorations, Halloween Decorations,* and a few unlabeled boxes. The next wall housed the washer and dryer, a small sink, a folding table, and a sewing table. The wall at the back of the house had two more shelves with more boxes, some labeled and some not. The fourth wall, which was to the left of the stairs as you walk down, was bare.

The next set of photographs moved a little closer in and focused entirely on the floor. Adam's stomach started to turn as he looked at the graphic pictures. Four bodies, badly beaten and burned, were just to the right of the stairs. The first photographs were of the father, Gregory Dutch. He was lying on his back, covered in blood-soaked clothing and his face was battered to the point that he was unrecognizable. The left side of his head, just above his ear was caved in and his shirt had several puncture marks all in the upper chest area. Blisters from the intense heat of the fire could be seen on his legs and arms. There was a small notation at the bottom of the board that stated his body had been penetrated with the sharp end of a claw hammer 18 times.

Adam shifted down and positioned himself in front of the next cork board. The heading on top of the board said, "Gwen Dutch, six-year-old female". The photographs that followed showed a small white female lying on her stomach. The back of her head was caved in so badly that her brain matter was exposed through her bloody blond hair. There was a small stuffed teddy bear that was covered with blood right next to her body. Her arms were outstretched toward her father as if she were reaching out to him to be comforted before she died. Her right femur was obviously broken and could easily be seen through her pant leg. According to the notation, Gwen had been stabbed ten times and her head caved in with the blunt end of the claw hammer.

Moving along, the next board had the name, "Allison Dutch, age ten". Allison's body was even worse than her little sisters. She was photographed lying on her left side, just a few feet away from her younger sibling. Adam couldn't distinguish any facial characteristics of the little girl, nor could he tell what color her hair was. There were portions of her face that were completely ripped away from the skull exposing the muscle and bone underneath. Dark brown specks of coagulated blood appeared on what was left of her little face. The synthetic fibers from her pants were burned into her skin from the intense heat from the fire just like Melissa Dwyer. Adam couldn't look at the rest of the pictures so he moved down to the last board. One look at the badly burned body of Stephanie Dutch and he was done. He had to walk away.

Adam walked back over toward Bernie and sat down next to him with a feeling of sadness and anger coursing through his body.

"These are some sick fucks, Bernie."

Bernie shook his head but couldn't muster up any words to say. Adam just sat there numb, thinking about what the Dutch family had gone through before they died.

Thankfully, he didn't have too much time to dwell on his thoughts because he was brought back to reality by the sound of a familiar voice, "Alexander and Steckler, let's get going. We've got a two hour drive down to Bowling Green to shadow the forensics unit while they look through our truck."

That was all the two Stillwell County Detectives needed to hear. They popped out of their chairs and followed Detective Howell to a waiting Frankfort Police Department Suburban. The ride to the crime scene only took an hour and a half because Howell drove ninety miles per hour the entire trip. Bernie rode in the back seat with his seatbelt on, grasping tightly at whatever he could get his hands on.

"Holy smokes, Howell. I didn't think we were gonna make it here alive. Where did you learn how to drive, New Jersey?"

Howell let out a loud laugh, "No, I'm from Frankfort—born and raised."

The Suburban sailed into the city limits of Bowling Green with all thee detectives eager to get to the scene.

"You know where you're going?" Adam asked.

"Yeah, I got it punched into the GPS. It says we're five miles away."

The GPS directed them down the residential street of Nashville Road and eventually onto Lost Woods Avenue. They bypassed a long line of cars and news vans and drove right up to a Police Officer standing behind a strip of crime scene tape guarding the entrance to the Lost Circle complex.

"You boys are a little far from home, ain't ya?" the officer asked.

Detective Howell explained that they had made arrangements to follow the green pickup truck back to the garage and to shadow their forensics team while it was being processed. While Howell was explaining the details of their investigation to the officer, Adam looked through the windshield toward the activity and saw a flatbed tow truck waiting to load their pickup.

"I'll get ya'll where you need to be. Just give me a minute."

Howell watched as the officer walked back to his cruiser and got his cell phone. After a brief conversation, the officer returned to Howell and told him what to do.

"My supervisor told me to tell ya'll to park over there and wait. He'll be down here directly."

Howell pulled the Suburban past the entrance to the complex and waited for the supervisor's arrival. A few minutes later a sharply dress man, wearing a gold badge around his neck, approached the driver's side window.

Howell rolled down his window and started to introduce himself, "I'm Detective Howell, and these two gentlemen are…"

"I don't give a shit who you are. First of all, let me tell you that I don't appreciate you coming down here in the middle of my investigation. This scene is fucked up enough without me having to babysit you guys, too. So let me be perfectly clear when I tell you I don't want you touching anything or getting in anybody's way. As a matter of fact, I don't want you to even get out of your car while you're here. Are we clear on that, Detectives?"

"Crystal clear, Sir. You won't even know we're here."

"Good. You see that rollback over there? It will be pulling out of here in five minutes so sit tight. Once it leaves, you follow it back to our garage. One of our crime scene techs is already there waiting."

"Do we have any idea what vehicle the suspects are in now, Sir?"

"Yellow Honda Accord bearing Kentucky registration 1243-YRS."

Adam quickly pulled out his notepad and jotted down the tag number before he forgot it.

"I still didn't catch your name, Sir."

"Lieutenant James Anderson," he yelled as he walked away

"What a dick," Howell declared as he rolled up the window.

"He reminds me of Sheriff Lawson," Bernie added.

The three detectives watched from their position as the truck was loaded onto the flatbed, wondering what evidence from their crime scene might be inside. Adam scribbled down the make, model and tag number of the Ford F-250 crew cab pickup truck in his notebook and called Ms. Crags back in Stillwell to have her run both of the tags for him.

"That tag returns to a Jerry A. Wallard out of Cincinnati, Ohio. The vehicle was reported stolen by Mr. Wallard on December 17th according to the NCIC hit."

"Okay, can you also run Kentucky registration 1243-YRS?"

"Sure thing, honey. That returns to a Tyrone and Sharonda Adams out of Bowling Green Kentucky. Says here that they live on Lost Circle unit number two. The male was born in 1938 and the female was born in 1941. You need me to run anything else?"

"No, ma'am. Thanks for all your help."

Adam looked back at the notes he had taken while on the phone with Ms. Crags and passed along everything that he had just learned to his comrades. While they waited for the rollback to leave, Adam called Sergeant Bishop to pass along what he had found out so far and where he and Bernie were. Bishop didn't answer his phone so Adam left him a message detailing their trip. Just as Adam was hanging up, the rollback pulled off of Lost Circle so Howell put the Suburban in drive and fell in behind it.

Within 30 seconds Adam's phone rang, "Hey, Bishop."

"Did I hear you correctly? You two nitwits are in Bowling Green?"

"Yeah, there was a triple homicide and the pickup we were looking for was parked in front of the house. They think the bad guys are driving a yellow Honda Accord with Kentucky tag 1243-YRS. We're on our way to the garage to watch these guys process the truck now. They're still working on trying to identify a suspect."

"Was the house set on fire?"

"Nope, just three people murdered."

Bishop was pleased with their work and asked to be kept in the loop if anything else developed. Adam hung up the phone and looked out his window at the barren landscape for the rest of the trip. In no time at all, they were pulling up to a county owned facility that was surrounded by a chain-linked fence with razor wire perched on top. The sign on the gate read "City Garage and Bowling Green Police Department All-Purpose Facility". They followed the rollback through the gate and onto a narrow gravel road. As they drove farther into the facility, they passed two sets of gas pumps, three large buildings, and a parking lot full of busses. All the way on the opposite side of the property, in the dimly lit corner, stood an aluminum storage type building with a single roll up door in the middle and an office door on the left. The rollback driver hit his horn briefly and the door to the building opened for the truck to enter. While the truck was backing up to the door, Howell parked his suburban in the spot next to the office door. All three detectives got out of the car, walked up to the unlocked office door and entered into a small room with only a desk and a file cabinet. Standing in front of them was a shorter gentleman in his mid-thirties wearing a pair of blue slacks and a *Bowling Green Police Crime Scene Unit* polo shirt.

"You guys must be the Detectives from Frankfort and Stillwell. I'm Geoff Mager, the crime scene tech. I understand that this truck may hold some clues for you?"

Howell extended his hand toward Mr. Mager, "Yes, Sir. I'm working a quadruple homicide and these guys are working a single. This truck may have been used in both crimes as the getaway vehicle and we know it was stolen out of Cincinnati last month. Have your guys been able to identify any suspects yet?"

"Not to my knowledge. I was at the original scene for a while and recovered multiple prints. They're being run through the FBI database as we speak. That could take a few hours, or a few days. We have identified the victims though. The two older victims are Tyrone and Sharonda Adams. The younger victim is their granddaughter Tamisha Taylor. All three were bound with duct tape and had their throats slit. It was pretty intense in there."

Geoff turned around and walked through the door leading from the office to the bay and motioned for everyone to follow. The flatbed had already unloaded the pickup and left it in the middle of the large room. Geoff grabbed his evidence kit from the shelf and went right to work on processing the exterior of the truck for fingerprints. He pulled out his brush and applied a generous amount of black powder to the end. Almost instantly he was able to locate several sets near the door handles and on the windows.

"Nice prints," Howell stated.

"Yeah, I used to use a synthetic fiber brush, but then I heard about these. They're squirrel hair, which isn't as coarse. You have to replace them more often but to me they're worth every penny."

Geoff cut off a piece of clear tape and carefully placed it over the fingerprint powder that exposed the first print. Carefully he removed the tape, pulling off the print and placed it on a white three-by-five index card for preservation. As he continued gathering prints, each card was carefully marked with where they had been located and the time of removal.

Since there were no keys to the truck, Geoff had to use a Slim Jim to unlock the doors. Howell and Adam were right there looking over his shoulder as he doors opened. They were all excited at the prospect of what they might find. Adam and Bernie were just hoping that something inside would place the driver, and or vehicle in Stillwell County on the night of December 18th. Geoff popped the lock and opened the driver's side door. Immediately, everyone was hit with a stale smell of marijuana, alcohol, and rotten food. There were empty fast food containers all over the cab of the truck along with a ton of other trash. Geoff turned around and asked Bernie to go and get two new blue plastic tarps from the shelves behind them. Bernie grabbed the tarps, opened them up, and placed them on the floor of the bay for the sorting of the trash.

"Glove up, guys. I could sure use some help going through all this stuff."

Geoff photographed the entire truck before he started to move things from the cab to the plastic tarps. Everything from the front of the cab went on one tarp while everything from the rear of the cab went on the other. Howell concentrated on the items that came out of the back of the cab and found a black nylon purse. He opened it up, pulled out the matching wallet, and found Stephanie Dutch's driver's license in the clear plastic holder.

"Yes! It's Stephanie Dutch's purse!" Howell exclaimed.

As he went through the rest of the wallet he noticed that there were no credit cards in any of the slots and no cash. He stood up and excused himself to call his supervisors to let them know what he had found and to get them working on tracing any credit activity after the murders. He hoped that this information would yield some sort of surveillance video of their suspects. Adam focused his attention on all of the receipts that came out of the truck hoping to find something purchased in or near Stillwell. It took the four detectives two hours to thoroughly search the contents of the truck. Howell had hit a home run, while Adam and Bernie had struck out. There was absolutely nothing in the cab of the truck that Adam could use to put this suspect at his crime scene.

The ride to Frankfort and then back to Stillwell took a little over four and a half hours. Adam dropped Bernie off at his car and headed home. He was physically and mentally exhausted. He pulled out of the office lot and was driving south out of town when his eye caught a glimpse of a light off in the distance. It was the back porch light of Alexis Leighton's house high up on the hill. He looked at his watch and saw that it was already one in the morning so he bypassed her street and headed home. Adam pulled into his driveway and saw the glow of the television through the living room window. He put his car in park, walked up to the front door, and used his key to let himself in. After taking off his shoes and jacket, he walked around the corner to see that Rennae was still awake and watching a movie on the couch.

"Is everything okay, Rennae?"

"No, Adam. I'm sick of staying home alone all the time wondering where the hell you are and if you're alive. This has got to stop. It's either homicide or me. After this investigation is over you either go back to general investigations or I'm going back to Michigan."

Adam turned around without saying a word, and went to bed. If he had said what was really on his mind then a divorce would have been imminent. Instead, he walked up the stairs, closed the bedroom door behind him, and crawled into bed fully-clothed. At that exact moment, he was too tired to care.

Chapter 14

Adam stood under the steady stream of the shower with his head leaning against the opposite wall. He closed his eyes and thought about the case, hoping that today would be the day he could put a name with a suspect. He also hoped he would get a chance to see Alexis sometime during the day to make sure she was still fine with their New Year's encounter. A smile came to his face as he thought about that night. It had been a long time since he had felt that way about another woman. His marriage of 11 years was slowly starting to go south, and in the back of his mind he was elated that someone like Alexis felt he was desirable. The hot water felt good on his aching back, but it was time to come back to reality. Five minutes later he was dressed and in desperate need of a cup of coffee.

Adam walked down the stairs to see Rennae still asleep on the couch so he bypassed the kitchen and went straight toward the front door. The coffee would have to wait because he didn't want to endure another verbal assault before walking out the door. Adam heard the rain hitting the front porch as he sat on the stairs putting on his boots. Quietly, he opened the door and made a mad dash through the steady downpour to his cruiser. The cold rain hit his face sending a shiver through his body, waking him up faster than any cup of coffee ever would have. Adam could tell already that it was going to be a long day.

The rain had eased to a drizzle just before he entered town. Adam knew that the first order of business before going to the office was a cup of coffee, so he drove to the other end of town to the *Grub-N-Gas* and pulled into the lot. An excited smile came to his face as he passed by a familiar black Porsche at the gas pumps. His heart started to race and his palms became sweaty like a teenager with his first crush. He parked in the spot closest to the front door and ran inside to see Alexis standing there talking with a man he didn't know. He wiped the residual rain off his face and walked over toward the coffee pots in the back of the store hoping that she would see him. He was dying to know if she was still okay after what had happened between them.

Adam was pouring creamer into his coffee when he felt a slight touch on his shoulder.

"Hey there stranger."

He turned and looked down at the most beautiful brown eyes staring directly back at him. Her hair was pulled back and she didn't have on any makeup but Adam didn't care. Even unkempt she was absolutely gorgeous.

"Hello, Ms. Leighton. How are you?"

She hesitated for a second before answering, "I'm good. Are you?"

Adam looked at her inquisitively.

"Because after the other night I kind of felt bad. I mean, I did rape you in my basement."

A smile came to Adam's face, "You can't rape the willing, Ms. Leighton."

She smiled back at Adam and had a relieved look on her face.

"So, we can continue our arrangement?"

"Yes, we can continue our arrangement."

Alexis leaned in and put her lips close to Adam ear, "I'm so glad to hear you say that because I always get what I want, and right now, I want you. What are you doing right now?"

Alexis gave Adam a "Come-and-get-me" smile as she turned to walk out the door. Adam finished making his coffee and walked up to the front counter to pay.

"No charge, Detective," the clerk told Adam as he waved him past the register.

He walked out the door to see Alexis's tail lights headed south out of the parking lot toward her house. It took him a few minutes but he was able to catch up to her on Trimble Branch Road, just west of her driveway. He followed her up to the top and this time he drove all the way to the rear of the house and parked next to the back door. Alexis parked in the detached garage and met Adam in the court yard.

"Follow me… Detective."

Adam followed Alexis onto the back porch and into the kitchen. She closed the door behind them and walked slowly toward Adam.

"What would you like to do with me on this dreary morning detective?"

Adam tried desperately to think of something witty to say, but all he could manage to spit out was, "Anything that you would like, Ms. Leighton."

Alexis took Adam by the hand and led him into the sun room. She turned around slowly and pulled him to her. They kissed slowly at first, gradually building in intensity. Adam caressed her back as he pulled her closer and closer into him but Alexis suddenly stopped and pushed away from him.

"What's wrong?"

"Nothing, follow me upstairs."

Adam followed her up the grand circular staircase never taking his eyes off her. Every other stair that they climbed, she took off a piece of clothing. First she lost the sweatshirt, followed by the t-shirt and then her pants. Adam just laughed as picked up her discarded clothing and followed her up the stairs.

Alexis continued down the hallway toward her bedroom. Once inside the two made a move for the bed. Adam was tugging at his shirt while Alexis was unbuttoning his pants. In a matter of seconds Alexis had him naked and was on top of him. Just like the first time they were together, the moment was perfect. It was every bit as good as he remembered it form New Year's Eve, and just as quickly as it began, it was over.

"Do you mind if I shower here before I head in to the office?" Adam asked.

"Do you mind if I shower with you before WE head in?"

"Now you're talking, beautiful."

Adam looked down at his watch to see that it was already 6:40. He was due for the task force meeting in twenty minutes. Without warning, he jumped out of bed and fumbled to collect his clothes off the floor.

"Are you late for something?"

"Shit! I forgot I've got the task force meeting in twenty minutes. Can I take a rain check on our shower? I need to be out of here in five minutes."

"Sure thing. The towels are in the closet on the right as you walk in."

Adam was in and out of the shower in record time and it was a good thing he was only five minutes from the sheriff's office or he would have been in real trouble.

With a cold cup of coffee in his hand, Adam walked briskly into the conference room. Luckily he was right on time and walked in with Bernie, Bishop and Sheriff Lawson.

"You just get out of the shower?" Bernie asked.

"Yeah, it's been a hectic morning, Bernie. I'll fill you in later."

Everyone took a seat in their usual places except for Sgt. Bishop, who stood in the corner with two light brown folders in his hands. Once everyone was settled and quiet, Bishop walked over to Adam and plopped the folders on the table in front of him.

"Adam, I have some good news for you. Howell called me last night at three in the morning to tell me they had identified their suspects. Meet your potential killers."

"This is turning out to be a glorious day," Adam said with a smile.

"What's not included in those pages is that Clay and JJ are wanted for questioning in the murder of Clay's girlfriend up in Cincinnati on December 8th, of last year. I found that out when I ran them through our system this morning. These guys have been busy."

"Did you see any warrants on file for either of them?"

"Yes, there's one malicious wounding charge for Clay. Allegedly he stabbed a guy who was out for a run up in Princeton. A copy of that report is in the file."

Adam's eyes lit up as he looked at both of the folders in front of him. The first folder he looked at was labeled, in black magic marker, *Raymond "Clay" Whitley*. He opened the front cover to see the picture of a white male, with short brown hair staring angrily back at him. His piercing blue eyes were evenly spaced on his round face and his ears stuck out a bit. The bridge of his nose was crooked and scarred, like it had been broken in one too many bar fights. Thirty-four years of hate that had built up from a rough life could be seen all over the face staring back at him. Standing at just over six feet six, Clay was the kind of guy that if you met him in an alley, you would seriously consider running the other direction. Adam could tell from the picture that Clay was an angry and nasty man. Behind the mug shot were miscellaneous papers that outlined his lengthy criminal history that Adam would read over later.

Moving to the second folder, Adam read the name *Jimmy "JJ" Jebb*. Inside the folder was a similar array of papers, starting with a mug shot. Adam was looking at the exact opposite of Clay in this picture. Looking back at him was a twenty seven year old white man with calm eyes. His facial expression was not angry like the other photograph he had looked at. JJ's face was a little bit thinner with more normal-looking features. He had longer black hair that stopped just above his eyebrows and a slight goatee to accent his stubby nose. Adam flipped through the rest of the papers hastily, knowing that the real work had yet to begin.

Sgt. Bishop walked over to his seat and looked over at Adam, "That should keep you busy for the remainder of this morning. But for now, can you tell us what you guys found out in Bowling Green yesterday?"

Adam closed the folder on JJ, stood up, and addressed the group, "The crime scene guys let us help with the processing of the pickup. Howell was able to find the purse of his victim inside the vehicle, but we weren't able to find anything linking these guys to our case. I went through every piece of trash and receipt in that truck trying to put these guys in our neck of the woods. I got nothing."

The sheriff jumped up and angrily interjected, "That doesn't mean that they weren't here! I read Clay's rap sheet and he did a stint up the road at Big Sandy State Prison for robbery! He knows this area. Adam, you fucking dig and get this thing solved! You understand me?"

"Sheriff, I just found out who these guys are. I've…"

"Did I ask you to tell me their life story? No, I didn't! Get it done, Alexander, or I'll find someone that will."

The entire room fell silent as the sheriff, once again, took a hasty retreat out of the room and slammed the door behind him.

"What the hell is his problem?" Bernie asked.

Adam just shrugged his shoulders and looked over at Bishop.

"Hey, Sarge. Do you mind if I get going? I've got a lot of sleepless nights ahead of me until these sons of a bitches are behind bars."

"You got it, Adam. The First Sergeant and I need to talk to Bernie for a few minutes anyways. It seems that you're going to be losing his assistance for a day or two. Ms. Leighton has looked over Bernie's file on Bubba, and she has given him the green light to get a search warrant for his house on Beaver Valley Road."

"I thought the last informant flaked out on you, Bernie?"

"He did, but the task force has been working a new guy for me while I've been helping you with your case. They made three controlled buys from Bubba in the last six days, so we're going to hit the house with the search warrant tonight. I just got the word this morning that all this was going down."

"Good luck with that."

"Thanks, Adam. Hey, if it turns out that Clay and JJ didn't kill Melissa Dwyer, then maybe one of the

Woodchucks did. If that's the case then when I come back we'll hit those guys hard, okay?"

"Sounds like a plan to me. I guess having too many suspects is better than having none at all."

Adam stood up from his seat, walked out of the conference room, and made a beeline for his office. After turning on the light, he put the two files down on the desk and turned his notebook to a fresh page. It was time to learn everything there was to know about his new suspects. JJ had a short criminal history, ranging from breaking and entering to petit larceny and drug possession. He did time in the local jail for his crimes, but nothing that lasted longer than six months. Clay, on the other hand, had a more violent past. Adam counted seven assaults, three burglaries, three possessions with intent to distribute schedule two narcotics, five petit larcenies, and one attempted rape. All told, Clay had racked up eight felony convictions since his eighteenth birthday.

After reading everything that was in both files, Adam began piecing together a time line of their exploits.

<u>*Time Line:*</u>

1. *Tara Johnson – 12/05/08*
   a. *Girlfriend of Raymond "Clay" Whitley found murdered in a park in Cincinnati, Ohio. NCIC hit reveals that Clay and JJ are wanted for questioning in this murder. Have not been formally charged, but are suspects.*
2. *Melissa Dwyer Murder in Stillwell Ky. – 12/18/08*
   b. *White female found shot and stuffed into a closet. House set on fire.*
3. *Princeton Kentucky stabbing – 12-31-08*
   c. *Jarrod Stanley – Stabbed by Clay and JJ as he was out for a midnight run. Jarrod Stanley stated that they demanded money prior to stabbing him. Mr. Stanley survived his injuries and positively identified Clay and JJ as his attackers.*
4. *Dutch Murders X4 in Frankfort Ky. – 01-01-09*

   a. *Gregory Dutch – Father*
   b. *Stephanie Dutch – Mother*
   c. *Allison Dutch – 10 year old*
   d. *Gwen Dutch – 6 year old*
5. *Adams/Taylor Murders in Bowling Green Ky. – 01-06-09*
   a. *Tyrone Adams – Grandfather of Tamisha Taylor*
   b. *Sharonda Adams – Grandmother of Tamisha Taylor*
   c. *Tamisha Taylor – Girlfriend to Jimmy "JJ" Jebb*

Once the timeline was finished, Adam clicked the *print* button on his computer and waited for the finished product to spit out of his antiquated printer. While he waited, Adam took out a new three-ring binder and placed all of Clay and JJ's information inside. Once the printer was finished with the time line, Adam took the paper from the tray, three-hole punched it, and placed it in the very front of the binder.

The long days were starting to take their toll on Adam's body. He was more than a little fatigued from sitting behind his desk all morning, so he stood up and walked down the hall toward the kitchen for his afternoon caffeine fix. As he passed by Bishop's closed door, he could hear muffled yelling coming from inside. Bishop was pissed off about something, but there was too much background noise for Adam to hear anything specific. Fearing the he would get caught eavesdropping, he continued down the hall to the kitchen, poured himself a fresh cup of coffee, and walked back toward his office. It felt good to stretch his legs a bit. Midway down the hall, Adam heard Bishop yelling from inside his office.

"Adam! Get in here!"

He turned around and walked into Bishop's office to see him sitting behind his desk with his head in his hands.

"Is there a problem, Sarge?"

"Bernie's going to be gone for a while, so the sheriff took it upon himself to give us his dip-shit son-in-law to fill the void. You and Corporal David Gibbons will be working this together until Bernie can come back."

Adam sat down in the chair in the corner, not sure why Bishop was so angry. Gibbons was a decent street cop with good common sense, and Adam got along well with him.

"Why are you so angry? Gibbons is a good guy."

"Good guy? That idiot couldn't investigate his way out of a wet paper bag. The only reason he made it to the rank of corporal is because he knocked up the sheriff's daughter. I've had to cover up more of his mistakes in the past two years then I care to tell you about and I'm tired of it. You don't let him do a damn thing except sit next to you. You got that?"

"Sure thing, Sarge. I was planning on going to Cincinnati tomorrow to talk with their detectives about the Tara Johnson murder. I want to see if there are any similarities in our cases. When will Gibbons be assigned to us?"

"He is coming down the hall now, so he's all yours. I mean it Adam, he's to sit next to you and keep his fucking mouth shut. Understood?"

"Yes, Sir."

Adam sat quietly sipping his coffee, while waiting for Gibbons to arrive. After a few uncomfortable minutes, Sheriff Lawson turned the corner and walked into Bishop's office with Gibbons close behind.

"Adam, get David up to speed on the investigation," Sheriff Lawson instructed before he turned around and walked out the door.

Once he was out of earshot, Bishop took the opportunity to fill Gibbons in on his rules.

"Gibbons, this is Adam's investigation. DO NOT open your mouth unless he tells you to. You WILL NOT go off on your own, you WILL NOT follow up on any leads by yourself, and you WILL NOT conduct any interviews without one of us present. Your job is back-up only. Understood?"

"You got it, Sarge. Listen, I was just as shocked as you were to hear I was being assigned to this case. We're short-staffed in patrol and I just want you to know that I didn't ask for this. I was told."

Bishop shook his head in disgust and motioned for Adam and David to get out of his office. Adam walked out first and led the way down the hall to his small slice of heaven. After the door was closed behind them, Adam started to fill David in on the case.

"What do you know so far, David?"

"I only know what I learned that night on scene, which is that a dead chick was found in a closet with a meth lab in the room. Other than that, I don't know anything. It's been so busy on the street lately that I haven't had the opportunity to see what's been going on. You know that the holidays always bring out the best in people. 'Tis the season for suicides and domestic assaults. Oh, I did hear that Rocky sent you his love from beyond the grave."

"Everyone's a fucking comedian."

Adam handed David a large folder with all of the reports and case notes that he had compiled over the course of the investigation.

"You've got some work to do. I need you to make a copy of this entire folder for yourself and get this one back to me before you leave this afternoon. And then I suggest that you go straight home and start reading. We're headed up to Cincinnati first thing in the morning to meet with one of their homicide detectives. Read up on Clay and JJ and be here at six in the morning, I want to be in Cincinnati no later than nine."

"You got it," David said as he took the binder and disappeared into the copy room.

An hour and a half later, David was on his way home. As he drove out of town he kept looking over at the large three-ring binder that was in his passenger seat, wondering what was inside. As he pulled into his driveway, he was greeted by his wife, Lindsay, and their three boys who were all playing football in the front yard.

"You're home early, honey. Did you forget something?"

"No, your father decided to pull me from the street and have me help with the murder investigation that happened last month. Adam and I have to go to Cincinnati early tomorrow morning to meet with their homicide detectives and I have some light reading to do."

David held up the giant binder of paperwork to showed Lindsay what he would be reading for the remainder of the night.

"Okay, honey. The boys and I are going to my parents for dinner tonight so the house will be quiet."

David gave his wife a kiss and walked inside to the living room to get started.

Adam made the decision to stay at the office and keep studying up on his suspects. He checked all of his local databases to try to establish some sort of connection between Clay, JJ, and Stillwell County. Three hours later, the only relationship he was able to make was five years prior when Clay did two years for an attempted rape and assault charge at Big Sandy State Prison. Adam picked up the phone and called the prison to see if he could talk to someone in the records room.

"Big Sandy, this is Dillon, how can I help you?"

"Hey, Dillon. This is Detective Alexander from the Stillwell County Sheriff's Office. Is there anyone in the records room by any chance?"

"Yes, Sir. It's only 4:30 so there should be someone there. Hold on and I'll transfer you."

The phone rang twice and Adam was greeted with another voice.

"Records, this is Bryce."

"Hey, Bryce. This is Detective Alexander here at the Sheriff's Office. I was wondering if you could help me out with something. Five years ago you guys had an inmate by the name of Raymond Whitley. He is a white male with a birth date of 10/22/1972."

Bryce cut Adam short, "Oh, you mean Clay? Yeah, he was here. I still have the file sitting in front of me. You're the second person to ask about him today. He must be a popular fellow."

"What do you mean? Who else called asking about him?

"Your sheriff. He called here this morning asking all sorts of strange questions about Clay. Now, what information do you need?"

Adam sat still for a moment, with the phone up to his ear, and staring blankly at the wall. Then it hit him. He remembered the sheriff saying that he read Clay's rap sheet in the meeting this morning. He must have called the prison before the meeting.

"Hello. Are you still there, Detective?"

"Yes, sorry. Was Clay reprimanded in any way during his incarceration?"

"Let's see here. It says he was a model inmate and that he made trustee in six months."

"Did he have any violent contact with other inmates?"

"No reprimands for anything that I can see, and we're pretty strict on infractions and making sure that they get documented. Every cell search turned up negative results for contraband. All his reviews were good and he got out five months early for good behavior. I wish all our inmates were this good."

"Did he by any chance have any visitors while he was there?"

"Yes, he had three people on his list. Tara Johnson who listed herself as his girlfriend, Jimmy Jebb who is his nephew, and Tamisha Taylor who is listed as a friend. Is there anything else I can help you with, Detective?"

"No Sir, you've been very helpful. Thanks for your time."

Adam hung up the phone and pulled the timeline that he made out of his binder. Two of the three names on Clay's visitors list had been murdered. He knew that Tara Johnson was his girlfriend, but what he didn't know was the relationship between him and Tamisha Taylor. Adam picked up the phone and reluctantly placed a call to Lieutenant Anderson from the Bowling Green Police Department. He hoped the lieutenant would be in a better mood than he had been the night they met. Unfortunately he wasn't in the office so Adam left a message detailing what he had just discovered.

His next call was to the Cincinnati Homicide Unit to make contact with the detective who had worked the Tara Johnson homicide, but since it was after five, there was no answer on the main line. Adam, once again, left a message with the answering service letting them know that he was going to be coming up in the morning to discuss their two cases. After hanging up the phone, Adam decided to call it a day and go home. He knew he had to get some much needed rest before making the trek to Cincinnati.

Chapter 15

Bernie looked down at his watch and saw that the time was 10:15 pm. He had better pick up the pace if he was going to make it to the task force office by 10:30. He still had a few details to iron out before the briefing at 11:15. This was a major case for Bernie and if all went well, it could be the biggest bust of his career. He pulled off the highway onto the long gravel drive to the task force office and found that just about everyone was already there. He parked in the only available spot and walked inside to a packed house. Police officers, special agents from the state police, and sheriff's deputies were on both floors of the Task Force Office, waiting for the briefing to begin. Bernie bypassed the crowd and walked into his office to put a few last-minute touches on his paperwork.

"Hey, Bernie. I had everyone sign in as they walked through the door. Looks like we have more than enough people," First Sergeant Parr remarked.

"Why is everyone here so early?"

"I told them to come early so we could get a proper head count for the operations plan. This is a big bust and I didn't want anyone to be late."

"Thanks, First Sergeant. I appreciate you doing that."

"What time are you thinking you want to hit this place?"

"Around 12:30 in the morning," Bernie said as he pulled out a copy of the aerial photograph that he had printed earlier and spread it out across his desk for First Sergeant Parr to see. "I'm thinking we should put two forward observers in the tree line off Coal Street so they can keep their eyes on the house and record license plate numbers for us to use later."

"Sounds good to me, Bernie. I'll get two of my men out there now. How far away is the house from here?"

"It's about a 35-minute drive."

Bernie took the sign-in sheet from the first sergeant as he left the room and scanned the list to see who he had to work with. He counted 10 state police swat team members, seven task force members, three sheriff's deputies from Stillwell County, Captain Cubbage and First Sergeant Parr. Then he looked back at the aerial map and counted seven buildings on the property that would need to be searched before the night was over. Fortunately, only three of the seven had to be entered simultaneously. He had more than enough people to get the job done safely, so for the next 40 minutes Bernie sat at his desk making sure everyone was assigned to a strike team and that even the smallest detail was taken care of.

Satisfied with his preparations, he made copies for everyone, and walked upstairs to the conference room where First Sergeant Parr had them all assembled. He took his place at the front of the room and drew a rough map of Bubba's property on the dry-erase board. Once that was done, he handed out the packets of information that contained the operations plan, an aerial photo of the property, and Bubba's criminal history to each officer in attendance so they could follow along as they were briefed.

"We're going to execute a search warrant at 47 Beaver Valley Road in Martin, which is just south of the town of Stillwell. The search warrant is for the residence, curtilage, outbuildings, and vehicles on the property. If you flip to the first page of the packet I handed out, you'll see an aerial map of the property. It's approximately 22 acres with one big 10 acre field that's surrounded by woods. I counted seven buildings in total that need to be searched tonight and three of the seven need to be breeched at the same time. If you flip to page five I've divided everyone into three teams. Team Alpha will be going into Bubba's house. Team Bravo will be going into the detached four car garage next to the house and team Charlie will be going into the barn."

First Sergeant Parr's cell phone started to ring, prompting him to excuse himself into the hallway to take the call.

"Do we know which building the meth lab is in?" Captain Cubbage asked.

"No, Sir, we don't. Everyone that buys there goes into the main house, gets their dope and leaves. No one has actually seen the lab."

"Okay, then do we know who owns the property?"

"According to the tax map, the property is owned by our target for tonight's warrant, Derwin C. Bolden, aka Bubba. He is a white male born 07/07/51. He's six feet six inches tall and weighs two hundred and ninety pounds. He's a big boy so be careful."

"Excuse me, Detective," First Sergeant Parr interrupted. "The forward observers we put into the woods just called to report that Bubba's outside shooting in their direction. They don't know if he's aiming at them or if he's just out shooting."

"No kidding. Are they sure it was Bubba?"

"They said it was him. They also said that there's a ton of traffic going in and out of the driveway and on four wheelers through the hills."

"Well, now we know that he has guns in the house and he's a convicted felon. This just got a little more interesting."

Bernie continued with the briefing, "Turn back to the map and you'll see there's only one road going to Bubba's and it's surrounded by trees. My informant told me he has a sensor at the end of the driveway to alert him when someone is coming so we'll have to park on Coal Street and walk in through the woods." Bernie turned around and pointed to his map on the dry-erase board to show everyone where they would be parking. "Once everyone's in place, Team Alpha, which is my team, will knock and announce police presence at the main house. That will be the signal for teams Bravo and Charlie to make entry into their buildings. After we hit the house and everything's secure, we can have a few guys go back to get the cars and bring them up the driveway. Are there any questions?"

After a brief pause, Bernie concluded the briefing, "Okay guys, we're finished here. Let's break up into our strike teams and hash out any last minute concerns you may have. Team Alpha, please stay here with me. Teams Bravo and Charlie, you guys can meet downstairs. Hey, one last thing, make sure that someone in your crew takes a breeching kit just in case you encounter any locked doors. No surprises tonight. Everyone goes home."

Bernie waited for everyone to leave the conference room before he gathered his team around the dry-erase board to go over how they were going to make entry into Bubba's house.

"Jimmy, you're my ram man, so as soon as I announce police presence you shatter that fucking door. Don't even give that bastard a chance to respond. I have the search warrant so I have to be first in the door. Derek, you fall in behind me, Zach, you fall in behind Derek, and Jimmy will drop the ram and fall in behind you. Frank and Tim will take perimeter duty behind the house. Are we all clear on our assignments?"

Bernie looked at each individual in his strike team and affirmed that each of them was absolutely sure of their duty. After fifteen minutes of prepping in the parking lot, Bernie called everyone together one last time.

"Last chance for questions gentlemen. Once we get to the parking lot, it's light and sound discipline. Is everyone good?"

He looked around the silent crowd and his heart started to race. It was go time. "God speed, guys. Let's hit it!"

Bernie watched as everyone loaded up into their cars. Once the last door was closed he jumped in the passenger side of an unmarked Suburban and led the charge to Bubba's. The convoy of marked and unmarked police cars drove south through Stillwell on their way to Martin. As soon as they were past the town limits, Bernie picked up the mic to his in-car radio and gave out some last minute instructions.

"We'll be using tack two on your portable radios so make sure you're on that channel before we get to the rally point. We should be there in about ten minutes so get your game faces on."

Bernie called the dispatcher on his cell phone rather than use the radio just in case someone had a scanner and was listening in.

"Hey, Ms. Crags. We're getting ready to execute a search warrant on Beaver Valley Road in Martin. Can you alert the local rescue squad and have them stand by just in case? They don't have to leave the station, they just have to be ready to head our way if we need them."

"No problem, Detective Steckler. I'll take care of that now."

The long line of police vehicles pulled onto Coal Street and parked behind the shopping center. Bernie got out of his car and met up with the other members of Team Alpha.

"Team Bravo and Team Charlie, are you guys ready?"

Bernie was given the thumbs up from both team leaders and they were off through the woods toward Bubba's. Although the terrain was flat, there were numerous downed trees and sharp rocks that made their trek through the dark dangerous. About 10 minutes into their walk Bernie could see the light on Bubba's rear porch getting closer through the leafless trees. They approached the edge of the tree line and stopped for a brief moment to assess their surroundings. Bernie could see three cars parked in the driveway in front of the house with their head lights on and their engines running. Two of the three cars had people in the passenger seat so Bernie got on the radio and told everyone to stop and wait for his command to go. After the last car had left the property, Bernie gave the command.

"Go, Go, Go," Bernie whispered into the radio.

Team Alpha had the least amount of distance to cover so they gave teams Bravo and Charlie a few extra seconds to sprint to their target before they approached the main house. Bernie led his team of six toward the front porch, while the two perimeter guys peeled off and took their position in the rear to make sure no one ran out the back.

"POLICE SEARCH WARRANT!"

Like yellow jacket's swarming a threat to their nest, everyone moved in. Jimmy took the ram he had in his hand and splintered the front door giving his team access to the house. Bernie was the first man inside and saw Bubba running across the living room toward the kitchen.

"STOP, POLICE!" he shouted.

Ignoring Bernie's warning, Bubba ran toward the sliding glass door and tried to make his escape. As he stood there fumbling with the lock, Bernie sprinted toward him and lunged at Bubba's massive upper body. Bernie did his best to try to bring Bubba to the ground, but he just brushed Bernie to the side like he wasn't even there. It wasn't until Zach and Derek joined in that they were able to get him to the ground. It took everything all three of them had to get Bubba under control and in cuffs. After they had him subdued, the remainder of the team continued to sweep of the house for any other potential threats to their safety.

"Hey Bernie, I found this chick asleep in the back bedroom," Jimmy said as he lead the handcuffed female down the hall toward the kitchen.

Bernie was still in the process of catching his breath, "Okay, search the couch in the living room and have her sit there." He turned back and looked down at Bubba, "Are you gonna tell me where the dope is?"

"There ain't shit here. I'm gonna sue the hell out of you and your department. Go ahead asshole and look, you won't find a damn thing on this property."

"I intend to, Bubba."

Bernie helped Bubba up off the floor and moved him into the living room with the woman they had found and left them both on the couch. Bernie pulled the search warrant out of his raid vest and held it up to Bubba's face.

"I told you. There ain't shit here."

"Just shut the hell up and listen for once in your life. This is a search warrant for the property of 47 Beaver Valley Road. I am hereby granted permission to search this property for the presence of any narcotics or narcotics related equipment. You have the right to remain silent…"

"Save it, dipshit. I ain't gonna talk to you guys no how."

Bernie put the copy of the warrant on the table and left two of his team members in the house to guard Bubba and the girl while he walked outside to check on the other two teams. He passed through the hole where the front door used to be and down the front steps to the driveway. Teams Bravo and Charlie had just finished their cursory searches and were congregating on the dirt road in between the house and the barn.

"Did anyone look in the silo or the tractor shed yet?" Bernie asked.

"Yeah we did. The only thing we have left to search is the shed out behind the house," Bravo's team leader added.

Bernie looked back at his two team members who were on the perimeter during the initial entry and motioned for them to go and look in the shed. It only took a few seconds for them to report back.

"It's all clear, Bernie. There are just some old bicycles and lawn mowers in there."

"Let's get a couple guys to head back to the cars and start bringing them up here. I need two guys from each team to stand by the buildings you entered and make sure no one goes in or out. I'm going to go back in and start to question the lady we found in the bedroom."

Bernie returned to the house and took the woman into the kitchen so he could talk to her away from Bubba.

"You say one word and you know what's gonna happen to you, bitch!" Bubba yelled.

"Can you please loosen these cuffs? They're cutting off the circulation to my hands."

Bernie loosened the cuffs on her wrists before telling her to sit down at the kitchen table.

"I'm Detective Bernie Steckler, and you are?"

"Julie Roper."

She looked over at Bernie with a nasty scowl on her face. He knew instantly that getting anything other than her basic personal information was going to be next to impossible.

"Do you live here Julie?"

"Sometimes I stay here. I have a place back in Madison, West Virginia."

"So you're Bubba's girlfriend I take it?"

"You could say that. He's the father of my child so I come down here when I need some money."

"Do you know why we're here tonight?"

"I can take a guess."

"You mind telling me what your guess is?"

"Yes I do."

"So that's it then? Anything we find in this house we're going to charge you with too, so it's kind of in your best interest to start talking to me."

"No way. You heard what he said as we walked out of the living room. I ain't gonna tell you shit. I'll take whatever you guys charge me with and do you know why?"

"No, why is that?"

"Because at least I'll be alive in jail. We're done here, Detective."

Bernie stood Julie up and walked her back to the front room with Bubba. He sat her down on the couch and keyed up his radio.

"I need all team leaders to the front porch of the main house please so we can go over what we need to do next."

He walked out on the porch and waited for everyone to arrive. Within two minutes he had all the team leaders, and the guys who weren't already busy, waiting for his instructions.

"It's time to break everyone up into search teams. If you hit the garage, you search it. If you hit the barn, you search it. If you find anything that needs to be collected, mark it and I'll come by and get it later. Are there any questions?"

The teams scurried off again to complete their detailed searches of the outbuildings on the property. Bernie walked back in the house and began his search. He started with the living room under the watchful eye of Bubba but didn't find anything. The kitchen and bathroom yielded the same negative results. He walked down the hallway and searched two of the three bedrooms, carefully looking in every closet, dresser drawer, book, and air vent, again finding nothing.

"You find anything yet Bernie?" Captain Cubbage asked.

"Not yet, Sir. But I still have Bubba's bedroom to search. There's no way in hell that I can get skunked here."

"It's here, Bernie. We just have to find it. Don't get discouraged."

Bernie walked to the end of the hallway and into Bubba's bedroom. He started with the large dresser that was on the wall opposite the king-sized bed and opened every drawer, but found nothing. He searched the entire room with the same result, nothing. Not even the gun he was outside shooting earlier.

"Fuck Captain, I've searched this entire house and found zip. I sure hope someone found something in the other buildings."

Bernie walked down the hallway and into the living room. Bubba was still on the couch with a smug look on his face.

"Find anything, asshole?"

"Fuck you, Bubba. It's here and I'm gonna find it."

Bubba started to laugh out loud at Bernie's anger, "Yeah, good luck with that."

He was starting to get under Bernie's skin and he knew it. Bernie had to get out of the house and get some fresh air. He walked outside and down toward the four car garage to check on their progress. The search party was standing inside with the door closed trying to stay warm.

"Please tell me you guys found something. A fucking crack pipe. Anything."

"Sorry, Bernie. We didn't find anything. We even ran the vehicle identification numbers on all the engine blocks and the four wheelers along the back wall to see if they're stolen."

He walked out of the garage and up to the barn to receive the same grim news from that search team. Now it was time to panic. He knew that he was covered from any legal retaliation from Bubba because he had made several controlled buys of meth from this house and every informant had been made reliable. Each buy had been well documented with the evidence properly stored in the evidence locker back at the Sheriff's Office.

He keyed up the microphone on his radio, "All personnel please meet up at the main house."

He waited for everyone to congregate in front of the porch before they started the debriefing.

"I have no clue how but we didn't turn up anything in any of the buildings on the property. Everyone that isn't on the Narcotic's Task Force is released and I thank you for all your help and hard work. The rest of you guys please come inside for a minute while I finish with the paperwork."

Bernie walked back inside the house to execute the search warrant with no evidence found.

"Damn it's dark in here. Where is the light switch?"

He walked across the room to the door where the light switches were. He flipped the first one and nothing happened so he moved on to the second. No lights turned on after the second so he flipped the third and the lights came on. When he turned back around he saw that Bubba no longer had a smug smile on his face.

"Hey, Bernie. Get out here," Jimmy yelled.

Bernie ran outside and saw a single light coming off of Roundhead Mountain and headed toward the house. He recognized the high pitch wind of an engine echoing off the hillside, indicating to him it was a four-wheeler. Bernie ran down to the garage, hopped on one of Bubba's four wheelers, and drove recklessly toward the light trying to intercept it. But whoever it was had seen the police cars in the driveway, made a u-turn, and took off in the opposite direction.

Bernie raced across the driveway and down the fence line toward the corner of the property. Once he got to the tree line he found a small trail that went up onto the mountain so he darted up the trail without hesitation. About a half mile up the trail Bernie's headlight illuminated three four wheelers parked next to a dimly lit rundown shack. He slammed the brakes on his ATV and sought refuge behind a large tree 20 yards from the building.

Bernie pulled his gun from the holster and popped his head out to get a better look at what he was up against. Even in the sparse lighting he could see the building was in rough shape. Little beams of light could be seen through the seams of the poorly constructed frame and the only window was covered with cardboard to help keep out the cold winter air. Smoke poured out of a metal pipe that jutted out from the side of the building indicating that there was a heat source inside. Could this be the lab? Off in the distance Bernie could hear the hum of what sounded like a large gas generator running.

Bernie keyed up his radio, "Hey guys, if you can hear me there's a shack up here in one of the hollows of this mountain. Follow the trail at the end of the fence line and it'll bring you right to me."

In no time Bernie heard the roar of more ATV's headed toward him so he yelled out to the house.

"This is the Stillwell County Sheriff's Office! We've got you surrounded so you need to come out here with your hands where I can see them!"

He waited for a few moments with no answer from anyone inside the shack so he gave a second command with the same results. By this time three ATV's with task force members had reached his location and set up a perimeter to contain whoever was inside.

"This is your final warning. Come out with your hands up or I'm just gonna say fuck it and throw in a flash bang."

"OKAY! We're coming out," a familiar voice from inside yelled.

The door flew open and out walked all of Rocky's Woodchucks with their hands held high. The task force swarmed in and put all four of them on the ground and in handcuffs. Bernie looked over at Stuart Winston lying on the ground and motioned for Frank to bring him over to the ATV's where they could talk out of earshot.

"Hey Stuart, what's going on here?" Bernie asked.

Stuart just stared at the ground and didn't say a word.

"You know as well as I do that when we go over to where that generator is we're going to find what you guys have been up to. And when I find out I'm going to give the first person that talks to me the best deal when we go to court. I figured I would give you first crack at it since we've worked together in the past."

"Okay. What do you want to know?"

"Everything."

Bernie read Stuart his Miranda Rights before he started asking him questions. When he finished, Stuart agreed to cooperate and let the flood gates open.

"This is Bubba's lab. We started working for him full time after Rocky killed himself. We pretty much stay up here most of the time, cooking and delivering to Bubba's customers."

"How do you know when he needs dope down at the house?"

"He has a light switch next to his front door. When he turns it on, it turns on a light up here in the shack. One flick of the lights means one gram, two flicks means two grams and so on. I package the drugs, hop on the bike and bring it down to the house. Pretty simple actually."

"Are you guys cooking in that shack too?"

"Hell no. Those generators you hear over there are powering the stoves and the ventilation system for the cook. Bubba had two school buses buried underground a while ago. Right after Rocky killed himself we needed to make money, so we started to cook for Bubba."

Bernie couldn't believe what he was hearing. He walked with Stuart 50 yards through the woods to where two gas generators were running. One of the generators powered the industrial-sized exhaust fan that was sitting on top of a fresh mound of dirt. The second generator was powering the heat source that they were using to cook with.

Bernie pointed to the wooden stairs that went down into the ground, "You said there are two school buses down there?"

"Yes, Sir."

"How in the world did Bubba get them up here?"

"As soon as it gets daylight you can see there's an old logging road that runs up here from the main road in Martin. From what Bubba told me, he just drove 'em up here. His buddy has a backhoe and a bulldozer that they used to lower the buses into the holes after they were dug out. They're only about 10 feet or so underground."

"You know I'm going to ask you about Rocky. Did he kill Melissa Dwyer?"

"Detective Steckler, I've known Rocky for the better part of my life. He and my daddy were good friends while I was growing up. They even used to race against one another before he passed away six years ago. There's no way in hell Rocky killed Ms. Dwyer. We all really liked her and her kids a lot."

"Were you guys using her house to cook in?"

"If anything like that was going on, I didn't know about it, and that's the truth."

"Did Rocky know how to cook this shit?"

"Hell no. We even offered to teach him, but he said he didn't want to learn. I felt bad when I found out he was using the stuff. I always thought of him as an older brother and not a boss."

Bernie looked away from Stuart and over at the steps leading down into the ground. He wanted to go down to the lab to get a look at the operation, but stopped himself because he didn't know how well the exhaust fans were moving the toxic air in the confined space. He walked Stuart back over to the where Richard, Charles, and Stephen were sitting on the ground and told his guys about what he had just discovered. After giving them the lowdown he walked over to the shack and popped his head in to see what was inside. There was a small wood-burning stove along the back wall and three cots. There was a radio playing country music on the floor next to a wooden table with three chairs around it. Empty pizza boxes and fast-food wrappers were thrown all over the floor. On top of the table was what Bernie had been looking for.

"HOLY SHIT!" He yelled at the top of his lungs.

The other task force members came running over to Bernie to see what he was yelling about.

"What's the problem, Bernie?" Frank asked.

"Not a damn thing, boys. I just might be able to retire after this bust. There has to be at least half a million dollars and five handguns on that table." Bernie stated.

It was definitely the bust of his career, and potentially the biggest bust in Stillwell County History.

Bernie, Frank, and Tim walked the Woodchucks back down to the house while Derek stayed behind to guard the lab and the shack. With everyone back inside the living room, Bernie walked over to Bubba with a snide grin plastered all over his face.

"What do you have to say now, you fucking piece of garbage?"

Captain Cubbage looked over at Bernie, "What are you talking about. Where did these guys come from?"

"It appears that Bubba has two school buses buried up in the side of Roundhead Mountain that he uses to cook in." Bernie walked over to the light switch next to the front door, "See this Captain? When you flip this switch, it turns a light on up in a little shack signaling these guys to bring down an order. When I tried to turn on the light I was actually signaling Stuart to bring some dope down to the house."

Captain Cubbage was amazed, "No shit!"

"And guess what, Captain? In that shack on a little table is roughly half a million in cash and five handguns. Not too shabby for a nights work, huh?"

Captain Cubbage didn't say a word. He didn't have to because the look on his face said it all.

Bernie assembled everyone in the front yard and filled them in on what they had found up on the mountain. To his knowledge, this was the most elaborate meth lab that he, or anyone else in the state of Kentucky had ever unearthed. He tried his best to contain his excitement, but the smile that was plastered across his face revealed it all. At the end of his debriefing, he asked if anyone had any questions or concerns. When no one spoke up, he turned the floor over to First Sergeant Parr.

"That was some damn good work tonight, gentlemen. No one got hurt and we're all going home. We took a dangerous man off the street tonight and dealt a huge blow to the meth trade in eastern Kentucky. Enjoy it now, because as we all know, someone else will eventually pick up right where Bubba left off. That being said, I'm going to need the task force to remain on scene to help Bernie, while the rest of you can go home. Once again, thanks for your hard work tonight."

Bernie looked over the horizon and saw that the sun was just starting to come up. As much as he wanted to stand there and bask in his glory, there was still too much that had to be done. He had to go back to the sheriff's office to get another search warrant typed up for Roundhead Mountain; he needed to call the DEA and have them send up their clean-up crew to help get these buses out of the ground; he had to get Bubba and the Woodchucks back to the jail to get them booked; and he had to get the search warrants certified by the Clerk of the Circuit Court. It had been a long and rewarding night, but the day ahead would prove to be just as rewarding.

Chapter 16

Adam arrived at the sheriff's office at exactly six in the morning to find David sitting in the chair, next to his door. Too tired to hold a conversation, Adam put his key in the door and walked into his office to check his e-mail before they hit the road. He sat down behind his desk and turned on his computer. While he waited for the hard drive to boot-up he picked up his phone to check for messages. After the voice mail operator advised him he didn't have any, he hung up the phone and looked up at David, who was standing in front of him with a cup of coffee in each hand and the heavy binder under his arm.

"Coffee, Adam?"

David extended his arm without the binder under it towards Adam.

"Are you applying for the Secret Service or something?" Adam asked as he reached up and took the hot cup out of David's hand.

David was dressed sharply in a black pinstripe suit, white shirt, multicolored tie and black dress shoes. His badge was hanging from a silver chain around his neck and he had made sure he tucked his jacket behind his gun for everyone to see.

"No, I had no idea what to wear so I put this on."

"I'm just busting your balls. I sure do appreciate the coffee."

After a few minutes of fumbling around at his desk, Adam grabbed his leather bound notebook, a few pens, and his digital recorder before heading out the door for the three-hour drive to Cincinnati.

"Last chance for the rest room, brother, because once the wheels are in motion, we ain't stoppin'," Adam stated.

"I'll meet you at the car," David answered without hesitation.

The ride up to Cincinnati was quiet. Since Adam and David didn't have much in common, not a lot was said.

They did talk briefly about the case and what they hoped to accomplish by talking with the detective who had investigated the Tara Johnson murder, but that only took a few minutes.

The remainder of the trip seemed like it took an eternity, and David was excited to see they were finally crossing the state line.

"Welcome to Ohio. It's about damn time. You know Adam, I may just be a dumb country boy, but there's no way in hell that I would want to live here."

"I know what you mean. I get a nasty feeling every time I have to cross the river into this place."

Adam was on interstate 471 headed over the river and into downtown. Twenty minutes later they were on Broadway, in front of the homicide division of the Cincinnati Police Department. The station's parking lot was full, forcing Adam to drive a few blocks away to find parking on a side street. Once he found a parking space with high visibility and foot traffic, he pulled in next to the meter.

"An hour should do it," Adam said as he deposited his four quarters.

The walk to the station was cold and windy and the day's forecasted snow had been falling for the past twenty minutes. As they approached the dull gray, seven story building, Adam read the words "To Protect and Serve" in large letters suspended above the entrance.

"This place doesn't look so bad?" Adam stated as they gingerly walked up the slick snow covered stairs.

Adam reached out and opened the heavy glass door and was greeted with a blast of warm air that had a foul stench of body odor. As they walked into the large lobby, they looked around and noticed several homeless people scattered throughout, all trying to avoid the snow until they were kicked out at closing time. Adam and David were on sensory overload as they tried to take it all in, not knowing which way to look next.

"Maybe I spoke too soon."

“Can I help you?” A snide voice yelled across the lobby.

When neither of them answered, she tried again, this time a little louder, “I said, can I help you?”

Adam stopped in his tracks and looked across the lobby to see a receptionist waving him over to her desk.

When he finally got over to her, he answered, “Yes, ma’am. We’re detectives from Stillwell County, Kentucky. Would it be possible to speak to someone in your homicide division?”

“Do either of you have an appointment?” she rudely asked.

“No ma’am. We don’t.”

“What about identification? Do you at least have that?”

Adam and David both reached into their back pockets and showed the receptionist their sheriff’s office credentials.

“We were wondering…”

Adam was cut off immediately, “I’ll try to see if someone’s available, have a seat over there.”

It was obvious that arguing with the receptionist was going to get them nowhere but tossed out on their asses. David did as he was told and sat in the only available chair that wasn’t next to a homeless person. Adam, on the other hand, walked out the door, toward the street, looking for someone in uniform who might be more help than the receptionist. It didn’t take long for a well-dressed gentleman with a badge hanging around his neck to come walking toward him on the street.

“Sir, can I talk to you for a second?”

The young Cincinnati detective stopped and looked over at Adam, “What can I help you with?”

Adam introduced himself and gave the detective a brief rundown of why they were there.

The detective patiently waited for Adam to finish with his introduction and then extended his hand, “I’m

Detective Mundon, and today's your lucky day. I worked the Tara Johnson homicide. Come on in."

Adam followed the detective back inside and collected David who was clenching his notebook tightly and trying not to make eye contact with anyone. After they passed through the secure door, they walked down a series of hallways before coming to an elevator. Five floors later, the doors opened to another series of dimly-lit hallways. The homicide unit was on the back side of the building and it was obvious they needed more space. File cabinets that were filled to the brim with old cases lined the hallways. Perched on top of those same file cabinets were cardboard boxes that had case numbers and detective's names scribbled on them in black magic marker. Several detectives ambled around the room, each working on something different. Adam counted at least fifteen detectives sitting in different cubicles either on the phone or going through mounds of paperwork.

"Is it always this busy?" Adam asked.

"No, but you caught us with our pants down. We had a triple homicide this morning just outside the financial district. That's where I was coming from when you flagged me down."

Adam felt bad because he thought he was keeping the detective from his work.

"Do you want us to come back later on tonight or another day, Detective?"

Mundon looked back at Adam and laughed, "Brother, it's hit or miss around here. So if you come back another day, it might be just as busy. I can spare some time. Besides, I'm not working the triple. I was just down there giving those guys a hand. I'm assuming that you came up here to talk about Clay and JJ?"

"Yes, we did."

"Has anyone picked them up yet?"

Adam opened up his folder to take notes on their conversation, "No, not yet. As you may or may not know, they are suspects for seven murders and one stabbing in Kentucky."

"Yeah, we've been keeping close tabs on what's been going on down your way. Did you know that those two idiots are also suspects in a malicious wounding of a guy that lived down the street from them?"

"No, I didn't hear anything about a malicious wounding. What happened in that case?" Adam asked.

Mundon walked over to his file cabinet and retrieved two large three ring binders from the bottom drawer. He opened up the first binder to the report section to give Adam the 50-cent version.

"On October 15th of last year, two white males, matching the description of Clay and JJ, were seen breaking into a residence at 207 Renshaw Street. They were interrupted by the homeowner, who came home from work early because he was sick. He walked through his front door and was immediately attacked and severely beaten by the intruders. He was beaten so badly that the doctors at the hospital didn't think he was going to make it, so patrol called us to work the case. I arrived at the residence to find an absolute blood bath in the front hallway. They beat every square inch of his body with whatever they could get their hands on. Despite all odds, this poor bastard survived the beating. He's now confined to a wheelchair. He can't talk and for lack of a better term, they beat him retarded."

"Damn, that's pretty hardcore. What were they after do you think?"

Mundon looked down at his case notes and flipped to the back section.

"The victim in this case was a low level drug dealer, and some of the bigger players used his house to stash their dope. So, they were either there for the drugs or the money."

Mundon flipped back to the front of the binder and showed Adam some photographs from the scene. Adam looked at the pictures and saw two large pools of coagulated blood in the hallway just inside the front door. Two broken chair legs lay on either side of the hallway along with a cast iron skillet. There were three holes in the walls where the victim was violently thrown against them. Each hole was outlined in the victim's blood.

Adam continued to flip through the pictures with no reaction until he got to the pictures of the victim at the hospital. Although he felt sorry for the poor guy, it was nothing compared to what he had seen in Frankfort.

"Are you going to charge them with this, Detective Mundon?"

"I can't. No one is willing to talk."

"I thought I heard you say someone gave you a description? That person won't testify?"

"I had a little old black lady in her mid-eighties tell me, and let me make sure I quote her correctly." Mundon flipped through his notes until he got to the right page, "Here it is. She said, and I quote, "I seen these two white mother fuckers creeping around that house earlier in the day. But don't ask me nothing else. I didn't get a look at their faces." And since there aren't a ton of white people in that part of town, we were able to narrow it down to Clay and JJ pretty quick."

All Adam could do was laugh and say, "Good Lord."

"Now onto the Tara Johnson murder," Mundon continued as he closed the binder on the malicious wounding and opened a much thicker binder on the murder.

"What was the motive behind her murder do you think?" Adam asked.

"We haven't a clue. Her body was found five blocks away from her home in Fairview Park. Unfortunately, after hours, the park gets inundated with druggies and prostitutes, and Tara was both. She'd been arrested for possession and prostitution in the past, and was known to hang out in that park after dark. She did tricks for crack in the bathroom next to the playground. Several people walked past her body that morning thinking she was just a local drunk sleeping it off. At approximately nine in the morning, a jogger got suspicious after the third time she passed her body, so she went over to check on her. That's when she noticed that Tara wasn't breathing and called 911."

"Sorry to interrupt you, but do you mind if I record this? I don't want to miss anything."

"Not at all."

Adam pulled out his digital recorder from his jacket pocket, hit *record*, and placed it on the table in front of him.

Mundon continued, "Once we got there, we found Tara's lifeless body laying at the edge of the woods, with her skull bashed in. They did a real number on the back of her head." He pulled out a photograph of Tara's lifeless body and handed it to Adam.

"How long had the body been there, do you think?"

"We figure she had been there for at least a day and a half because rigor had come and gone. We canvassed the area around her body and were able to find her Ohio driver's license on the ground, just inside the wood-line. Her face was still intact, so I was able to make a positive identification on scene. I then ran her information through our DMV system and discovered that her boyfriend, Raymond "Clay" Whitley, had reported her missing the day before. After her body was removed from the park, we went to the house where Clay and Tara were living in the 2300 block of Wheeler Street to see if we could ask Clay a few more questions."

"Was he there?" Adam asked.

"No, he wasn't. But Tara's mother was. After we told her that her daughter was dead, she told us that the two of them had been fighting all day long on the day before she was reported missing and that she had heard Clay hit Tara a few times during the argument. Ms. Johnson was adamant she had seen her daughter, in their home, the morning before her body was found. That's when I came back to the station and looked up the missing persons report filed by Clay. He told the officer Tara had left the house two days before he called the police and that he hadn't seen her since. That's when Clay became our number one suspect."

Adam looked up from his note pad, "Was there any evidence left inside the house?"

"There was nothing that we could find. Although, the mom did say that there was an area rug missing from the master bedroom floor."

"Were you able to find it?"

"No, we weren't. I can tell you that it wasn't with her body when it was found, and it wasn't anywhere near the park. We even searched all the local dumpsters and trash cans looking for that thing. Since we didn't have anything linking Clay to the murder, he hung around town for a few more weeks before leaving for good."

"Did Clay say anything to Ms. Johnson before he left?"

"I have no idea. Ms. Johnson won't talk to us anymore. She's got it in her head that we aren't going to charge Clay with her daughter's murder and that we've given up on working the case. The last thing she said to me, before slamming the door in my face, was that our department was run by a bunch of idiots that couldn't care less about her daughter."

"You're making friends everywhere you go, huh? Did Clay have a job around here?"

Mundon flipped through the three-ring binder to the "Clay" section and perused his basic information.

"He was a self-employed as a handyman with some condominium complexes around the area, but no real full-time employment."

"Do you remember if he had any scheduled maintenance on December 17th or 18th of last year?"

"I'm not sure, but we can drive over to the condo offices and check. They're only a few miles down the road from here."

"Do you mind showing us the way?"

"Not at all. Just let me notify my sergeant that I'm going with you guys."

Detective Mundon walked out of his office and down the hall. A few minutes later he returned with his supervisor's blessings to chaperone Adam and David around the city.

"You two ready to go?" Mundon asked.

Adam and David both stood up, eager to get going, "Lead the way," Adam answered, as he pointed toward the exit.

The two detectives followed close behind Mundon as he navigated them out of the building the same way he had led them in. Once they were outside, they walked to Adam's unmarked and quickly hopped inside to escape the snow.

"Where to?" Adam asked.

Detective Mundon gave Adam turn-by-turn directions until they were in the parking lot of Hook Manor Condominiums. There was a large banner that hung over the office door bragging that they had several vacant apartments with the cheapest rent in the city, and after he looked at the grounds, Adam knew why. The off white stucco walls were in sorry shape, part of the roof was covered with a large blue tarp, and there was trash scattered all over the property. The dumpsters were overflowing with trash and there were several cars on jack stands in the parking lot. The place was an absolute dump and it didn't get any better once they were inside the rental office. Adam did his best to dodge the cockroaches that darted across the floor and in-between his feet. The whole place made his stomach turn.

"Can I help you?" The receptionist asked.

"Yes, ma'am. I'm Detective Mundon from the Cincinnati Police Department and these two gentlemen are Detectives from Stillwell, Kentucky. Do you have a minute to answer a few of their questions?"

"Certainly. What questions do you have?"

Adam cautiously approached the desk and opened his leather binder, making sure that nothing he had touched any surface in the rental office.

"We're looking for information on Raymond "Clay" Whitley. We understand he worked here as a handyman."

"That's right. He did."

"Can you tell me if he was scheduled to be here on December 17th or 18th of last year?"

"Is Clay in some sort of trouble?"

"You could say that. We're investigating a murder and his name came up in the middle of it."

"Seriously? Clay was always such a nice guy. I guess you never really know a person, huh?"

The receptionist stood up and walked to the file cabinet a few feet behind her desk. A few seconds later she brought back a large ledger book, sat back down at her desk, and opened the book to the back page.

"Okay, Clay was scheduled to fix three sinks and five toilets on December 17th, but he never showed up. It says here that the manager of the property tried calling him several times on the 17th and 18th, but he didn't answered his phone. And he still hasn't come back to get his last paycheck."

"Is it possible he was working at another complex at the time?"

"Nope, we have four complexes in this area that are all run by the same management company, so every tenant that needs maintenance calls here to schedule. The manager would then call Clay and let him know where and when he had to show up. Is there anything else I can help you with?"

Adam smiled briefly because he knew Clay could have had plenty of time to drive three and a half hours to Stillwell on the day of Melissa Dwyer's murder.

"No, ma'am. You answered all of my questions. Thank you for your time."

The trio turned and walked back to Adam's car in the parking lot. The snow had now started to fall faster and the flakes were getting much bigger.

"I think I need a hot shower and a tetanus shot after being in that place," Adam announced.

"Believe it or not, that was the cleaner of the four properties. We went to all four of them while trying to hunt

Clay down. Do you guys want to try talking to Ms. Johnson before you head on back to Stillwell?"

"Sure, we can give it a try."

Adam pulled out his cell phone and called Bishop to let him know what was going on while David took his turn behind the wheel and drove to the Johnson house following Mundon's directions. The drive was surprisingly short considering the time of day and the weather. David turned onto Wheeler Street and parked in front of 2308. The house was well maintained and not what he had pictured a mass murder's residence to look like. Adam could tell the exterior had been recently painted and the front porch looked inviting to passers-by.

Mundon looked over at Adam, "I'm going to stay in the car, guys. The mother's first name is Angela and she's a little standoffish. I may have forgotten to mention this earlier, but she threw a glass of lemonade in my face before she slammed the door the last time I was here. Good luck."

Adam and David got out of the car and walked up the front steps to the house. As they approached the porch, they could hear several small children running around the house. Adam stopped and listened at the front door for a few seconds, out of habit. He didn't hear anything out of the ordinary so he knocked. A few seconds passed before a small child answered the door.

"Hello there, is Mrs. Johnson home?" he asked.

The child ran away from the door, down the hallway, and returned with a frail-looking elderly black woman. She walked slowly and with an obvious deformity to her left leg. She was short with gray hair and the wrinkles of a hard life scattered all over her face.

"Whatever it is you two want, you can keep on walkin' 'cause I ain't got a damn thing to say to you."

Adam pulled his badge out of his back pocket and held it up to the door.

"We're Detectives from Kentucky, ma'am. Can we please come in and talk to you about Clay?"

"Why would I want to talk to you two assholes? I already told your kind that I'm through talking. If ya'll don't give a shit about my baby girl, then I don't give a shit about ya'll."

"Ma'am, we need your help. We wouldn't be here if it wasn't important. Please?"

"You can talk from there. I can hear you just fine."

"I understand that you don't trust us, but we're investigating a homicide that happened in Stillwell County, Kentucky, and we believe that Clay and JJ are the culprits."

Ms. Johnson held her hand up to stop Adam from talking.

"Well, there was a murder committed in this house and the police don't give a shit. Clay murdered my baby girl and these asshole cops ain't doing a fucking thing."

"Ma'am, if we can get Clay and JJ charged with our murder then we're going to seek the death penalty. Plus they've killed seven more people all over our state. There's no way in hell that they won't be put to death."

Ms. Johnson began to tear up as she spoke a little softer to Adam, "I'm sorry, Detective. I know I was rude, but the police around here are jerks. That monster took my baby girl's life and the police say they have no evidence to charge him. I'll do anything that I can to get them behind bars. How can I help you guys kill Clay and JJ?"

"May we please come in and talk to you?"

Ms. Johnson opened up the door wide enough for Adam and David to walk inside. They followed her down a narrow hallway to the kitchen and had a seat at the table. Adam opened up his notebook to a clean page and started asking more questions.

"When was the last time you saw Clay?"

"The week after they murdered my baby, I kicked him out of the house. I have no idea where he went after that."

"Have you ever known Clay or JJ to carry a gun or any weapons?"

"I've never seen him with any guns, but he carried a knife all the time. He was a handyman, you see. So he had tools on him at all times."

"Do you know if either Clay or JJ has any family in Kentucky?"

"They both have family down there. Clay's family is in Frankfort, Louisville, and Lexington. His mother lives in Frankfort I think. And from what I remember, JJ was dating some girl in Bowling Green. Other than that, I don't know of any other family they have."

Adam continued to ask Mrs. Johnson questions about Clay and JJ for the better part of an hour, but didn't get the smoking gun he was after. He handed Ms. Johnson a business card and copied down all her contact information just in case he needed to talk to her again.

"Ma'am, I'm truly sorry for your loss, and I hope we can make things right on our end. If you remember anything else or have any questions, please don't hesitate to call."

Mrs. Johnson thanked them for their dedication and escorted them to the door. The snow was falling heavily and it had started to accumulate on the roadway. Mundon was still in the passenger seat, talking on his cell phone, waiting patiently for Adam and David to return. Adam got behind the wheel and drove back to the homicide unit in the city.

"Thanks Detective for taking us around the city today. We couldn't have done this without your help. Do you collect police patches?" Adam asked.

"If you have one I won't turn it down."

He unzipped the front zipper to his leather carrying case and pulled out two Stillwell County Sheriff's Office patches and handed them to Mundon.

"Thanks for the patches gentlemen, and drive carefully going home."

"Hey, if you guys get enough evidence to charge Clay and JJ, are you going to swear out warrants?" Adam asked.

"We've talked about that in the office at length. I think we concluded that since Ohio doesn't have the death penalty like you guys do, it would be a shame to charge these guys up here and have them fight extradition back to Kentucky. I know your state will do the right thing."

He got out and left the passenger side door open for David to climb in before walking into the Police Department. David took his seat, closed the door behind him and the two deputies were headed south toward home. Adam stomach started to rumble so he looked down at the clock to see that it was 5:30 in the evening.

"You hungry, David? Dinner's on me tonight."

David started to laugh, "Yeah, I'm starving. I was beginning to think that you didn't eat."

Adam pulled off the interstate onto the first exit he came to once they were back over the river in Kentucky. They grabbed a couple of burgers from the drive-through and continued south, fearing they were going to get stuck in the nasty weather.

The snow followed them all the way back to Stillwell and the four-hour trip left Adam exhausted. He pulled into the lot and let David out at his car.

"See you tomorrow, David. I'm going home and straight to bed. I'll do my report in the morning when you do your supplement. See you around 8:30 or so?"

David slowly nodded his head as he turned around and walked directly to his cruiser. It was late and all Adam wanted to do was slip in between his covers. He quickly made the short drive home to find all the lights were off in the house and Rennae's car wasn't in the driveway. He parked in his usual spot and walked through the back door into the kitchen. He turned on the light and found an envelope with his name written on it propped up against the salt and pepper shakers on the table. He let out a sigh, because he knew what it was going to say. Adam bypassed the letter and went right to the fridge to get a beer. After taking two big swigs he returned to the table and sat down. He drank the entire beer never taking his eyes off the envelope. Three beers later, he was ready to read the letter. He picked up the envelope, slid out the single sheet of paper, and read;

Dear Adam,

These last few months have been really stressful for both of us and I know I said I would try to be more understanding about your job. But I just can't. You're never home, you hardly ever call me to let me know that you're okay, and you never answer your phone when I call. I've put a lot of things on hold for you and your career and I'm going to tell you right now that I'm not doing that anymore. I'm 26 years old and I want children. You probably don't know this because every time I bring up the subject, you start talking about something else. I've asked you several times to go back into general investigations or even go back to the street, but you have not done that. I have asked you several times to just pick up the phone and call me, but you can't even do that. So I have gone home to Michigan to be with my family and to take a break from us. You have a lot of thinking to do in the meantime. I don't expect a call from you tonight, but I do expect a call from you in the next week or so to let me know what you want to do. You need to decide if you want this marriage to work or if you want to simply end it the way things are. This is entirely up to you. I still love you very much Adam, but my life here isn't the life that I want. It's the life that you want. I hope to hear from you soon.
Love,
Rennae

Adam stood up, walked over to the refrigerator, and pulled out three more beers before sitting back down at the kitchen table. His was already feeling the effects from the previous three beers because the only food he had consumed was a cheeseburger four hours ago. He was half-way through his sixth beer before he was able to finally take his eyes off the letter. He had to, he needed another beer. Adam stood up, walked back to the refrigerator, and opened up the door to see six remaining beers. There was no way in hell he was going to go to bed before finishing them off. He knew that he had to go to work in the morning, but he didn't care, because tonight he was going to drink Rennae out of his mind.

Chapter 17

Adam woke up to the sound of his cell phone ringing somewhere near his head. Startled by the noise, he lifted his head off the floor and looked around. The remnants of an empty twelve pack were scattered across the kitchen floor where he lay, and the refrigerator door was wide open. He blinked his eyes slowly and shut them again because the light intensified his already pounding headache. It was then that he realized he had passed out in the middle of the kitchen floor in the same clothes he had come home in, and the letter which had sent him running to the bottle was pressed against his face. He reached in-between the empty bottles and grabbed his cell phone.

"Hello."

"Adam, where the hell are you?" David asked. "It's ten in the morning and Bishop is looking for you. He's about to send a unit by your house to see if you're still alive. Are you okay?"

"Yeah I'm fine. I wasn't feeling well when I got home last night, so I took some Nyquil. I must have slept through my alarm. Can you tell Bishop that I'm sick and won't be coming in this morning please?"

"Sure thing, and I hope you feel better."

Adam picked himself up off the floor, leaving all the empty beer bottles where they were and stumbled over to the couch. His body was sore all over from sleeping on the hard floor and his head was pounding. As he lay down on the couch and closed his eyes, the room began to spin.

"Oh shit!"

He sprang up off the couch and ran for the hallway bathroom to empty the remnants from last nights exploits into the toilet. Five minutes and fifteen dry heaves later, he was back on the couch. Adam leaned over toward the coffee table and grabbed the remote to see what daytime crap was on television. Instead of the usual talk shows and soap opera garbage which was normally on, he tuned in right in the middle of a press conference with the Chief of Police for the City of Mayfield.

"At this time, we have an elderly couple who was found murdered in their residence on Dowdy Street. We're not releasing their names until family members can be notified."

As he slowly sat upright to watch the television the phone rang. Adam answered on the third ring to an angry Bishop on the other end of the line.

"Adam, you had better get your ass in here right now!"

Adam didn't have the strength to argue with Bishop, "Sir, I have a fever of over 100 and I just took a pretty heavy dose of Nyquil. I'll be in the office a little later after this fever breaks."

There was silence on the other end of the line and then a loud click. He knew he was in deep shit, but it was either take the write up or lose his job because he was still drunk. Adam lay back down and was asleep as soon as his head hit the couch.

He woke up several hours later to the sound of someone pounding on the back door. He looked over at the clock and saw that it was now seven at night. Surprisingly he felt a lot better as he stood up to answer the door. Outside on the porch were Bishop and Gibbons. He knew this wasn't going to be a pleasant conversation by the expression plastered on Bishop's face. Adam placed his hand on the doorknob and looked back to see all the empty beer bottles still all over the floor. He slowly opened the door and motioned for them to enter.

"What the fuck Adam! We have two more people murdered in Mayfield and here you are drinking?"

Adam didn't say a word as he turned around and located Rennae's letter still on the floor. He reached down, picked it up, and handed it to Bishop to read. After he read the letter to himself, his attitude immediately changed.

"You should've let me know, Adam. How long ago did she write this?"

"I came home last night and found it on the table. One beer turned into twelve, and before I knew it, I was passed out on the kitchen floor. I'm sorry I lied to you, Sarge. It won't happen again."

Bishop gave Adam the once over, "You ready to get back to work? Because we really need you right now to look into this latest incident. I already put in a call to the Mayfield Chief and asked to be kept in the loop. He told me that they think Clay and JJ were responsible for this because a yellow Honda Accord was seen leaving the area with two white male passengers. I may need you two to take a trip down there. Who knows, maybe something of Melissa Dwyer's will turn up inside that car."

"Just let me take a quick shower and I'll meet you guys at the office. I'm fine to drive, Sarge."

"Take your time, Adam. We'll see you in an hour or so. David and I are going to get something to eat. Do you want anything?"

Food was the last thing on Adams mind, so he declined the offer, hit the shower, and twenty minutes later headed for his car. For the first time all winter there was a measurable amount of snow on the ground. After Adam had brushed off his car, he slowly made the drive to the office via the unplowed roadways. As he pulled into the snow-covered parking lot, he saw several work-release inmates, wearing their bright orange jumpsuits, shoveling the walkways and putting down salt. He parked in his usual spot and walked toward the building.

Out of the corner of his eye, Adam saw Bernie and several of the task force members walking into the jail with Bubba and Rocky's Woodchucks in cuffs. Bubba, being his usual loud self, was yelling at the top of his lungs that he was going to have all the task force members fired for making a wrongful arrest while Richard, Stuart, Charles, and Stephen walked silently behind. He was happy Bernie had been able to make an arrest and bring Bubba down, but he would much rather have been working with him on the Dwyer homicide.

Adam walked inside the building and down to the investigations wing. Bishop and David were inside Bishop's office eating their dinners and watching the news.

"Any news from Mayfield, Sarge?"

"Not yet, but I did talk with their Chief again. He said they have the FBI down there helping process their scene since we have two serial killers on our hands. He also said they lifted several prints from inside the garage that belong to Clay and JJ. Looks like it'll be the death penalty for both of these guys."

Bishop continued to eat, paying close attention to the news broadcast. The plan was to wait until the ten o'clock news and if nothing new transpired then they would call it a night.

"Go make me another sandwich, Adam," Bishop commanded.

Adam let out a laugh as he walked out of Bishop's office and down toward his. He wanted to update his timeline with the recent murders before returning for the news broadcast.

Ten o'clock came and went with nothing new on the murders. Bishop was about to call it a night when his phone rang.

"This is Bishop."

Adam hit the mute button on the remote, silencing the TV, just in time to hear Bishop's one sided conversation.

His facial expression turned sour for a few seconds before he responded, "Right now we just need to get these guys so we can interview them. I understand that we have zero physical evidence tying them to our scene. Yes, I understand all of that. How about this, we'll be in touch with you if we need anything. Yeah. Bye."

Bishop didn't even thank the person on the other end of the line before hanging up, peeking Adams curiosity.

"Who was that, Sarge?"

"That was Special Agent Who-Gives-A-Shit from the FBI. He was wondering if we needed their help with our homicide. Well, you know how the rest of the conversation went."

Adam chuckled momentarily as Bishop changed the channel to one of the major news networks. Much to everyone's surprise, they were talking about Clay and JJ. A reporter was standing outside the home of the elderly victims and was reporting live.

"According to several of their neighbors, the couple has lived on this street for 56 years."

The picture on the television changed to an older female with a microphone shoved in her face.

The caption on the bottom read, "Deloris Young, neighbor of the victims." The short, white-haired lady spoke softly and with a gentle southern drawl about the incident.

"Yes, they've been my neighbors for as long as I can remember. We played cards together every Thursday night and I'm going to truly miss them. They were wonderful people with kind hearts. Simon and Maryanne will both be missed very much."

The reporter took the microphone away from the lady and turned back toward the camera.

"The Chief of Police is scheduled to give another press conference here shortly. Hopefully he will be able to give us more insight into these gruesome murders. This is Ronald Grissom reporting live from Mayfield, Kentucky. Back to you guys at the station."

The picture on the television changed once again to a dapper young man who was dressed in a white shirt and a green tie. The caption under the news desk read "Murder Spree Across Kentucky" with the news anchor intently describing the timeline of Clay and JJ's exploits.

"Starting off in Cincinnati on December 5th, Raymond Whitley and his nephew Jimmy Jebb are suspects in the murder of Whitley's girlfriend, Tara Johnson. Her body was found in a local park just blocks away from their home with the back of her head severely beaten. That's when the two allegedly took their killing spree on the road, next in Princeton Kentucky. Here Raymond and Jimmy demanded money from a man who was out for an evening jog. When he refused to hand over his wallet, Raymond pulled out a knife and stabbed the man repeatedly. So far, he's the only victim who has survived."

The reporter went down the list of the rest of the massacres only giving a brief synopsis of each murder. After the two-minute segment was done Adam looked over at Bishop who was still stuffing his face.

"They didn't mention our murder. I wonder why?" Adam asked.

"I'm not sure. I've told everyone that these two are our suspects."

"What do you think, Sarge? You want to call it a night?"

"Yeah, let's call it a night, gentlemen."

The three tired men picked themselves up and walked outside to a cold blowing snow. Bishop waited for David to get into his car before he approached Adam.

"Hey, Adam. Go ahead take tomorrow off. If anything happens, dip-shit or I will take care of it."

"You really don't like him, huh?"

"Nope. Now go home and relax. That's an order."

"Thanks, Sarge."

Adam closed his car door and started the engine. As he pulled out of the lot, he gave Bishop a wave and briefly thought about calling Rennae, but instead he called Alexis to see what she was doing. The phone rang into her voice mail so Adam left a message telling her that he was finished for the evening and going home. After hanging up, he grabbed a quick cup of coffee at the Grub-N-Gas and continued towards home.

The snow was really starting to come down making the road conditions slick. It looked like four inches had already fallen and the weather report predicted at least two or three more over the next few hours. Adam was half way home when his phone rang. He looked down at the caller id to see it was Alexis calling him back.

"Hello, Ms. Leighton. How are you this cold and snowy night?"

She had a cheerful tone in her voice, more so than usual.

"I'm doing well, Adam. I'm up here at my grandfather's distillery for the weekend. We're celebrating his 75th birthday tomorrow. I wish you could be here with me."

Adam thought about making a trip up to Paris, Kentucky, but was brought back down to reality as the snow steadily hit his windshield.

"Me too, that would be a lot of fun. I assume the attendees will be a who's who of the elite Kentucky society."

"You could say that."

For Adam's entire drive home, the two of them talked about absolutely nothing, the way two people who meet for the first time do. He didn't want to hang up but decided that catching up on all the sleep he had been missing for the last few weeks was more important.

"I'm just now pulling into my driveway. Will you be home on Sunday, or are you making it a long weekend?"

"I'm thinking of heading home after the party tomorrow night. Will you be around?"

Adam contemplated telling Alexis that Rennae had left him, but decided against it. He didn't want anything to change about their relationship.

"Bishop gave me tomorrow and Sunday off, so I'll be around. Just let me know what time you'll be home and I'll try to meet you there."

"Okay, Adam. Have a good night's sleep and hopefully I'll see you Saturday night or Sunday if you can swing it."

"That sounds great."

Adam hung up his phone and walked into the dark, empty house with a smile on his face. But as soon as he turned on the light, he looked down at the floor where the empty beer bottles were strewn on the kitchen floor and was instantly reminded of Rennae's leaving. The good feeling he had was now gone. The letter she wrote was staring him in the face as it lay there on the kitchen table. He picked it up and re-read it, still in disbelief about what it said. After a few minutes of staring blankly at the words, Adam was brought back to reality by a rumble in his stomach.

Instead of standing there feeling sorry for himself, Adam decided to clean up the kitchen and make something to eat. With the last empty bottle in the trashcan, he walked over to the almost empty pantry, and weighed all his options. He knew he wasn't in the mood to cook, so his eyes gravitated toward the canned goods. After sifting through can after can of cream-of-whatever, he was able to find the last can of calm chowder hiding all the way in the back. He heated up his bounty in the microwave, grabbed a few stale saltine crackers, and retreated to the living room to watch the news. He grabbed the remote off the coffee table and turned to the local news to see the same reporter from earlier standing in front of the Mayfield house.

"Chief Dillon stated he would be holding a press conference in the morning to give us more details. At this time they still haven't released any motive for the killings. Back to you at the news desk."

Adam ate his dinner while he watched the rest of the news but he really wasn't paying attention. A ton of different thoughts were going through his head ranging from the homicide, to the incredible sex he has had with the county's commonwealth attorney, to Rennae's leaving him. He was sad his wife was gone, but he was also a little angry that she went back on their agreement. He vividly remembered her saying he could work this last murder and then he had to make a change. Why did she change her mind all of a sudden? Did she find out about Alexis and their affair on New Year's? Or was she just tired of being home alone in a hick county all the time? Whatever her reasoning, Adam was having a difficult time understanding it. He had every intention of going to Bishop after the investigation was over and asking for his job in patrol back.

He knew he couldn't go back to working general investigations after working major cases. He would go crazy telling people that he was sorry about their smashed mailbox all the time.

Adam looked down at his phone and saw that he had one missed text message from Alexis.

"Hey Adam, just headed off to bed and was thinking about you. I'll try to text you later on tomorrow. I kind of wish I were hanging out with you right now instead of with all these old bourbon distillers and senators. It makes for a boring night if you ask me. Hope to see you soon. Sweet dreams."

A smile came back to Adams face as he deleted the text. He couldn't get Alexis out of his head. He wanted to be with her but knew the right thing to do was eventually try to patch things up with his wife. Either way, he knew he would have to call Rennae in the next few days to see where things stood. Adam turned off the lights and headed upstairs, content with calling it a night. He walked into the bathroom, took off his shirt and pants, and threw them on the floor next to the hamper. After brushing his teeth, he grabbed a fresh tee shirt from his dresser drawer and crawled into bed. Tomorrow had to be a better day.

Adam opened his eyes and looked over at the alarm clock to see that it was already two in the afternoon. He contemplated going back to sleep, but decided to get up and try to go for a run instead. Walking over to the window, he could see the snow was still falling lightly, and by his estimation there was at least 5 inches on the ground. He went to the closet and pulled out his winter running gear and walked down to the kitchen to get something light to eat. In his mind he wanted to get at least seven or eight miles in but decided that five would be okay too. He ate a small bowl of oatmeal along with a cup of coffee and went out for his run. Once again his mind was swimming with emotions and thoughts he could not control and before he knew it he was running into town. Looking at the GPS on his watch, Adam saw that he had already run five miles.

The five miles back to his house went by just as quickly as the trip into town. Once back in his kitchen, Adam shed his wet jacket and went over to check his phone which was charging by the sink.

"Five missed calls, all from an unknown number? I wonder who in the hell that could be?"

Scrolling through his menu, he was able to see he had two text messages. One was from Bernie, and the other was from Alexis. Saving the best for last, he looked at Bernie's text first.

"Hey Adam, I talked to Bishop and I'm just checking in to see if you need anything. Give me a shout later and we can go out for a beer or something."

Since Alexis was out of town, Adam thought that a night out on the town might be a good idea to take his mind off of everything. Now for the text he really wanted to read.

"Hey Adam, just wanted to let you see what you're missing by not being here with me."

Below the message was Alexis standing in a full length evening gown looking as stunning as ever. As much as it pained him to delete the picture, Adam knew that leaving any evidence behind was a bad idea. After getting rid of the picture he decided to give Bernie a call.

"Hey Bernie, you have any plans for tonight or can we still go out for that beer? I could sure use a night out"

"I was wondering if you were gonna call. Sure, we can head out for a beer if you want. I need to go to the office to take care of some paperwork, but afterwards the boys and I were gonna grab a beer or two. You want me to pick you up at nine or do you want to meet me at the office?"

"I think I'll drive in and meet you at the office. I have a few things I need to update with my case anyways. See you there in a few."

Adam hung up the phone and gave Alexis a quick call before going up to take a shower.

"This is Alexis Leighton, commonwealth attorney for Stillwell County, please leave me a message after the sound of the tone and I will get back to you as soon as possible."

Adam decided to not leave her a message and went upstairs to clean up.

The roads still had not been properly plowed which made for another slow trip into town. As Adam walked into the office he saw Bernie packaging and cataloging evidence from his big bust the other night.

"You need any help, Bern?"

"No, Bro. I'm almost finished with this. You go and take care of your shit and then we're out of here. Three of my guys are meeting us at The Still House at nine."

The Still House was a local bar that was over by the college. Since the kids were out on Christmas break, they were assured of having a quiet evening without all the students making asses of themselves. Adam couldn't wait to play a little pool, throw some darts, and have a few beers to help forget things for a while. Paperwork completed, Adam followed Bernie down the street.

Three beers in, Bernie tapped Adam on the shoulder, "You see those two guys down there?"

Adam looked down the bar to see two rather large locals having a disagreement.

"I bet you the guy in the red shirt destroys the guy in the black shirt."

"You're on!"

The two detectives settled back on their stools, paying close attention to what was happening at the other end of the bar.

"Have we figured out what they're fighting about yet?" Adam asked.

"No, but it's about to get physical."

No sooner had Bernie gotten the last word out of his mouth, than the guy in black let fly a haymaker that connected square on the jaw of the guy in red.

"Are we gonna step in Bern?"

"Fuck no, let the local Police Department do some work for a change."

The female bartender picked up the phone and frantically dialed 911. She asked for the rescue squad as well because the guy in the red shirt was out cold and bleeding all over her floor.

"Pay up, bitch." Adam gloated.

After the three ring circus calmed down and Mr. Red and Mr. Black were on their way out, Bernie decided to ask Adam how he was doing.

"You know, Bernie, I knew she was tired of me being a detective with the long hours and stuff, but she didn't have to walk out on me like this. She gave me an ultimatum, and then backed out on it. I just don't get it."

Bernie really didn't know what to say, so he just let Adam do the talking, offering his two cents every once in a while. Adam went down the laundry list of problems they were having and admitted to having his own flaws, but not admitting to the whole demise of his marriage being his fault.

"I guess I'll just have to wait and see what she does. But until then, it's boy's night out, every night!"

Bernie let out a laugh knowing damn well they would both be divorced if he went out every night.

Adam looked down at his watch to see that it was already midnight.

"Well Bernie. It's time for me to head on home."

Bernie looked down at his watch and then back at Adam.

"You pussy. It's only midnight. Tomorrow's Sunday and you ain't got shit to do. What's up?"

"Nothing, Bro. I just want to get in another run tomorrow. Felt good to get back out there."

Bernie picked up the tab for their night's debauchery and the two went their separate ways. As they walked out of the Still House, Adam noticed the snow had finally stopped falling.

"Drive safe, Bern."

Bernie looked back at Adam, "You too, brother."

Chapter 18

Adam's afternoon run went just like the one the day before. It was cold at the start, but he quickly warmed up along his out and back route. Once safely at his house, he walked over to his kitchen counter and picked up his cell phone to see that he had missed a text from Alexis.

"Hey Adam, I was just wondering what you're up to today. I'll be home around two or so if you can swing on by. I'm looking forward to seeing you a little bit later."

The time on the top of his phone said it was already three fifteen.

Adam hit the reply button on Alexis's text, "Hey, I just got back from a run. If you're home, I'll take a shower and come over. I have a little time to spare if you do."

He placed his phone back on the charger and went upstairs to take a shower. In record time he was back down in the kitchen checking to see if Alexis had responded. Much to his dismay, she hadn't.

Adam put his phone in his pocket and walked into the living room to see what was on the TV and to wait for Alexis to return his text. Almost immediately he found himself immersed in old reruns of the Andy Griffith Show. He loved the show because Barney reminded him of a few of the town police officers he had interacted with over the years and Stillwell had its fair share of town drunks. Earnest T. Bass was about to throw another brick through the Mayberry Sheriff's Office window when Adam heard the sound of his phone ringing. His heart began to race, hoping it was Alexis, but he was let down when he looked at the LED screen and saw that it was Bishop.

"I thought you said I could have the weekend off. What gives?"

"Well, if you don't want to know that Clay and JJ are currently surrounded by the Nashville SWAT team, at Clay's father's house, then I'll talk to you later."

"No, no. Are you at the office?"

"No, but I'll be headed that way in a few minutes. The wife has me taking down the damn Christmas lights from the gutters."

"I'll be there as soon as I can, Sarge."

Adam shot up off the couch and rushed out of the house toward his car. While in route to the office, he called David to tell him about the new developments and that a trip to Nashville might be in their immediate future.

"Seriously, they have them surrounded?" David asked.

"Yeah, now get dressed and come to the office. I'm pulling into the lot as we speak."

"I'm on my way."

Adam ended the call on his cell phone and pulled into his assigned parking space in the back lot. He knew he had a few minutes to kill before everyone got there so he went inside and made a pot of coffee. While he waited for it to brew, Adam walked down the hall and jiggled Bishop's office door to see if it was unlocked. When the handle didn't turn, Adam pulled out a credit card from his wallet and let himself in. After he was inside he turned on the news, took a seat and put his feet up on Bishop's desk.

"You comfortable?" Bishop scoffed at Adam.

"They haven't said anything about Clay and JJ on the news yet. How did you hear about this?"

"How the hell did you get in here? I know I locked the door before I left."

"They taught us how to pick locks in the first grade up in Detroit. Now, back to my original question, how did you hear about this?"

"I got a call from Detective Howell in Frankfort. They're working closely with the FBI, who gave him a call about an hour ago. Supposedly, one of the detectives who work for the fugitive apprehension division in Nashville got a call from an informant telling him that Clay and JJ were there. SWAT mobilized immediately, surrounded the house and confirmed with Clay's father that the two were in the basement. As of 30 minutes ago they were barricaded inside the townhouse with negotiators attempting to make contact."

Adam diverted his attention to the big screen TV hanging on Bishops wall as the breaking news was just coming in.

The caption under the news desk read, "Murderers Take Refuge in Music City." The news anchor handed the broadcast off to a field reporter who was standing in front of a Nashville Police Cruiser with its blue lights flashing. Off in the distance Adam could see three sets of blinking red lights from helicopters jockeying for position over the house. One of them had the spotlight shining on a single unit in a row of townhouses. Occasionally the camera would change from the ground to an aerial view from one of the helicopters, giving a great bird's-eye view of the scene. There were numerous marked police cruisers, with blue lights flashing, making a perimeter for containment of two full city blocks. Adam looked down at his watch and saw that it was six in the evening and returned his attention back to the television.

"We're live at the Sam Levy Housing Projects, just outside of Nashville, where sources have confirmed that Raymond Whitley and Jimmy Jebb are inside one of these townhouses. Negotiators have made contact with the pair and they're refusing to come out. Nashville Police are using their armored vehicle to help evacuate the residents of other townhouses in the complex. Because the suspects are believed to be the "Kentucky Serial Killers," every precaution is being taken to protect the public. The occupants of the complex are being told to remain inside their homes until they can be safely evacuated by the armored vehicle. I've been told by the local authorities that protocol dictates they try to do everything they can to come to a peaceful resolution. They hope the suspects can be persuaded to surrender, but they are willing to go in and get them if absolutely necessary."

Adam became too anxious watching the coverage so he excused himself to go get a cup of coffee. After he was inside the small kitchen, he checked his cell phone to see if Alexis had called or texted. There was one missed call with no message from her, so Adam called her back to let her know that he wasn't going to be able to make it over to her house right away.

Alexis answered her phone with a very seductive, "Hello, detective."

"Hey there, Alexis. I have some bad news. Well good news and bad news. The bad news is that I won't be making it over to your place for a while. The good news is that my suspects, Clay and JJ, are surrounded in Nashville by the local authorities. I'm thinking that David and I may be headed that way in the next few hours depending on how it all plays out."

"Well that is good and bad news. Please be careful and let me know when I can see you again."

"You'll be the first to know, trust me. I'll talk to you later."

Adam hung up the phone and walked back into Bishop's office with three fresh cups of coffee.

"Did I miss anything?"

Bishop took one of the cups out of Adam's hands and placed it on his desk.

"No, same old shit so far. Like rats in a hole, they're gonna have to smoke 'em out."

The picture on the screen was still the same—with the helicopters flying in the distance. Then the camera angle changed to an overhead shot from one of the choppers with a close-up of the townhouse that Clay and JJ were holed up in. From an aerial view they were able to see one row of town homes in the Sam Levy Housing Project. The grass was tall, there were broken toys scattered throughout the front yard, and the chain link fence was broken in half rendering it useless. The green siding was discolored and a majority of it was barely hanging on. There was a single remaining shutter that hung over one of the front windows and the back yard resembled the neighborhood landfill.

The broadcast at the scene was interrupted a few times with other top stories from around the country and the world. After each story, they returned to the Sam Levy Housing Project with a camera trained on the armored car evacuating families.

"We've just seen a second armored vehicle, this one from the state police, arrive at the scene. It seems that eight or nine of the residences on the block have not yet been evacuated. The Nashville Police and their armored vehicle have been working hard to get the remaining families out safely, but they needed some help from the state to speed things up. I don't know if you can see this, but another SWAT truck has just showed up and I've counted another 10 SWAT team members in addition to the seven that are already here."

Adam and Bishop watched as the camera panned over toward the SWAT team, who were congregated next to the command post. The heavily armed team members were quickly ushered inside the large motorhome to be briefed on the situation. Uniformed officers were scurrying in the background relieving one another on the perimeter. Noticing that it was seven o'clock, Adam felt bad for everyone who had to remain outside. The temperature in Nashville was only a few degrees higher than in Stillwell. If they didn't surrender soon, it was going to be a long, cold night.

Adam, David, and Bishop were watching the broadcast when Bishop's desk phone rang, taking everyone's attention away from the television.

On the second ring he answered, "Investigations, this is Sergeant Bishop."

"Yes, Sheriff. I see what's going on."

Bishop held the phone away from his ear for a few seconds and acted like he wasn't interested in what Lawson was saying.

"Sure thing, Sheriff. I'll let you know as soon as they're in custody."

David looked over at Adam and mouthed, "He's at some dinner for the town council."

Adam nodded at Gibbons and went back to the television. The story unfolding in front of them was more like a movie than a homicide investigation. Adam had mixed emotions about how he wanted the standoff to end. A small part of him wanted them to go down in a hail of gunfire. Their bodies pierced by hot lead, ripping through their skin, making it a slow and painful death. He wanted them to feel the same pain they had inflicted on all of their victims. The remaining part of him wanted them to be brought to justice through the Stillwell County Judicial System. To see them sit in his courtroom, in front of his judge, sentenced to death at the hands of his jury. That would be the only reason he would want them to live. But either way, they were as good as dead.

Time slipped away from the three deputies as they sat, watching the broadcast of the standoff. Bishop made several calls to Detective Howell checking on the status of things but got his voicemail every time. Adam was already on the computer getting directions to Nashville, thinking they could make it to the scene in just under five hours. He wanted to be there when they interviewed these guys to make sure they didn't forget to inquire about their murder.

"Bishop, when can I drive down to Nashville with David?"

"Hold your horses, boy. They haven't even got the guys out of the house yet. And who is to say they'll come out alive. To be honest with you, I hope they kill the sons of bitches so we can close this case without a trial."

Adam was contemplating making another pot of coffee, but decided against it when he realized that it was already ten o'clock.

"You guys want a pizza or something else to eat?" Adam asked.

"Pizza sounds good to me. David, is pepperoni and sausage good for you?"

David didn't respond but rather pointed up toward the television.

"BREAKING NEWS FROM NASHVILLE. Raymond Whitley and Jimmy Jebb were taken into custody moments ago by the Nashville Police Department SWAT Team. According to Lieutenant Brian Gilliam, SWAT team commander, Raymond Whitley sustained minor injuries during his capture, while Jimmy Jebb gave up without a struggle and is being transported back to the homicide division for questioning. We'll have more on this in five minutes when Nashville Police Captain, Andre Chriswell, commander of the Criminal Investigations Bureau, will be giving a press conference."

All eyes remained on the television until the press conference convened. The camera was pointed at the side of the mobile command center when the white shirted captain walked into view. He stood at a makeshift podium, which housed numerous microphones from the many news organizations that were following the apprehension.

"I'm Captain Andre Chriswell from the Nashville Police Department. Tonight at approximately 9:46 pm, Raymond Whitley and Jimmy Jebb were taken into custody by our SWAT officers. Mr. Whitley sustained some non-life-threatening injuries prior to being taken into custody. He refused to obey the commands of our officers and therefore, they used the amount of force necessary to make the arrest. One of our officers was injured during the arrest and was transported to the hospital for treatment. He's expected to be okay and released within the hour. Mr. Jebb obeyed all of the commands that were given to him and was taken into custody without incident. Are there any questions?"

The captain pointed to the different reporters in the crowd singling out those from the major news outlets first. The questions were coming at the Captain from every direction and he did his best to make sure he answered as many as possible. Many of the reporters were asking questions about the other murders and trying to confirm rumors which had been spreading since January 1st, but the Captain refused to speculate. Roughly five minutes into the questioning, the Captain held up his hand to indicate that the conference was over. It was obvious that everyone wanted answers to questions that he couldn't answer, so he turned his back on the reporters and disappeared into the command bus, leaving everyone dissatisfied.

Bishop looked over at Adam, "Now we just have to play the waiting game. I know those guys are going to eventually take them down to homicide and try to get a confession."

"I just hope they don't screw anything up for us by doing that."

"Nah, they have a pretty high murder rate down there. I'm sure they know what they're doing."

"I hope you're right, Sarge."

"Well, boys, looks like you two are on your way to Nashville in the next few days. I figure that extradition back here is going to take a few months and it's going to be interesting to see who gets them first. I think we should wait a few days to let the dust settle and see if they confess before we proceed. Besides, I have a feeling that if you were in Nashville tomorrow you'd be in a very long line waiting to talk to these guys."

"Very true, but if I can get in there and get confessions out of these guys I can get warrants for them before they get back to Kentucky."

"Just relax, Adam. I'll see what I can do about getting you in there to talk to these guys in the near future."

David didn't say a whole lot but was excited about the opportunity to accompany Adam on the interviews.

"Do you need me to do anything, Adam?"

"Yes, David. I need you to get every detail about these guys together for us to use. Go over their criminal histories with a fine-toothed comb. I want you to know everything that they've ever done from robbery to jaywalking. For every offense listed I want you to contact that agency and get copies of the reports if you can. If they won't fax it over and ask you for a subpoena, then just ask what the case was about. I'm going to start going back through all my notes and get our questions together. This might be a giant waste of time because I know these guys will play it hard and lawyer up, but we better have all our ducks in a row just in case. I'm headed home for the night. Is there anything else you want me to do, Bishop?"

"No, I'll see you two in the morning."

After three hours of looking over his case notes in bed, Adam turned out his light and tried to close his eyes. After about fifteen minutes of tossing and turning, it was obvious that he wasn't going to get any sleep, so he turned the light back on and grabbed his notes. While he looked over page after page he thought about how he was going to handle sitting across the table from two serial killers. He had worked with the worst of the worst back in Detroit, but it hadn't been his job to get a confession. This was by far the biggest case of his career and he didn't want to screw things up. His apprehension turned to fear when he thought about the possibility that Clay and JJ hadn't kill Melissa Dwyer. What would he do then? He gradually regained control of his thoughts and concluded that he would just have to take everything one step at a time, but first he had to get past these two suspects.

Adam looked over at the clock and saw that it was almost time for him to get up and get going. But just before his alarm started chirping, Adam let his mind wander to the murder he had worked five months ago. He had to laugh because the circumstances around that homicide were pretty funny. One night, Earl Crippon came home from the local watering hole and found his wife in bed with the preacher from their church. Earl had two shotguns sitting inside the closet, one was filled with slugs for hunting and the other was filled with rock salt to keep the neighbors dogs away from his chickens. He meant to grab the shotgun filled with rock salt but grabbed the wrong gun by accident. Earl shot the preacher in the back as he was trying to jump out of the bedroom window, naked. Adam remembered walking into the bedroom for the first time and seeing the preacher's bare ass staring back at him. What a night that had been.

Adam was instantly brought back to reality by the buzzing of the alarm clock on the bedside table. He groggily went through his normal morning routine and headed into the office without a cup of coffee. It had been a few days since Rennae had left and there were no groceries left in the house. He parked his car and before he could get out he was met by Bishop standing next to his door.

"You aren't going to believe this, but they got a full confession from Clay last night. A full fucking confession! You and David need to get down there as soon as possible. I already called the Nashville P.D. to let them know you are on your way. They told me to have you look for Detective Frank Riddell and he'll be expecting you sometime this afternoon. Here's the credit card for gas, hotel, and food. Go easy on me. This isn't a vacation."

A surge of adrenaline shot through Adam's body, and for a brief moment he forgot about his desperate need for coffee. Without another word, he snatched the credit card out of Bishop's hand, threw his car in reverse and drove home to get some clothes for the trip. As he was pulling into his driveway, he pulled out his cell phone and called David to let him know the new developments.

"What's up, Adam?"

"I'm coming to your place to pick you up in the next half hour. Clay actually gave a full confession last night, so we're on our way to Nashville to see if we can hear it with our own ears. Pack a bag just in case we need to stay down there for the night."

Adam could hear the cries of children in the background followed by the David's wife yelling at the boys to stop hitting one another.

"I'll be ready when you get here."

Adam hung up the phone and ran inside his house to throw some clothes in a suitcase and get on the road. Fifteen minutes later, as he was pulling into David's driveway, he saw David waiting on his front porch. He threw his bag into Adam's trunk and the two were off to Nashville, hopefully, to put an end to this case.

Chapter 19

Adam drove around the Nashville Police Station three times before having to expand his radius on the city streets in search of a parking space. Fifteen minutes later, he was able to find one five blocks away. David dug in his pockets and found four quarters for the parking meter while Adam made sure he had enough blank paper in his leather notebook, just in case they wouldn't let him take a copy of the confession back to Stillwell.

"You ready for this, David?"

"As ready as I'll ever be."

Adam made sure the car was locked before he and David started back toward the Nashville Police Department. As they walked, Adam noticed that the majority of the parking spots were taken up by either Nashville police vehicles or large SUV's with tinted windows and Federal Government license plates.

"Damn feds are everywhere," Adam commented.

"Yeah, this does seem like a little bit of overkill."

Within a few minutes, Adam was opening up the front door to the police station and walking up to the receptionist in the lobby.

"Can I help you gentlemen?" she asked.

Adam flashed his credentials and answered, "Yes, ma'am. We're here to see Detective Frank Riddell."

"Why don't you two have a seat over there in the lobby and I'll page him for you."

After taking a seat, Adam picked up a magazine on bicycling and turned to the section detailing the routes of this year's Tour de France. He loved watching the tour and under different circumstances he would have loved to have read the article, but today his only interest was in getting a confession. After a few minutes of mindlessly flipping through the pages, Adam placed the magazine back on the coffee table and anxiously stared at the secured door next to the receptionist. It didn't take long for a sharply dressed detective to walk into the lobby and over toward him.

"Are you two from Stillwell County Sheriff's Office?"

Adam jumped to his feet and extended his hand, "Yes sir, we are. I'm Detective Alexander and this is Corporal Gibbons."

"I'm Detective Riddell. You two can follow me to the homicide unit and I'll fill you in back there."

Adam was so intent on following Riddell back to the homicide wing that he completely ignored everything else. They were led down a series of long hallways and eventually into a conference room with surveillance monitors and recording equipment along the back wall.

"Have a seat and I'll be right back with the transcripts of Clay's confession."

David took a seat at the round table, while Adam walked to the back wall to see what kind of equipment they used. As he was looking at one of the monitors he saw a detective questioning a white male with a very familiar face in one of the interview rooms.

"David! That's JJ in the interview room!"

Adam looked for the volume control for that particular monitor but was unable to find it.

"I wonder if they'll let us talk to him?" Adam inquired out loud.

"That probably wouldn't be a good idea, Detective," Adam heard from over his shoulder. When he turned around he saw Detective Riddell standing in the doorway with two small stacks of paper in either hand. He walked in the room, placed the transcripts on the table and continued, "As you know, there are a few other agencies that have an interest in getting their hands on these guys."

Adam walked away from the back wall and took a seat at the table in front of one of the transcripts.

"I can appreciate that, Detective Riddell. But it also never hurts to ask. Now, what can you tell us?"

"I was the one that brought Clay from the scene back here to the homicide unit last night. If you turn to page three, you can see that Clay was properly mirandized before any questions were asked, he initialed next to each Miranda warning and verbally acknowledged he understood his rights. If you flip to page four, that's where the interview starts. Now, I'm going to tell you right away. I've been doing this job for 15 years, 10 of which has been spent here in homicide, and let me tell you, this is the coldest son of a bitch I've ever dealt with. Just wait till you get to the Dutch murders. It made me sick just listening to him."

Adam looked at the last page of the transcript and saw that it was ten pages long.

"Does Clay admit to everything in here?"

"Almost everything, Detective. I asked him about your murder a couple of times and he denied it. I even tried to trip him up by asking him what he did with the gun they used. He didn't bite. But don't get discouraged, we have JJ in the interview room right now with another detective. He's been instructed to ask JJ about your murder, so I'll let you know when it's over. And just to let you guys know, Tennessee law requires a subpoena for those transcripts, so I'm going to need them back when you're finished. While I'm gone, feel free to take whatever notes you may need, if you catch my drift. I'll be at my desk if you need me."

Adam turned to page three and began reading the interview.

***Riddell**: Today's date is January 12, 2009, and I have in front of me Raymond "Clay"* ***Whitley**. Mr. Whitley has been read his Miranda rights and has agreed to talk with me today. Is that correct Mr. Whitley?*
***Raymond Whitley**: My name is Clay. Call me Clay or this interrogation is over. You understand me?*
***Riddell**: Okay, Clay. Have you been threatened or promised anything today for talking to me?"*
***Raymond Whitley**: No, you haven't promised me shit. But I'm a dead man anyways so I'm gonna' just talk.*
***Riddell**: Okay, Let's talk about December 15th, 2008. Your girlfriend, Tara Johnson, was found murdered in a park,*

blocks away from your home. Can you tell me what happened?

***Raymond Whitley**: Yeah, that bitch was up my ass all day long buggin' me for money. She wanted to go out and smoke crack and not come home for a few days. I told that bitch I wasn't givin' her shit and she needed to get the fuck away. But she didn't. Later on that afternoon she looked at me and told me that she would fuck me if I gave her money, so I told that bitch to meet me in the bedroom in an hour. JJ was in the living room playing video games so I asked him to help me kill this bitch. We came up with a plan, so JJ went upstairs and hid in our bedroom closet with a big ass lead pipe. The plan was for him to watch me fuck this bitch, and when she sits up on top of me, he comes out the closet and smacks her in the back of the head with the pipe.*

***Riddell**: And is that what happened?*

***Raymond Whitley**: Yeah, that's what happened. But the little pussy didn't hit her hard enough. He came out and half-assed it. She went to the ground but she didn't go out. She just laid there all dazed. Like she was high or something.*

***Riddell**: What happened next?*

***Raymond Whitley**: I had to take the pipe and finish the job myself. I hit that bitch seven or eight more times in the head before she stopped breathing. Since she got blood all over the rug, JJ and I wrapped her dead ass up in it and carried her down to my work truck. JJ and I drove around for a few hours trying to figure out what to do with the body. Fuck, we even bought weed from a dude with that dead bitch in the back. When we were drivin' down the main street I saw the entrance to the park where she normally smokes crack, so I drove in and around to the back where she fucks dudes for money. I dumped her body there. I figured it would take someone five or six days to find her but I guess not. Fuck that bitch.*

***Riddell**: What happened to the rug that you used to carry the body?*

***Raymond Whitley**: We put that shit in a dumpster a few blocks away.*
***Riddell**: Then what did you two do?*
***Raymond Whitley**: We smoked the shit out of that weed I bought to calm down. Then I come up with the plan to report the bitch missing. Stupid ass cops bought it too. We even hung around town for a few more days.*
***Riddell**: Now before that, there was a report of a guy that was severely beaten. Do you know anything about that?*
***Raymond Whitley**: Fuck that dude. He was a snitch and a drug dealer anyways. Next.*
***Riddell**: Now let's go to December 18th, to Stillwell County, where a woman named Melissa Dwyer was found murdered and her house set on fire.*
***Raymond Whitley**: Stillwell? Where the fuck is Stillwell County?*
***Riddell**: You did time in Big Sandy State Penn. That's in Stillwell County.*
***Raymond Whitley**: We didn't do anything in Stillwell County. Don't try to pin no shit on us that we didn't do, man. Not like it matters though. We're headed for Death Row as it is.*
***Riddell**: Okay, how about on December 31st, in Princeton Kentucky. A gentleman named Jarrod Stanley was stabbed in an attempted robbery.*
***Raymond Whitley**: Yeah, JJ was driving me around that night when we ran out of beer. I didn't have any cash money on me so we started looking for someone to rob. This dumb ass dude was jogging down the street, so I get out and ask for his wallet. He tells me he ain't got no money so I stab his ass a few times hoping he would just give it up. He took off running and I was too drunk to chase his ass, so I just got back in the truck and we drove off. I knew that fucker had money too. How bad did I cut him?*
***Riddell**: He survived and he positively identified you as the one who stabbed him, according to the FBI report we have.*
***Raymond Whitley**: The FBI was chasing our asses around?*

Riddell: *Yes, the FBI was working with the local authorities chasing you guys around.*
Raymond Whitley: *What next chief? I'm getting tired here and I don't know how much longer I'm gonna want to talk.*
Riddell: *January 1st, 2009, a family of four was found murdered in their basement in Frankfort, Kentucky. What can you tell me about that incident?*
Raymond Whitley: *We were driving around all hung over and shit from the night before. JJ and I got high and drunk with a couple of bitches down the road. So we were looking for a place to get some fast cash. We needed to get back to Cinci and I had zero funds. So we drive down this street with some nice ass houses, but it didn't look like anyone was home at any of them. Till we get to this one house. The storm door was closed but the front door was open. It was the only one like that on the whole fuckin' block. That's why we picked that house. I go up to the door and this white dude answers. I ask if I can use his phone because my truck is broke down. He looks over my shoulder and see's my hood up on the truck in the street so he lets me and JJ in. While I fake a call to a friend of mine, JJ looks around and sees that it's just him, his wife and two little girls. So I drop the phone and pull out my knife to stab the dude in the chest. You know, to let them know we mean business. After I stab the dude, he fell to the floor and that's when JJ runs over and throws the two girls on the floor and tells them to shut the fuck up. I ran over to the wife and put the knife to her throat and told the dude that he either gives us the money or his wife is dead.*
Riddell: *Were you able to get any money?*
Raymond Whitley: *Fuck no. Dude says he didn't have any. But before I can ask again, the doorbell rings. That's when the white lady tells me that she's expecting a friend to come to the house to help her with something. I pull the knife tight against her neck and tell her to go answer the door and tell her friend that she's sick. Before I let her go, I told her that if she tells her friend that we were there, I was going to kill her entire family.*

***Riddell**: Weren't you worried that she would tell her friend to call the police?*
***Raymond Whitley**: No, I heard the whole conversation. When she comes back we try to tell them that we won't hurt them if they just give us the money. Dude kept telling us he didn't have any. So I ask about an ATM card or Credit Card. Dude says he had a credit card but that was it. I look at JJ and he says we should take them down to the basement to tie them up before we leave. I walk with the dude and the white lady to the basement door with the knife to dudes throat. Once we get there I push her down the steps and slash dudes throat. He falls down the stairs and lands on the white lady. JJ grabs the two little girls by their hair and follows me down the stairs. I grab the white lady and put the knife to her throat too. I tell her one more time to give up the cash or everyone dies. She started to cry and said she didn't have no money, so I look over at JJ. He picks up this claw hammer he finds on a shelf next to the washer and dryer and smacks the small white girl on the back of the head with that shit. Blood flew fucking everywhere. So the little white girl falls to the ground near the dude, but she ain't dead yet so I stomp on her leg till it breaks and JJ come over and finish her off with the claw hammer. I seen her brains hit the floor. The white lady tries to get away from us and run up the stairs so I tackle her. She hit me in my face so I slit her throat and stab the shit out of her over and over. I stabbed that bitch at least 50 times I think. I stomped on her leg till it broke too. JJ walks over to the older white girl and just goes fucking crazy on her. She didn't know what hit her. She was the last one to die. She watched us kill her entire family and she didn't make a sound. I think she pissed herself before JJ went crazy on her. I had to pull him off. As we were going back upstairs, dude was still trying to breathe so I put my boot on his throat till he stops moving. He was already dead, he just didn't know it yet. JJ gets the gas can from the corner and pours it all over the bodies.*

***Riddell**: Is that when you set the Dutch family and the residence on fire?*
***Raymond Whitley**: No, JJ and I go upstairs and look for the money for a few minutes, but when we don't find any we go back down stairs and set that shit on fire. It went up quick too. JJ grabbed some cookies and the white ladies purse, I think from the counter, as we ran out the door to my truck.*
***Riddell**: Cookies and a purse were the only things you took from that house after you killed the entire family?*
***Raymond Whitley**: Looks like it. Next?*
***Riddell**: On January, 6th of this year, your pickup truck was found at a residence in Bowling Green, Kentucky, and three residents were found murdered in a townhouse.*
***Raymond Whitley**: Yeah, that shit was JJ's idea. He was fucking this bitch Tamisha over there and he wanted to go and get some. So he drives us over there and we meet up with her. She was going on about how much she hates living in Bowling Green and that she wants out. So after her and JJ do their thing, he asks if Mish can come with us. I didn't want that bitch around because I used to fuck her back in the day and she can't keep her mouth shut, but I agree to hear the plan they got. JJ and Mish wanted us to go into the house and make it look like a robbery. First we would tie up the old dude and the old lady.*
***Riddell**: Did she know who these people were?*
***Raymond Whitley**: Yeah, they were her grandparents.*
***Riddell**: So did you agree to it?*
***Raymond Whitley**: Yeah. So JJ and I wait till it's all dark and we break into the townhouse. The old dude and old lady were watching television in the back room. I pull out a knife and smack the old lady in the face. Old dude gets out of the chair so I knock his old ass out. We tie em' up and put them back in the back bedroom. JJ ties up Mish too to make it look real and shit. I start loading up the truck with the TV and the stereo. They old, so not much shit in that house was worth stealing. I come back inside after the third trip and JJ is all scared and shit. I ask him what his fucking*

deal is and he takes me back to the bedroom where Mish is at. When he put the duct tape over her mouth he put it over her nose too. The bitch suffocated to death. I start laughing because that shit was funny. JJ is kind of upset about it, so I slit her throat in front of him. Don't know why I did it, but I did. JJ rips the knife out of my hand and walks to the back bedroom where the old dude and the old lady are. He starts stabbing the shit out of them like he did the little girl. Except this time I just let him go to town. After he tires himself out we leave my truck there and take that yellow piece of shit that they had and get the hell out of there.

Riddell: *Where did you and JJ go next?*

Raymond Whitley: *We drive toward Missouri. JJ and me has some family in St. Louis that would hide us out. They cool and all.*

Riddell: *But you ended up in Mayfield next. What happened in Mayfield?*

Raymond Whitley: *We decided that they would be looking for us in St. Louis, so we decided to go down to stay with my old man in Nashville instead. It was just starting to get dark and JJ and me needed some money. The money we took off Mish's grandfather didn't last long. Cheap bastard. We drove down a few streets and we saw this old white couple unloading groceries. She had her purse on her shoulder so we was going to do a grab and run. But the old bitch wouldn't let go of her purse. So I stab her and the old man too. She went right down, but the old man took six or seven sticks to take down. I had to drag the bodies inside the house so no one would see them. I took the old lady's purse and two of the bags of groceries. JJ was waiting at the end of the driveway, so I hop in and we drive to Tennessee. That old bitch was loaded too. I got $300 dollars from her and $200 out of the old dude's wallet. That night we ate like kings. Shit, we even got to sleep in real beds. We got a hotel in Jackson, and stayed two nights before going to my dad's house. The next day you pig mother fuckers pulled us out of the basement.*

Riddell: *Now back to Stillwell County. You had nothing to do with the murder of that lady?*
Raymond Whitley: *Do you honestly think that I would tell you all that shit, in detail, and then lie to you about killing that lady. Like one fucking murder is gonna' make the difference if we live or die? Why are you so interested in that lady anyhow?*
Riddell: *No particular reason. She was found Shot in the chest and burned in a house fire, just like the Dutch family.*
Raymond Whitley: *I ain't never used no gun on nobody, ever. I like to knife people, in case you missed it.*
Riddell: *So you've never owned a firearm?*
Raymond Whitley: *Did you not understand me? No. Never.*
Riddell: *Why did you guys decide to do this?*
Raymond Whitley: *Say what?*
Riddell: *I mean it seems senseless to go out and kill 10 people for no good reason. Or did you two have a reason?*
Raymond Whitley: *You think we're psycho, don't you?*
Riddell: *I never said that. I'm just trying to make sense out of all this.*
Raymond Whitley: *JJ and me been talking about going on a killing spree for a few years now. We've read about a ton of different murders in the papers and thought about how cool it would be to go out and do some of that shit for real. It even got to the point where we started to research that shit.*
Riddell: *Any murders in particular catch your interest?*
Raymond Whitley: *There were these three dudes from the west coast, Los Angeles I think, who we read about a few years ago. Their lives were almost identical to ours, so we picked them. Fuck, we even planned that shit out so it all happened on the same dates. I mean, don't get me wrong. We improvised a little with some of the details since there were only two of us, but for the most part, that shit was on-point.*
Riddell: *Were you able to accomplish what you set out to do?*

Raymond Whitley*:* *Yep, and then some. Those two old people were a bonus.*
Riddell*:* *Do you mind telling me which murderers you guys were copying?*
Raymond Whitley*:* *You're the fucking detective. You figure that shit out on your own fucking time. Listen, we're done here, man. Take me to my cell.*
Riddell*:* *So you're saying that you want to terminate the interview at this time?*
Raymond Whitley*:* *Fuck you!*
Riddell*:* *I'll take that as a yes. This concludes the interview of Raymond "Clay" Whitley.*

Adam looked across the room at David, who was still reading the confession and taking notes.

"How much more do you have to read, David?"

"I've got three pages to go. Give me another five minutes or so."

Adam got up from the table with a sick feeling in his stomach. How in the world could two people be so cruel, heartless, and sick that they could treat another human being—especially children—as they did? He walked out the door into the homicide unit and looked for Detective Riddell and found him just across the hall, sitting at his desk reading the transcript from JJ's confession.

"Detective Riddell, that was some nasty stuff."

"I warned you that it would be. In all my years I've never met someone who was so callous. He actually laughed a few time during the interview when he was describing the murders. Like when he was talking about JJ accidentally killing Tamisha. He thought that was the funniest thing ever. He laughed for at least a minute."

Adam looked down at the desk and saw that Riddell had JJ's confession.

"You have better news for me with JJ's confession?" Adam asked.

"Here's a copy, if you care to reread the entire series of events through another psycho's eyes."

The thought of that made Adams stomach hurt even more. And for some reason he thought about the Dutch girls' last few minutes on this earth. How little Gwen Dutch clung to her stuffed teddy bear for comfort as she was being bludgeoned to death. It was almost overwhelming.

Adam took a deep breath and responded, "I really don't want to, but I guess I'm going to have to."

He reached out his hands and took JJ's confession back to the conference room to read it.

Three quarters of the way through the confession, Adam looked up at David and interrupted his reading, "Hey, David. These guys didn't kill Melissa Dwyer."

David stopped reading for a second.

"I don't know, Adam. They have ties to our area and they definitely had the time to do it. No one can account for their whereabouts on the 17th of December, including them. I still think it's possible."

"David, why in the hell do you think that these guys would confess to nine different murders in Kentucky, deny killing our victim, and then go right back into how they claw hammered a six year old clutching a teddy bear?"

"I hear what your saying, Adam. I just thinks it's a little early to be saying they didn't do it is all."

"Sorry, David. It's just after reading all this I don't think that they did it. These aren't our murderers."

Chapter 20

Adam and David both handed back their copies of the confessions to Detective Riddell and expressed their appreciation for his time.

"Thanks, Detective. It's a shame they didn't confess to our murder, but I guess you win some and you lose some," Adam stated.

"I know the feeling, Detectives. You work so hard on a case by following up on every lead, only to be let down time and time again. This happens to all of us on a daily basis. Good luck to you guys, and in the meantime, I'll get Clay and JJ back in the interview room on another day to see if they waver on any part of their story."

Adam and David both shook Riddell's hand and walked back to their unmarked, parked outside.

Adam thought about spending the night in Nashville, but decided to push straight on through and get back to Stillwell. David tried to bring up the interviews and the case a few times during the six-hour ride, but Adam didn't want to hear anything he had to say. Instead, Adam kept mentally going through his notes trying to figure out what, if anything, he was missing. He kept thinking about the green pickup truck in the driveway with the lettering in the rear window. Was it possible that a neighbor could have seen that truck parked in the driveway all the time, killed Melissa, and used it as a ruse to cover up their tracks? He thought about the diary that Melissa Dwyer had kept and what she had said about Rocky being verbally abusive toward her. Could Rocky have had enough time to kill Melissa and get out of there within the time frames Mr. Mastus and Sheila Potts had given him? Where was the evidence? All fingers pointed to Rocky, but he wasn't ruling out the possibility that someone else could have done it.

Adam pulled into David's driveway just after one in the morning. David grabbed his things out of the trunk and disappeared into his house without saying a word. Adam was too tired to care about hurting his feelings, so instead of trying to make amends, he drove to his house to crash for the night. All the way home, he was consumed by the turn of events in this case. He couldn't stop thinking about the fact that Melissa Dwyer's killer could still be out there, and although he had nothing tangible, Adam knew for sure that Clay and JJ weren't his murderers. His last thought before turning into his driveway was just how was he going to proceed on Monday with the investigation. To his surprise, when he rounded the corner, Adam noticed that Rennae's car was parked in her normal spot. He parked next to her and walked in the back door to see Rennae sitting at the kitchen table, staring out the window.

"Hey, wasn't expecting to see you here."

"Where have you been? I've been here for the last eight hours."

"I was in Nashville working on this case. If I had known you were going to be here, I would have called to let you know."

"You calling and letting me know where you are? That would be a first."

"Listen, Rennae. I've had a terribly long day and I'm not in the mood to argue with you. Can we please just go to bed and talk about this tomorrow? I have the day off since it's Sunday. Please?"

Rennae put her coffee mug in the sink and followed him upstairs. Adam climbed directly into bed with his clothes on, bypassing his normal nightly routine. Rennae followed suit and lay there beside him. Adam gave her a gentle kiss on the cheek before turning off the lights and falling asleep.

Adam woke up at his usual 8:00 sharp, and rolled over to see Rennae sitting on the side of the bed, staring out the window. Slowly he took inventory of his body for any unnecessary holes, and when he didn't find any he relaxed a little bit.

Adam broke the silence, "You want to go for a run?"

Rennae turned around with a tear rolling down her cheek and replied, “That sounds good to me, honey.”

Adam smiled at her and got out of bed. He walked around to her side and gave her a quick hug before going into the closet to get ready.

“I’ll be ready in a minute.”

Adam got undressed and was in the process of putting his running pants on when the closet door opened. Rennae was standing there completely naked looking at him.

“So, are we still going out for a run?”

“Later. Come back to bed please.”

Adam walked out of the closet and closed the door behind him. Rennae grabbed Adam gently by the hand and pulled him back into bed. She pulled the sheets over their heads and looked deeply into Adam’s eyes.

“I’m sorry I left, Adam.”

Adam put his hands around her waist and drew her tight to him. He gently placed his lips on hers for a brief moment before pulling his head away.

“Listen, we have our problems. All couples do. Let’s talk about this in a little while please.”

Adam and Rennae had been making love for over a decade, but that particular time was more intense and more sensual than either of them could ever remember. Completely content, Rennae rolled onto her side and looked over at her husband.

“Can we talk now, please?”

She was just about to say more, but Adam cut her off, “Its okay, Rennae. I understand completely why you did it. And in the future I promise to call you more often and be more open about what I’m doing. I do want to spend more time with you, doing things that we enjoy, like running and biking. After this investigation is over, we’re going on a long vacation—two weeks at least. But most importantly, I don’t want to lose you.”

Rennae just lay there smiling at Adam, “I have something important to tell you.”

"What is it?"

"I'm pregnant. You're going to be a father."

Adam sat on the edge of the bed in complete silence, not knowing what to say.

"Can you please say something, Adam? You're scaring me."

"Rennae, that's the best news I've ever gotten!"

He leaned over and gave Rennae a big hug and kiss before standing up and looking her in the eyes.

He jumped back and started flexing his tiny muscles while yelling, "That's right baby, I'm all that is man!"

Rennae started to laugh and Adam could see a sense of relief come over her face.

"When did you find this out, Rennae?"

"I had a sneaking suspicion a few weeks ago. I guess that's why I've been so moody lately. New Year's Eve, I was sick from the baby, not the flu. When I woke up the next day feeling normal, I knew something was up. Plus I was late, so I went and got a home pregnancy test when I was in Michigan. When the results were positive I went to the doctor's to confirm it yesterday morning. After I found out for sure, I packed up and drove straight home to share the news with you."

Adam and Rennae got dressed and went downstairs to get a late breakfast before going for their run.

"How far you want to go, babe?" Adam asked.

"Five or six sounds good to me. I ran 10 two days ago."

The two laced up their shoes and headed away from town on a back country road. The sky was still a light shade of gray with puffy white clouds rolling in. The hills looked so calm and peaceful all tucked in under a blanket of fresh powder. All Adam could hear was the crunching of the snow under their feet followed by both of their heavy breathing as they ran. At about mile four, the snow started to fall slightly. At mile five the flakes were the size of quarters, building up on the roadway. And as they turned into their driveway at mile six, there were blizzard-like conditions with winds gusting at 30 to 40 miles an hour.

"Good thing we're home. If this keeps up, I'm not going to work tomorrow either."

Rennae looked over and laughed, "You'd go to work even if they said a nuclear bomb was headed this way, just to get caught up on your reports."

"So, what do you want to do tonight? I'm assuming by the weather report that we'll lose power at some point. I'm going to go out to the wood pile and stack a ton of firewood, for the stove, on the back porch. While I'm doing that, can you get the air mattress out so we can sleep down here tonight and fill up the bathtub with water so we can flush the toilets?"

Rennae nodded her head and walked into the kitchen to check out their food situation. As she opened the pantry and the refrigerator, she saw that they were both almost empty.

"Well, at least you've been eating all the leftover crap. We need to go to the store to get some food for the next few days."

"Okay. We'll go in a few minutes. Just let me get the fire going."

The parking lot at the only grocery store in town was packed with cars. Adam dropped Rennae off at the front door and drove through the lot to find a spot. Ten minutes later, he was parked in the back row and walked in to find Rennae. Once inside, Adam wandered aimlessly until he found Rennae staring into one of the almost empty freezers in the frozen foods section.

"Take your pick, Adam. They've got frozen fish sticks and French fries or frozen meat loaf. Everything else is gone in this place. I hope you like soy milk with your cereal, because that's all they had."

All they could do was laugh as they picked over what was left in the store. There wasn't a loaf of bread, a carton of eggs, a gallon of milk, or a single roll of toilet paper to be found in the entire store.

The sole check-out line was at least twenty people and it took them fifteen minutes to get to the clerk.

"Mr. and Ms. Alexander, how are ya'll today?"

Adam smiled back at the female clerk, "We're doing just fine Ronda. How are the kids?"

"Everyone in my house is fine, although I haven't seen them in a few days. Been stuck here."

"I bet you have. When is the next semi going to be here to restock the shelves?"

"They've been promising to be here for the last two days, but now that we've got this new storm going on, your guess is as good as mine."

"Well, you have my number if you need anything Ronda, and I mean that. If you need anything at all, just let me know."

"Thank you, Mr. Alexander. I sure do appreciate that."

Ronda rang up the last item and placed it in the bag. Adam paid for his harvest of frozen bounty and walked back to their car that was parked in the middle of east nowhere.

"She was awful friendly, Adam. Who is she?"

"That was Ronda Conyers. She's the older sister of Mary Jo Conyers, who was found murdered on the interstate a few years back. She's the nicest lady and unfortunately she's married to a piece of shit. He beats her when he gets drunk. I've tried to get her some help, but since he actually has a good job and doesn't hit the kids, she stays with him."

Rennae looked down at the ground and shook her head, "That's really sad. It also makes me appreciate what I have a little bit more."

Rennae grabbed onto Adam's arm tightly as they walked through the snow to the car. Once they were there, he opened Rennae's door for her and closed it after she was seated. Adam secured the groceries in the trunk, returned the cart, and then began the long drive home.

Later that evening, the power went out in the house, just as Adam had predicted. Rennae resorted to the pioneer-style of cooking by opening up two frozen meals and cooking them on top of the wood stove in a cast iron skillet. Adam grabbed a few candles, lit them, and placed them in various places around the room so they could see. It was going to be a long night, but thanks to the woodstove, it would be reasonably comfortable downstairs. Adam lay down on the couch and took the opportunity to catch up on some reading. He had recently started a new murder mystery, but because of the case, he hadn't gotten very far.

"How do you like your frozen meat loaf?" Rennae asked with a smile.

Adam chuckled and replied, "Hot," before going back to reading his book.

While their meals cooked on the woodstove, Rennae pumped up the air mattress and placed it in the middle of the living room. She carefully put the sheets and a comforter on it, trying to make it as neat as possible. After their mediocre meal, the two crawled into their make-shift bed in the middle of the living room floor, said their goodnights, and in no time, Rennae was out like a light. Adam stayed awake for a little while longer reading his book. At times he found himself looking at Rennae as she slept and wondered about what the future held for the two of them. He was going to be a dad, and it was time to make things right by ending his relationship with Alexis. With that important decision made, he put his book on the coffee table and closed his eyes.

Adam woke up to the sound of his cell phone ringing at seven the next morning. He quickly snatched the phone and looked down to see that it was Bishop calling him.

"Hey, Sarge. What's up?"

"You've got to come in today, Adam. The sheriff wants a sit down with you, me, and David to discuss the case."

Adam stood up and went to the window.

"Sarge, there's two feet of snow on the ground, and I don't have a four wheel drive vehicle. I'm stranded out here."

"I'll send the National Guard out to get you if I have to. The sheriff is all fired up and wants to see us within the hour."

"Okay, then you need to send the troops to come and get me. I'll be ready to go in ten minutes."

Adam ended the call and turned around to see Rennae laying next to the fire looking over at him.

"Sorry, baby. I have to go in for a bit."

Rennae smiled back, "It's Okay. You go and do what you need to do. Can you stack some firewood next to the back door before you go, please?"

"Sure thing."

Adam was placing the last piece of wood on the back porch when a green Humvee came plowing up his driveway.

Bernie popped out of the back door and yelled up to Adam, "Come on bitch, the Germans are invading!"

Adam busted out laughing, "Okay, douche bag, let's go to war."

He crawled in the rear seat of the Humvee next to Bernie, who had the biggest little kid smile on his face.

"You kill me, bro. How long have you been out here riding along with these guys?"

"Pretty much all morning. We've been out checking the roads for the road crews, getting the hospital employees to work and picking our guys up."

"Damn, you have been pretty busy. I wonder why the Sheriff is in the office today?"

"I don't know, but he didn't seem too happy when we went and got him this morning."

The Humvee pulled into the only cleared parking lot in town. Adam looked out to see guys in bright orange suits with shovels and bags of salt busily clearing away all the snow from the rear parking lot. Adam quickly jumped out of the Humvee, punched in the code to the back door, and let himself into the office. As soon as he walked through the door, the smell of fresh coffee hit his nose and the warm air hit his body. It had been almost twelve hours since he had experienced electricity and he didn't know when it would be restored at home. He could have kicked himself for not bringing in fresh clothes and a towel, because he could have showered in the jail before returning home. Adam walked into the kitchen and poured himself a cup of coffee. He sipped it all the way down the hallway enjoying every drop.

"Adam, get in here please," Bishop beckoned.

His train of thought was derailed by the booming sound of the sergeant. Adam rounded the corner into Bishop's office and saw that the sheriff and David were already there waiting on him. Sheriff Lawson gave Adam the once over before returning his attention back to Bishop.

"Nice of you to shower and look professional before coming to this meeting, Adam. And why the hell weren't you here on time like everyone else?" Sheriff Lawson sneered.

"Sorry, Sir, but my house doesn't have power, we're on a well, and you don't provide me with a four-wheel-drive vehicle to make it in here on days like today."

Bishop looked over at Adam and could see that he was about to let the Sheriff have it.

"Adam, we're here to discuss what you and David learned in Nashville. What can you tell us?"

Adam looked angrily over at the Sheriff and then back at Bishop.

"Well, I'll be honest with you. I don't think that Clay and JJ are our killers."

Sheriff Lawson looked over at Adam and in a raised voice asked, "Based on what Alexander? You read one fucking confession!"

"Sir, with all due respect, there was nothing in that truck belonging to our victim when they found it in Bowling Green. They've never been known to use a firearm, only knives and razor blades. The only ties to this area were several years ago when Clay was incarcerated at Big Sandy Penitentiary for a robbery charge. And to top it all off, they confessed to ten murders and one malicious wounding in two states. I read the most horrible confession detailing the brutal murder of a six year old girl. The detective then asked Clay about our victim here and he said they didn't kill anyone in Stillwell. Then he went right back to a description of killing JJ's girlfriend and slitting her throat for no fucking reason. And for the record, I read two fucking confessions."

Sheriff Lawson jumped up and shouted at Adam, "You worthless piece of garbage, how dare you cuss at me me? David and Bishop, get the hell out of here, NOW!"

The two did exactly as they were told in record time and closed the door behind them. Sheriff Lawson walked over to where Adam was sitting in the corner and hovered over him.

"Now you listen to me, you little maggot. You will make all your reports indicate that Clay and JJ are our murderers. I don't care what their confessions say. You will make this stick or so help me God, you will not only lose your fucking job, but I will follow you all around this country and make sure that you never have another job in law enforcement for as long as you live. Do you understand me? Was that clear enough for you to understand?"

Adam just sat there, completely in shock. Sheriff Lawson stood over him waiting for a response.

When none came he yelled, "I'm waiting for a damn answer!"

Adam could see the rage in the Sheriff's eyes and face as he stood there trembling.

"Yes, Sheriff. I understand."

Lawson turned around and left the office in his usual fashion. Bishop and Gibbons reappeared once the Sheriff was well out of sight.

Adam looked at Bishop and then over at David, "You little fucking weasel. You gonna run to daddy every time you don't agree with something I say?"

"Fuck you Adam! He asked me what happened in Nashville so I told him!" David yelled.

"Fuck me? NO, FUCK YOU! What exactly did you tell him, huh? That all the evidence points to someone else, but you have a hunch so I'm wrong? That I disagreed with the sheriff's errand boy and hurt his little feelings?"

"Both of you shut the fuck up. David, get out of my office. I don't want to see you anywhere near this investigation. Do you understand me? And before you go and blab your big mouth, I don't care what your fucking daddy has to say. This is my investigations unit and I will assign who I see fit."

David stood up and pointed his finger at Bishop, "You just signed your own death warrant, Bishop."

"Do you think I give a shit? Now get the hell out of my office."

Adam waited for David to walk out the door, "Thanks Bishop, but you didn't have to do that. Now we're both in deep shit."

"I hate to break it to you kid, but I was in deep shit before today. I told the Sheriff that I didn't want David on my wing when he assigned him to take over for Bernie."

Bishop sat back in his chair, knowing that his time as the head of investigations was short. He opened his desk drawer and pulled out two cigars.

"You want a cigar short timer?"

"No thanks, Sarge. I'm going back to my office so I can figure out what I need to do next."

Adam went back to his office and slumped down in his chair, trying to recall everything that had just happened. No matter which way he sliced it, the Sheriff was asking him to falsify his records to make a murder conviction stick to two guys that, in his mind, didn't do it. He needed to talk to someone about all of this to get a second opinion, so he called his best friend in the department.

"Bernie, you still at the office?"

"Yeah, bro. What do you need?"

"Can you come to my office? I have something I want to talk about with you."

"Sure thing. I'll be there in a few minutes."

Adam sat back and waited for Bernie to come into his office, his mind in a whirlwind of thought. Bernie walked around the corner into his office and took his usual seat across from Adam.

"What's up?"

"Close the door."

Bernie closed the door behind him and sat down across from Adam, "What's this all about?"

Adam sat silent for a few seconds, contemplating how he was going to open the conversation.

"The sheriff just threatened me, Bernie. He said I either make the charges against Clay and JJ stick or he's going to fire me. What the hell am I going to do?"

Bernie sat back in his chair and stared at Adam with an inquisitive look on his face.

"What in the world are you talking about? Clay and JJ didn't kill Melissa Dwyer?"

"All of the evidence that I've got says that they didn't do it."

"It sure is nice of you to fill me in on this now. Some friend you are."

"I'm being serious, Bernie. He said that I better make it stick, or he was going to fire me. And not just fire me, but make sure that I never work in law enforcement again. Rennae is pregnant and I need this job. What am I going to do?"

"Wait, what? Rennae is pregnant? Is she back?"

"Yeah, she came home two days ago and told me that she was pregnant. She said that she wanted to work things out. What am I going to do? No matter how bad these guys are, I can't try to convict them without any evidence and if they didn't do it, the real killer is still out there."

"Now I understand why she left you. Your communication skills need some serious work."

"Nice. Really nice, Bernie."

The two detectives just sat there in silence. Bernie wanted to congratulate Adam but knew that it wasn't the right time. Instead, he tried to come up with a solution to get Adam off the hook.

"What about this? If you put together all of the evidence and hand it over to the commonwealth attorney and she doesn't think there is enough to convict, then you're clear."

"That's good in theory, but he told me to change my reports to point the finger at Clay and JJ. If he goes over those reports and doesn't approve of them, I'm screwed. I guess the long and short of it is I'm going to be fired, because I refuse to lie about something this important."

Chapter 21

Bernie and Adam talked about his unfortunate situation for about an hour before they both decided to call it a day. Adam was just about to turn off the lights and head for the nearest Humvee to take him home when his desk phone rang.

"Investigations, this is Alexander."

The voice on the other end of the line was a familiar one.

"Hey, Adam. This is Howell, from Frankfort PD. I see from the weather forecast that you guys are snowed in."

"Yeah, we've had three feet of snow over the last few days. What can I do for you, Sir?"

"I actually have some good news for you. I did a subpoena for Clay's cell phone records and it seems that one of the calls made on his phone hit off a cell tower in Hillsboro on the day of your murder. He made that call at approximately three fifteen in the afternoon. As the crow flies, Hillsboro is roughly eighty five miles northwest from you guys. If you give me a fax number I can fax this over to you."

"Did you call Bishop and let him know about this?"

"No, I figured he had enough on his plate. Besides, you're the primary investigator, right?"

"I am indeed. Thanks, Howell. I really appreciate the help."

Adam gave Howell the fax number before hanging up and waited impatiently by his machine for the transmission to arrive. Three minutes later, five pages of cell phone records were sitting neatly in the tray. Adam thumbed through the pages and saw that the dates of inquiry were between December 1st and January 1st. He had hoped that Howell would have subpoenaed all the way up to today's date, but he hadn't. The calls prior to their murder primarily originated in the Cincinnati area but after December 13th the calls spread into Kentucky.

He looked down at the cover sheet and saw a note from Detective Howell at the bottom that stated, "As you know, you're going to have to subpoena these for yourself in order for it to admissible in your trial. Happy Hunting."

Adam decided to keep this new information to himself for the time being because he wanted to double check and make sure there were no other calls placed on that phone after Clay and JJ were picked up. But then he thought that if he didn't inquire any further he would be able to obtain warrants for their arrest based on all of the circumstantial evidence alone and the Sheriff would get off his back. He could always decide to not prosecute further on down the line if he were to find definitive proof that Clay and JJ were innocent of his charges. Adam reluctantly turned on his computer and pulled up a blank report to document his new findings. He typed up his narrative, carefully choosing his words and making sure he said all the right things.

"This should keep the Sheriff off my back for a little while."

Adam printed out his report and took a copy down the hall to Sheriff Lawson's office. The Sheriff's secretary was not in due to the weather, but he could see that his light was still on down the hall.

"Sheriff, you in?"

A few seconds later Adam saw the sheriff's head pop out from around the corner. "What the hell do you want, Alexander?"

"Just letting you know about some new evidence that just hit my desk. If you have a minute I'll fill you in."

Sheriff Lawson came out of his office and stumbled down the hall toward him. Adam could tell right away that something wasn't right.

"What is it?"

Adam smelled alcohol on the Sheriff's breath, but after the scene they had had earlier, he didn't dare say a word.

"Well, Sheriff, I just got Clay's cell phone records for December 1st through January 1st, and it seems that a call that was placed from his phone that hit off a cell tower in Hillsboro, just outside of Morehead on the day of our murder."

The Sheriff's gruff tone took an abrupt turn after hearing the news.

"That's fantastic news, Adam. We really need to get those murder warrants right away. The public has been breathing down my neck on this and, as you know, it is an election year. We're all under a lot of stress to get this solved. Come on in my office and let me pour you a scotch."

Adam couldn't stomach spending any more time with Sheriff Lawson than he had to, so the thought of having a drink with the man was out of the question. He quickly had to think of an excuse to get out of the office, and for the first time in his life he actually had a good one.

"If it's okay with you Sheriff, I just found out this morning my wife's pregnant. Can I take a rain check?"

"Well congratulations to you and the wife. When do you think can you present to Ms. Leighton?"

Adam hesitated for a minute before answering. He knew that there was a lot more that he had to look into before he even entertained the thought of getting warrants, but he told the Sheriff what he wanted to hear.

"As soon as the Commonwealth Attorney's office is open, I'll be ready to present."

Sheriff Lawson extended his hand toward Adam, "Good job, Detective. I look forward to the seeing you in action in the courtroom."

Adam walked back to his office to lock up and go home. Just before he turned off his light, he looked out the window to see that the snow was still falling fast. It was then that he remembered he hadn't driven in to the office today. He picked up his phone and called the dispatch center to arrange for the National Guard to take him back home.

"Hey, Ms. Crags. Can you see if the Guard can run me home please?"

"You got it honey. The guys are here watching TV in the dispatch center. I'll have them meet you in the back lot in five minutes."

Adam hung up the phone and turned everything off before locking the door behind him. While walking toward the back parking lot, he ran into Bernie.

"You aren't going to believe this, Bernie."

"What's up?"

"After you left my office I got a call from Detective Howell. He was able to track down Clay's cell phone records through January 1st, and get this—there was a call placed in Hillsboro on December 18th. I went back to drop off a copy of my report in Sheriff Lawson's mailbox a little while ago. I wasn't expecting him to be there, but I saw that his office light was on. When I called out to him, he came stumbling out of his office and almost fell down. He was completely blitzed. I'm talking shit faced, Bernie."

Bernie laughed hysterically for a few seconds.

"I always wondered what he did back there when his secretary was gone."

"What should I do, man? The cell phone records were only for one month and I have a feeling that if I subpoena the next month, there will be calls placed after they were picked up. That means that someone other than Clay or JJ had the phone."

Bernie agreed with Adam but interjected, "Well, who's to say that his phone wasn't left at his dad's house in Nashville and one of his relatives decided to use it until they cut it off?"

"See Bernie, that's why I want you back on this case. You're always thinking. But that still doesn't help me out with the Sheriff wanting me to falsify my reports. I'm screwed."

Adam and Bernie walked out back to see that a Humvee was already waiting to take Adam home. He climbed into the vehicle and was safely transported back to his house where Rennae was waiting for him.

“You done for the day honey?” Rennae asked.

“Yeah, today was the craziest day I’ve ever had. I’ll fill you in over a stove cooked frozen meal.”

Adam was going to fill Rennae in about everything that happened during the day, but decided against it. He didn’t want to worry her about possibly losing his job and cause undue stress on her and the baby. Instead, he told her about the investigation and everything that had transpired up to this point. After dinner Adam tried to read more of the book he had been reading the night before, but he just couldn’t concentrate. He was worried about how he was going to be able to convince the Commonwealth Attorney that Clay and JJ were their murderers with what little circumstantial evidence he had. He realized it would be up to the defense to prove that Clay didn’t make the call, but in his mind that wasn’t enough to base his entire case on. Adam put his book down for a minute and thought about what he was going to present to Alexis. He also thought about how he was going to tell her that he could no longer see her. No matter what, they were both professionals and would have to work together despite any differences they might have. He blew out the candle and did his best to get a good night’s rest.

Adam woke up an hour earlier than usual so he could shovel off both of his cars and the driveway. He wanted Rennae to be able to get out and get to the store because they were running out of frozen meals. After a quick breakfast and an even quicker shower, he was on his way into the office. The roads were now plowed, and with the temperature just above freezing, the snow was starting to melt. Adam turned on the radio to one of the local stations and heard *Eighteen and Life* by Skid Row. Naturally he cranked up the volume and sang his heart out like he was Sebastian Bach, live at the Roxy. His concert was cut short when he turned onto Court Street and saw four news vans with antennas extended.

"What the hell is this shit?"

Adam parked his cruiser and double-timed it into the office. Moving down his hallway, he noticed that all the detectives' offices were empty, except Bishop's.

"What gives, Bishop?"

"I know, Adam. I told him this wasn't a good idea, but he decided to call it anyway."

"I haven't even presented to the Commonwealth yet. I don't even think we can get warrants with the shit case we have."

"You're preaching to the choir. He had it in his head that he was going to announce that Clay and JJ were our killers and we were going to prosecute. I just walked in 30 minutes ago and he had already called the press conference."

"Bishop, I got the cell phone records yesterday. Your buddy, Detective Howell, faxed them to me. He only subpoenaed for one month. I bet if I were to get the current records, that phone would still be in use. I don't know how many times I have to say it. These aren't our killers."

Bishop sat back in his chair and turned on the press conference that was going on outside. On the screen in front of them was Sheriff Lawson, standing tall in his dress uniform behind a podium. He was leaning forward slightly, talking into several microphones, which were poised in front of him to capture every word.

"Ladies and gentlemen, thank you for being here on this chilly morning. I'm here to announce that we have identified our murder suspects as Raymond "Clay" Whitley and Jimmy "JJ" Jebb. They have been apprehended in Nashville Tennessee and are awaiting extradition back to Kentucky. My detectives have been working tirelessly since December 18th, when we learned of Melissa Dwyer senseless murder."

Bishop turned off the television, "I can't even listen to this shit."

Adam shook his head in agreement.

"Hey, why were you so late this morning?"

"I had to shovel the driveway so Rennae could get out."

"Next time let me know, please. Now get your sorry ass to work."

"Sure thing, Sarge. If you need me, I'll be in my office getting my case together for the Commonwealth."

Adam stood up and walked out of Bishop's office and into his own. He turned on his light and computer to print copies of his entire case for Alexis to look over.

"Adam, get back in my office!"

Adam scurried back to Bishops office and stood in the doorway.

"What's up?"

Bishop had his phone pressed against his ear, listening intently to what was being said on the other end of the line. He even broke out his note pad and started to jot a few things down. Adam walked the rest of the way into Bishop's office and took his usual seat.

Bishop hung up the phone and looked over at Adam, "That was the transportation officer for Nashville Police. He said that as he was driving Clay and JJ to court, he overheard Clay tell JJ that if it keeps the needle out of his arm, to confess to the murder in Stillwell."

"Did he say it like that? Because if so, that means nothing. That confession will never make it into court."

Bishop ripped the single page of paper off of his pad and handed it to Adam. On it contained the name, badge number and phone number for the transportation officer who had heard the conversation between Clay and JJ.

"Make sure you call this guy back and talk to him, okay?"

Adam nodded his head and went back into his office. He picked up his phone and dialed the number that was given to him.

"Transportation, Riley."

"Hey, Officer Riley, this is Detective Alexander from the Stillwell County Sheriff's Office. Do you have a few minutes to fill me in on what you heard today?"

"I sure do, Sir. What would you like to know?"

"What exactly did Clay and JJ say to one another today on their way to court."

"Clay was telling JJ that he was as good as dead and that JJ needed to say whatever he needed to in order to keep himself alive. Clay then got real loud, like he wanted me to hear him. He told JJ to make a deal with you guys and to tell you that he would turn on Clay in order to get life in prison on all of the charges."

Adam took meticulous notes on everything that Officer Riley was saying to him. "And your opinion, Officer Riley? Why do you think he told JJ to say that?"

"In my opinion, he said it to save JJ's ass."

"My thoughts exactly."

"Well, if you need me for anything else, sir, you have my cell phone number. You can call me anytime."

"Oh, can you tell me how the extradition hearings went today, Riley?"

"Like I told your sergeant earlier, they went well. Neither Clay nor JJ is going to fight extradition. They'll be headed to Frankfort in a few hours and should be there by tonight."

Adam ended his conversation with Officer Riley and walked back to Bishop's office. As he rounded the corner he saw Sheriff Lawson sitting in one of the chairs across from Bishop.

"Is this a bad time?" Adam asked.

"Hell no, Detective. Please come in and join us. Bishop tells me that you guys watched the press conference this morning. Sorry I didn't tell you about it earlier, but I just wanted to get it out of the way."

The room fell awkwardly silent for about 15 seconds. Bishop, as usual, broke the silence.

"You looked good up there Sheriff. Don't know if you heard yet, but Clay and JJ are headed up to Frankfort as we speak."

"Well that's good news. I figure it'll be a few months before we can get our hands on them."

Bishop turned to Adam, "I filled the Sheriff in on what that transportation officer had to say."

"Yes he did, and it sounds like we can put all this behind us after the trial. Have you gone and presented to the Commonwealth yet, Adam?"

"No, Sheriff. I need to type up this newest report and then I'll head that way. I'm making copies of everything for Ms. Leighton now."

"Good. Let me know when we can bring these guys to Stillwell for arraignment."

Sheriff Lawson got up and walked out of Bishop's office.

"Bishop, I just got off the phone with that transportation officer. This shit isn't going to fly at all. I want to go to Frankfort and interview Clay and JJ before I get these warrants."

"I'll call Howell and make the arrangements for tomorrow, but right now you need to go see Ms. Leighton and at least let her know what we have."

Adam returned to his office and retrieved the entire packet he had prepared for Alexis. The walk was a short one across the street to the courthouse and ultimately to the commonwealth attorney's office. Adam walked in through the double doors and to the elevator. Once on the fifth floor, he walked in through another set of double doors into Alexis's office. She was sitting at her solid oak desk behind a mountain of papers.

"You have a minute, Alexis?"

She looked up from the file she was reading and gave Adam a smile.

"For you, I have several minutes. Are you prepared to present your evidence for the murder of Ms. Dwyer?"

"I have a packet for you that contains a lot of information, but little or no evidence. As a matter of fact, the only thing that I have against Clay and JJ is a shaky confession that was made in the back of a transportation van on the way to the courthouse in Nashville. According to the transportation officer, Clay told JJ to confess to our murder to keep him off death row."

"Well, based on that confession alone, you can get warrants for murder."

"Alexis, I'm pretty sure that these aren't our guys, but I'm getting a lot of pressure from the sheriff to make this stick."

Alexis stood up from her chair and walked around the desk to the front where Adam was sitting. She was wearing a short black skirt and a white button-up blouse that was semi see-through. She cleared off the area that was directly in front of Adam and hopped up on the desk. She slightly opened her legs exposing the black thong she was wearing.

"When can we meet to discuss this case in detail, Detective Alexander?"

Adam smiled and immediately changed the subject.

"I don't think that we have a case here, Alexis. That's the problem."

"Well, if you don't think that we have a good case here, then don't apply for the warrants."

"I have no choice on this one. I took the liberty of filling out a criminal complaint based on all of the information that I have so far. I am here to request a warrant for murder under Kentucky state law 507.020, for Raymond Whitley and Jimmy Jebb. Both suspects have confessed to the murder of Melissa Ann Dwyer in the presence of a transportation officer."

Alexis hopped off the desktop and retreated to her computer to start typing out the warrants that Adam requested. While she typed, she kept looking over at Adam, trying to gauge what he was thinking.

"Penny for your thoughts."

Adam stood up and walked over toward her window. He looked out over the town of Stillwell for a few seconds trying to think about what he was going to say.

"Spit it out Adam. You're not going to hurt my feelings one bit."

Adam turned around and looked solemnly at Alexis.

"Rennae came home the other day and told me that she was pregnant. I'm going to be a father."

"And that means what exactly?"

"It means that I can't continue our arrangement. I need to try to make things work with my wife."

Alexis went from angel to devil in the blink of an eye. She jumped up from behind her desk, keeping her finger pointed at Adam the entire time.

"Let me tell you something, Detective. You started this whole affair and now you expect me to act like nothing ever happened?"

Adam sat down in the nearest chair and stared at Alexis with a confused look on his face. His heart started beating a million times a minute. Adam was actually scared of the woman who was standing across from him. How could she be so kind and gentle one minute and a complete psycho the next?

"I don't understand, Alexis. I thought you wanted this relationship to be discrete. You would be in just as much trouble as I would if this leaked out."

"Yes, but I'm the heiress to a multimillion dollar bourbon distillery and you would be out on your ass with no job, no wife, and a child support payment every month which would amount to what I spend on a Sunday night dinner. I would be just fine."

"Come on, Alexis. I never meant for it to be like this. And you knew from the beginning that I would never leave my wife."

"Shut the hell up, Detective. As soon as I finish typing out these warrants I want you out of here. And you had better tread lightly around me from now on, you got that? You'll never know if or when I'll spill my guts about us. Have fun living with that for the rest of your life. Oh, and from now on, you need to deal with my assistants for all your legal questions. You step one foot inside this office and it's all over. You got that?"

"I understand completely, Alexis."

"It's Ms. Leighton to you, Detective."

Fifteen uncomfortable minutes later, Adam had arrest warrants for Clay and JJ. His next stop was Sheriff Lawson's office to let him know that the warrants were in hand and that they would set an arraignment date to get them in Stillwell after they were served. The sheriff shook Adam's hand and thanked him for all his hard work on the case. He walked out of the office with a heavy heart, knowing that he was premature in getting the warrants. As he sat on one of the benches in the lobby, he thought long and hard about what he had just done. It wasn't until he felt a hand on his shoulder that he looked up. Bishop was standing over him with a perplexed look on his face. Adam had to say something.

"Any word on whether or not I can interview Clay and JJ tomorrow?"

"Yeah, Howell will be expecting you first thing in the morning."

Adam stood up and turned away from Bishop, but he paused briefly just before walking out the lobby door.

"Bishop, after this case is over, I want off homicide. I may even be putting in to go back to patrol."

"Now why in the hell would you do that? You're the best detective I have."

"Rennae came home the other day. She's pregnant."

"Holy smokes, Adam. That's good news. It's going to suck losing you, but I understand. You want Bernie to go with you tomorrow?"

"If you don't mind, yes I would."

"Not a problem. I'll get him reassigned to you right now."

Chapter 22

Adam walked through the double doors of the lobby and out into the cold January air. He strolled around the block of the courthouse a few times to clear his head, but no matter how hard he tried, he felt like he had betrayed the badge he so proudly wore. He had compromised his morals and caved in to the Sheriff without even putting up a fight. Although he had a lot on his plate, this particular situation was eating at him worse than the affair he had had with Alexis and her threat to spill her guts about their relationship. On his third trip around the court complex, Adam looked up at the sky and saw that the sun was getting ready to set. He walked over to his car and sat in the driver's seat with his head down on the steering wheel. While he waited for the engine to warm up, he concluded that everything was now out of his hands and he would just have to roll with the punches from here on out.

Adam lifted his head, put his car in drive and started for home. As he drove out of town he saw Angel's Flower Shop coming up on the left. He had never come home with fresh cut flowers for Rennae and he figured that today was the best time to end that dry spell. He pulled into the parking lot, walked into the building, and moseyed up to the counter to order her favorite flowers. While the florist was arranging the long-stemmed red and pink roses, he picked out a blank card and filled it out:

Dear Rennae,

I know that we've had our ups and downs over the years and our lives have taken different paths from what we had originally intended. But I just want you to know that I'm more in love with you today than when we first got married. I can't wait to be a father, because I know that with your help, we will be a great team. I also told Sergeant Bishop today that after this case was completed, I was off homicide for good. I hope these flowers and all this news makes you happy, because the only thing I want is to see you happy. I love you, Rennae, with all my heart.

Adam

He placed the card inside an envelope and tucked it into the baby's breath with the arrangement. After paying, Adam drove home to spend some time with his wife—the soon-to-be mother of his child. As he drove up the driveway, Adam saw Rennae on the front porch shoveling the remaining snow off the steps, so he parked in his normal spot and emerged with the flowers in his hands. Rennae looked up and smiled at him as he moved toward her.

"I don't believe it! Let it be known, on this day, my husband has brought me flowers for the first time in eleven years."

Adam looked at her and smiled, "That's because this is the first time I've ever screwed up in eleven years baby."

Rennae let out a giggle as Adam handed her the roses and told her to read the card. Tears ran down her face as she read what he had written.

After she finished, she gave him a big hug, "Thank you, Adam. I really needed this. Let's get out of the cold."

Adam followed Rennae in to the kitchen and watched her put the roses in a vase.

While she was carefully arranging the flowers, she turned to him with a suggestion, "Let's go out tonight and celebrate. We can eat at Monica's and then go to the movies. *Paul Blart; Mall Cop* is playing."

Adam shook his head with a smile on his face, "Sounds good to me, baby. You go and get ready and I'll call for movie times."

Rennae was gone for a few minutes and returned wearing sweatpants and a West Virginia University sweatshirt. Adam was still on the phone with the movie theater, learning that the next showing was in two and a half hours. They would have plenty of time to get some supper and make it to the movie.

"We've got plenty of time to eat and get down to Coal Run for the movie. You ready to get going, baby?"

"I sure am."

Adam locked the front door behind them as they walked out of the house toward the car. He opened Rennae's door for her and then went around the car to let himself in. They were both smiling simply from being in each other's company, for the first time in ages. Adam pulled into town, drove toward Monica's, and immediately noticed a line outside the door.

"You want to try the Still House?" Rennae suggested.

"No, that place is a dive. Let's just see how long the wait is going to be. We've got two hours before the movie starts. Adam let Rennae out at the corner and parked the car down the block. When he came to the front door, he saw that Rennae was already inside sitting at the counter with an open seat next to her.

"Gotta love the counter service," Adam said as he sat down. "Bernie and I eat here all the time."

The two chatted amicably while they waited for their food to arrive. The place was packed with just about everyone from town and it seemed that their conversation was interrupted at least half a dozen times with friends coming over to congratulate Adam for solving the murder. Luckily, once their food arrived, everyone left them alone to enjoy it.

"I saw Sheriff Lawson on the news this morning. He said you guys were extraditing Clay and JJ back here as soon as possible. When do you think the trial will be?"

"Well, I got murder warrants for Clay and JJ, but I'm not so sure they did it."

Adam looked over his shoulder and saw that the nearest person was only a few feet away, which was way too close for him to be talking about the case.

"There are too many people here, I promise to fill you in at home tonight before we go to bed. Tomorrow is going to be interesting. Bernie and I are headed up to Frankfort to interview them."

"You're going to be sitting across the table from a serial killer? I will never understand how you can talk to people like that."

"Well, someone has to do it. And to be honest with you, I have a few questions that need to be answered."

The remainder of the evening went smoothly. Both Adam and Rennae enjoyed their time together and made it home before ten. As they got ready for bed, Adam filled Rennae in on the case and how he had his doubts about who the killer or killers were.

"So you don't think they did it, huh?"

"I really don't. My first suspect killed himself and these guys are only confessing to save JJ from the death penalty. I hate to say it, but I'm afraid the killer is still out there. "

Adam turned out the light, gave Rennae a kiss, and fell asleep.

The alarm clock went off at six in the morning for the start of another long day. Coffee in hand, Adam drove to the office to pack up his notebook, get Bernie, and drive to Frankfort to meet with Detective Howell. With Bernie back riding shotgun, the two reunited detectives headed north out of town.

"Glad to have you back, Bern. David really wasn't much of a conversationalist."

"Yeah yeah, I'm going to kick your ass for getting me back on this case. I could be at home sleeping right now."

"Shut up. It's not like your job is important or anything."

Bernie shot Adam the same look his wife gives him when she gets mad.

"Just drive, asshole."

"Yes dear," Adam snidely retorted.

Adam drove for a few minutes in silence before turning to Bernie, "Can I trust you to keep your yap shut?"

"Yeah, what's up?"

"I think I royally screwed up, Bernie. I had sex Alexis Leighton."

"Wait, what? You did what? And you didn't tell me?"

"Yeah, she wanted to keep it a secret. The first time was at the New Year's Eve party. She took me down into a safe room she had built in the wine cellar. The second and last time was early one morning while I was on my way to work. I kinda took a detour over to her place. But when I was in her office the other day getting the warrants for Clay and JJ, I tried to break it off because Rennae's pregnant. She went fucking psycho on me. She told me I didn't make the rules and she would decide when it was over. I'm scared, Bernie."

"I don't know what to tell you Rocky, I mean Adam."

"Screw you."

Bernie and Adam continued to talk about what he should do with Alexis for the remainder of the drive. In no time, Adam was parking in the same spot he had used a little more than a week ago.

"You ready for this, Adam?"

"To be honest with you, I'm really nervous. I've dealt with some shady characters back in Detroit, but never a serial killer."

Adam called Howell and let him know that they were about to walk into the lobby. Minutes later, he came through the side door in his usual disheveled state.

"Hey, Adam. I have Clay and JJ back here in separate rooms. You can either interview them one at a time or you can do one and Bernie can do the other. It's up to you."

"I've read enough of what you guys were doing while I was off the case. I don't mind talking to JJ," Bernie said.

Adam nodded his head and pointed toward the secured portion of the building for Howell to lead the way.

Once back in the homicide wing, both Adam and Bernie secured their weapons in the lock boxes that were hanging on the wall. They continued down the hall until Howell stopped at two wooden doors with plastic "Interview Room" signs hanging over each door.

Howell turned to the detectives and pointed at the doors, "Okay guys, Clay is in here and JJ is in there. I'll have two uniformed officers standing by the door just in case. When you're finished, just knock and they'll let you out. Good luck, Detectives."

Adam took a deep breath and put his hand on the doorknob to let himself in the interview room. He slowly opened the door to see Clay sitting at a small table with a can of soda and a bag of chips in front of him. His eyes narrowed as Adam walked into the room.

"Now, just what the fuck do you want?" Clay asked.

Adam stood at the door for a second and looked Clay over from head to toe. His face was bruised and his eye was still swollen from the beating he had gotten while being taken into custody in Nashville. His hands and feet were chained together leaving him barely enough length to reach for the chips and soda. Adam walked over to the table and placed the large file from his case on the table and sat down in the only other chair in the room.

"I'm Detective Adam Alexander from the Stillwell County Sheriff's Office. Can I get you another soda or bag of chips?"

"Cut the small talk. What the fuck do you want to talk about?"

"Well, I have to read you your Miranda rights and then we can…"

"I heard that shit a thousand times. Just fucking ask what you want to ask."

Adam took out his digital recorder and placed it on the table in front of Clay and hit the record button, "Sorry, but I still have to read them to you."

After he finished with Miranda, Adam cut right to the chase.

"I don't think you killed Melissa Dwyer. I think you're just saying you guys did to keep JJ off death row."

Clay sat up in his chair and had a surprised look on his face.

"Now why do you say that? How do you know we didn't kill that lady?"

"First of all, where's the gun?"

"I tossed it in the woods on the side of the road."

"Okay, what caliber gun did you guys use to kill her?"

"Fuck if I know. JJ stole it from some dude back home, I just took it from him and pulled the trigger."

"Right. Why did you choose Melissa Dwyer and how did you get to her house?"

"We was just drivin' around. Came to the house and did what we did."

"And what was that? Where did you leave her body? What room in the house specifically?"

"I can't remember all that shit. We killed that lady, plain and simple. We did it. Well, I did it. I pulled the trigger."

Adam jumped up and slammed his hands on the table, "Bull Shit! You didn't kill Melissa Dwyer, because you two were in Cincinnati at the time. You didn't leave town until December 30th. Now who has your fucking cell phone?"

For the first time since his capture, Clay dropped the hard ass routine.

"Listen Detective. I respect that you've got a job to do and that you want to make sure the right person goes to jail, but I gotta protect my interest too. JJ's gonna testify that I killed that lady to help keep him off death row. I did it. You hear me? I did it."

Adam dropped his head and looked at the floor for a minute.

"Listen, Clay, please understand where I'm coming from. I live in a small town, where lots of people depend on us to keep them safe. You were man enough to admit what you guys did, and I respect that more than you'll ever know. But now I'm asking you to be man enough to admit what you didn't do. There may be a killer running around my town and if you take the blame he might kill again."

Clay turned his head away from Adam and stared off into the distance. Adam sat patiently, never looking away, waiting for his answer. He could tell that Clay was struggling with doing the right thing and telling him the truth, but unfortunately for Adam, the devil won again.

"We did it. We killed that lady. I'm done talkin' to you."

"Fine Clay, if that's the way you want to play it. I have here an arrest warrant for Raymond Whitley, aka Clay, for the murder of Melissa Ann Dwyer."

Adam stood up and knocked on the door to let the guard know they were finished talking and to take custody of Clay once again.

"Can you take Clay back to his cell until we're ready to get this warrant officially served and notify your Commonwealth Attorney of our intention to bring these guys to Stillwell to stand trial."

Adam stood outside the interview room and watched as Clay was taken down the hallway and back over to the adult detention center. The other uniformed officer was still standing outside of Bernie's interview room door, so Adam decided to sit in on the rest of his interview.

"JJ and I were just talking about the Yankees. He's a fan too."

"And the rest of what we are here to discuss? How's that going?"

JJ sat back and shook his head, changing his demeanor instantly, "Yo, I'm done talking. Let's get this shit over with."

Adam pulled out JJ's arrest warrant and had him taken out of the interview room and back to the jail. Once the door was shut Adam looked over at Bernie, "Well, what did he have to say?"

“He said that Clay killed our lady. Said he shot her, left her in the house and they set it on fire.”

“Did he say where he left the body and what caliber gun they used?”

“He sat down, looked me in the eye and said they killed our lady. The next words that came out of his mouth were, ‘I want a lawyer’. So we just started talking sports. He likes the Yankees and the Jets.”

Bernie could tell that Adam was starting to get pissed off.

“What did you want me to do, Adam? He said that they did it, and then asked for a lawyer.”

“I’m going to investigate a little further and prove that they didn’t, and I don’t give a fuck what the sheriff says.”

Adam walked down the hall to look for Howell and found him sitting at his cubicle eating a huge ham sandwich and drinking a soda.

“Hey, Howell. When you got the subpoena for Clay’s cell phone records, did you happen to get them for JJ’s as well?”

Howell sat up in his chair and pulled the file from the back corner of his desk.

“I sure did.”

“Did he make any calls the day of our murder?”

Howell took the log out of his case file and handed it to Adam. After looking at the paper, he made a discovery.

“See here Bernie, JJ made a call to a number in Tennessee from Cincinnati on the night of our murder. No way that they could’ve been in Stillwell County. Now I just need to find out who has Clay’s phone. Let’s get Clay and JJ served and go home.”

On the way back from Frankfort, Adam picked up his cell phone and dialed the number that was attached to the subpoena. Not expecting an answer, he was surprised when he was greeted with the sound of a female voice on the other end of the line.

“Hello.”

"Please don't hang up on me. This is detective Adam Alexander from the Stillwell County Sheriff's office. Who am I talking to?"

The female on the other end became belligerent, "That's none of your damn business. You already have my family in jail."

"Listen, I know he didn't kill our victim and I don't want to see them get convicted of something that they didn't do."

There was no response on the other end of the line.

"Can I please meet with you so we can talk? Five minutes of your time is all I need. Please?"

"Meet me at North Park Baptist Church on Broadway Road in Lexington. I'll be there in one hour."

Adam turned to Bernie with a perplexed look on his face. Knowing full well the consequences of his actions, he drove in the direction of Lexington to meet with the cell phone user. Once in the parking lot of the church, Adam turned off his car and looked down at the clock. They still had another 20 minutes before his interviewee was to arrive.

"You hungry Bernie? There is a ton of fast food joints down the road?"

"No thanks. I just want to meet this chick and get the hell out of here."

Bernie looked out the window at the snow covered landscape. His mind was instantly taken back to the partially burned house on the night of the murder. A chill came over him as he thought about Melissa's badly burned body, discarded like trash in the closet. He knew that being with Adam could get him in trouble with Sheriff Lawson, but he didn't care. He wanted justice for Melissa and her family.

"Here she comes, Bernie."

He looked back at the entrance to the parking lot and saw a heavy set white female striding toward them. Without even hesitating she got in the back seat of the car and ordered Adam to drive to the interstate.

"I can't be seen talking to no cops. And by the way, this meeting ain't free, if you know what I mean."

Adam did as he was told and hopped back on I-74 south. He looked in his rear view mirror at a woman with no emotion on her face. She slumped down in the back seat until they were well outside the city limits before she sat up and held her hand out for payment.

"I'll make it worth your while, trust me. Can you tell me who you are please?" Adam asked.

Adam discretely pulled out his digital recorder and placed it on the seat next to him to document the interview, while Bernie sat quietly with his arms folded tight to his body, never once making eye contact with the woman in the back seat.

"I'm Ashleigh Simmons. My mother is Clay's sister."

"Do you have the cell phone that I called you on?"

"Yeah, I have the phone. Clay bought it for me two years ago for a birthday present."

"Has he had your phone in the last two or three months?"

"No, it's my phone. He bought it for me. He has his own damn phone and I can give you that number. It's one of those pay as you go things that you can get from any convenience store."

Ashleigh looked through her contact list and read the number out loud.

"Do you know where Clay and JJ were on Sunday, December 18th, Ashleigh?"

She looked around the interior of the cruiser for a minute before answering.

"That's two weeks after Tara was killed. They were still up in Cincinnati. I remember because they didn't leave there until just before New Year's. I talked to JJ a few days before then and he was sayin' some crazy shit, like they had to get out of Cinci like real soon. I didn't ask what he was talking about because I just figured he was high or some shit like that."

Adam diverted his eyes from the road and looked at Bernie with disgust. “Well, that’s all we needed Ashleigh, where do you want us to drop you off?”

“Back near the church would be fine with me.”

Adam gave Ashleigh $30.00 out of his own pocket for her trouble and dropped her off behind the church.

After she closed the door and was out of sight, he looked over at Bernie, “Damn it! What am I going to do now?”

“I’m pretty sure that was a rhetorical question, but you’re going to have to drop the charges against Clay and JJ.”

“I know, but they still have to make an appearance in court to have the charges dropped. As soon as we get back, I’ll draft a subpoena for the phone records for the number that Ashleigh gave us. That will be the true test of where these two were.”

“Are we gonna tell Bishop or the Sheriff about what we learned here today?”

“Hell no. Let’s just see what we get with the new subpoena. I’ll write my report about Clay saying he confessed and you hammer out one about what JJ said to you. That should keep everyone happy for the time being.”

“Why do you think the Sheriff cornered you in Bishop’s office and told you to alter your reports?”

“The only thing I can think of is because it’s an election year and someone is running against him for the first time in forever.”

“Yeah, I heard that too. Aaron Delzatto from the town police is running this year. He’s a good guy and actually has a shot at winning. That’s enough to put Lawson on edge right there.”

Adam continued to engage Bernie in small talk the entire way back to the office parking lot. The two emerged from Adam’s car, tired and hungry.

“Why don’t you go home, Bernie. You can write your supplement to the case tomorrow.”

“You ain’t gotta tell me twice.”

Adam turned away from Bernie and walked in the back door of the office. His first stop was in the kitchen, where he poured himself a large cup of coffee.

Bishop was on his way out the door when he saw Adam in the kitchen, so he stopped and asked, "Well, how did it go today?"

"Fine. It went fine, I guess."

"Fine? Can you please elaborate a little bit more on that?"

"They confessed to our murder. Clay said he did it while JJ watched."

"Well that's good news right?"

"Yeah, good news, Sarge."

Bishop knew that something was wrong, but decided to let it go for the time being.

"Okay, just get your report finished for tonight and I'll read it first thing in the morning. Keep up the good work."

Adam walked into his office and turned on his computer. He sat and stared at the screen for at least ten minutes before he began to type his first words. This situation was delicate, so he needed to choose his words very carefully. Omitting the entire interview with Ashleigh from his report, Adam printed out three copies, and left one each, for Bishop and the Sheriff, in their mailboxes. Ten minutes later he was at home, filling Rennae in about his day over a warm bowl of beef stew.

Chapter 23

The next morning, Adam drove into the office to get the subpoena for Clay's phone records typed out and over to Judge Watson for his signature. The sooner he had the information that he was looking for, the sooner he could drop the charges and start looking for the real killer. With the signed subpoena in hand, he returned to his office and faxed a copy over to the legal department of Mobile Incorporated. He waited for five minutes before calling to make sure they had received his request. After listening to his list of options, Adam pressed *seven,* and was transferred directly to the service manager.

"Mobile Incorporated legal division, how can I help you?"

"This is Detective Adam Alexander with the Stillwell County Sheriff's Office. Did you, by any chance, receive the subpoena for cell phone records I faxed over to you guys a little while ago?"

"I did, and I'm pulling up those records as we speak. You know that we only keep the numbers dialed and received. We don't retain any text messages."

"I do, and I appreciate your quick response. All I'm really looking for are the numbers and the coordinates for the cell towers that the calls originated from."

"Not a problem, Detective. I'll print all of this information out and fax them to you within the next few minutes."

Adam sat on the edge of his chair, staring at the fax and waiting for the information he had requested. Five minutes later the machine was spitting out page after page of Clay's phone records. Adam grabbed the papers from the tray and raced down to Bernie's office so they could decipher them together.

"Pull up the cell towers for Mobile Incorporated, Bernie. I've got all the coordinates for Clay's cell phone here."

Adam put all the pages in order by date and took out his yellow highlighter to mark all the outgoing calls made on December 18th.

"Okay, Bern. I have seven calls made on the day of our murder. You ready?"

Bernie had the comprehensive list of all the cell tower locations used by Mobile Incorporated in front of him, broken down by state and county.

"Go ahead, Adam."

"Okay, they're all from the same coordinate 407.00635."

"You were right, that tower is in downtown Cincinnati."

"Looks like we need to talk to Clay again."

Adam took the cell phone records and moved toward Bishop's office to let him know what he had just discovered. He was excited that he had debunked Clay and JJ's confession because now he could start looking for the real killer. The only thing that worried him was Sheriff Lawson's threat, and how he was going to tell him he jumped the gun with his press conference. There was no way Adam was going to convict two innocent men, no matter how disgusting they were. He barged through Bishop's door to find him watching the morning news and sipping on a cup of coffee.

"What's up, Adam?"

"I have some good news and some bad news. The bad news is that there's no way that Clay and JJ killed Melissa Dwyer."

"And how can you be so sure of that?"

"On our way back from Frankfort yesterday I called the cell phone number that I got from Howell, and Clay's niece answered. She told me that Clay bought that particular phone for her over two years ago and he's never used it. Then she gave me Clay's personal cell phone number which I got the records for today. All calls were made and received in Cincinnati on the 18th. And now that I look further, there's no outgoing activity after January 12th."

Bishop put his head in his hands and looked down at the floor. He had hoped the investigation was behind them after Clay and JJ had confessed, but he, like Adam, knew they had to move in another direction.

"And the good news, Adam?"

"There isn't any. But, I'm beginning to think that Rocky may have been our guy all along. All we can hope for now is that the forensics lab has some good news for us. The ballistics information and all the DNA evidence are going to be crucial at this point."

"Damn. Well, go type up your report while I break the bad news to the Sheriff. He ain't gonna like this one bit."

Bishop stood up and walked toward Sheriff Lawson's office while Adam went to his office to type up his narrative.

He had just pulled up a blank report on his computer when he was interrupted by his door slamming shut and the sheriff screaming at him, "You couldn't leave well enough alone could you, Alexander?"

"Sheriff, they didn't do it, which means the real killer…"

"I told you that if you didn't make those charges stick I was going to make you pay. Well, guess what? It's time for me to live up to my end of the bargain. Detective Alexander, you are hereby terminated as a Stillwell County Sheriff's office employee. Hand over your badge and gun immediately."

Adam sat in silence, not knowing exactly what to think.

"And furthermore, I know that Detective Steckler was with you when you went out on your little side investigation. His ass is gone, too."

"Sheriff, that was all me. Bernie had nothing to do with it. He also didn't have any idea about our previous conversation. It was all me and I take full responsibility."

"Badge and gun! NOW!"

Slowly, Adam took his Detective's badge off his belt along with his service weapon and handed it over to the Sheriff.

"I need all your files. Every bit of paperwork in this office belongs to me."

Adam pulled out his keys from his pants pocket, took the file cabinet key off the ring, and placed it on the desk.

"Now, grab your personal shit and get the fuck out. I'll have a deputy escort you to your house to get my uniforms and anything else that belongs to this office."

Adam started to take his cruiser key off his key ring when Sheriff Lawson inched up to him and whispered in his ear, "I told you not to fuck with me, boy."

Adam stood still for a moment, frozen by the situation.

"I said get your shit and get out."

Adam was in the process of packing up when Bishop came running into his office, "Sheriff, you can't fire these men for doing their job."

"I can fire these men for whatever reason I want to. The way I see it, they engaged in a rogue investigation outside of Stillwell County without permission from a superior. That's conduct unbecoming and that's the grounds I'm terminating them under. And you better shut your damn mouth Bishop, or you're next."

Adam took a few minutes to pack up his personal pictures and important numbers into a large evidence box while two Deputy Sheriffs looked on. They were given explicit instructions from the Sheriff not to let Adam take files or loose paper from the office or they too would be fired. He walked down the hallway with seven years of his law enforcement career as a detective crammed into one box. The whole process was beginning to seem surreal. Once outside, Adam climbed into the passenger seat of a marked sheriff's cruiser and was driven to his home. The Deputy that drove him home didn't even have the common decency to look him in the eye or offer up any condolences.

These people used to be his family. Adam would have taken a bullet for any one of these guys and this is how they repaid him for his loyalty.

He climbed out of the passenger seat and walked in the rear door to the kitchen, where Rennae was sitting reading the paper.

"What's going on, Adam? Why are these deputies here?"

"I got fired today, baby. I'll fill you in after they leave."

Rennae couldn't help but start to cry, worried about their future. Adam went upstairs to the closet and retrieved every piece of clothing that said Stillwell County Sheriff's Office on it and handed them to the goon standing over his shoulder.

"Now get the hell out of my house!" Adam yelled.

The two deputies did as they were told and walked out of the house the same way that they had come in. Adam stood behind Rennae in the kitchen and put his hand on her shoulder as she wept uncontrollably.

"Adam, what in the hell just happened?"

"I was fired today for no damn reason, Rennae. I'd love to fill you in, but right now I need to go find a job."

"Where are you going to go?"

"To the only place that I can think of. I'm going to beg Chief Evans from the Stillwell Town Police for a job. I'll be back in a bit."

Adam grabbed the keys to his personal car and drove back into town. He was still shaking from what had just happened, but the need to find work superseded his anger. Eleven years as a deputy sheriff, down the drain. Adam pulled onto Court Street just in time to see Bernie being escorted out the front door with a box of his personal belongings and his head hung low. He screeched to as halt in the visitor spot in front of the court house and told Bernie to put his things in the front seat.

"Come with me Bernie. This is bullshit."

The two men, now civilians, marched into the front door of the police department and asked to see Chief Evans. Five minutes later they were in his office explaining why they had been fired and begging him for a job. Chief Evans sat across from them, with his mouth wide open, as Adam explained the situation.

"He did what? Adam, you're the best general investigator they've got and Bernie, you're the best narcotics investigator they've ever had. Why the hell did he fire you two?"

Adam laid it all out there on the table while Chief Evans looked on in disgust. He told the Chief about every nasty encounter he had had with the sheriff, every conversation where he had been told to falsify documents, and why he and Bernie were ultimately fired.

"You mean to tell me that he fired you because you went to Louisville on your way back from Frankfort following up on a lead?"

Adam nodded at the Chief and went on to say that he knew Clay and JJ were confessing to a crime they didn't commit. He was just about to tell Evans about the cell phone records when Adam heard the lobby door to the Police Department slam shut followed by the sound of Darla, the chief's secretary yelling, "Sheriff Lawson! You can't go back there! Chief Evans is in the middle of a meeting!"

"Screw his meeting. I want those two clowns thrown out of this building!"

Chief Evans stood up from behind his desk and waited for the Sheriff to come barging into his office while Adam and Bernie both sat still, anticipating a barrage of insults to be hurled at them by Lawson. Right on cue, Chief Evan's door flew open.

"Evans, these two were just fired for conduct unbecoming and disobeying direct orders. I demand that you throw them out of this building immediately. They have absolutely zero credibility and can't be trusted to wear any uniform or badge. They're a disgrace to law enforcement."

"Well Sheriff, you're too late. I just hired these two officers and they start immediately. So if you wouldn't mind, get the hell out of my office."

Sheriff Lawson turned to Adam and pointed his finger in his face, "Don't you think this is over. Not by a long shot. I'm going to the county executives in the morning and filing formal complaints against both of you. This job won't last long."

Chief Evans slammed his fist down on his desk and yelled, "Lawson, I said get the hell out of my office!"

Sheriff Lawson's face turned three shades of red before he turned around and walked back to his side of the building.

"Sorry about all this, Chief," Bernie said.

"It's not your fault, gentlemen. I have two road positions open that need to be filled. Unfortunately, I can't put you back on the investigations wing right now, but when the spots open up, you two will be the first to know."

Adam and Bernie both stood up and extended their hands toward Chief Evans.

"Thanks, Chief. We won't let you down," Adam stated.

"Not a problem. The way I see it, you two just saved me the time and money of hiring and training two inexperienced people. Please, sit back down so we can go over a few more things."

Adam and Bernie did as they were instructed and sat back down to discuss their salaries and duty assignments. At this point, they were both happy that they would only be taking a two thousand dollar pay cut a year to work the street.

"I can also give you guys the same shift if you want. I have two midnight slots available, one on A-side and the other on B-side. One of the A-side guys recently asked to be transferred to the other midnight shift, so that would give me two openings for A-side."

“That would be great, Chief. When do we start officially?” Adam asked.

“The beginning of the next pay period sounds good to me. We get paid every two weeks as opposed to every month like you’re used to, so four days from now. You two need to head down the hall and get fitted for uniforms, bullet proof vests, gun belts, and all that other stuff so you can get to work. And then you need to go to the range to qualify. Oh, and stop by Human Resources on your way to the range. They’ll have some paperwork that you’ll need to fill out by tomorrow so we can get you processed. Now let’s go on over to the courthouse so we can get you two sworn in.”

Without hesitation, Adam and Bernie followed the chief across the street to the courthouse to be sworn in by the clerk of the circuit court. Once in front of the clerk, they happily raised their right hands and solemnly agreed to uphold the constitution of the United States, the laws of the Commonwealth of Kentucky, and enforce the ordinances set forth by the Town of Stillwell. Adam reached across the counter and grasped his shiny new patrolman’s badge in his hand. A smile spread across his face as he looked down and studied every detail on his new shield. It was beautiful. With his sense of pride restored, Adam put his badge in his pocket and walked with Chief Evans and Bernie back to the office to get fitted for the rest of their gear.

“I’ll call Sergeant Rankin and see if he’ll be able to get you down to the range today to qualify. I can’t have my officer’s walking the streets without a weapon.”

Chief Evans picked up his desk phone and made a call to the operations bureau of his department to see if the range was open. Thirty minutes later the two new hires were down at the range qualifying under the watchful eye of Sergeant Rankin. Bragging rights went to Adam because he shot a ninety eight percent to Bernie’s ninety seven percent.

On the drive back to the police station, Adam looked over at Bernie, “I’m sorry that I got you fired. I know you really liked working narcotics.”

"You did the right thing, which is exactly what I would have done. And you got me a new job five minutes after I was fired, so I can't be that mad at you."

"Thanks, Bro. You're a damn good man and a damn good friend."

"Is this the part where we hug it out?"

"I was trying to be nice for once, and you go and ruin the moment."

Bernie let out a laugh, "I appreciate the sentiment. Now can we go and get the rest of our shit so I can go home and try to explain this to my wife."

Within the next twenty minutes, Adam and Bernie walked out onto Court Street carrying two huge bags full of duty gear and brand new gray uniforms. They walked over to Adam's car parked on the street to find Bishop leaning against the passenger side door.

"I heard you two assholes were in the Chief's office begging for a job."

"Yeah, we had to do something to put food on the table," Adam answered.

"I guess I'll be seeing you two on the road then."

Bernie looked at Adam and then back at Bishop, "You got demoted?"

"Yep, I'm now Deputy Bishop assigned to the midnight's squad under Corporal fuck-stain Gibbons."

Adam cringed, "Ooooh no. That stings a little bit, huh?"

"You ain't kidding, brother. The first time that little fucker snaps at me, I will knock his ass out."

"So we all got screwed today, huh? I say we all go out for a beer before we head home," Bernie suggested.

Adam pulled out his cell phone and called Rennae to let her know that everything was ok. And for the first time that he could remember, he asked for her permission to go get a beer with the guys before he came home. With her permission given, it was off to the Still House for a well-deserved beverage.

Four beers in, Adam started talking about the Dwyer homicide with Bernie and Bishop.

"What are we missing here guys? We have to be missing something."

Bernie already had that glazed look in his eyes because he was hammered, "I don't care about that case no more. And we don't have the reports, so fuck it."

"I still have all my cases at home. I copy everything and keep them in a file in the basement. I have every case I've ever worked, including this one. We need to get our hands on the ballistics information."

Bishop put both fingers in his ears and pretended he didn't hear anything.

"Seriously guys, I'm not letting this go. If Lawson thinks that he got the best of me then he can think again."

Bishop chugged the remainder of his beer and excused himself to the restroom. While Bishop stumbled off toward the bathroom, Adam looked over at Bernie and saw him staring off into the distance.

"Well, I see that talking to you is going to be useless, Officer Steckler."

"Just let it go for tonight, Adam. You can continue to get yourself in trouble tomorrow, so let's just play some pool and forget today ever happened. Please."

"You know that I'm not going to let this go."

"Yeah, I know. But do me a favor. This time, keep your investigation to yourself. I don't want to get fired twice in one month."

Bishop returned from the bathroom and ordered a basket of wings and some nachos to help absorb the alcohol in their systems. While waiting for the food, the three reminisced about all the fun that they had had together over the years. For a while, they were able to forget about their troubles and just enjoy the moment. Even as their food hit the table, they continued to tell stories and laugh about things that would make a normal person puke. Things that people outside of law enforcement would never see or understand.

Adam was the first one to call it an early night. He called Rennae and had her pick him up because he was way too drunk to drive and he didn't want to risk running into a deputy on the back roads. While he waited for her to arrive, he thought about how strange it was that this morning he had been a detective working a homicide and now he was a town police officer, about to be pushing a cruiser on the road. As he sat on the cold bench outside the bar he let his mind wander back to the night of the murder. He was mentally inside the house looking at the picture of Melissa and her kid's, on the bedside table. They all looked so happy. Why did her face look so familiar to him?

Rennae arrived within ten minutes and took Adam home. She didn't even have the car in park before Adam was out of the passenger seat and on his way down to the basement. He pulled out a box labeled "Christmas Stuff" from under the stairs and went over to the couch. He sat down and pulled out his files on the Mary Jo Conyers murder and the Melissa Dwyer Murder. He pulled out both of their photos and placed them side by side on the coffee table.

"Mother of God! They could be twins!"

Adam looked over his shoulder and saw that Rennae was standing directly behind him with her arms folded.

"What in the world are you doing, Adam?"

"Rennae, look at this?"

Rennae walked over and looked at the two photographs, "They look alike, so what."

Adam pulled out the ballistics report from the Conyers murder and confirmed that she was found on the side of the road with a nine millimeter bullet hole in her chest.

"Mary Jo was murdered with a nine millimeter, and Melissa was killed with a nine millimeter. They both look alike. They were both around the same age when they were killed and they were found within two miles of one another. There are too many similarities for it to be a coincidence, Rennae."

Adam rifled through the files for a bit longer and decided to make a call to his buddy Darren Walker from the state lab. At this point, only he could tell Adam if his theory was correct.

"Put that phone down, Adam. You sound like a damn drunken fool. Call him in the morning, please."

Adam put his phone back in his pocket and left the files scattered on the coffee table. As he shut the light off, he looked back at the pile of papers and hoped that he was on to something.

The next morning, Adam paced back and forth in his kitchen waiting for nine o'clock. At precisely one minute past nine he was on the phone with the state lab.

"Hello, Kentucky State Police Division of Forensic Science Lab, this is Vikki, how can I help you?"

"Hey, Vikki. This is Detective… Sorry, this is Officer Alexander, is Darren Walker in please?"

"Yes he is. Please hold while I get him for you."

The transfer took a few minutes, but eventually Darren picked up the phone.

"Listen Adam, I'm not supposed to be talking to you at all right now. And I sure as hell am not going to be talking to you over a recorded line. What's your cell phone number and maybe I'll call you back. But we will not discuss this case, do you understand?"

"Sure thing, Darren." Adam gave him the number and ended with, "Hope to hear from you soon."

Almost the entire day went by while Adam waited for the call. He had run all his errands and turned in all the necessary paperwork that his new agency required for health insurance and payroll. On the drive home his cell phone rang.

"Darren. I didn't think that you were going to call."

"Trust me, I gave it serious consideration."

"I am guessing that by now you know I'm no longer working the case."

"Yes, your former employer, Sheriff Lawson, called us yesterday afternoon looking for the ballistics results from your murder. When I told him that I hadn't finished it yet he went crazy. I transferred him to my boss who then came back to me and said to put a rush job on the case. I had started it two days ago and just finished it this morning. When I told my boss that I was going to call you with the results, he informed me that you had been terminated and that I was to call the sheriff directly with the information and no one else. He specifically said that only the sheriff was to get the ballistics report."

"What did you find out?"

"Adam I can get fired for this. You're not even an employee of the sheriff's office any more."

"Come on Darren, please. Something crazy is going on here and I need to figure it out."

"Well, after I examined the bullet I entered it into the National Integrated Ballistic Identification Network to compare it to other unsolved cases throughout the state."

"And?"

"I got a hit. The bullet that was taken out of your dead lady was fired from the same gun that killed Mary Jo Conyers. "

"I knew it!" Adam yelled."

"Oh, there's one more thing you don't know yet. All that meth lab equipment that was in the room tested negative for methamphetamine hydrochloride or any precursor chemicals. It was clean as a whistle. You didn't hear any of this from me, Adam. You got that?"

"Not a problem. Thanks, Darren."

Chapter 24

Before continuing home, Adam hung up the phone and made two frantic phone calls to Bernie and Bishop. After a little persuasion, and the promise of free beer, they both reluctantly agreed to meet at Adam's house later that evening to discuss the new developments in the case.

When asked what the developments were, Adam just told them, "Come on over and I'll fill you in then."

He pulled into his driveway and ran down to his basement to sort through the case files before the pending round table discussion. He was in the middle of looking over both cases when he was interrupted by Bishop walking down the stairs to his basement, followed by Bernie ten minutes later.

"Well, what's the huge news that you have to tell us about?" Bishop smirked.

"I just got word from one of my inside sources at the state police forensics lab and guess what?"

"What?" Bishop asked.

"Are you two ready for this?"

"Yeah, I'm on the edge of my seat with anticipation," Bernie commented.

"The same gun that killed Melissa Dwyer killed Mary Jo Conyers."

The room fell silent for a period of thirty seconds or so as Bernie and Bishop tried to wrap their heads around what they had just heard.

"And Bernie, all that meth equipment that you collected and sent off to be tested came back negative for meth or any other toxic chemicals."

"You're kidding? That glass triple neck flask is pretty damn hard to get your hands on. Just getting caught with one is a felony."

"Bernie, do you remember if Rocky had any ties to Mary Jo?"

"Not to my knowledge. Mary Jo was a country girl with no education and she worked on the farm with the rest of her family. She wasn't exactly Rocky's type if you know what I mean."

"Bishop, Rocky was how old, forty-four?"

"Yeah, he was born in nineteen sixty-five, so that sounds about right."

"Melissa was born in seventy five, making her thirty four years old. Mary Jo was killed five years ago and she was born in seventy, making her thirty four years old at that time. Check this out."

Adam held up the photographs of both victims for Bernie and Bishop to see. Once again, the room fell silent.

"They could be twins," Bernie stated.

"I know I'm not crazy, guys. We have too many similarities here to be a coincidence. Something isn't adding up. What are we missing?" Adam asked.

"I don't know, but I can tell you that Rocky's name never came up during Mary Jo's investigation," Bernie added.

"Are you sure about that?"

Bernie took the Conyers case folder and started to look through the file.

"Okay, it says here that Deputy David Gibbons received the call from dispatch for a disabled motorist. When he arrived on scene, he found an abandoned vehicle on the side of the road, with the keys still in the ignition. David said in his report that he had gone through the vehicle without gloves on and accidentally contaminated the scene because there was no evidence of foul play inside or around the car. He also said he had looked for the registration in the glove box and center console so he could try to identify the owner. He was on his way back to his cruiser to run the tag on the car when he looked over his shoulder and saw what looked like feet sticking out of the bushes. When he went over to investigate, he saw Mary Joe with a bullet hole in her upper chest. He started CPR but she was DOA at the hospital."

"Do we know anything else? Did any of Mary Jo's family members work for Rocky?" Adam asked.

Bernie scoured the case file for any association but was unable to come up with one. Slowly, the evening slipped away from them as they discussed possible scenarios and theories. Adam walked over to his fridge to get another beer and realized that they had gone through an entire case of Pabst Blue Ribbon.

"Shit, we need more beer."

Bishop looked over at the clock and saw that it was almost eleven, "Can I make a suggestion please? Now that we know the sheriff has the ballistics and the lab results let's see what he does with it. He may appoint someone else to my position and have them drop the charges and keep going with the investigation. And if he doesn't then we can confront him with it later on. Or at least give that information to Ms. Leighton for her to use against the sheriff later on."

"Yeah, I nominate Adam to meet with Ms. Leighton to discuss the case," Bernie stated with a smirk.

"Fuck you, Bernie."

"Am I missing something here?" Bishop Asked.

"No, you're not missing anything. Bernie is just being an asshole."

At the conclusion of the meeting, everyone was in agreement that they would keep a close watch on the case through Bishop and the newspapers.

Weeks turned into months with no news about the charges against Clay and JJ being dropped. To make matters worse, Sheriff Lawson appointed none other than his own son-in-law to the position of Sergeant in charge of the Criminal Investigations Bureau and the lead investigator for the case. Adam tried on several occasions to sit down with David to discuss the case but every time he was told to mind his own business. It was looking like they were going ahead with the charges and Adam couldn't let that happen. Even if he had to go to the newspapers, he was going to see this one through.

Adam, Bernie, and Bishop spent a lot of time together working the midnight shift on the mean streets of

Stillwell. It took them a little while to wrap their heads around the fact that they were no longer detectives, but eventually they were able to see that there was a lot less stress pushing a cruiser. Not to mention the fact that all the brass were at home and not standing behind you, breathing down your neck. Adam and Bernie usually hit the street after roll-call and wrote a couple tickets to satisfy their supervisor before screwing off the rest of the shift. If there weren't any calls-for-service pending, the three would meet at the Grub-N-Gas, just after one in the morning, and gossip about what was going on in their respective departments.

One spring evening, Adam leaned back against his patrol car sipping a cup of coffee in the parking lot, waiting for Bernie and Bishop to arrive for their bull session. The temperature was finally warm enough for them to enjoy their conversations outside of their patrol cars without a jacket. A few minutes later, all three were spinning lies and swapping tales, as usual.

"Have you been on any good calls lately, Bishop? Bernie and I haven't done shit."

"Not really, just your typical stupid stuff. Larcenies from cars, domestic disputes, nothing to write home about. How's the town treating you two?"

Bernie looked over at Bishop and said, "Like a baby treats a diaper."

"That's not true. It ain't so bad. With overtime, I make more here than at the Sheriff's Office. Plus I applied for a federal job with the DEA."

"Good for you, Adam. I know you'll go far. I always wondered why you and Bernie were here in the first place. Both of you guys have college degrees and you're smart. I'm just a dumb ass local boy and am stuck here forever, but you two can go anywhere you want."

Adam thought about it for a minute and decided that Bishop was right. He wanted better for his family, and now that Rennae was pregnant he had some serious decisions to make. Bernie on the other hand saw things differently.

"I grew up in the city and absolutely hated it there. It's always go, go, go, with no slowing down. This is the life for me, guys. I'm not going anywhere."

While Adam leaned inside his car to see if his cell phone was fully charged he asked Bishop, "What's the latest with our case? Anything new?"

"Well, that dickhead David is still going forward with the charges against Clay and JJ. They're going to be in town tomorrow for their arraignment. I overheard him telling Captain Cubbage that the case was strong and that Ms. Leighton is handling it herself."

Adam just shook his head in disgust, "Fuck this shit, something has to be done, and now."

"Whoa, Adam. What are you going to do?" Bishop asked.

He didn't say a word as he walked past Bernie and Bishop, hopped in his patrol car, and drove south out of town toward Sheriff Lawson's house. He was so angry about what was going on that he didn't care about the consequences. He pulled into Lawson's driveway and charged up to the front door. He saw that all of the interior lights were off, but he pounded on the door anyway. A minute later, Sheriff Lawson came to the door wearing his robe and fumbling with his glasses. His wife stood silently behind him with a look of concern on her face and wondered what the commotion was about.

"What do you want Alexander? This conduct of yours is a disgusting display of disrespect. I'll make sure this gets passed along to your superiors. Goodnight!"

The Sheriff tried to turn away, but Adam grabbed onto his arm.

"You want to discuss this in front of your wife, or do you want to save what little fucking dignity you have left? I know what you're doing. I know it all."

Sheriff Lawson turned to his wife, told her to go back to bed, and that he would be up in a few minutes.

Once she was clearly out of sight, Sheriff Lawson turned back to Adam, "Exactly what do you think you know, Son?"

"I know all about the ballistics. I know the gun used to kill Melissa Dwyer was also used to kill Mary Jo Conyers. And I know the meth lab in the house was an afterthought, put there to throw us off the trail. It tested negative for any toxic substances. I didn't put two and two together until tonight. The night I walked in on you in Bernie's office, I found out that you were in mine, too. You were pulling the ballistics information from our files. But what you didn't account for was that I keep copies of all my cases at my house. You're covering up for someone, and when I find out who, I'll take great pride in bringing you both down."

Sheriff Lawson hung his head, turned around and walked back inside his house, closing the front door behind him. Adam stood on the front porch and watched all the interior lights turn off before he walked back to his patrol car.

On his way back to town he took a deep breath and realized what he had done. He pulled into the parking lot where he had left his two friends and found them still standing in the same spot. Adam got out of his patrol car, still shaking from adrenaline.

"What in the world did you just do, Adam?" Bernie asked.

"It's probably best that you don't know, Bernie."

"Seriously, Adam, what did you just do?"

"I drove to the sheriff's house and I told him I knew what was going on. I told him that once I found out who he was protecting I was going to take them both down."

Bernie and Bishop both had a look of shock on their faces.

"And then what did you do?" Bernie asked.

"I waited for him to say something, but he didn't. He just turned around and walked back inside his house. That's when I left and came back here."

No one knew what to say. They just stood there in silence for a few more minutes. Eventually, Bishop decided that he was going to head into the convenience store to use the bathroom and get some more coffee. It was only three in the morning and everyone had four more hours to kill before his shift was over. Adam decided to leave Bernie and Bishop in the parking lot and drive around town for the rest of the night. For the remainder of his shift, he worried that Sheriff Lawson would call Chief Evans to make a formal complaint. He was also kicking himself in the ass for letting his emotions get the better of him. He needed this job and getting fired for a second time would surely hinder his chances of getting hired with the DEA.

Thirty minutes before they were supposed to get off Adam and Bernie were dispatched on one more call that took the remainder of their shift and then some. Adam had to take a report of a larceny from a pick-up truck where the victim didn't lock his tool box. Bernie grabbed his fingerprinting kit and attempted to lift prints from the tool box, but the diamond plating made it impossible.

"Bernie, you can stop trying, I'm just going to give this guy a case number and call it a night. It's his own damn fault his tools were stolen."

Just as he was about to key up his mic to ask the dispatcher for a case number he heard the emergency tones sound twice through his portable radio.

"All units. All units. Shots fired at 311 Court Street. One gun shot heard at this time."

Bernie raised his head, "It's probably one of the jail deputies unloading his gun again. I sure hope they didn't shoot anyone this time."

"You're probably right, Bernie."

Adam keyed up his mic and asked for a case number, but when there was no answer he became worried.

"Hey, Bernie. Let's go to the office just in case."

Adam turned to his larceny victim and told him he would return later on in the morning to give him a case number for his insurance claim. The two officers got back into their cars and drove to the station, not entirely convinced that everything was okay. Adam pulled into the front parking lot with Bernie directly behind him.

"I'm telling you bro, this is probably nothing."

"I hope you're right, Bern. It looks like we're the first ones here."

Adam had just put his hand on the lobby door when he heard a second gun shot.

"Shit, that came from the Sheriff's Office side!"

Without hesitation, they were inside the lobby with their guns drawn. Adam punched in the code to the secured door and burst through to avoid being in the fatal funnel for too long. They cleared the four rooms on the administration hallway and were about to turn left toward the patrol bureau when they heard noises coming from Sheriff Lawson's office.

"Sheriff Lawson, are you okay?" Adam yelled.

There was no response, so the two cautiously headed all the way down the hall to his office door, which was wide open. Adam peered around the corner and saw a lifeless body laying face down on the floor with a pool of blood forming around the torso. Sheriff Lawson was sitting at his desk with a semi automatic pistol to his head and tears coming down his cheek. Adam realized that he was in danger of being the next victim, so he moved back away from the doorway.

"Sheriff, put the gun down and let's talk."

"Go to hell, Alexander. I know the drill. I refuse to spend the rest of my life behind bars."

Adam looked down at the floor again to try and identify the body, but it was positioned so all he could see was the torso and the feet. There was no way that he could have moved forward anymore without putting himself in the line of fire, so he stayed where he was.

"Sheriff, who's the dead guy on the floor?"

"I tried over and over to keep him out of trouble. I tried to give my daughter and grandkids a good life. I only wanted the best for my family. Please, God, know that. Please, God, forgive me."

"Sheriff what are you talking about?"

Sheriff Lawson started to yell at the top of his lungs, "HIM! That no good murdering piece of shit son-in-law of mine! He killed those ladies! He said that the voices in his head told him to do it, but I know the truth. He was trying to fuck those whores and they turned him down. He wasn't crazy. He was just a cheating piece of shit who couldn't handle rejection. NOW LOOK AT YOU! Look what you did to my family!"

Adam tried to calm the situation, "Sheriff, put the gun down and talk to me. Just put it down. I won't come any closer."

"You of all people should be happy, Alexander. You get to solve two murder investigations and you get to see the two people you hate the most, dead."

"Sheriff, I don't want to see anyone dead."

Bernie heard movement down the hallway, so he backed away from Adam to tell the incoming officers to hold their positions. They didn't need anyone else inside to make matters worse. Bernie popped his head around the corner and saw that Bishop was coming down the hallway with two deputies in tow.

"Don't shoot, it's me, Bernie. I'm coming around the corner."

"We got you, Bernie. Come around the corner."

Bernie holstered his weapon, walked around the corner displaying his hands, and motioned Bishop to come up to him.

"What the fuck is going on, Bernie?"

"It's the Sheriff. He's shot David twice and now he's in his office with a gun to his head."

"What the fuck, why?"

"Apparently David killed Melissa and Mary Jo. Bishop, you come with us." Bernie looked over at the other two deputies and gave them explicit instructions, "You two, post up at the door and don't let anyone else in here. Make sure the next group of incoming officer's surrounds the building and secures all the exits. Keep everyone else out."

"Copy that."

The two deputies did as they were told and retreated out the secure door into the lobby, while Bernie and Bishop walked back up the hallway to cover Adam.

"You're wasting your breath, Alexander. There are no other options for me. I covered up one murder and I tried to cover up another one."

"Well, if you're just going to kill yourself, can you do me a favor? Where is the nine millimeter that David used to kill those women?"

"I told the dumb ass to get rid of the gun after the first murder, but apparently he was too STUPID TO FOLLOW ORDERS!"

"Sheriff, calm down. Where's the weapon?"

"I have it to my head. So when I'm finished blowing my brains out, this gun will have killed four people. Think about that Adam, four people dead with one gun. How could I have been so STUPID!"

Adam could tell the situation was getting more volatile by the minute, so he made one last attempt to talk the Sheriff down.

"Sheriff please don't do this. You have so much…."

"Alexander, I am not coming out of this office alive. That's a fact. I was in the process of getting this letter written when dip-shit walked in the door. I was going to do this later today when everyone was here, but I suppose it's going to work out better this way. All you had to do was get Clay and JJ take the fall. That's all you had to do."

"Sheriff, that wasn't the right thing to do and you know it. I had to do my job and try to get the real murderer off the streets."

"Well, I did your job for you. And now it's time to get this murderer off the streets. Tell my wife and daughter that I love them."

Adam didn't have time to say another word before he heard the third gun shot. Weapons drawn, he, Bernie, and Bishop all rushed into Sheriff Lawson's office to see him sitting behind his desk with blood dripping down his left temple. Bits of brain matter, skull, and blood covered the cinderblock wall just beyond the exit wound. They all heard him exhale one last time before his body went limp and lifeless. Adam walked around the desk and looked down that the nine millimeter that was on the floor just below the Sheriff Lawson's outstretched arm. He was looking at the one piece of evidence he had been in search of for the past five years. How could one little piece of metal and plastic cause so much trouble? That one gun had almost destroyed his marriage, kept him awake at night, and had caused a constant fear that someone else would fall prey to its powers.

But that was all over now. He was saddened that things had ended the way they had, but happy it was over. He looked over at the Sheriff's desk and saw a piece of paper underneath an expensive looking pen. It was the letter the Sheriff had been in the process of writing. Adam looked down at the letter on the desk and read what the Sheriff had written:

To Whom It May Concern,

I'm sure by now you are all wondering how a horrible tragedy such as this could have occurred in our peaceful little community. It happened because I allowed it to happen. You, the people of Stillwell County, voted me into office twice, with the expectation that I would do my best to protect and serve you. But that was not to be. Not only did I allow a murderer to go free, but I also employed him, allowed him to stay married to my daughter, and I even invited him into my home. I allowed a violent man to walk the streets among you, I gave him a badge and a gun, and I turned him loose. I turned him loose to take the lives of two young and beautiful women who had their whole lives ahead of them. If that wasn't bad enough, I turned my back on good, hard working deputies to protect this monster. I got so wrapped up in trying to protect my job and my freedom, that I forgot to do what was right. I forgot why I had become an officer of the law. I forgot why I placed my left hand on the bible, raised my right hand to God Almighty, and swore that I would uphold the laws of the State of Kentucky and uphold the Constitution of the United States. I'm not going to pretend that I am somehow the victim here, that I was merely protecting my family. I am just as guilty as the man who murdered Mary Jo Conyers and Melissa Ann Dwyer. So that is why I am taking the easy way out and taking my own life. I am truly sorry for the black eye I have given this department and I am truly sorry for the pain I have caused everyone along the way. Please accept my apology; it was never my intention to have anyone get hurt.

The letter ended there. Adam walked back around the desk and took a long look at Sergeant David Gibbons lying on the floor. His mind went back to all the times that they had been together. He tried to remember all the car rides, all the meals, all the discussions they had had. Had there been any clues that Adam hadn't picked up on because of who he was? He had spent five years of his life looking for a killer who had been working beside him the entire time.

He keyed up his shoulder-mic and broadcasted to everyone on scene, "We have two confirmed dead inside the building. Be advised that this is going to be a Sheriff's Office investigation, so go ahead and notify their personnel that they need to clean up this mess."

Adam looked down at David's lifeless body and fought back the anger that was beginning to build. Bernie, who had been standing in the doorway with Bishop, could see Adam's face getting red, so he grabbed him by the shoulders and turned him toward the door to get him out of the office. But before he could usher him out, Adam abruptly turned back and spit on the back of David's head.

"I hope you rot in hell you bastard."

Acknowledgements

What exactly does one say when four years of torment and utter frustration comes to a close? Four years of staying up all night, trying to put words down on a page that not only fit together, but portray exactly what you're trying to say. Let me be the first to tell you, it ain't easy. Some weeks I could barely eek out a sentence, while others I could hammer out five pages. To me they were all beautifully written works of art, but to my editors… Not so much. And that was the hardest part of all—putting myself out there, only to have my hard work returned to me with TONS of red ink all over the pages. But that's how you learn. That being said, there are a ton of people that made this all possible and I would like to take this opportunity to say THANK YOU!!!!

Along the way I've had some pretty awesome people lend their time and expertise to make this novel what it is. First and foremost I'd like to thank Karen Washburn for putting me on the right track. I know that the first edition of this story must have had you cringing when you first read it, but you didn't give up on me. Thanks for all your words of encouragement.

To my grammar and content editor, Elaine Blackmore, thank you for not taking it easy on me. After looking at the same pages for so long, I missed a lot of things that you picked up on right away. Your attention to detail and my misuse of the English language was impeccable, and for that I thank you.

To my Alpha Readers: Dave Fox, Missy Katinsky, Matt Carson, and Adam Mancini… Well, not so much Adam Mancini, but the rest of you, I thank you for your time and comments. You guys really helped make this a better story.

What would a book be without a cover? When I first asked Tim Bzdak for help, I simply explained to him my vision and he told me that he'd take care of it. And take care of it he did. It turned out better than I ever could have imagined. Because of your vision, I now have an eye-catching cover that will make people stop in their tracks. Thank you.

And last, but certainly not least, I would like to say thank you to the man, the myth, and the legend…Frank Sheridan. Without you, I never would have realized that I had this in me. You were the one that opened my eyes to the joys of writing, and for that, I am grateful.

Thank you to everyone for your continued support and I hope you enjoy reading this as much as I enjoyed writing it.